My Cousin Caroline

The acclaimed Pride and Prejudice sequel series

The Pemberley Chronicles:
Book 6

DEVISED AND COMPILED BY
Rebecca Ann Collins

SOURCEBOOKS LANDMARK™
AN IMPRINT OF SOURCEBOOKS, INC.®
NAPERVILLE, ILLINOIS

By the Same Author

The Pemberley Chronicles
The Women of Pemberley
Netherfield Park Revisited
The Ladies of Longbourn
Mr Darcy's Daughter
Postscript from Pemberley
Recollections of Rosings
A Woman of Influence
The Legacy of Pemberley

Published by Sourcebooks Landmark, an imprint of Sourcebooks, Inc.
P.O. Box 4410, Naperville, Illinois 60567-4410
(630) 961-3900
FAX: (630) 961-2168
www.sourcebooks.com

Originally printed and bound in Australia by SNAP Printing, Sydney, NSW, October
2001. Reprinted December 2004 and March 2007.

Library of Congress Cataloging-in-Publication Data

Collins, Rebecca Ann.
  My cousin Caroline / devised and compiled by Rebecca Ann Collins.
     p. cm. — (The Pemberley chronicles ; bk. 6)
  Originally published: Sydney : SNAP Printing, 2001.
  1. England—Social life and customs—19th century—Fiction. I. Austen, Jane, 1775-
1817. Pride and prejudice. II. Title.
  PR9619.4.C65M9 2009
  823'.92—dc22
                              2009021799

Printed and bound in the United States of America
VP 10 9 8 7 6 5 4 3 2 1

Dedicated to
Jenni, Sue, and Colin,
with my love.

An Introduction . . .

CAROLINE'S STORY IS RATHER SPECIAL.

Ever since I devised _The Pemberley Chronicles_, in which she was to develop from a pretty young girl into a personable young woman, Caroline Gardiner and her Colonel have nagged at my mind. It is almost as though they demanded to have their own story told, rather than be just a subplot in the love story of Elizabeth and Darcy.

He was one of Jane Austen's most promising minor characters in _Pride and Prejudice_, and she was chiefly mine.

Jane Austen's depiction of Colonel Fitzwilliam leaves one in no doubt that he was an agreeable and attractive gentleman, lacking only adequate wealth to make him also an eligible bachelor. It was not difficult to devise some means by which he could acquire sufficient income and independence to permit him to follow his heart, albeit a few years later and with another young woman.

Caroline Gardiner proved, as she matured, a useful foil to the silliness and irresponsibility of her cousin Lydia and also helped demonstrate Jane Austen's conviction that the Gardiners—a sensible and refined middle-class family embodying some of her own values—could well teach any gentleman's daughter a thing or two about decorum and style.

The wedding of Elizabeth and Darcy, and Jane Austen's particular mention of their continuing intimate friendship with Mr and Mrs Gardiner, afforded me the opportunity to bring Colonel Fitzwilliam and Caroline Gardiner together, and the rest, while it may not be history, is not difficult to imagine.

Given Elizabeth's affection for her young cousin and Mr Darcy's sincere regard for the Gardiners, there was scope for an interesting interplay of relationships between the families.

The marriage of Caroline and the amiable Colonel combines the two social strands that come together in *Pride and Prejudice*, both equally valued by Jane Austen herself: the traditional codes of gentlemanly behaviour and the decent, sensible middle-class virtues of the Gardiners, of whom Elizabeth is so justly proud. Each supports the other, and in the success of their union, the contention that honourable behaviour is not the exclusive preserve of one class of society is reaffirmed.

Because the time line of *My Cousin Caroline* crosses all the stories in the Pemberley series so far, it opened up possibilities of looking at some of the other characters again: Robert and Rose Gardiner, Richard and Cassandra, Lydia and Wickham, and even Darcy and Elizabeth, as they settled into their marriages and faced new challenges.

Perhaps best of all, it was a chance to revisit the days when Mr and Mrs Bennet, Lady Catherine de Bourgh, and the impossible Mr Collins were still with us. Their demise in Book One of *The Pemberley Chronicles* upset many readers; I hope their return, even for a short spell, will please some of them.

As for Caroline herself, it was easy to invest her with intelligence and courage as well as beauty and let her go, knowing she may stumble, as most romantic young persons do, but never fall. She is no paragon of virtue, but she has resilience and strength. Her life spans a period of historic change for women in late Georgian and Victorian England. Not all of them meekly accepted the strict boundaries society laid down for their lives; many worked actively to help the poor and advance causes that governments mostly ignored. Some, like Florence Nightingale, were positively modern in their activism.

Caroline Fitzwilliam fills the role well. She is a loving, loyal daughter, wife, and mother, but she is her own woman—almost incorrigibly so. She enjoys living passionately but will not abdicate any of her responsibilities.

It has been an absolute pleasure to tell her story in *My Cousin Caroline*; I hope all those readers of the Pemberley novels, who have written to ask for more, will like her too.

RAC 2001.

Website: *www.geocities.com/shadesofpemberley*

For the benefit of those readers who wish to be reminded of the characters and their relationships to one another, an aide-memoire is provided in the appendix.

Prologue

It was the absence of noise, rather than the excess of it, that roused Colonel Fitzwilliam from his sleep.

He lay awhile in bed, letting his eyes become accustomed to the semi-darkness, hearing nothing, wondering vaguely where he was.

He was confused at first, by the unfamiliarity of the environment in which he found himself—a large soft bed in a spacious room, instead of the cramped quarters on board *The Viking*, where the water slapped at the ship's timbers and the winds soughed through her sails all night long. Slowly, he began to recall they had been due to berth at Portsmouth and yes, he remembered now, he had been ill while at sea, very ill indeed.

Unsure and curious as to his present surroundings, Fitzwilliam rose from the bed, glancing momentarily at himself in the mirror, noted he was wearing someone else's night clothes, and still somewhat unsteady on his feet, walked over to the window. Drawing aside the heavy, blue brocade curtains, he looked out, not as he had expected, upon the narrow streets of the busy sea port of Portsmouth, but at a sunlit garden below, bounded on one side by a high wall and sloping gently westwards to a terrace, which, when one looked further, afforded a most seductive, distant view of a bay.

There appeared to be no one about, except a gardener pruning a hedge. The building, of which he could see another part extending out towards the terrace, was an early Georgian construction, such as one might see in any prosperous coastal resort.

Bewildered, he was about to return to his bed, contemplating further how he might have come to be in this place, when there was a knock on the door. A servant entered, bearing a tray, which he set down upon the table beside the window.

"Good morning, sir," he said as he moved to pour out a cup of tea. "Mr Jarrett said you were not to be disturbed, sir."

"Mr Jarrett! Of course." Fitzwilliam knew then that this must be Southampton and asked quickly, "Is your master home?"

The man shook his head. "No, sir, he is gone into the town. He had some business in the High Street. But he did give instructions that you were to be allowed to sleep as long as you wished—he said you had been very ill on the voyage, sir."

Fitzwilliam nodded, acknowledging the truth of this assertion, as he sat down to enjoy a most welcome cup of tea.

Slowly the recollections returned; indeed now he remembered it all quite clearly; John Jarrett, his school mate, colleague, and fellow traveller on *The Viking*, had invited him to stay at his family's home in Southampton.

It seemed such a long time ago—all those weeks, those interminable, hot days and nights crossing the Indian Ocean, and the huge seas pounding the ship as she ploughed into the Atlantic; it had felt like an eternity. For much of the last fortnight at sea, he had indeed been very ill; feverish, unable to eat or sleep, waiting only for the voyage to be over. It had been months since they had sailed from Colombo, Jarrett and he, both leaving the Eastern colonies to return permanently to England.

Jarrett was going home to be married and Fitzwilliam, when he learned that there was a spare berth on board *The Viking*, had leapt at the opportunity to return a couple of months earlier than planned.

The footman had left the room, and as he sat down to more excellent tea and fresh buttered toast, Fitzwilliam recalled again the difficult conditions they had endured on the voyage. The ship returning to England after completing a tour of duty escorting vessels of the East India Company across the China Sea, where they were forever in danger of being boarded by pirates, had called to pick up supplies in Colombo. Jarrett and he were fortunate indeed to obtain passages on a naval vessel, rather than the merchant trader they had been expecting. The abominable conditions on board some of them were legendary. Jarrett's own naval connections had helped secure them the berths and Fitzwilliam had been profoundly grateful to his friend.

He had barely finished his breakfast when the door opened and Mr Jarrett appeared.

"Fitzwilliam! Thank God, you are looking a good deal better this morning. I must say I am relieved. How do you feel?"

The colonel, looking rather sheepish, admitted that his head was still somewhat sore and his tongue felt dreadful!

"Is that all? You'll live then. I confess I thought when we got you here that we were going to have to call in Doctor Price. You looked very miserable indeed, my man thought you had caught some wretched fever—the kind spread by mosquitoes in the tropics," he said, looking very anxious.

Fitzwilliam hastened to reassure him. "I do not believe it was anything as serious as that; it was probably a combination of the cramped quarters, the foetid air below decks, the heat, and the wretched weather that affected me. I confess I am not a good sailor, nothing would have got me into the navy—I assure you, not even Nelson himself could have persuaded me to put to sea in a howling gale! But, as you see, I am much recovered, now that we are back on *terra firma*, and I shall soon be as right as rain."

His friend laughed. "I am so pleased to hear you say that—two nights ago, I would have said you were fit only for the infirmary!"

"I have much to thank you for, Jarrett, including my night clothes, I see. You have been most kind."

Jarrett laughed, "Ah well, you did not believe I would leave you to the tender mercies of some dockside publican in Portsmouth, did you? Your trunks and bags have all been transported here and safely stored. The servants will bring them to you, whenever you are ready."

Urging his friend to take his time and promising to see him at dinner later, Jarrett left to attend to the various matters that awaited his urgent attention. He was being married in a fortnight. He had a good deal on his mind, a plethora of things to arrange, and not a lot of time to spare.

Colonel Fitzwilliam, on the other hand, had all the time in the world.

The servant returned, removed the remains of his breakfast, fetched his clothes, which had been cleaned and pressed, before preparing his bath. He bathed and dressed slowly, savouring the pleasures of being back in the kind of comfortable environment he had enjoyed for most of his life.

Going downstairs and finding no one about, he decided to explore the garden and perhaps take a walk into the town. Fitzwilliam did not know Southampton well, having only visited it when he was a very young lad at school. But he had heard a great deal about it from Jarrett, whose family had lived here for many years, ever since his grandfather retired from the navy.

It was his very first visit to the Jarretts' family home—a commodious, well-constructed house, solidly built in Georgian style, set in a smallish garden where a green lawn bordered by laburnum and roses sloped down towards the water. As there was not a great deal to hold his attention, Fitzwilliam walked on, pausing on the terrace to admire the prospect which took in the bay and away to the west—the New Forest. It was, he thought, a remarkably salubrious spot and it did not surprise him that Jarrett, while at sea, had spoken of the place so fondly and with such nostalgia.

Coming away from the terrace, he sought to make his way into the town, whither he assumed his friend had gone. As he walked, conscious of the particularly pleasing mildness of the day, his thoughts turned to his reasons for returning to England. Growing suddenly impatient of the indolence induced by long afternoons in the tropics waiting to be back in England, he had begun to long for home. Thoughts of Derbyshire brought memories of his cousin Fitzwilliam Darcy and Pemberley, which was as close to a home as he had ever known. The two cousins were very close and their joint guardianship of Darcy's sister, Georgiana, had drawn Fitzwilliam even deeper into the fold of the family.

Darcy had been married some three years to Miss Elizabeth Bennet. Fitzwilliam could not deny his own interest in her and knew he looked forward to seeing her again. He had admired her immensely and enjoyed her company. Of course, now she was his cousin's wife, they could only ever be friends. He hoped they would be good friends, but wondered why, at this moment, that did not seem a very consoling prospect.

Having spent close to an hour acquainting himself with the attractions of the town, its gracious buildings lining clean streets, he was retracing his steps when his friend Jarrett appeared, looking most upset.

As he approached, Fitzwilliam greeted him with a jest, "Jarrett, my friend, for a man about to be married, you look uncommonly worried and harassed."

Jarrett stopped right before him and said, "Yes, that is because I am, very worried indeed. I have come out in search of you, to ask a favour. I need your help, Fitzwilliam, this is truly a crisis. Will you help me?"

Fitzwilliam laughed lightly. "Seeing you have very likely saved my life, I can hardly refuse. But what is your problem and how can I be of assistance?" he asked.

At this Jarrett, who had turned to walk back towards the house with Fitzwilliam, declared that he had received bad news that morning, in a letter which had arrived from his cousin in Winchester, who was to have been his best man at the wedding.

"He has been struck down with the measles and expects to be confined to his room for a fortnight at least. So you see why I am in such a pickle. I am without a best man, unless you would be so kind as to step into the breach. Would you, Fitzwilliam, please?" he pleaded.

"Good God!" Fitzwilliam exclaimed. "I don't know that I could. I do not know many of your family, nor anyone in the bride's party." But he was soon persuaded by the realisation that his friend needed his help and Fitzwilliam was a most amiable and obliging man, who found it exceedingly difficult to refuse such a request.

"It will mean staying on with us until the wedding in twelve days' time, but since you had made no mention of any urgent plans, I hoped you had none. Had you, Fitzwilliam?" Jarrett asked apprehensively and Fitzwilliam said quietly, "None that cannot wait a week or two; I do have business to attend to in London, friends to see at Westminster, and thereafter, I am for Derbyshire and Pemberley."

"You lucky dog," said Jarrett, who had never been to Derbyshire but had heard much of Pemberley from his friend and claimed to envy him the hospitality he enjoyed at that great estate.

As they made their way back to the house, they talked again of the future and what each hoped to accomplish, but once at the house, plans for the wedding were uppermost in their minds and Fitzwilliam knew he had to stay. Quite clearly, his friend needed him now.

The last wedding he had attended had been that of Darcy and Elizabeth three years ago. Then too, he had been best man, he thought wryly, recalling the happy occasion at a country church in a small village in Hertfordshire.

Returning to his room, he asked for his trunks to be brought upstairs, so his clothes could be aired and made ready for the occasion. Jarrett's bride-to-be was from Eastleigh and they were to marry at the chapel at Winchester, where both Jarrett and Fitzwilliam had attended school.

It would probably be a nostalgic occasion for all of them, he thought as he opened up his trunk and extracted a leather satchel filled with letters and papers. They had all been hurriedly packed when the news came of a berth available at short notice on *The Viking*. Some were old letters and, with little to do for the rest of the afternoon, Fitzwilliam took them over to the desk by the window, intending to put them in order. He would need to re-order his life and business now he was back in England, he thought, and getting his correspondence organised would be a good start.

Amongst the papers was a sheet of music copied out by hand, to which was attached a note in a pretty, round hand, obviously written by a young girl. Picking it up, Fitzwilliam remembered the song and the time he had sung it at the house of Mr and Mrs Gardiner, Elizabeth Bennet's aunt and uncle. Later, in a nostalgic mood, he had asked for a copy to be purchased and sent out to him in Ceylon, where he was stationed at the time.

It was young Miss Caroline Gardiner who had copied it and sent it with the note, explaining that there were no printed copies to be had in the shops and she hoped the handmade one would suffice.

It had done very well, he recalled with a smile. Fitzwilliam had sung the song many times since, alone or as a duet with other young ladies, but he had always remembered the first time he had sung it with young Miss Gardiner, when they had been accompanied on the pianoforte by Miss Elizabeth Bennet. He recalled that Miss Gardiner had a very sweet, clear voice and remembered also how they had met at the wedding of Darcy and Elizabeth.

Elizabeth had introduced them a few days previously, when they attended the rehearsal at the church.

"Colonel Fitzwilliam," she had said, "I would like you to meet my cousin Caroline, who is to be one of the maids," and there in front of him had been a pretty girl, probably not more than twelve years old, but a very self-possessed young person indeed.

Fitzwilliam, always the gracious gentleman, had bowed as he took her outstretched hand, saying gallantly, "And a very pretty maid too; I am very happy to meet you, Miss Gardiner."

She had coloured slightly at the compliment and said in a perfectly modulated voice, "And I am very pleased to meet you, Colonel Fitzwilliam, for my cousin Lizzie declares you are almost the nicest gentleman she has ever met—excepting Mr Darcy, of course."

Fitzwilliam and Elizabeth had looked at one another in astonishment at these words, spoken without a trace of artfulness or coquetry, and while Elizabeth had managed to say something light and witty, poor Fitzwilliam had been left in total confusion.

Someone, he could not recall who it had been, had remarked, "Out of the mouths of babes, eh, Fitzwilliam?" adding to his embarrassment and Fitzwilliam had wished he could have disappeared into thin air, except Miss Gardiner had said gently, "You must not fret, Colonel Fitzwilliam, we shall all miss our dear cousin Lizzie. Besides, you do know, do you not, that the bride never marries the best man?"

Looking sharply across at her, he had wondered if she was being pert just to needle him, but soon realised that, with her cousin Miss Elizabeth Bennet as a role model, young Miss Gardiner was probably practising her wit and meant no harm at all. When she'd smiled sweetly and said, "Hadn't we better join them, else we shall not know what to do or where to sit tomorrow, and that will not do," he had forgiven her completely.

⁂

After the wedding, Fitzwilliam had become better acquainted with the Gardiners, whom Darcy had recommended to him without reservation as a family of great integrity and remarkable good taste. Seeing that Mr Gardiner was in trade, being the owner of a lucrative business situated in Cheapside, this was high praise from Darcy, and Fitzwilliam was soon to discover that it was completely justified.

He'd visited them at home and had been invited back to dine with them often. Both Misses Gardiner—Caroline and her younger sister Emily—had proved to be charming and accomplished girls, with a good deal more to say for themselves on a variety of matters than any of the young persons of a similar age he had met before. Free of silliness and puffery, they were a credit to their parents, as was their brother Richard, whom Fitzwilliam had met when he had been home from boarding school. Impressed with the entire family and particularly with the business acumen and great good sense of Mr Gardiner, Fitzwilliam had promised to keep in touch.

This he had done faithfully, even after accepting a position overseas in the new Colonies of India and Ceylon. He had told no one at the time, but in his heart, he had known that he could not easily and swiftly get over his fascination for Elizabeth Bennet.

Ever since they had met, by a happy chance, at his aunt's estate, Rosings Park in Kent, he had been bewitched by her beauty, intelligence, and wit, but quite apart from his own financial situation, which had precluded his making her an offer at the time, it had become perfectly plain to him that his cousin Darcy was besotted with the lady. Though it had taken an inordinate amount of time to resolve, Fitzwilliam had had no doubt of the outcome. He had never seen his cousin so deeply in love before.

Once the couple were engaged and their mutual affection was clear to all, the situation had become almost intolerable, and when at last they were wed, Fitzwilliam, after performing his duty as best man with admirable composure, had decided he was going to take the first available posting overseas.

Now, he was home again and planning to leave soon for London and thence for Derbyshire and Pemberley.

Darcy's letter, inviting him to stay, sending his regards and those of his wife and sister, who was soon to be married, was in his pocketbook as he prepared for his journey to London.

So too was a letter from Mr Gardiner, with whom he had been in regular communication while in the colonies, on matters of business and politics. It offered him the opportunity to invest in the Commercial Trading Company, which Mr Gardiner had acquired to pursue and develop trade with the colonies. Messrs Darcy and Bingley were partners already and Colonel Fitzwilliam was welcome to join in their enterprise, he had said.

Included in the letter was an invitation to join the family on Boxing Day to celebrate the fifteenth birthday of their eldest daughter—Miss Caroline Gardiner.

END OF PROLOGUE

MY COUSIN CAROLINE

Part One

Chapter One

THE GARDINERS HAD MOVED TO Oakleigh Manor near the village of Lambton in Derbyshire at the beginning of 1817, leaving behind their life in London but not Mr Gardiner's flourishing business interests.

Indeed, Mr Gardiner's commercial enterprise had grown so satisfactorily over the last few years, he had acquired another warehouse and a new manager to run the office he had established at Cheapside.

The expansion of trade with the colonies and prospects of new contracts in the Caribbean and South America meant the need would soon arise, as he had predicted, to set up offices in Manchester and Liverpool, from where the bulk of their cargoes would be carried to the world. His partners, Messrs Darcy and Bingley, readily agreed.

The move to Derbyshire had made Mrs Gardiner, who had been born and raised in the village of Lambton, very happy indeed. She was now within a short journey of both her favourite nieces, Elizabeth Darcy and Jane Bingley. It had also brought new pleasures into the lives of her young daughters, Caroline and Emily, who had ready access to the natural beauty of the county their mother loved so passionately and as well to the treasures of Ashford Park and Pemberley. Through their cousins Jane and Elizabeth, they were introduced to a new social circle and the very special attractions available at Pemberley, where they could read in the great library, practise in the music room, admire one of the finest art collections in the country, or wander at will among its splendid grounds.

For young Emily, an indefatigable reader, the library was a virtual heaven, while Caroline's love of walking in the parks and woods around the estate could never be exhausted. Each day, there appeared a new vista to behold or a prospect to admire at Pemberley.

Thither they had planned to go today and waited only for the carriage to be brought round to the front porch, when the post was delivered to their father, who was finishing his breakfast. Recognising a letter that had clearly been posted overseas, Mr Gardiner reached for it immediately. It came from Colonel Fitzwilliam, writing from Colombo, where he was awaiting the arrival of a ship that would convey him to England before Christmas. He had received Mr Gardiner's letter, he wrote, with its invitation and promised he would be back in time to celebrate Christmas at Pemberley and attend Miss Gardiner's birthday party on Boxing Day. He wrote:

> *They are both singularly important events and I would not miss them for anything. I look forward with much pleasure to seeing you, Mrs Gardiner, and your family again, but even more importantly, Mr Gardiner, sir, I am interested in taking up your proposition of a partnership in the Commercial Trading Company. This is a matter we shall address when we meet. I trust that your proposal has already been discussed between yourself and my cousin Mr Darcy and has his support.*

Mr Gardiner read the letter out to his family with much satisfaction. Mrs Gardiner was very excited at the news it contained.

"Does this mean Colonel Fitzwilliam will invest in the company?" she asked and her husband answered cautiously, "He may, my dear, we shall need to have a serious talk first and ascertain what Colonel Fitzwilliam expects from a partnership and how much he is prepared to contribute. I do not mean in terms of money alone, but in time and effort to run the company and organise the work that must be done. We live in a time of great competition and there are many similar companies waiting to take advantage of the opportunities available to us. We need sound management and hard work if we are to succeed in the next decade."

"Will Colonel Fitzwilliam live at Pemberley, Mama?" asked Emily.

Her mother answered firmly, "I doubt that he will," and Mr Gardiner agreed with his wife, "No indeed, he is a very independent gentleman and will not wish to be obligated to his cousin Mr Darcy for too long, although I know Mr Darcy would be quite happy to accommodate him at Pemberley. I believe he will acquire his own place soon enough; I gather from his letters that he has done remarkably well in the colonies and does not lack for funds."

At this point, Caroline, who had been silent throughout the conversation asked, "Do you think Colonel Fitzwilliam will stand for Parliament, Papa?"

Mrs Gardiner was astonished at her question.

"Parliament, why, Caroline, whatever gave you that idea?" she asked.

Caroline shrugged her shoulders. "I do not really know, Mama, except I overheard Papa and Mr Darcy speaking of it a few days ago and I heard Mr Darcy say that Colonel Fitzwilliam appeared to be interested in joining the reform movement and may well stand for Parliament."

"If he did, I would vote for him," said little Emily with childish enthusiasm. The colonel had always been a favourite with her.

"Emmy, you are very silly indeed. You cannot vote and neither can I. Ladies do not vote, do they, Mama?" asked Caroline and her mother smiled and took up her book as they moved to the parlour.

"Sadly, you are right, Caroline; if we could, however, I'd wager anything you care to name we would send a better bunch of members to Westminster."

Everyone laughed at this and Mr Gardiner was moved to say, in mock surprise, "Now now, my dear, you are beginning to sound like those dreadful revolutionaries across the channel!" which remark brought much mirth and laughter from Caroline, who had heard all about the revolutionary women of France and did not like the sound of them at all.

The arrival at the front porch of the carriage interrupted their conversation and the girls raced upstairs to put on their bonnets.

Soon, they were on their way, Mr Gardiner to his business in Matlock and Mrs Gardiner and her daughters to spend the day at Pemberley.

Together with many advantages, the move to Oakleigh Manor had brought the Gardiners a new set of social responsibilities, of which they had little or no experience in London. The deepening recession in the country meant that hundreds of people, who had once earned sufficient to keep their families in reasonable comfort, found themselves in greatly reduced circumstances, some driven to depend upon the charity of their neighbours to feed their children.

Led by the two families whose estates encompassed most of the district, the Darcys and the Camdens, groups of men and women worked with their local churches to organise the collection and distribution of food and clothing to the needy, so that none would starve or face the Winter without shoes or warm clothes. On their estates and at Oakleigh Manor, tenants and workers were permitted to take firewood to warm their homes or game to feed their children without the fear of being arrested and brought before the magistrate for thieving.

Elizabeth was not able to assist actively, since she was close to being brought to bed with the Darcys' first child. Despite the excitement that inevitably attended such an event, Cassandra Jane was born without much fuss or fanfare in the midst of a Summer storm. She was pronounced by Caroline to be "the most beautiful little girl I have ever seen," and no one disagreed with her. Cassy Darcy was destined to be a favourite in the family.

She was certainly the very centre of her parents' universe.

In July of the same year, the families journeyed from Derbyshire to Longbourn in Hertfordshire for the wedding of Kitty Bennet to Mr Jenkins, the rector at Pemberley.

Caroline and Emily were bridesmaids, and this time, being three years older than when they had followed their cousins Jane and Lizzie up the aisle, they attracted a good deal of admiration. Emily, being rather small in stature, still seemed like a pretty child, but Caroline had developed into quite a beauty. Her figure was slender though well formed and graceful in both appearance and movement; she caught the eye of many an admirer in the congregation at the church and at the wedding breakfast that followed. While she was neither timid nor shy, there was in her general manner an artlessness that was appealing, suggesting a most engaging quality of innocence. Yet, she was at all times, in her behaviour, a model of modesty and decorum.

Her mother was exceedingly particular to counsel her daughters, and Caroline provided on this occasion an absolute contrast to the silliness of her cousin Lydia Wickham. Lydia's determination to flaunt her charms and flirt with any man who was available to do so had already caused adverse comment and not a little embarrassment to her elder sisters. Jane and Elizabeth observed the conduct of their sister and her husband with sinking hearts.

Encouraged by Mrs Bennet, whose own high spirits had been in no way curtailed by age, Lydia and Wickham paraded and preened for all to see.

"Why is it, Lizzie, that I cannot bear to look at them, because I know they will inevitably be engaged in some activity that will draw undue attention to themselves and cause me to cringe with embarrassment? How is it they have no shame at all—neither of them?" asked Jane.

Elizabeth, knowing well the truth of her sister's words and already inured to the condition she described, urged Jane not to let their foolish sister spoil the occasion for them.

"As I remarked to my Aunt Gardiner only a moment ago, Lydia and Wickham are both quite brazen in their disregard of people's opinions. They appear oblivious to the fact that most people in this room are well aware of their elopement and the circumstances of their subsequent marriage."

"Oh, do regard Wickham now," said Jane in a despairing voice, "look how he simpers and smiles and courts the approval of everyone he talks to; he will flatter and flirt with every woman in the room who will tolerate his antics. Oh Lizzie, just look at him!"

Elizabeth's eyes followed her sister's and alighting upon Wickham, who had just bowed low and kissed the hand of Caroline Gardiner, whom he appeared to be engaging in conversation, she said, "Good Heavens! He is trying out his charms on Caroline. Our poor young cousin does not know the detail of his background, does she, Aunt?" and she turned to Mrs Gardiner, only to find that her aunt, having witnessed exactly the same scene and being even more wary of Mr Wickham than her nieces, had evacuated her chair with speed and was making her way across the room to where some of the young people were gathering for a dance.

As she approached, Wickham, who had been standing inordinately close to young Caroline, allowing her no means of escape, stepped back and Mrs Gardiner pointedly interposed herself between them and asked after the health of his wife and children.

"And how does the air of Newcastle suit your wife and family, Mr Wickham? I trust they are all well?" she asked and Wickham, unabashed, switched his charm from the daughter to her mother, launching into a description of domestic felicity which he claimed to enjoy with his dear Lydia and their two little boys. Having successfully distracted him from her daughter, Mrs Gardiner turned to Caroline.

"My love, I believe your cousin Lizzie wishes to see your gown—she had not seen it until today and longs to see the embroidery close up."

Caroline obliged, and as she moved away, Mr Wickham, his eye attracted by the charms of yet another young woman, excused himself and went to join in the dancing.

Mrs Gardiner soon returned to her place at the table.

"His hypocrisy is quite breathtaking," Mrs Gardiner told her nieces, "it was as if he and Lydia had the happiest of marriages, yet we all know the truth of it. The man's a disgrace!"

Caroline, who had been too young at the time to know the detail of Wickham's infamy and Lydia's notorious affair with him, was nevertheless well aware that the man was *persona non grata* at Pemberley. On rejoining her cousins, she declared quite firmly that if Mr Wickham had been the very last man left on earth and he had proposed to her, she could not have accepted him.

Elizabeth was curious to discover the reason for this revulsion.

"Why do you say that, Caroline?" she asked. "After all he is both handsome, after a fashion, and his manners are certainly calculated to please."

Caroline looked at her with some astonishment at first, before she realised that her cousin Lizzie was being sarcastic.

"That may well be, Cousin Lizzie, but there is about him something, I cannot say what, for I do not know him at all well, but I do know I could never trust him, however charming he may try to be or however well he may try to present himself. He is the kind of person who could never win my confidence. Poor cousin Lydia, it must be dreadful to be married to such a man."

Even as she spoke, Jane and Elizabeth exchanged glances, recalling how easily they had been taken in by Wickham's charm and apparent openness, when they had been older than Caroline. Elizabeth in particular recalled how she had been deceived by him into upbraiding Mr Darcy, and her cheeks burned with shame at the memory. How had young Caroline come so directly to the right judgment when they had all been so wrong?

A cold shiver ran down her spine as she remembered how near she had come to disaster herself, defending Wickham, defaming Mr Darcy, and almost, but for the merest chance, letting her feelings run away with her good sense. She had her aunt and Mr Darcy to thank for her escape.

It was with some relief that they saw Mr Darcy and Mr Gardiner approaching, and as Elizabeth rose with a welcoming smile, her uncle asked, "Are we ready to leave, ladies?"

~❦~

Returning to Derbyshire, Mrs Gardiner and her daughters became involved in helping Elizabeth organise the parish church fair at Pemberley. In the absence of the rector Mr Jenkins and his wife, who were on their honeymoon in Wales, it had fallen to Elizabeth to do the honours. While Mr Darcy and her Uncle Gardiner were busy establishing offices in Manchester, Elizabeth had borrowed Caroline for the day to assist her with setting up the stalls in the garden of the rectory.

"I do miss Kitty at times such as these. It is very good of your mama to let me have you to help" she said and Caroline, who was devoted to her cousin Elizabeth, made light of her tasks.

"I am perfectly happy to help, Cousin Lizzie, and Mama did not mind at all. She had to take Emily to Derby to get her some material for a new coat; she is growing so fast, she is taller every day and has outgrown all her Winter clothes," Caroline explained as they got busy with the tasks at hand.

Elizabeth was constantly surprised at her cousins' accomplishments in artistic pursuits and matters of a more practical nature. Both Misses Gardiner were deft and quick at sewing and cooking, while Caroline was especially favoured in her mastery of the pianoforte and in her singing. As she proceeded with sorting and arranging things with a minimum of fuss, Elizabeth, who did such tasks as a matter of duty, wondered at the way Caroline seemed to find genuine enjoyment in it.

Unlike her own mother, Mrs Bennet, who'd had little inclination to have her daughters learn any domestic skills, which she considered to be beneath them, being the daughters of an impoverished gentleman, Mrs Gardiner, despite her husband's relative affluence, had insisted that Emily and Caroline were well schooled in housekeeping while also acquiring a good education and artistic skills.

It was while they were thus engaged that Caroline asked Elizabeth a question, which, while it was certainly not impertinent, succeeded in surprising her cousin.

"Cousin Lizzie, I know you and Mr Darcy and indeed my own mama and papa have a very poor opinion of Mr Wickham and Cousin Lydia. I do not doubt for a moment that it is with good reason, but I wonder, would you mind telling me why this is so? What was it brought about this general lack of regard for them, for it is very plain to see?"

So taken aback was Elizabeth by this unexpected query, as much by the substance of the question as by the casual manner in which it had been asked, that she was silent for quite a few minutes.

Confused as to how she should answer her cousin, how much or how little to reveal, what construction to place on Wickham's deception of herself and how much of Mr Darcy's story concerning his sister Georgiana she need tell, Elizabeth's discomfiture was obvious and, conscious she may have embarrassed her cousin, Caroline apologised.

"I am sorry if I have discomposed you, Cousin Lizzie, I had no intention of doing any such thing. If it is a subject that causes you pain or unhappiness, pray do not feel you must answer... I am sorry... I probably should not have asked..."

Elizabeth, roused to protest, said quickly, "No, Caroline, you were not wrong, you have asked a perfectly understandable question and you are entitled to an answer. I hesitated only because I had thought your mama may have already revealed something of the matter to you, but as she has not, it falls to me to enlighten you. I have some reservations because there were several persons other than myself and Lydia involved at the time, and I was sensible of the fact that they have not authorised me to speak of it.

"Still, you are my cousin and you do, unhappily, see the Wickhams from time to time, and there cannot be any harm in your knowing the facts of the matter. Indeed in the circumstances, it may even be argued that it is my duty to acquaint you with them."

And so the tale was told over an hour or more of a late Summer's afternoon in the garden of the rectory at Pemberley.

As Elizabeth told it, she spared neither herself nor her sister Lydia, admitting her prejudice and imprudence as well as Lydia's stupidity but, most of all, making it clear how deeply her husband Mr Darcy had been wounded by Wickham's despicable conduct and subsequent defaming of him to all and sundry in Hertfordshire and elsewhere.

Caroline, while being old enough at the time to understand that her cousin Lydia had, through her elopement with Wickham, done something very foolish that had caused a great furore in the family, had little knowledge of Wickham's previous history and even less of the role played by Mr Darcy in bringing the entire distasteful episode to a relatively satisfactory conclusion.

Elizabeth's narration, revealing as it did the benevolence and magnanimity of Mr Darcy as well as the iniquity of Wickham, while it shocked young Caroline to the core, also served to explain why Mr Darcy was held in very great esteem by her parents. It also made even clearer the reason for Elizabeth's deep regard and love for her husband.

When Elizabeth had finished the tale, it was time to return home for tea. As they walked through the grounds of Pemberley, Caroline spoke with real feeling.

"Thank you very much for telling me, Cousin Lizzie. I am very grateful, not only because it has opened my eyes to the misbehaviour of Mr Wickham and Cousin Lydia, but because it has helped me to see why you love Mr Darcy so very dearly. He must surely be a very good, kind man and you are fortunate to be his wife."

Elizabeth inclined her head gently, acknowledging her cousin's simple words, and her voice was soft when she spoke. "I am indeed, Caroline; he is without exception the best man I have ever known. I cannot imagine being married to anyone else."

Approaching Pemberley House, they noticed the Gardiners' carriage in the drive; Mr Gardiner and Mr Darcy had clearly returned from their journey to Manchester.

Caroline said, "Papa is back, I see; he is of exactly the same opinion about Mr Darcy. He and Mama believe him to be one of the finest gentlemen they have had the honour to meet," and as her cousin coloured at this compliment to her husband, added, "They are very good friends now, I think."

Lizzie could not but agree. "They certainly are, Caroline, and Mr Darcy has great respect and affection for your parents," she said.

As they arrived at the steps of the house, the two gentlemen came out to greet them, followed by Mrs Reynolds, who invited them into the saloon to partake of an excellent afternoon tea.

❧

As Caroline Gardiner returned to Oakleigh with her father later that evening, she was unusually quiet, causing Mr Gardiner to become concerned that she had worked too hard and was overtired.

"Have you had a very tiring day, my dear?" he asked, but she smiled and shook her head.

"Oh no, Papa, but it has been a most revealing day. I learnt a great deal from Cousin Lizzie today."

"Indeed?" said her father, but thinking she meant personal matters, ladies' talk, he asked no more and she made no further mention of it.

Her mother and sister, back from Derby several hours, greeted them with lots of questions and promises of a good dinner.

That night, Caroline, when she retired to her bedroom, took out her diary and wrote:

I was for a little while afraid that I had offended my dear cousin Lizzie by asking such a question. It had never been my intention to pry, but I had long wondered what Mr Wickham had done wrong, apart from elope with Cousin Lydia and flirt outrageously with every woman he meets, to warrant such grave censure.

Yet, even if I had known all of Mr Wickham's behaviour, I might never have discovered Mr Darcy's goodness of heart had I not asked the question.

Furthermore, it has shown me quite plainly how very easy it is for a young woman to be gulled and deceived if she, in ignorance of the whole truth, believes the word of a man of whose character she knows little.

Why, even my cousins Jane and Lizzie were both taken in by Wickham's friendly and seemingly open nature, and their judgment would never be questioned in such matters.

Oh that it were possible to tell the true nature of a man's heart from his countenance or understand his character from his words alone!

I have resolved that I shall marry no man whose heart and character are not open and known to me, no man whose words I cannot wholly trust.

A fine thought indeed, Caroline, but where is such a man to be found?

There cannot be more than one Mr Darcy, surely?

Chapter Two

UNBEKNOWNST TO THE DARCYS AT Pemberley, Colonel Fitzwilliam had left Southampton after his friend Jarrett's wedding and journeyed to London. Having arranged to stay a few days at his club, he proceeded to Westminster, where he was shocked by the chaotic situation obtaining in the country. The Parliament appeared merely to reflect the confusion and disillusionment that was abroad in the land.

Even before leaving for the colonies some three years ago, Colonel Fitzwilliam had become aware of the general contempt in which the Royal family and in particular the king's eldest son, George, was held. His Regency had started most inauspiciously, with public dissatisfaction moving quickly from the pathetic old King George III, now completely out of his mind, to the extravagance and arrogance of the Prince of Wales and his courtiers.

Their wasteful ways, their unrestrained lifestyle, and their complete disregard for the sensitivities of the people whom they seemed determined to outrage on every occasion had made them the butt of satire and the focus of public loathing. Like many others of the time, Fitzwilliam had regarded them with a mixture of ridicule and anger.

However, nothing he had seen then had prepared him for the degeneration that had taken place over the past three years. No longer were the Regent and his brothers the mere butt of jokes; they were thoroughly hated.

Ordinary people who had great sympathy for the poor demented King resented the antics of the princes, who wasted a fortune in gambling and other nefarious pursuits while unemployed men and women watched their children starve or die of malnutrition or disease. Even the middle class, solidly conservative for many years, had lost faith in the monarchy and were demanding reform.

Meeting two of his former colleagues, who were now members of the Commons, Fitzwilliam dined with them and learned that the Reformists were active everywhere. Mostly men of the Whig Party, they were out of favour with the Regent and did not spare their words in denigration of him and his courtiers.

"He will thwart every attempt to bring in even the simplest reforms, and as for extending the franchise, you can but dream," said one, while the other, a man who had been with Fitzwilliam in the army until the defeat of Napoleon, declared, "Unless the reform movement wins this battle and delivers significant change, England will not only become the laughingstock of Europe, we will likely see revolution in our streets."

When Fitzwilliam protested, "What? Never, not in England, surely?" they both assured him he was wrong; the people were very restive indeed.

"Mark my words, Fitzwilliam, unless there is a genuine movement towards reform of the Parliament, we are in for a great deal of trouble. The Midlands are seething with Radicals," said his friend.

Fitzwilliam was very shocked.

"What is to be done?" he asked. "Clearly the Regent is no supporter of such policies as the abolition of slavery and the reform of the Parliament."

"He is not, and unless sufficient numbers of members in the Commons can influence the government, we will have achieved nothing."

Gradually, Fitzwilliam, who had begun the week with a somewhat luke-warm desire to support the reformists, was now determined to be involved. There was, he declared, no more important goal than the furtherance of reform in England.

Leaving London, hoping to leave some of the chaos and depression behind, he set out for the Midlands. Travelling north and west through the heartland of England, he was appalled by what he saw. The swift spread of mining, manufacturing, and mechanised farming was in evidence everywhere, changing utterly much of the countryside.

On reaching Birmingham, he broke journey and called on a friend of his youth, one Tom Attwood, who he discovered was actively involved in the agitation for reform. With him were several others, young and old, rich men and workers, who had committed to the cause. The conclusion was inescapable. All thinking men with an interest in their nation were moving in the one direction. It was a direction that appealed strongly to Fitzwilliam's sense of justice and rectitude.

Taking the coach to Derby, he hired there a private vehicle to convey him and his luggage to Lambton. He was happy to see, as they journeyed towards Pemberley, that here at least the countryside remained unspoilt. It was early Autumn and a cool breeze was rustling the leaves of trees that had only just begun to turn to gold, bringing back for Fitzwilliam, who had endured three years in the tropics, a most nostalgic memory.

Having made some preliminary enquiries, he took rooms at the inn, bathed, changed out of his travelling clothes, and continued his journey to Pemberley. As they drove the five short miles through the approaches to the great estate, where he had spent many happy months with his cousins Darcy and Georgiana, Colonel Fitzwilliam recalled his last visit.

He had come to say farewell to Georgiana and the staff, especially Mrs Reynolds, before returning to London to take up his appointment to the colonies. Darcy and Elizabeth were on their wedding journey and were not expected to return to Pemberley until Christmas. He remembered Georgiana, handsome but still rather gauche at sixteen. He had hoped her new companion, Mrs Annesley, who seemed a well-educated woman, would help her overcome some of her awkwardness.

He had subsequently met up with the others quite by chance in London when Darcy, Bingley, and their new brides had been invited to the Gardiners' and he had been of the party too. The recollection of that evening brought back many memories.

Now, here he was returning to Pemberley, and there was uncertainty about his plans; he was unsure of many things, except he was very glad to be back in England.

As the vehicle approached Pemberley House, the sun slanting down through the trees to the west of the building gilded the glass windows and cast great pools of indigo shadow on the lawn. Fitzwilliam could remember it exactly as it was. He was glad very little had changed here.

At the entrance he was met by a servant who greeted him, and then Mrs Reynolds, who welcomed him most effusively, declaring that the master and mistress would be very pleased to see him, she was sure, even if he was a month early.

"They were not expecting you this early in the season, sir, but I know they will be very happy to see you and looking so well too, if I may say so, sir."

When he asked if Mr Darcy was at home, she replied, "No, sir, he is gone with Mr Gardiner to Liverpool; they are expected to return in time for dinner. But Mrs Darcy is home and she has Mrs Gardiner with her. They are taking tea on the west lawn."

Fitzwilliam knew this was the moment he had most wished to avoid. Meeting Elizabeth without her husband at her side, seeing her while in his heart he still remembered his own tender feelings for her, he knew it was not going to be easy. As he made his way across the front of the house to the west lawn, he heard voices, not Elizabeth's or Mrs Gardiner's, but young, girlish voices. Someone was reading poetry, a familiar poem by Wordsworth; not a favourite of his but popular with young ladies, he had discovered.

A gentle, well-modulated voice spoke the words, as he hung back to listen.

> "Never did sun more beautifully steep
> In his first splendour, valley, rock or hill
> Dear God, the very houses seem asleep
> And all that mighty heart is lying still..."

As she finished, there was applause from her audience and he heard Elizabeth say, "Well done, Caroline, that was very good."

Fitzwilliam knew then that the young voices must belong to Mrs Gardiner's daughters: Caroline, whom he remembered as a pretty girl with a very appealing singing voice, and her sister Emily, who was only a child at the time he had left for the colonies.

Walking quickly along the path, Fitzwilliam approached the group seated on the lawn and added his appreciation.

"That was very well spoken, Miss Caroline," he said, and everyone turned around, startled to see him standing there in front of them.

Elizabeth had jumped up from her chair.

"Colonel Fitzwilliam! What are you doing here?" she cried.

Smiling, unabashed but apologetic for startling her, he kissed her hand and greeted her affectionately.

"Mrs Darcy, Elizabeth, please forgive me, I know I am not expected until the end of the month, but I had the rare chance of a berth on a naval vessel leaving Colombo to return to England and I could not resist it.

"I have been eager to return ever since I received Darcy's letter."

Seeing Elizabeth again after several years, now an even more handsome young woman, a wife, and recently a mother, he was struck by her beauty. There was also the quality of openness and warmth of feeling that he had found so appealing when they had first met. She had changed very little; her charm was still fascinating.

This time, it was part of the role she played as Mistress of Pemberley, gracious and welcoming, inviting him to take tea as a fresh pot was brought, asking after his health and his journey down from London, wanting to assure him he was welcome to stay at Pemberley.

Turning to Mrs Gardiner and her two daughters, who had sat quietly while Elizabeth plied him with questions and poured out his tea, Colonel Fitzwilliam found Mrs Gardiner no different to when he had last seen her: pleasant, intelligent, and amiable as ever. He remarked at the happy coincidence of their meeting at Pemberley, and she mentioned that Mr Gardiner had received his letter.

He then turned to tell Miss Caroline Gardiner again how well he had enjoyed her reading of Wordsworth. Only then did he, looking directly at her, notice for the first time how very different she was to the pretty little girl he remembered from three years ago. Caroline had risen from her place and was standing by the table, getting her mother a cup of tea. She was taller, he noticed, and there was a new gracefulness to her figure as she moved. Her gown was elegantly simple and her hair styled in a more grown-up, upswept fashion. The delicacy of her features was enhanced by a subtle blush that was surely more maidenly than childlike, he thought.

Fitzwilliam was quite enchanted.

Sitting down beside her, he talked some more and their conversation turned upon the book of poems from which they had been reading.

Fitzwilliam confessed he had purchased a copy in London, Emily asked if he had a favourite poem, and so it was they came to read the lines by William Blake, the visionary poet.

Even as he read it with Caroline joining in, he could hear in her voice the passion of youth, as she trembled when she spoke Blake's inspirational words,

"Bring me my bow of burning gold,
Bring me my arrows of desire
Bring my spear, O clouds unfold,
Bring me my Chariot of Fire.
I shall not cease from mental fight,
Nor shall my sword sleep in my hand
Till we have built Jerusalem
In England's green and pleasant land."

As they finished, Mrs Gardiner and Elizabeth applauded enthusiastically, but Caroline seemed rather shy; however, before Fitzwilliam could speak, they heard footsteps approaching at great speed and Mr Darcy, having just that moment returned from Liverpool and heard the news, appeared, almost running into his cousin in his haste. They greeted one another with warmth and great affection, and soon arrangements were being made to have Fitzwilliam's things fetched from Lambton. He must stay at Pemberley; they would hear of nothing else.

Later that evening, Mr Gardiner arrived and the three friends, now also business partners, were soon deep in conversation as Mrs Gardiner and Elizabeth took the two girls upstairs to bed. Mr Gardiner was delighted to see Fitzwilliam; he had not expected him back in England for a month or more. The colonel regarded Mr Gardiner with enormous respect, both as a businessman and friend. Indeed, he had an exceedingly high opinion of the entire Gardiner family.

Meeting like this, unexpectedly at Pemberley, brought back many pleasant memories of evenings spent together at the Gardiners' home in London; evenings of warm hospitality, excellent entertainment, and interesting conversation such as he could rarely find elsewhere in London at the time. He recalled that it had been quite a wrench to say farewell before leaving for the colonies.

Fitzwilliam had much to discuss with Mr Gardiner and his cousin Darcy. He had maintained a regular correspondence with both men over the years and wanted to know their views on his present plans.

He told them of his desire to join the reform movement, and it was soon clear to Darcy and Mr Gardiner that his commitment to the cause was sincere and serious.

"I am resolved that we must demand reform in the Parliament and the extension of the franchise to the middle class, the men who create the wealth that makes England the foremost trading nation in the world and yet have no voice in her government," he declared and as always, Mr Gardiner, prudent and wise, counselled caution, urging him to consider carefully the implications and consequences of committing to one or the other of the political parties.

"Would you be prepared to stand for Parliament, Colonel Fitzwilliam?" he asked, to which the colonel replied with some alacrity, "Yes, if need be, I will."

Elizabeth and Darcy, who had previously discussed Fitzwilliam's possible ambition to enter Parliament, exchanged glances but said nothing. He had been quite certain but she not so sure Fitzwilliam had the will to do so.

Later that night, she acknowledged that her husband had been right.

However, he did admit that he had not anticipated the energy and enthusiasm with which his cousin had entered the lists on the side of the reformists.

"He is totally resolved upon this course, Lizzie, it has become a *cause celébre* with him, I think. But he means to accomplish several other things too; we have discussed half a dozen at least, already. He tells me he wishes to purchase a farm in the neighbourhood."

"Does he seriously mean to settle here?" asked his wife.

"He certainly does, and enter into a business partnership with your uncle Gardiner as well," Darcy replied.

Elizabeth was concerned, wondering if this burst of energy could last. This was so different to the Fitzwilliam she remembered—a young man with little ambition, somewhat irritated by his lot as a younger son with no fortune or title, but a man nevertheless with a sense of fun and certainly no burning desire to do much more than enjoy the comfortable style of life his place in society afforded him.

Darcy sought to reassure her. "Well, my dear, he is older and more mature; life in the colonies has taught him responsibility if nothing else. Furthermore, he is no longer the dependent and disadvantaged younger son, waiting on his father's generosity for an allowance; he has a reasonable income from his investments and a small fortune in property overseas. He is able to follow his inclinations now, whereas before, he was bound by his circumstances to be cautious," he explained.

Elizabeth was interested to pursue this further.

"Does this mean he is now able to follow his heart in matrimonial matters as well as his inclination in politics?" she asked.

Darcy's answer was emphatic. "Undoubtedly, there can be no constraint upon him on that score, except in matters of character and disposition, of course."

Elizabeth smiled. "And Lady Catherine would not pursue him as vigorously as she might have done before?"

Her husband knew she was teasing and, anticipating her next question, said, "There is no way of knowing how assiduously Lady Catherine may prosecute her cause; Fitzwilliam is a particular favourite of hers."

"As you were?" interposed his wife.

"Indeed, but while one may not predict her actions, we can say with certainty that Fitzwilliam's fortune is now considerably more than anything she could take away from him. His assets have an increasing value, based as they are upon trade, the fastest growing enterprise on earth." Darcy smiled and, turning to regard his wife, added, "No, Lizzie, my dear, I think he will be free to make whatever choices he wishes. We must hope and pray they will be the right ones for him."

❧

Sometime later, contemplating her husband's words, Elizabeth realised that Colonel Fitzwilliam was clearly a changed man, very different to the one she had met some four years ago when visiting Charlotte Collins at Hunsford. It appeared he was back from the Eastern Colonies a man of independent means, mature and decisive, politically active, seeking to purchase a property, and with the capacity to marry a woman of his choice, unimpeded by the dictates and prejudices of his aunt, Lady Catherine de Bourgh, or anyone else.

That, at least, gave Elizabeth some satisfaction, for she knew from personal experience that Lady Catherine would dearly wish to arrange a suitable match for her now much more eligible nephew. To see her thwarted yet again would give Elizabeth particular pleasure.

Writing to her friend Charlotte Collins, she could express her feelings candidly, knowing Charlotte could keep a confidence.

My dear Charlotte, I am sure you will be delighted to hear that the amiable Colonel Fitzwilliam, Mr Darcy's cousin and Lady Catherine's nephew, is back from the colonies, where it seems he managed to make a small

*fortune, which now renders him independent of his aunt and his father. A
singularly satisfactory situation you will agree, I think.*

*Mr Darcy tells me he has plans to go into business, enter Parliament,
and acquire a property as well. This sounds suspiciously like a man who
may be preparing to take a wife and I look forward with great interest to
see who the lady of his choice may be and—and this is the most pressing
question—will his aunt approve of her. To be thrice disappointed in the
marriage partners of her dear nephews will be a grievous blow to Lady C's
pretensions indeed, do you not agree?*

Having despatched her letter to the post, Elizabeth came downstairs to
find Mr Darcy and Colonel Fitzwilliam deep in discussion in the sitting room.
Fitzwilliam had sought Darcy's opinion on a property, a small freehold farm
near Matlock, which Mr Gardiner had mentioned as a prospect worth considering. Fitzwilliam, having seen it already, was most enthusiastic and urged his
cousin to accompany him so they could inspect it together.

It transpired later that Darcy had tried to counsel him against undue haste,
but to no avail.

"He is quite determined, my dear, so it is probably best that I take a look at
this property, if only to assure myself that he is making the right decision."

"Did you assure him that he could stay at Pemberley as long as need be?"
asked his wife.

"I most certainly did, Lizzie, but he is in no mood to procrastinate; he insists he
must see this place and he *must* have my opinion. If he finds it suitable, I'll wager my
estate that he will probably purchase it before the week is out," he replied.

Elizabeth was, by now, quite certain there had to be a lady involved.

"Perhaps he is secretly engaged and means to impress the lady," she said,
but her husband shook his head.

"I am sorry to disappoint you, my dear, but I have asked him, quite bluntly,
and he has given me his word this is not the case. Indeed, there is no suggestion that he is intending to impress a prospective bride or anyone else with
pretensions of being the lord of the manor; he tells me he seeks only to acquire
a solid house with some acreage of farm and woodland. He means to be a
farmer," Darcy explained, to his wife's consternation. This did not sound like
the Fitzwilliam she knew at all.

When, on the following Saturday, the Darcys gave a dinner party at

Pemberley to make Fitzwilliam welcome, almost everyone in the neighbour-hood attended. The colonel, a regular visitor to Pemberley since his college days, was well liked and had many good friends in the district. Now, he was back and the news that he had acquired a fortune in the colonies and was still single seemed to have increased his desirability as an acquaintance. All his friends and some of his relatives attended, and Doctor Grantley, who was to marry Georgiana Darcy in the Spring, travelled up from Oxford to be present.

Elizabeth and Mrs Reynolds had spent many hours planning the occasion, and the dinner was a triumph, with much fine food and wine.

Afterwards, there came the usual calls for entertainment—dancing and music. Elizabeth and Georgiana obliged, and then young Miss Gardiner, whose clear, youthful voice had been enhanced by training and practise, sang a beau-tiful English air to general applause.

While she was putting her music away, Colonel Fitzwilliam joined her and Elizabeth at the pianoforte and invited Caroline to sing with him the duet they had performed together some three years ago, on the eve of his departure. Caroline had the music, and Elizabeth, though she could not recall it very well, was soon persuaded to accompany them as before. The song was then so delightfully rendered it held the company entranced, with the servants reluctant to bring in the coffee and sweets lest they should break the spell.

Amidst the applause that followed its conclusion, Colonel Fitzwilliam gallantly kissed Caroline's hand, and this time, she blushed as she curtseyed deeply before returning to her place beside her cousin Jane. Only then did she realise that she was trembling.

Elizabeth was curious to discover how Fitzwilliam had recalled the words of the song so well. He confessed he had never forgotten them. The song, he said, had haunted him and he had requested a copy, which the Gardiners had kindly provided. "It soon became my favourite party piece," he said and Elizabeth teasingly pressed him further.

"And did you always find a partner willing to sing it with you?"

"Oh yes," he replied, "but never one who could match the original for perfect harmony and sweetness. As you heard, Miss Gardiner has a most enchanting voice."

Elizabeth, perhaps hearing rather more in his words than he had intended to convey, thought he was probably enchanted by more than Miss Gardiner's voice, but said nothing, not wishing to spoil such a happy occasion.

The visit to the farm at Matlock turned out to be a great success, if one were to judge by the general approbation of those who journeyed thither the following week.

Everyone wanted to go, including Mr and Mrs Gardiner and their two daughters. Afterwards, opinions varied little.

Mr Gardiner thought it was good value and Darcy agreed—if that was the sort of property Fitzwilliam wanted, he should purchase it as soon as possible, he advised. Fitzwilliam declared it would suit him very well indeed, and Mrs Gardiner said the kitchen garden and orchard were superior to hers at Oakleigh. Elizabeth found it to be rather small, influenced no doubt by the accommodation at Pemberley, though she did admit the house had character and style, and needed only some refurbishment to be comfortable. Caroline, though she said little, thought it near to perfection. Only at home in the privacy of her bedroom did she reveal her thoughts to her diary.

It has been such a strange day. The journey to Matlock to see Colonel Fitzwilliam's choice of a property was generally uneventful, except Emily chased after a dog and fell over!

The property, situated in a cul-de-sac off the main Matlock road, is quite beautiful. It is a little place, perhaps half the size of Oakleigh and nothing when compared with Pemberley, but its situation and aspect are delightful.

Rarely have I seen a place more romantically situated than this one.

It sits in a small scoop of land filled with wildflowers and rampant mint, a pretty farmhouse with its own orchard, stables, and barns, surrounded by a green meadow sloping down to the river. And all this in the shadow of the Peaks, with the woods and the gorge below them.

Mama thought it pretty, Papa said it was good value, and for myself, though I never would have said so aloud, I could not have imagined a more perfect setting for a music room than the long space upstairs that runs the length of the house, affording from all its many windows such splendid views of the Peaks as to make one want to sing with joy!

What bliss to live in such a place! How fortunate is Colonel Fitzwilliam to have secured it.

When I expressed my views to Colonel Fitzwilliam (about the music room, not the part about singing with joy!) to my surprise, he agreed at once. "It will be perfect for just such a purpose, Miss Caroline," he said.

No one else in the party took much note of this, but later when we were preparing to leave and Mama had gone to comfort Emily, whose foot was aching from having fallen over in the meadow, he returned to my side and said in quite a serious voice, "That was a very clever idea, Miss Caroline. If I do decide to purchase this property, the upstairs room will definitely be a music room. I cannot think of a more appropriate use for it, and when it is ready, I hope you will play and sing for us there one day."

I thought he was just being polite, as he always is, but he did sound quite sincere and I do believe he meant it.

The early arrival of her sister Jane's baby daughter Emma completely absorbed Elizabeth's mind, and she quite forgot the concerns of Colonel Fitzwilliam and his farm, including her own opinion of his association with her cousin Caroline.

Little Emma Bingley, everyone agreed, was going to be a beauty like her mother. Her doting father could not stop boasting to all and sundry about his lovely wife and daughter, and no other topic was considered more worthy of any expense of time. Every visitor had to be shown the child, so they might agree with her father. Mr Bingley was in his element.

And then, it was almost time to start preparing for Christmas again.

Colonel Fitzwilliam, meanwhile, had contacted his lawyers and set in train the necessary arrangements for the purchase of the property at Matlock, well satisfied that it would suit his purposes. Mr Gardiner and Mr Darcy had both agreed that it was a sound investment.

In another matter, however, he was not to be so fortunate.

His ambitions to enter Parliament were thwarted when he failed to gain the support of sufficient numbers of men in the Whig Party to enable him to stand for the Commons under the reformist banner in the forthcoming election. The deteriorating situation in the country had given him hope that youth and enthusiasm would carry the day, but he had not the kind of immediate influence that he needed to obtain endorsement.

Disappointed and determined to try again, he called on the Gardiners to break the bad news to them and, finding the family deep in their preparations for Christmas and Caroline's birthday celebrations, he discarded his disconsolate mood and stayed to help.

The Gardiners' sons, Richard and Robert, were home from college and, together with their sisters, helped cheer him up.

The warmth and friendliness of their household, so very different to the way it had been in his own somewhat austere childhood home, appealed to him, and when they made him welcome, he could not resist their hospitality. He stayed to dinner and came again the following day and the day after that, always finding matters of business or pleasure to take him there and engage his attention.

꧁꧂

It was not until Boxing Day, however, that he began to understand that his pleasure in visiting Oakleigh seemed to have more and more to do with the Gardiners' eldest and loveliest daughter, Caroline.

He spent the entire afternoon in an agony of indecision and anticipation, during which time he had sorely tried the patience of his hostess, Mrs Darcy, by enquiring of her, on three separate occasions, at what time their party would be leaving for Oakleigh.

When finally they arrived at the Gardiners' residence, fearing he would betray his feelings, which he had only just begun to acknowledge to himself, he then forced himself to behave with the utmost propriety and restraint, bordering almost upon indifference to Caroline.

On first seeing her as she entered the room with her father, he barely met her eyes before disappearing into an ante-room simply to avoid committing some unforgivable indiscretion that would give him away. She looked particularly appealing, in a gown of cornflower blue silk, with her dark hair done in a new Grecian style, and Fitzwilliam was sure she would have many partners.

To his relief, Caroline's cousin James appeared to have been assigned the role of her escort for the evening, and it was he who led her into the first dance. Having previously extracted from her a promise of two dances later in the program, Fitzwilliam kept his distance as a seemingly interminable queue of brothers, friends, cousins, and uncles had to be allowed to dance with her before he could claim his reward for his patience and discretion.

When he did, however, she appeared so genuinely delighted that he was certain she must have sensed something of his eagerness. As he bowed and asked for the honour of this dance, she smiled and took his hand and accompanied him to the centre of the room, saying softly, "I was beginning to think you did not find the music to your taste, Colonel Fitzwilliam, so rarely did I see you dancing tonight. Indeed, I wondered if you might not dance with me at all," then seeing the outraged expression upon his face, she added quickly, and with a charming smile, "I see I was mistaken and am very happy to have been so."

As they danced, they spoke but little, and it may have seemed to those observing them that they were merely a particularly well-matched pair of dancers, but in Elizabeth's mind there was no doubt at all. Clearly, Fitzwilliam was fascinated by her young cousin; whether he knew it or not, it was plain to her. Whether young Caroline knew was quite another matter. Whatever the answer, Elizabeth did not fail to notice that they danced only with one another for the rest of the evening, until supper was announced and the musicians took their rest.

As they went into the dining room, her sister Jane, always alert to a romance in the making, did not improve matters when she commented that Caroline and Fitzwilliam made a very handsome pair, to which Elizabeth could only reply that none but a blind man would fail to see that they were also very much in love.

On returning to Pemberley, Colonel Fitzwilliam, who had been unusually quiet during the short journey from Oakleigh, thanked his host and hostess and went directly to his room. Elizabeth wondered whether her husband had noticed what she had, but it had been a long day and Darcy seemed tired; she refrained from questioning him on the subject, planning instead to observe both Caroline and Fitzwilliam over the next few weeks to ascertain if anything more were to proceed from tonight.

Elizabeth had often seen couples appear to be strongly attracted to one another at a ball or a dinner party, where the romantic music and the general ambience might encourage such impressions, yet on later reflection, their attraction often failed to survive the cold light of day, not to mention the disapproval of their families. Of the latter, she expected there may well be a considerable amount in this case, on account of the difference in their ages.

Fitzwilliam was probably thirty-two years old while Caroline was just fifteen; Elizabeth would not have been surprised if their apparent fascination with each other, which had been so plain to her that night, was somewhat short-lived. Still, she would watch closely, because as far as she knew, her young cousin had never been in love before and it would not do for her to be hurt, especially not by Mr Darcy's cousin.

~᭟~

Caroline, meanwhile, feeling astonishingly alert and bright at the end of what had been a very long and exciting day, lay in bed, wide awake, unable to sleep. The evening had been more than memorable; it had been unique in her experience. One subject engrossed her thoughts, and as she turned it over in her mind, she knew she was afraid to admit, even to herself, that she was probably on the very verge of falling in love with a man almost twenty years her senior—who until a few months ago, she had regarded only as her father's friend and business partner.

Yet, since his return to England in early Autumn, something had changed between them. There was no denying it; she had been aware of it from the very first day, when he had arrived whilst they were reading poetry on the terrace at Pemberley and they had read William Blake's poem together. Since then, they had talked often of Blake and why "Jerusalem" was Colonel Fitzwilliam's favourite poem and gradually, she too had begun to respond to its stirring message.

He had been delighted when she, having committed the poem to memory, had spoken it again as they had walked in the grounds of her father's property, and he had told her of the despoiling of the moors and meadows of the midlands with coal pits and slag heaps and the cramming of thousands of former rural men, women, and children into hideous mills and mines all over England. When they spoke of the children in the mines, there had been tears in her eyes.

They had met again on several occasions, always with their families around them, and each time she had become conscious of his attention to her. Though he had said nothing explicitly to mark her out, it was there in his manners and actions, in small but significant ways and in the way he seemed to watch her, even when she was not in his immediate circle.

When he spoke with her, it was neither in a patronising manner, nor in that foolish, flattering way that men like Wickham used to flirt with young girls. But there was a special attention, a more personal communication that she could not fail to sense each time they met.

He would listen as if everything she said was important to him, and when he spoke to her, she remembered every word, every expression exactly. With no other man of her acquaintance had it been so.

When at the Pemberley party, they had sung together the same English lyric they had sung three and a half years ago, when she was a mere girl; Caroline had felt the difference and she had trembled, not because she was young and shy, as her cousin Jane had thought at the time, but because she was conscious that they had sung so well together, enjoying it so much, even she had been surprised and touched by it.

When Fitzwilliam had taken her hand in his and kissed it, as the assembled guests applauded, all manner of hitherto unknown sensations and feelings had flooded through her, leaving her flustered and confused. Her deep curtsey had been as much to hide her confusion as to acknowledge their appreciation.

Caroline Gardiner was a romantic young person, but she was neither foolish nor naïve. She knew in her heart that if she permitted herself to fall in love with Colonel Fitzwilliam, it would not be a matter of flirtation and silliness but would inevitably lead to a deeper attachment, should he wish it. She knew she would not be able to contain her feelings.

And therein lay her dilemma; for while she was aware of a change in her feelings towards him, she was, as yet, unsure whether, on his part, there was any desire for an affection deeper and more significant than mere friendship. It would need to be a deep and sincere affinity, if she were to respond to it as she wanted to. Else, she knew well, it would end only in misery and Caroline was unready for that risk.

As if silence would help protect her secret feelings, she resolved not to speak of the subject to anyone, certainly not before Colonel Fitzwilliam had spoken to her.

"If he does care for me as deeply and truly as I do for him, he will want to tell me before long. He must wish to discover if my feelings are the same. Until he does, I shall keep my counsel and no one shall know how I feel," she resolved.

What anxiety or pain lay ahead for her, she knew not. That there may be some of that to endure, she was well aware. Yet, despite her refusal to even contemplate such a situation until she knew his mind, Caroline could not keep her innocent thoughts from returning again and again to the possibility of loving and being loved by him as a most welcome and pleasurable prospect, as she drifted into sleep in the early hours of the morning.

The New Year brought no resolution to Caroline's predicament, for Colonel Fitzwilliam had to travel to London on business with her father. On the morning they were to depart, he called to say farewell to the family, and her brothers monopolised him, while the bustle of servants loading Mr Gardiner's trunk and papers into the carriage surrounded them. Only moments before they were to start, while Mrs Gardiner had rushed upstairs to fetch some missing item of her husband's luggage, did he approach her as she stood in the hall and say in a friendly though not especially intimate or affectionate manner, "Miss Gardiner, Caroline, I must say good-bye now, but I promise I shall return with a copy of your favourite song by Mr Handel, of which we spoke on your birthday, and I hope we shall soon hear you sing it for us."

In mentioning the song "Where e'er you walk...", which they had both commended, was he, she wondered, reminding her discreetly of her birthday, on which occasion they had heard it admirably performed and wished they had a copy of the music so they too might learn to sing it?

It was also the last evening on which they had spent so much time together and all so pleasantly that each had seemed not to want to break away until the carriage for Pemberley was about to leave and Fitzwilliam had to go.

Did he expect from her some response other than the simple line: "Thank you, Colonel Fitzwilliam, I shall look forward to learning it."

She was not to know, for Richard and Robert were back to shake his hand and her mother was coming downstairs. There was time only to give him her hand and say, "I shall pray that God speed you and Papa safely on your journey."

At which, he smiled, kissed her hand, and was gone to enter the carriage, followed by Mr Gardiner. Caroline watched from the window on the landing until the vehicle was hidden from sight by the ancient oaks that gave the property its name and then went quietly up to her room.

❧

After some weeks of separation, they met again at Georgiana Darcy's wedding, on a fine Spring morning at Pemberley.

Caroline had dressed for the occasion with more than usual care, knowing he would be there. As the cousin of the bride and one of her guardians, Fitzwilliam would be prominently involved, she thought, and would probably not notice her in the midst of the large and distinguished party assembled at Pemberley.

Even the redoubtable Lady Catherine de Bourgh and her daughter Anne were attending, gracing Pemberley with their presence for the first time since the marriage of Darcy and Elizabeth, of which Her Ladyship had so disapproved. Elizabeth had informed them of this with some glee, suggesting mischievously that Her Ladyship was probably hoping to catch her nephew's wife out in some social *faux pas* that would, in retrospect, justify her objections to their union.

As Her Ladyship's nephew, Fitzwilliam would be kept busy, Caroline was certain, waiting upon his aunt and paying attention to her daughter.

Which was why she was so surprised when he appeared at her side as she waited with her family to see the bride and groom arrive at the banquet, and asked if she would do him the honour of letting him escort her into the dining room.

So taken aback was Caroline that she almost forgot to thank him for the music he had sent her through her father. Mr Gardiner, who on his return from London always brought them gifts, had pointed out that this was one gift he had not chosen, for being a fairly plain man he was no connoisseur of the delights of Mr Handel's music, but the colonel had assured him that Caroline knew all about it. Oddly, this had caused no comment among the Gardiners.

When she did remember and thanked him very nicely, her father's remarks provided an appropriate opening to their subsequent conversation, which, as these things often do, led from one matter to another and extended without difficulty over the entire duration of the banquet.

Meanwhile, Elizabeth, overwhelmed by her responsibilities as hostess and her desire to ensure that every detail was right for the great occasion, was totally distracted from her resolution to observe the pair. She therefore failed to notice that Fitzwilliam and Caroline had been together during the meal, nor did she note the ease with which they then settled down to converse exclusively with one another over the next two hours.

As for her husband, Mr Darcy had been observing, with his father-in-law Mr Bennet, the performance of Mr Collins at his most obsequious best as he tried using every possible stratagem to ingratiate himself with Doctor Grantley. It was a plan he had conceived ever since he had learned from Lady Catherine herself that the learned gentleman was a theologian of repute at Oxford and likely to rise to high places in the church. Hopes of preferment had risen in Mr Collins's breast.

"The fellow never gives up, does he, Mr Darcy?" quipped Mr Bennet and his son-in-law had to agree.

"No indeed, sir, I have never seen anything or anyone that could stop him when he is determined to promote himself."

Mr Bennet, whose regard for his son-in-law had risen on every occasion upon which they had met, was determined to tell Mr Darcy of at least one instance when the intrepid Mr Collins's efforts had been brought to a halt: when he had first arrived at Longbourn intending to marry one of his five young cousins and had set about pursuing Lizzie with great determination.

"He began his campaign with a sermon on matrimony and financial security, but Lizzie would have none of it and put a stop to him very firmly. So astonished was he at being turned down by her, having no doubt assumed that any one of the girls would be grateful for his offer, he left in high dudgeon to visit the Lucases, returning less than twenty-four hours later engaged to Miss Charlotte Lucas. Mrs Bennet was furious, but Lizzie and I were mightily amused. We were sorry for Miss Lucas, though; the man's an idiot," said Mr Bennet, chuckling at the memory of that encounter.

Mr Darcy, who had heard his wife's version of the story and enjoyed Mr Bennet's dry sense of humour, was about to ask his father-in-law a question about his own role in the failed proposal of Mr Collins when a gentleman rose to speak. A colleague of Doctor Grantley, he had travelled with him from Oxford to be his best man.

"Let us hope he is not going to be as longwinded as Mr Collins or we shall be here all day," said Mr Bennet, who tired easily of sermons and high sententiousness, and Mr Darcy agreed.

"It is difficult to believe that Mrs Collins is not heartily tired of him; he would try the patience of a saint!" he said, only to be assured by Mr Bennet that as far as he could judge, the lady was a loyal but not uncritical wife.

"Jane and Lizzie are her closest friends," he said, with a wry smile. "I do believe they know rather more of the matter than we do. Mrs Collins, I would say, has the measure of the man."

With the attention of the guests concentrated upon the bridal couple, their retinue, and families, Fitzwilliam and Caroline found time to talk of the myriad of matters which they had stored up to tell each other over the weeks when they had been apart.

Fortuitously for them, Georgiana's companion, Mrs Annesley, sat to one side of Fitzwilliam, sobbing quietly through most of the meal, so devastated was she at losing her "dear Miss Georgiana", while young Robert Gardiner, who was more interested in the food than in small talk, sat beside his sister and ate very well, undisturbed by any attempt at polite conversation. It was the ideal situation for a couple who had so much to say to one another that all other conversation must be an unwelcome distraction.

Yet Fitzwilliam, mindful of his situation and solicitous of Caroline's feelings, was amiable and pleasant but said or did nothing that would have led to any embarrassment to her or her parents.

Behaving with perfect decorum at all times, he struggled hard to keep his feelings concealed, for Caroline's beauty and sweetness of disposition were especially appealing upon this day.

Caroline, unaware that the man she was falling in love with was as concerned about his feelings as she was, despite the delight she had experienced at seeing him again and being singled out by him for attention, was a little disappointed that he had said nothing that gave her any indication of his intentions. She wrote in her diary that night:

> *It is difficult to believe that he does not care for me when he singles me out and behaves with such graciousness towards me and shows so much respect to Mama and Papa, but I wish he would let me see if his feelings are more than a general affectionate friendliness as one might feel for a sister or indeed a cousin like Georgiana, of whom I know he is very fond indeed. It would mean so much to know if one was truly loved.*

Poor Caroline; it seemed there never was a young woman more deeply loved who had so little knowledge of it. For Colonel Fitzwilliam was involved in a great deal of soul searching and, like Caroline, had determined to keep his feelings to himself until he had resolved his own dilemma. That he was in love with Miss Gardiner he had already acknowledged to himself. Indeed, the question had engrossed his mind for several weeks. Uncertainty on that score did not pose a problem.

The colonel's difficulty arose from the fact that he was clearly the only person in the Gardiner family, or among their relations and acquaintances, who did not still regard young Caroline as a child.

To him she had been transformed over their years apart into a lovely young woman with a mind of her own and a very particular appeal. To her parents, her aunts, and uncles, however, she remained their little girl.

He had no doubt that to Mr Gardiner, who had spoken often and with great affection of his family on their journey to London, she was still "my little Caroline."

He had tried to discover how Elizabeth might regard the situation, perhaps even canvass the possibility of approaching Mr Gardiner, but he had found no appropriate occasion in the midst of preparations for Georgiana's wedding to broach the delicate subject with her.

Impossible then to continue to let a warm and affectionate association grow between himself and Caroline, whose fondness for him seemed to be increasing each time they met. It was something he had become very aware of and while uncertainty existed about the propriety of his situation, he was beginning to feel some degree of guilt in allowing it to develop.

What, he wondered, would Mr and Mrs Gardiner say if he declared his feelings for Caroline and asked for their permission to propose marriage to her? Would they welcome it because they liked and respected him? Or would they be appalled that he, a man of three and thirty years, worldly wise, and well versed in society, was asking to marry their fifteen-year-old daughter? Might they be angry and accuse him of taking advantage of her youth and innocence?

Even worse, what if they were so outraged, they forbade him to see her again and perhaps sent her away from Oakleigh to her uncle's place in the next county?

What would that do to Caroline and how might she regard him then? Would she not feel he had trifled with her tender feelings, like some insensitive scoundrel, and betrayed her at the first sign of difficulty?

And what of Darcy and Elizabeth, he wondered? Would they understand and sympathise with him or take the part of the Gardiners, who were their dearest friends?

These and other terrible possibilities assailed him, and the speculation, though without foundation in fact, kept him sleepless on many nights.

How was he to resolve them, he wondered, for resolve them he must or give up all hope of Caroline and flee to London, abandoning his plans of settling permanently in the district.

Thus, in the midst of one of the happiest occasions seen at Pemberley in years, with every reason to be pleased with the world and a strong feeling that the young woman he loved was almost certainly willing to return his affection, Fitzwilliam could not avoid a sense of unease and apprehension, lest it should all suddenly come to naught.

~⋎~

That matters came to a head much sooner than either Fitzwilliam or Caroline had anticipated was due largely to chance.

The year following Fitzwilliam's return produced in England a mood of sullen anger and depression, following a collapse in the textile industry, and the loss of thousands of jobs. The rural poor, many of whom had been evicted from their small holdings and cottages by enclosures, had migrated to the industrial towns in search of work. They had been promised jobs in the mills of Manchester and other textile towns, but the work had not lasted and many found themselves on the streets again, this time on the cold, unfriendly streets of the towns, where along with hundreds of others, they waited upon the charity of strangers.

Fitzwilliam had been summoned to a meeting of men of the reform movement, who, together with prominent Whigs like Sir Francis Burdett and Lord Brougham, were demanding reform of the Parliament, while pamphleteers like Cobbett argued for more radical measures.

The atmosphere in the Midlands was not conducive to amicable discussion; there had been a spate of violent machine breaking and attacks on mills and mill owners, and the government had increased the penalties for such offences to hanging or transportation.

Returning from a business trip to Liverpool, Mr Gardiner arrived at Pemberley to report that there were fears that goods on the docks may be burned, there was real anger in the streets, and many traders were boarding up their warehouses.

The news infuriated Fitzwilliam, who had arrived not long before him.

"What do they propose to do?" he demanded, "hang or transport half the population of the Midlands?" Impatient and angry, he jumped up, vowing to join Cobbett and the radicals, no matter what the government might bring against them. His voice rising with frustration, he declared, "If that is the only way to get our voices heard, I fear I shall have no alternative. I can no longer stand by and do nothing."

Clearly, Fitzwilliam was outraged, and both Mr Darcy and Mr Gardiner were generally in sympathy with him, but neither were likely to advise that he join the radicals. Draconian measures brought in by the government would soon see him exiled or worse. With no seat in Parliament and no formal endorsement from a party, not even the protection of a title, he would surely be placing himself in great jeopardy. Mr Darcy advised moderation and Mr Gardiner, whose daughters had been spending the day at Pemberley with their cousin, counselled caution. Having extracted a promise that Fitzwilliam would do nothing without consulting him, he left with the two girls for Oakleigh.

Later, Elizabeth sought out her husband, determined to take up with him a matter of some importance, which had been causing her considerable concern all evening.

When first he heard what she had to say, he was both surprised and unwilling to take the matter as seriously as she did.

"Lizzie, dearest, are you sure? Is it not possible that young Caroline has misunderstood the situation? She is, after all, at a very impressionable age, and while I am aware that Fitzwilliam is fond of her, I had believed it to be quite an innocent affection when you consider that she is a mere child."

But Elizabeth was adamant; there was no misunderstanding, she was certain of it. She told him how she had found young Caroline in tears after hearing Fitzwilliam's outburst and his threat to join the radicals. On further questioning, she had been left in no doubt that there was, at the very least, a very close bond between them, one that suggested to her the existence of feelings far deeper than friendship.

"She confessed that she loved him and has as yet told no one of her feelings. She was absolutely miserable, Darcy. Could you not speak to Fitzwilliam?" she pleaded, and seeing his reluctance, said, "He is your cousin and respects and values your advice in all things."

Darcy's lack of enthusiasm for such a mission was plain and with good reason.

"My dear Lizzie, you more than anyone will understand my absolute determination never to interfere in the romantic affairs of my friends and relations ever again, having caused so much misery by my last effort," he protested, but Elizabeth pleaded, "I do understand, dearest, but can you not see that we cannot turn a blind eye to this situation, now it has been revealed to us? I know I shall blame myself if Caroline were to be hurt and my aunt Gardiner will never forgive me for not trying to prevent it."

Darcy was sceptical of their hopes of success.

"Do you honestly believe, my love, that we could prevent it, if both Fitzwilliam and Caroline had their hearts set upon it? As I said, I have noticed no more than a general fondness on his part, which I thought quite natural. She is accomplished and beautiful, with a most endearing nature. I did not believe there could be more to it, but I may well be wrong. However, while I appreciate your concern for Caroline, remember, Lizzie, he is no Wickham and I do not believe for a moment that there is any similar danger to her. Caroline is much more sensible than Lydia, and I would wager my entire estate on Fitzwilliam's honour and integrity.

"But I do understand your anxiety, and if it would ease your mind, I am prepared to see him to ascertain, if he is willing to confide in me, what his intentions are. Will that satisfy you?" His wife's gratitude, affectionately and extravagantly expressed, assured him that it would.

⁓⋎⁓

Some days later, Elizabeth went to visit her sister Jane Bingley at Ashford Park in the next county, her arrival preceded by a note which stated that her purpose was "to acquaint you with a matter of great delicacy and importance to someone very dear to us all."

Her husband, on the same day, travelled the short distance to Matlock, hoping to find his cousin alone at the farm, where he was supervising some refurbishments to the house he had recently purchased.

Fitzwilliam was pleasantly surprised to see him arrive. "Darcy, it is good to see you—much as I enjoy having this place improved, there is little I can do except watch the men at work. I was just beginning to be bored and your company is most welcome."

Darcy was at first awkward, apologising for intruding upon him and then urging him not to misunderstand the purpose of his visit.

"I do not mean to interfere in any way in your life, Fitzwilliam; I believe you are sufficiently responsible to conduct your personal affairs with good sense and honour, and if you were to tell me to be gone and say no more, I shall do so at once."

By this time, his cousin was thoroughly bewildered. "Darcy, to what do you refer? Why would I ask you to be gone? Have I offended you in some way? Surely, there is nothing we cannot discuss after all these years? I understand that you may find my views on some political questions rather radical, but you have known my mind on these matters…"

Darcy had to interrupt to explain that his concern was not with matters political at all. Apologising again for what he might deem to be gratuitous interference in his personal life, Darcy asked in the most conciliatory tone he could muster if Fitzwilliam would care to reveal to him, in strict confidence, his intentions towards young Miss Caroline Gardiner.

Awkwardly, but reasonably, he explained that his wife Elizabeth was anxious lest Caroline, being both young and impressionable, may have misunderstood fondness for something deeper and more serious.

"Elizabeth's concern is for Caroline and for her parents' feelings. She has no criticism of you whatsoever, Fitzwilliam, and neither have I," he said.

Fitzwilliam listened, his face flushed, his eyes downcast. He was unaccustomed to subterfuge, and the strain of concealment as well as the fear of causing offence had taken their toll upon him. Darcy was pleased to see there was neither anger nor resentment in his voice when he spoke, conceding Elizabeth's right as Caroline's cousin to enquire and exonerating Darcy of any charge of interference.

First, he assured his cousin that Caroline, despite or probably because of her tender age and innocence, was in no danger at all of being hurt in any way by him.

"I love her dearly, Darcy, and wish to marry her," he said simply, taking Darcy's breath away with his forthright declaration. He had not expected such a clear answer.

Continuing, Fitzwilliam revealed that he had realised after Christmas, certainly after Caroline's birthday celebration, that he was falling in love with her. Afraid at first to admit it even to himself and terrified lest her parents should discover his feelings for the daughter they still regarded as a child, he had done his best to conceal them.

"To make matters worse, it was becoming increasingly clear to me that Caroline reciprocated my undeclared feelings for her, sensing probably, as women intuitively do, that she was loved. Each meeting only confirmed my belief, and while I was naturally delighted, I was also fearful, lest we betray our feelings to others. Try as I might, I could not suppress my own affections nor discourage hers, innocent and tender as they were, without wounding her, which was the very last thing I wished to do."

"Why did you not come to me or confide in Elizabeth?" asked Darcy. "We would have listened to you, at least."

"I was afraid you may well berate me for taking advantage of her innocence and youth. I remember how furious you were with Wickham when he tried..." but Darcy interrupted him abruptly.

"The man was a villain, Fitzwilliam, a blackguard who was using my sister's innocence for his own ends to be revenged upon me and enrich himself. There is no comparison!" His anger at the recollection was obvious.

"Nevertheless, I feared your censure and Elizabeth's. I am almost thirty-three years old. Caroline is just fifteen. I feared most of all that a premature revelation might mean that I would lose her altogether."

Darcy could see how deeply his cousin's feelings were engaged. He experienced some degree of surprise, for while he had known Fitzwilliam to be passionate about politics, he had never seen him similarly committed in love.

"What do you intend to do now?" he asked, feeling much sympathy for him in his present predicament.

Imagine then his astonishment, when Fitzwilliam replied quietly, "It is done already, Darcy. I could no longer bear the uncertainty, nor could I continue to deceive the Gardiners, who have been exceedingly kind and hospitable to me. It would have been unthinkable that I sign up to a partnership with Mr Gardiner, as we have agreed, without acquainting him with my feelings for Caroline.

"A week ago, while Caroline was at Pemberley, I called on Mr and Mrs Gardiner and told them everything that I have told you. I placed myself in their hands; I gave them my word that I would do nothing, tell no one, not even Caroline, unless and until they had given me permission to speak. I asked for no marriage settlement, Darcy, proposing instead to settle the entire sum left to me, by my mother, upon Caroline when we are engaged, so she may have her own allowance, and despite my yearning for her, I have promised that we shall wait to be married until she is sixteen."

Darcy was silent. His cousin had astonished him; never in all their acquaintance had he known Fitzwilliam to be so determined and to act in such a decisive manner. Previously, in matters of the heart, he had been notoriously dilatory and irresolute, unwilling to take the first step. This time, clearly he was irrevocably in love.

"What did they say?" he asked and before he answered, Fitzwilliam said, "I told them also, as I tell you, Darcy, that while I have felt a passing fancy for two or three young women in my time, never have I loved anyone as deeply and with such pure affection as I do Caroline."

Darcy felt for his cousin, understanding how he must have suffered.

"Does she know of your feelings?" he asked.

Fitzwilliam looked somewhat disconsolate. "I pleaded with them to let me tell her, because I knew how much it would please her, but both Mr and Mrs Gardiner wished me to wait awhile. They are understandably cautious, Darcy; Caroline is very precious to them and they are concerned that, at such a tender age, she may not know her own mind, or being swept away by her feelings, may make the wrong decision. However, they have assured me of their affection and regard, commending my discretion and the honesty of my approach to them."

Darcy was impatient to discover more. "And when will they give you their answer?"

"I am to call on them on Sunday. Darcy my dear fellow, I can only ask that you wish me the very best of luck, for I love her dearly and should they refuse me, it would be a most devastating blow!"

Having spent some time reassuring his cousin and promising, if applied to by Mr Gardiner, to give him the best recommendation ever as a prospective son-in-law, Darcy left Matlock to make the journey of some twenty-five miles to Ashford Park, where Elizabeth and Jane awaited his return, eager for news. He looked forward to seeing Elizabeth's face when he told her of the success of his meeting with Fitzwilliam.

The two sisters had waited all afternoon for Mr Darcy's return, having gravely discussed the situation in which their cousin Caroline and Colonel Fitzwilliam were placed. No strangers to the vicissitudes of love and courtship, both Jane and Elizabeth had much sympathy for their cousin. They hoped Mr Darcy would arrive with good news, and they were not disappointed.

Glad to be able to assure them that there was no bad news in store and indeed, by Sunday, they may have some very good news, Mr Darcy concluded one of the most delicate missions he had ever been called upon to undertake.

When it was all explained, Mr Bingley, who had hitherto not been privy to the matter, expressed both amazement and pleasure at the new development, while Jane was completely delighted. She had been the first to sense the romance and was happy to learn that the situation was as she had hoped it would be. Her gentle, affectionate heart was finally satisfied.

Elizabeth was very proud of her husband's efforts. As they journeyed home that night, he was anxious for her approval and she made her appreciation very clear.

"You did very well indeed, my love, I am pleased and relieved that the matter is now in the hands of my uncle and aunt Gardiner. They will do what is best for Caroline and I hope it will make us all happy. I shall never forget your kindness and I thank you from the bottom of my heart."

~♥~

By prior arrangement with their mother, Caroline and Emily were invited to spend the day at Pemberley on the following Sunday, while unbeknownst to them, Colonel Fitzwilliam journeyed to Oakleigh to keep his appointment with their parents.

The Gardiners greeted him cordially and plied him with refreshments before Mrs Gardiner left the room, leaving the two men together. Then, with carefully chosen words, Caroline's father explained how very dear she was to them and with what deep concern they would view any proposal for her hand in marriage, especially at such a tender age.

"Caroline is a very special person, Colonel Fitzwilliam, as you no doubt have realised. She is affectionate and kind, even to the point of being an incurable romantic, but she is also strong, loyal, and has the highest principles Mrs Gardiner and I could teach her."

He was at pains to explain that his daughter would never marry for mercenary reasons.

"Neither money nor social status can influence her. She is well provided for, and though I am not by any means a rich man, none of my children will be in want when I am gone. I have ensured that, and they, especially Caroline and Richard, are aware of it, which does mean she has no need to marry in order to keep the wolf from the door, so to speak."

As Fitzwilliam listened, he went on, "She does, however, value sincerity and genuine goodness, as we do. Mrs Gardiner believes that Caroline has appreciated what is estimable in your character—she has gathered this in her conversations with her, and of course, Mr Darcy, for whom we both have the highest regard, speaks exceedingly well of you."

Seeing Fitzwilliam's countenance lighten, as he silently thanked his cousin for his support, Mr Gardiner added, "I have not consulted Mr Darcy about your proposal of marriage, but his recommendation of you for a partnership in the business was of the highest order; I cannot imagine that it would be any different in this instance. Furthermore, when I first knew you, Colonel Fitzwilliam, I judged you to be a man of honour and good character; nothing in my own observation of you since your return from the East has caused me to doubt that earlier judgment."

As the colonel bowed to acknowledge his kind words, Mr Gardiner continued, "However, you will accept, I am sure, that when it comes to giving our dear Caroline in marriage, I am entitled to be particularly careful. She is the jewel in our family. Which is why, knowing you to be a gentleman I can trust, I have placed a few conditions upon you, which if you are willing to fulfill, you may speak to Caroline of your proposal. Should she accept you, as I believe she may, you shall certainly have my blessing."

Fitzwilliam could not keep from smiling, so great was his delight, as he asked, a little impatiently, what the conditions were that Mr Gardiner had laid down for him.

When told they could become engaged but would have to wait until Caroline was sixteen before they could marry, and that Caroline, who would receive from her father a portion of shares in the company, be permitted to hold them in trust as her own property, Fitzwilliam had no hesitation in agreeing.

The matter being amicably settled, the two men partook of a quiet drink together before the colonel, still smiling, left for Pemberley.

After a very pleasant day, spent mostly walking in the grounds and reading in the library at Pemberley, Caroline and her sister Emily went upstairs to dress for dinner. When Elizabeth's maid Jenny came to say that Colonel Fitzwilliam had arrived and was in the sitting room with Mr Darcy, Elizabeth knew she had to prepare her cousin for what was to follow. Having avoided any mention of the colonel all day, it was time to reveal what had been in train, and when she did so, Caroline was most apprehensive.

"Oh dear cousin Lizzie, do you think Mama would have been very angry?" she asked, but Elizabeth reassured her, reminding her that her mama was "one of the kindest and wisest persons I know."

Once downstairs, they were met in the hall by Mr Darcy.

"Ah, Elizabeth, Caroline, there you are," he said, adding a little lamely what they all knew already, "Fitzwilliam is here," and though he said no more, Elizabeth judged from his countenance that all was well.

Caroline, with a little encouragement from her cousin, composed herself and entered the saloon, where Fitzwilliam waited. He was standing by the window, looking out over the park; when they entered, he turned and came to greet them. First Elizabeth, whom he thanked with affection for her care and concern, and then Caroline, to whom he held out both hands in a manner that proclaimed openly for the first time, without inhibition or unease, the closeness of their relationship, and as Elizabeth watched, Caroline went willingly into his arms.

Not wishing to intrude upon their happiness, Elizabeth slipped away to join her husband, who had earlier heard Fitzwilliam's account of his meeting with the Gardiners. She knew there would be no heartbreak for Caroline, but she hoped Darcy would enlighten her further and to this end, drew him away to another part of the house, where they could speak undisturbed.

Of the lovers newly acknowledged, suffice it to say that tears were shed as he took her in his arms and told her of his love and her parents' blessing, but they were without exception tears of joy. The anxiety and apprehension of the last few months had disappeared in but a few moments, to be replaced by the hope of greater happiness to follow.

Never in her young life had Caroline known such delight, nor imagined such bliss, as she now experienced. Unskilled at coquetry, unwilling to feign surprise, and unable to pretend, she confessed the full extent of her love for him, and the colonel, having kept his feelings under strict restraint for several weeks, could now, in the privacy afforded them at Pemberley, express with the deepest ardour and sincerity, the warm sentiments which Caroline had so wanted to hear and could promise to return in full measure.

Like many brave lovers before them, but possibly with greater determination than most, they resolved then and there that their love would be so strong as to overcome every future adversity.

Chapter Three

THE CHILD OF A CONVENTIONALLY happy marriage with siblings to whom she had always been expected to set an example, Caroline Gardiner had carried upon her young shoulders a not inconsiderable weight of expectation.

Seeing her cousins Jane and Elizabeth marry the men they loved, men whom her parents held in the highest esteem, Caroline had hoped, and indeed wished, that she too may one day meet such a man. Yet, she was aware that it was not common for gentlemen of honour and quality to be found wandering the dales of Derbyshire in search of eligible young women to wed.

Since she had felt no particular interest in any of the young men of her acquaintance and her only male cousin was already spoken for, Caroline, though only fifteen, had begun to contemplate seriously the advantages of spinsterhood. The pleasures of her happy home and the love of devoted parents would not easily be exchanged for marriage, she had decided, unless it was to an exceptional man she could love without question. It was not, however, an option she ever canvassed with her mother or her cousins, who would have laughed her to scorn. Her general sweetness of temper, her accomplishments, and her beauty would certainly get her a good husband, they would have said. But Caroline was not so sure.

The reappearance of Colonel Fitzwilliam after some three years in the Eastern colonies had changed all that, and despite the initial heartache and anxiety, Caroline's happiness was now so overwhelming as to be irresistible. Other members of the family seemed to "catch" it like children caught the measles. The Gardiners all appeared infected with the euphoria that surrounded Fitzwilliam and Caroline.

Writing to her friend Charlotte Collins, Elizabeth expressed her astonishment at the phenomenon.

My dear Charlotte,

How I wish you could have been here with us at this time, although I do understand that Mr Collins's chaplaincy and parish responsibilities must be onerous and will, of necessity, keep him at Hunsford. If however you should have the opportunity to make the journey to Pemberley, you will see a most amazing transformation in two people of whom we are both quite fond.

Let me first break the news.

Colonel Fitzwilliam, Mr Darcy's cousin, is engaged to be married to my cousin, Caroline Gardiner. Now, Charlotte, before you accuse Mr Darcy and me of matchmaking, let me hasten to assure you that this couple had done all that themselves, before Darcy and I were even aware of their interest in one another. As you know, Colonel Fitzwilliam is recently home from the eastern colonies a more prosperous and energetic gentleman than when he left England three years ago.

Having negotiated a partnership with my uncle Gardiner in his Commercial Trading Company, it seems Colonel Fitzwilliam has also discovered that a marriage partnership with their daughter Caroline was essential to his continued happiness and she likewise, having fallen in love with the colonel, the two are now engaged.

Charlotte my dear, you may well berate me for my flippant tone, but do not accuse me of poking fun at these fortunate lovers, for I have certainly not forgotten the joys of courtship. However, I cannot believe that I, at any stage of my life, wandered around Meryton resembling a beacon, which is how one would describe my fair cousin and her Colonel, so clearly radiant are they with happiness. One cannot only be happy for them, one must surely pray that nothing will ever mar their joy.

I believe Lady Catherine has been informed, by her nephew, of his engagement to my cousin. I wonder if she will ask them to Rosings; it is doubtful, seeing she holds my uncle's mode of earning an honest living as placing him beneath her notice.

We are not going away at all this Winter, seeing as our second child is due before Christmas. Dear Charlotte, I must ask for your prayers for a safe and speedy delivery.

Meanwhile, please look after yourself with great care until we meet again.

Yours etc...

Elizabeth Darcy

While Elizabeth's attention was totally concentrated upon the child that was soon to arrive, Caroline found herself being drawn inevitably into Fitzwilliam's political career. It had opened up an entirely new world to her, and she was enjoying it immensely.

Momentous changes were sweeping England, with the shocking consequences of economic depression apparent everywhere. Bankruptcies, evictions, and forced sales were a daily occurrence, and resentment grew among the dispossessed.

In August of 1819, an incident took place that came to be written in the history books in the kind of ironic language usually reserved for satire.

Some sixty thousand unarmed workers held a mass meeting at St Peters Field, near Manchester, and when the magistrates panicked and sent in sabre-wielding troops on horseback to attack and disperse them, killing eleven and wounding hundreds, millions around England and Europe were horrified by the savagery of the incident. Henceforth, in a parody of the Heroes of Waterloo, this action came to be called The Peterloo Massacre, soon becoming an unmitigated disaster for the government.

While Fitzwilliam, keeping a promise to his Caroline, had not travelled to St. Peter's Field that day, he had plenty of informants who had, and the *Matlock Review*, now jointly owned by the Tates and Sir Edmond Camden, told the whole gory story. When Caroline heard the details of the incident, so outraged was she by what she had learned, she decided to call on Mrs Tate, who managed the newspaper for her son Anthony, and place before her all the information Fitzwilliam had obtained, begging her to persuade the editor to speak out strongly.

She was not disappointed.

No decent English heart could not but be ashamed that Englishmen had spilt the blood of other ordinary, hardworking English men and women, whose only crime was to demand a fair hearing and Parliamentary reform,

…wrote the editor of the *Review*, ensuring a place in history for the "Martyrs of St Peter's Field."

Fitzwilliam, whose political career was gradually taking shape, realising the implications of the public outrage, campaigned wholeheartedly from then on, together with other radicalised middle-class men, warning that reform was essential if England were not to go down the path of France into mayhem and chaos. It was a cry that may not have been taken seriously prior to the massacre at St Peter's Field, but since then, it resounded around the country like an alarm, alerting men to the possibility of disaster.

❧

Following the birth of their son, William, Elizabeth invited her father, Mr Bennet, to visit Pemberley again. Wary of the cold Derbyshire Spring, he waited until the weather was warmer before arriving, taking the opportunity provided by his wife's departure with her sister Mrs Phillips for Ramsgate. Mr Bennet missed his elder daughters terribly and always enjoyed visiting them.

While he was there, they had an unexpected visitation from Mr Collins, bearing a message from Lady Catherine de Bourgh. He came unaccompanied by his wife, who had been brought to bed recently with their third daughter Amelia-Jane. Elizabeth was disappointed, fearing Mr Collins's presence may spoil their pleasure of her father's company. But Mr Bennet was not. Determined that if he must endure the company of Mr Collins, he would enjoy it, he used this rare opportunity to engage Mr Collins in various conversations, asking a number of seemingly innocuous questions, which Mr Collins answered with such a degree of seriousness and pomposity that the rest of the company struggled not to laugh outright.

They were entertained daily by these curious dialogues.

When Mr Collins claimed at breakfast that he had seen his patron-Lady Catherine de Bourgh only moments before leaving for Derby, Mr Bennet remarked, "Ah how very auspicious for you, Mr Collins," and then asked, in a quiet voice, "I trust you left Rosings in fine condition and Her Ladyship in good health? And Miss de Bourgh and Mrs Jenkinson?" and as Mr Collins, his mouth full, nodded violently, he went on, "And of course those superb horses that draw her Ladyship's barouche? All well?" to which the garrulous Mr Collins, pleased to be asked for such important information, swallowed hurriedly and replied with enthusiasm, "Oh yes indeed, Mr Bennet, how very good of you to ask; the Rosings estate, which is of course the largest in that part of England, is in excellent condition as is Her Ladyship. She boasts that she hardly ever needs to see a doctor," adding with a sigh, "But dear Miss de Bourgh, now she has a very delicate constitution and Doctor Burroughs visits her regularly, but this being Summer she is in reasonable health and so is Mrs Jenkinson, who is a good sturdy woman—strong as an ox, Her Ladyship says. They are all in fine fettle."

"Excellent, excellent!" responded Mr Bennet. "In fine fettle, eh? Hear that, Lizzie? The horses too, Mr Collins?"

"Oh indeed, sir, I saw them only an hour before I left Hunsford, conveying Her Ladyship into town. They were in very fine fettle indeed."

To which Mr Bennet, eyes sparkling, said, "Excellent, excellent," again and Lizzie, no longer able to restrain her laughter, excused herself, blew her nose violently, and ran from the room, only to find her husband skulking in the corridor. He too had escaped, unable to contain his mirth.

"Lizzie, I am sorry, but your father is right, the man's an idiot and doesn't even know he is being gulled."

"Oh Darcy, it is most unkind of Papa and you! How can you be so wicked? Papa encourages him so he can make a fool of himself and you encourage Papa! Shame on you. I am glad poor Charlotte is not here."

Darcy did not appear very contrite.

"Lizzie, your father would never have done anything that would have embarrassed Mrs Collins, of that I am quite certain," he said. "As you can see, he is simply engaging in some harmless fun. Collins takes himself so seriously, he cannot see it."

Later that day, there was more when the Bingleys arrived from Ashford Park to join them for dinner. Mr Collins, seemingly encouraged by Mr Bennet's show of interest in the subject, launched into a long and detailed monologue on the historic chapel at Rosings, which was now Lady Catherine's private chapel.

"It is soon to be refurbished. Her Ladyship is particular about these matters and wishes the work to be done right; she has sought my advice on the matter," he declared portentously.

"Which no doubt you are very happy to provide?" asked Mr Bennet.

"Of course," said Mr Collins, appearing to preen himself and grow a full inch in stature as he contemplated the prospect, "it would be a great honour to do so."

"And what is the nature of the refurbishment required to be done in the chapel?" asked Mr Darcy, who knew Rosings well.

"There is much to be done, sir, some problems in the roof, I believe," replied Mr Collins, and Mr Bennet muttered softly to himself, "Bats perhaps?"

"Bats?" exclaimed Bingley very loudly, not comprehending this at all.

"In the belfry," quoth Mr Bennet and once again, poor Elizabeth was seized by a fit of coughing and had to leave the room, "It must be the lid on that pepper pot—I shall tell Mrs Reynolds, we should have it replaced," she cried as she fled.

But Mr Collins was undeterred. Jane and her husband were quite bemused at the way he blundered on, barely stopping to put food in his mouth, when asked by Mr Bennet, "Apart from the roof, what other work needs doing, upon which you are to advise Her Ladyship?"

"Ah," replied he with great gravity, "there is a brown stain on the marble floor beside the altar, which may have been caused by blood!" at which Darcy almost choked, as he went on, "We must devise some means of eradicating it. And I do believe one of the stained glass windows, of which there are seven, may need replacing. Her Ladyship is unhappy with its design."

"And *you* are to advise on all these matters, Mr Collins?" Jane asked quite innocently, to which he replied, with a gratified smile, "Ah yes, Mrs Bingley. I shall have that honour."

"Of course you have studied these subjects, Mr Collins?" said Mr Bennet, pursuing his hapless quarry, "as a result of which, you are no doubt quite an authority now on the subject of bloodstains on marble and the style of stained glass windows?"

To the complete astonishment of everyone at the table, including Lizzie, who had since returned to her place beside her father, Mr Collins simply swallowed the last scrap of pudding, smiled at them, and said with the breathless arrogance of the truly ignorant, "No indeed, not at all, but Lady Catherine has asked me for advice, so I shall give it, having considered all the possibilities, in due course."

Mr Bennet was heard to say quietly, as if in awe of such self-importance, "Amazing, absolutely amazing," and from the others there was a stunned silence, which was broken only when the port was placed upon the table and the ladies, relieved, withdrew to the drawing room.

Jane was immediately concerned. "Oh Lizzie, Papa is being very mischievous in baiting poor Mr Collins. Do you not think so?"

Elizabeth smiled. "I did think so, at first, Jane, but the man is such an arrogant fool, I doubt he feels it at all. It certainly has not stopped him pretending that he will single-handedly supervise the restoration of Her Ladyship's private chapel! Besides, as Darcy says, Papa is having such harmless fun, it would be unfair to censure him."

"Oh Lizzie, you are become as cruel as Papa," said Jane, giggling helplessly. The sisters went upstairs together, for Jane wanted another look at little William, the brand-new heir to Pemberley, and Elizabeth was happy to show him off to her sister while leaving Mr Collins to the mercy of the gentlemen.

When the Gardiners and Colonel Fitzwilliam came to dinner some days later, Mr Collins had, mercifully, departed for Kent, there to embark upon his contemplation of marble floors and stained glass windows in Lady Catherine's chapel. But Elizabeth and Mr Bennet kept their visitors entertained with countless tales of his short stay at Pemberley.

"He was ever so grateful for being received with such generous hospitality, he would not stop thanking us, especially Mr Darcy, on every possible occasion," said Elizabeth, and her father pointed out that Mr Darcy must clearly be back in favour with Mr Collins's patron, Lady Catherine de Bourgh.

"He was so obsequious, Mr Darcy, it was quite clear he was angling for a further invitation, perhaps to do the honours at your cousin Colonel Fitzwilliam's wedding to Miss Caroline," Mr Bennet suggested, to which Caroline cried out in protest, "Oh no, we cannot have Mr Collins, he has such a solemn countenance, more suited to a funeral, I think, that I shall not keep a straight face during the ceremony and Emily will surely giggle."

Colonel Fitzwilliam intervened to say he had no intention of being married by Mr Collins, who was sure to preach a tedious sermon and send everyone to sleep.

"In any event, we shall be married in the parish church at Lambton, among the people whom I hope to represent in Parliament. Mr Collins is unlikely to be disappointed at not being asked to officiate there. It is a simple village church. Now, if it were Pemberley, that would be quite another matter," he said.

There was general agreement that Mr Collins's social ambitions would not be furthered on such an occasion, therefore his unhappiness would be short-lived.

"Besides," added Colonel Fitzwilliam, "we shall probably see quite enough of him next Christmas. We are invited, together with my brother James and his family, to Rosings."

"To Rosings?" Elizabeth could hardly believe her ears and even Mr Darcy looked surprised.

Clearly Lady Catherine had not let her contempt for Mr Gardiner's commercial occupation affect her attitude to her nephew's engagement to Caroline.

"Yes indeed. I received a letter from her Ladyship—she says she would have liked to see us before the wedding, but it would not be convenient—so next Christmas it must be."

"And are you looking forward to it, Caroline?" asked Elizabeth.

Colonel Fitzwilliam looked at Caroline, who smiled sweetly and said, "Colonel Fitzwilliam says he is quite sure Lady Catherine will have no reason not to approve of me; he has written her a long letter…"

"Filled with so much praise of Caroline that Lady Catherine, if she had any objections, has been soundly trumped," Mr Bennet concluded and added, "And so she should be, for there is no young lady more deserving of universal praise and approval than my dear niece, I am sure."

Caroline blushed as everyone agreed that Mr Bennet was absolutely right. Elizabeth agreed too; but she could not help feeling some degree of sorrow for her friend Charlotte, as she contrasted her situation—being married as she was to Mr Collins, quite the silliest man she had encountered in all her life—with that of Caroline, Jane, and herself.

Her young cousin had had the great good fortune to have found in Colonel Fitzwilliam a near perfect partner. Not only were they devoted to one another, but already, they seemed so well attuned to each other's ideas and hopes that they anticipated one another's thoughts and words and appeared in complete harmony. Yet, there was not a hint of domination on his part or manipulation on hers.

Jane was especially pleased with the remarkable degree of good sense and decorum that characterised their conduct.

"It cannot be easy for either of them, Lizzie, having to wait almost a year before they may marry, while loving one another so deeply; yet, at no time do they behave in an unseemly or outrageous manner as to embarrass those in whose company they are."

Elizabeth, who recalled the appalling behaviour of her sister Lydia, even before she was married to Wickham and often afterwards, had to agree.

Mrs Gardiner, speaking to Elizabeth, had expressed her own satisfaction.

"The colonel is the perfect gentleman Lizzie," she said. "I confess I had some reservations because of the great difference in their ages, but since they have been engaged, I have had not a moment's anxiety. I trust him completely and so does Mr Gardiner."

Clearly the Gardiners had taken Fitzwilliam to their hearts.

Later, after their guests had departed, Elizabeth and Darcy discussed Lady Catherine's invitation to Fitzwilliam and Caroline, and concluded that his aunt was probably shrewd enough to realise that Colonel Fitzwilliam, being the youngest son of his titled father, may be considered quite fortunate to have won the hand of an accomplished and charming young woman, who was also very well endowed with an income of her own as a result of her father's hard-won prosperity and benevolence.

"I have no doubt that Fitzwilliam has made it quite plain to my aunt that he intends to marry Caroline, and she has realised that, having no longer any control over him, she must make the best of it," said Darcy, while Elizabeth laughed and added, "You mean she will not make a fuss because she knows she will not be heeded and will probably look foolish for having done so?"

"You are probably quite right, my love," he said as they retired to bed, presuming that Lady Catherine, having failed to prevent their own marriage, was probably wary of proceeding along a similar path again.

Elizabeth was happier now than at any time of her life. Not only did she feel deeply loved and blessed with her husband and children, she had the great satisfaction of seeing how well her father liked and admired Mr Darcy.

During this visit, Mr Bennet had had ample opportunity and time to observe and understand not only the degree of his daughter's happiness, but as well, the extent of her husband's benevolent contribution to the community in which they lived. It was something of which he particularly approved.

Mr Bennet, who had often expressed outrage at the lack of education received by English children, who were left to grow up illiterate unless their parents were rich enough to afford a private tutor or governess, was particularly impressed by Mr Darcy's efforts, together with the parish councils of Pemberley and Kympton, to provide schooling for the children of the villages on his estate.

Both his daughter Kitty and young Caroline were full of praise for their benefactor, and Elizabeth was proud to hear her husband speak out against the injustices he saw in society.

In the course of conversation, replying to a question from Caroline, Mr Darcy had censured the repressive actions of the government.

"I am uncomfortable with a government that supports the demands of the privileged and represses the poor. I do not accept that birth has anything to do with it. It is a question of responsibility for your fellow men. I believe, as my father and grandfather believed, that those of us who are fortunate in life must play a part in helping those who are not. Not just by doing charitable deeds and giving to the poor, as all of us do, but by taking responsibility to contribute materially to the improvement of their lives, because in the end, to do so will improve the community in which we must all live."

As Caroline cheered, aware that Fitzwilliam was of a similar mind, Elizabeth looked across at her father, who was watching his son-in-law with obvious approval. Mr Bennet had never suspected this side of Darcy's character.

Later he confided in Elizabeth his great pleasure at hearing her husband express such noble sentiments.

"He is a man of principle and compassion, Lizzie; I know now why you defended him so passionately when I expressed some reservations about him. I hope you have both forgiven me. I see I was much mistaken," he said.

Elizabeth smiled and took his arm as they walked. "That was all in the past, Papa, and I was as much to blame as anyone for having misled you about his character. Perhaps my greatest happiness has been in learning how very wrong we all were when we permitted our prejudice to influence our judgment of him. I am truly ashamed of my own attitude at the time. My Aunt and Uncle Gardiner recognised that he is a good and generous man, and once I learned the truth, I knew you would grow to like him as they did," she said.

Her father urged her not to be hard upon herself. "So he is and you are a fortunate young woman, Lizzie. I am so very glad you made the right choice."

Elizabeth did not have to ask what he meant; she knew only too well how apprehensive her father must have been when she had seemed enamoured of Mr Wickham and even toyed with the prospect of marrying him. Marry Wickham! The very thought sent a shiver through her. How grateful she was to have been spared that humiliation!

Turning to look at the rest of the party, who were settling down to a game of cards, she said, "I think Caroline and Colonel Fitzwilliam are set to be very happy too, do you not agree, Papa?" to which Mr Bennet could only answer with a wholehearted, "Indeed I do, Lizzie. What is more, I know from my conversations with your Aunt and Uncle Gardiner that they are completely happy with the match. Fitzwilliam is plainly a sensible and intelligent young fellow as well as being devoted to Caroline."

Elizabeth readily concurred, adding that she had once had reservations on account of the disparity in their ages, but these had soon been dispelled.

"Mr Darcy believes that, as in the case of his sister Georgiana and Dr Grantley, such a difference could be an advantage, bringing stability and strength to a marriage," she said, to which her father replied quietly, "Ah yes, he is right, Lizzie, though its continuing success does depend rather more upon the good sense and understanding of the partners. Where these are present, together with affection and respect, then age will present no hindrance to felicity."

There was in his voice a hint of regret, a rueful quality, that reminded Elizabeth of her father's own situation in life.

Captivated by youth and good looks, he had married a woman of weak understanding and unstable disposition, realising too late that his imprudence had put an end to any hope of real domestic happiness. His elder daughters Jane and Lizzie had both been well aware of the sad lack of any esteem or understanding in their parents' marriage.

Looking to change the subject, lest it should cause her father pain, she sought in her mind some other matter to address when, to her immense relief, the door opened and Mr Darcy came to join them.

He brought news that was sure to lift Mr Bennet's spirits.

An invitation had been received from Sir Thomas Camden for Mr Darcy and his guests to visit Camden House, where a rare collection of books had recently been received into the library.

"It includes the diary and notebooks of one of our first explorers, and I am assured by Sir Thomas that it is quite absorbing." said Darcy.

"Mr Darcy, I can think of nothing I would like better," said Mr Bennet, and Elizabeth noted how swiftly her father's mind was engaged as they talked together eagerly of the earliest possible date on which they could arrange a visit to Camden House. No trace remained of his earlier melancholy mood.

Chapter Four

THE YEARS FOLLOWING THE DELAYED coronation of George IV were not particularly glorious or happy ones for most of the people of his kingdom.

While the King appeared more concerned with his private affairs and the desire to wreak vengeance upon a recalcitrant Queen, whom he wished to discard, the government lurched from one crisis to the next.

Dominated by a high Tory faction, they had set their minds against reform as firmly and implacably as the King had refused to allow his legal wife to be crowned in the abbey with him.

Repressive measures against those who demanded change, such as the infamous Six Acts, meant that all but the most determined or foolhardy of Reformists like Cobbett and Hunt were driven underground or overseas. Meanwhile, gentlemen farmers and absentee landlords alike continued to enclose farms and common land, evicting rural families, whose only recourse was to the work house or the grimy tenements of factory towns, where they either worked or stole to eke out a living.

In the Midlands, where unemployment was rising, agitators and machine breakers plagued the lives of the few men—usually middle-class entrepreneurs—who kept some industries running and contributed to the expansion of trade.

Mr Gardiner was confident that it was the only route out of the despair that had gripped the country. As he was fond of reminding everyone he met, not all of whom agreed with him, "Free commerce, not protectionism, is the solution. Only trade will bring Britain out of depression." Mr Darcy, convinced he was right, supported his view, but many did not.

Amidst all this gloom and unease, on a bleak North Country morning, church bells rang out across the village of Lambton and a large crowd of relations, friends, and neighbours turned out to see Caroline Gardiner and Colonel Fitzwilliam married.

The colonel, having consulted his father-in-law and his bride, had invited the entire village of Lambton as well as his own tenants and workers from his property at Matlock. Housed in a large marquee erected upon the lawns of Oakleigh Manor, everyone who attended, from Sir Thomas and Lady Camden to the humblest tenant-farmer and his nine children, was made welcome. It was something unheard of in the village and very much appreciated by the people Fitzwilliam hoped to represent in the Commons after the next election.

Thankfully, Lady Catherine de Bourgh, being unwell, did not grace the occasion, else she might have suffered a seizure from the shock of it.

It was a phenomenon that certainly left Mrs Bennet, who had arrived from Hertfordshire with her husband and her sister, Mrs Phillips, speechless for several minutes. Never had she found herself in such motley company.

"I cannot believe my brother has invited all these common folk to Caroline's wedding, Mr Bennet," she said, when she finally found her voice. "Why, half of them must never have polished their shoes!"

"You are probably right, my dear, that is if they ever had shoes to polish at all; of course, the other half probably have far too many pairs of shoes and servants to polish them too!" said her husband, and Mrs Bennet, feeling extremely vexed at not being taken seriously, flounced away to find someone else who would listen to her.

She had no luck with her sister-in-law Mrs Gardiner and her husband either. When she attempted to tell them how well their daughter had done by "catching the dear Colonel," who had "done very well for himself in the colonies," Mrs Gardiner, by now her son-in-law's greatest advocate, pointed out that Colonel Fitzwilliam had worked exceedingly hard to make his fortune. She then proceeded to deliver the *coup de grace*, by adding pointedly that, "He is very well established now, and our greatest comfort comes from knowing that

Colonel Fitzwilliam is devoted to Caroline; indeed, we cannot think of anyone else to whom we would so gladly entrust our daughter's happiness."

Having intimate knowledge of the effort that had been required on the part of Mr Darcy and her own husband to bribe Wickham into marrying Mrs Bennet's daughter Lydia, Mrs Gardiner had a distinct advantage over her sister-in-law. Mrs Bennet knew it and retreated quickly.

Poor Mrs Bennet, it seemed no one wanted to hear her opinion. Even her daughter Jane, to her great surprise, contradicted her when she tried to suggest that Lady Catherine's absence must signify her disapproval of the match. Jane was happy to inform her mother that it meant no such thing; in fact, the happy couple had been invited to spend next Christmas at Rosings. Her Ladyship, she said, was genuinely indisposed. By the time the couple had left on their wedding journey, Mrs Bennet had been silenced and was seen concentrating her attention upon more of the excellent fare that had been provided for the wedding breakfast.

~✥~

For Caroline, memories of her wedding would always remain a blur of activities and faces seen through tears; tears she had vowed never to shed on this her happy day. She'd forbidden all her relations and friends to weep; yet tears had come unbidden at the moment of parting from her family.

Only then, when she saw her father and mother and they embraced as they said farewell, did she fully realise the enormity of the step she had taken; leaving her warm and secure family for the uncertain life of a very young woman married to a rising politician.

But in her heart, she felt she was right.

It was hard to tear herself away, even as Fitzwilliam waited patiently, having given again his promise to her father that he would do everything in his power to make his daughter happy.

Yet, once having left her home, Caroline turned with so much love and loyalty to her husband that neither was left in any doubt of their feelings nor of the rightness of their decision to marry. Theirs was an unusual marriage. It was one of those unions which seem at the outset to bring out the doomsayers, of whom there were many, only to have their gloomy prognostications proved utterly wrong.

During the first years of their marriage, Caroline experienced a wider range of feelings than she had known in all her happy young life and, together with her husband, learned also the lessons of love in marriage.

Realising, while they enjoyed their intimacy, that married life was not all passion and ecstasy, though there was a good deal of that for they loved one another deeply, they discovered too the many simple pleasures that came in its train. Together with fun and laughter, there was disappointment and, inevitably, anguish. From none of these did she shrink, accepting and absorbing everything into a greatly enriched existence.

Setting up home at Colonel Fitzwilliam's farm at Matlock was one of her keenest pleasures, as each day brought fresh excitement and new responsibilities. With the guidance of a mature and loving husband, Caroline found no difficulty managing her new home, despite the very great differences between their farm and her parents' home at Oakleigh. Whereas Mrs Gardiner employed several maids, a cook, and menservants to do her bidding around the house and grounds, Caroline and Fitzwilliam had only a few servants, as society might expect, since theirs was to be a working farm, not a squire's manor.

They found they had no need of a large staff and seemed happy with a couple of trusted personal servants, a maid or two, and a good cook to look after them, while the majority of farm labour was drawn from the neighbouring village. Fitzwilliam was quite determined that he would not play the country squire; rather, he put himself forward as a farmer, a man who would represent all their interests in the Parliament, because he knew and shared their concerns.

Caroline explained it to her mother as a sensible measure, which her husband had undertaken as a matter of principle as much as for practical reasons.

"Fitzy says," she said, using the funny little sobriquet that only she was ever permitted to use, "he wants to provide work for the people of the village, the farmhands, and their families. They do not need to learn to bow and curtsey or polish the silver, he says, they need to work as they have always done, on the land. Many have lost their own farms in the enclosures, and this is a chance for them to do the work they are good at doing,"

Her mother looked doubtful. "Surely, Caroline, they could benefit just as well by learning to serve at table, make beds, or run a household," she said, unaccustomed to this new theory of household management, but Mr Gardiner agreed with his son-in-law and daughter.

"What good would it do? They would only learn to be servants, never their own masters. Now, on the farm, where they know the land and have the skills to work it, they could be achieving something worthwhile.

"I think your husband is right, my dear," he said, making Caroline's eyes shine. To have her father's approval for the man she loved was all she asked.

"Thank you, Papa, I knew you would approve; besides, Mama dear, I really do enjoy having only a few servants, there is not a great deal to do at the moment and until there is, I am perfectly content," she said.

Mrs Gardiner had no cause to doubt her daughter's words.

Throughout the year, which proved to be busier than expected, Caroline not only appeared content and happy, she worked harder than ever to help her husband in his campaign for Parliament. It soon became her chief preoccupation.

Certain of standing at the next election, Fitzwilliam worked assiduously to advance the cause of reform and Caroline was always at his side, learning every day and bringing her own special talents to promote his cause. A charming wife, with the happy gift of being able to put complete strangers at ease while they listened to his message, was an asset most politicians would covet. Fitzwilliam was proud of her and took her everywhere with him. Whether among the farmers and country gentry of Derbyshire or the Reformists and their supporters in the city, she was his most effective ally; some said, his secret weapon.

However, not everything was perfect in Caroline's new life.

She never spoke of it to anyone, not even to the husband she so dearly loved, but her life lacked only one thing to make it complete. Seeing all her cousins, Kitty, Lizzie, and Jane, with their children, Caroline longed for one of her own, and it showed in her eyes when she played with them. Only Jane seemed to understand and feel for her, yet she never mentioned it. Sensitive to her cousin's feelings, Jane remained discreetly silent but understood Caroline's longing.

Happily, that was soon to change, when in the Summer of 1822, Caroline knew her dearest wish was to be fulfilled. Fitzwilliam was delighted, and between them, they appeared to share their happiness around, conveying a sense of bright optimism to all who met them at a time when optimism was sorely needed. The year had not been a good one for the people of England, and two things symbolised the incipient despair that many felt, even as they went about their work amidst a climate of growing discontent that reached from the lowliest to the very highest in the land.

The shocking suicide of the Foreign Secretary, Lord Castlereagh, a man at the peak of his political career, seemed such a senseless act, it could only be explained as a personal cry of rage. It shook the confidence of everyone at

Westminster, and even those by whom he was widely hated could not deny that he had worked tirelessly to prevent another eruption of war in Europe. Colonel Fitzwilliam, who had been in London at the time, was severely shaken.

"I met Murder on the way, He had a face like Castlereagh!" raged the poet Shelley, expressing in savage satire his anger at policies of the government. Yet, a few months later, Shelley—whom Castlereagh would have regarded as a dangerous radical—was gone too, drowned in the Aegean Sea while making a futile attempt to help the Greeks in their struggle against tyranny.

For Caroline, who had idolised Shelley ever since she had read his "Ode To a Skylark," it was a bitter blow, one she wept over inconsolably, bemoaning the loss of "the brightest and best of our land, Keats and Shelley, both gone within a year of each other..."

So harrowing was her grief, Elizabeth was concerned for her health.

But when, in the final months of Autumn, her son Edward was born, Caroline was transformed. Soon she became the mother she had longed to be. Supported by her family and the devotion of her husband, she settled into a contented domesticity which overwhelmed all her other preoccupations.

When, a year later a daughter, Isabella, arrived, Elizabeth was astonished at the change in the young girl, who had wept in her arms for the lost poets, now a devoted mother, whose children were her chief concern.

"She is so altered, I could scarce believe it," said Elizabeth to her husband, as they returned from a visit to the Fitzwilliams' farm.

But Mr Darcy pointed out that Caroline was intrinsically an intelligent young woman and reminded his wife that he had predicted she would soon recover from her romantic melancholy. Elizabeth laughed and admitted that he had been proved right again.

Caroline enjoyed the role she had longed for, doted upon her children, and spent as much of their waking hours with them as she could, to the point where her mother was heard to complain that the nurse they employed was being paid well for very little work.

When, however, it was time to help her husband in his campaign, collecting signatures for petitions or handing out pamphlets, Caroline had no doubt of her duty either. Frequently, with one or both of her children, the nurse, or her sister Emily, she would set out in her pony trap to carry Fitzwilliam's message to the farms and villages around Matlock.

Even though the majority of people could not vote, Fitzwilliam believed it was necessary to inform them of the issues, the need for reform in the Parliament, and the extension of the franchise, because, he said, "If ordinary men and women do not know what benefits the franchise can bring, they will think it not worth fighting for. If we are to convince them that it is to be their government one day, we must help them understand how that will be so."

Determined to do her part, Caroline and her young family would take his campaign to the people at markets, fairgrounds, coaching inns, and public houses as well as isolated farms around the area.

Concerned that she should not overtire herself nor put her children in jeopardy as she travelled around, Mrs Gardiner appealed to her husband to intervene. "Could you not speak with Colonel Fitzwilliam? She will listen to him," she said, but Mr Gardiner was proud of his daughter's spirit and tenacity.

"Caroline will undertake only what she knows she can successfully complete. She is too sensible to bite off more than she can chew," he declared confidently. Mrs Gardiner could only pray he was right.

Marriage to Fitzwilliam had broadened Caroline's horizons, giving her access to a new world of political and social causes, which she gladly embraced. Not in a naïve or sentimental fashion, but with clear understanding and deep concern. She was a romantic at heart, but she was also a perceptive young woman. That his ideas meant a great deal to her husband she knew and took them up with enthusiasm, promoting them to everyone she met.

To the increasing astonishment of her older cousins Jane and Elizabeth, who led much more leisurely married lives at Ashford Park and Pemberley, Caroline threw herself into Fitzwilliam's political activities whilst still managing to retain the warmth and intimacy of her family life.

While Jane and Lizzie may have marvelled at her capacity for hard work, they could have no doubt at all of her happiness.

⸎

The Summer of 1830 was a particularly significant one.

Not one but two unexpected deaths; King George IV and Mr Collins, both not greatly lamented, save by their immediate families, passed away suddenly, with consequences unforeseen and unexpected.

The death of the king caused a general election to be called, in which Fitzwilliam was again a candidate, this time with even more hope of fulfilling his plans for effecting reform; while the demise of Mr Collins materially affected the lives of many people, from Mrs Collins and her three daughters to Mr and Mrs Bennet and their family.

For a start, no longer did Mr Bennet have to endure the complaints of his wife, detailing her fears of being turned out of Longbourn by the Collinses. With the death of Mr Collins without a male heir, the estate reverted to Mr Bennet.

The return to England from Paris of Richard Gardiner, Caroline's brother, who had been training to be a physician, was fortuitous and welcomed for a variety of reasons. Mr and Mrs Gardiner were happy to have their son back at home after several years away in Edinburgh and Paris, while Caroline, who knew her brother had a strong sense of justice and a sound social conscience, hoped he would help with her husband's political campaign. Health care was a crying need throughout the country, nowhere more than in the factory towns and isolated villages of the Midlands.

Caroline knew her brother's views on the subject were identical to those of her husband. He would speak out about it, and Richard's voice would be listened to; she was sure of it.

Meanwhile, a new radicalism was rising among the middle classes who had hitherto no voice at all in the Parliament, filled as it was with large numbers of members from pocket boroughs, who owed their places in the Commons to patronage rather than principle. Middle-class professional and businessmen, responsible for some of the most lucrative enterprises in the country, were beginning to join the clamour for Parliamentary reform, but as long as George IV sat upon the British throne, it could have got no further, for the king would not call on Lord Grey to form a ministry.

When, however, it became clear following the elections that Wellington could no longer command a majority in the Commons and Lord Grey was invited by the new King William IV to lead a government, the hopes of Fitzwilliam and his fellow reformists were reignited.

With the Whigs back in government, hopes were high, especially with men like the popular Viscount Althorp and Lord John Russell committed to reform.

During the fifteen months that followed, there was to be a tumult of political and social agitation, the like of which had not been seen in England for many years.

The Fitzwilliams, the Gardiners, together with their son Richard and his friend Monsieur Paul Antoine, both recently arrived from France, and

Sir Thomas Camden were dining at Pemberley when Mr Anthony Tate, the nephew of Sir Thomas, lately down from Cambridge, was announced.

A fine-looking young man, he had all the self-assurance of the wealthy and good manners besides. Apologising for his late arrival, he broke the news that had delayed him. He had received a message from Westminster that a committee had been set up within the Parliament to draft a Reform Bill, which was *"to satisfy all reasonable demands of the intelligent sections of the community for reform of the Parliament."*

Chief among the men on the committee was Lord Russell, a dedicated reformist, who had given his word that he would introduce a bill for the reform of the Parliament and electoral system.

Colonel Fitzwilliam was jubilant at the news, but Tate, who was part owner of the *Matlock Review*, appeared less certain.

"Do you honestly believe, Colonel Fitzwilliam, that the Whigs will want to give up their share of the rotten boroughs? They are as keen on preserving their privileges as the Tories; it is because they have had a taste of defeat that they've taken up the cause of reform," he said.

Mr Darcy, who had previously cautioned against over optimism, tended to agree with young Mr Tate, but Fitzwilliam, though in a minority, was prepared to argue that Lord Grey had given a commitment to the Reformists before the election and would surely deliver upon it.

"Grey is an honourable man. I trust him," said the colonel.

Anthony Tate was unsure. "Even if what you say is true and Grey does keep his promise and produce a bill for reform, the Tories will scream blue murder as soon as it is presented. Mark my words, Fitzwilliam, they will claim there will be chaos and mayhem, that England will disappear under a rising tide of revolutionary excesses; indeed, they will so terrify the populace that very soon there will be no reasonable voice to be heard supporting it."

There was laughter as he spoke and when he stopped, there was a sudden silence, as if everyone around the table had realised the chilling truth of his words. Then into the pool of quiet dropped Caroline's voice, not loud but very clear.

"If this is so, Mr Tate, is it not the sacred responsibility of us all to speak out and contradict it, to tell people that reform is not revolution, that there are many benefits to be had by ridding our country of a rotten system that denies most people the right to vote?"

It is unlikely, though not entirely impossible, that Anthony Tate had ever before been addressed in such a manner and on such a subject by a lady—except perhaps his mother, who was a remarkably outspoken and liberal-minded woman. He was a young man of intelligence, education, and shrewd understanding, who was soon to control the *Matlock Review*, yet he found he had no answer for Caroline except to say, with a shrug of his shoulders, "Indeed, Mrs Fitzwilliam, you may be right, but you will admit, I am sure, that the forces ranged against reform are powerful, and who in the community has the courage and the means to rebut them?"

Directly addressed, Caroline felt she had to respond.

"I am surprised, indeed, that you should ask, Mr Tate," she said, and by this time, almost everyone around the table was listening with interest. "Surely it is those who control the press who wield the most power, for you have the means to inform ignorant people of the truth, have you not? The *Review* has campaigned diligently for a school and a hospital for the children of our area; is it not an even greater cause to lead the campaign for reform, so people may vote for those that govern them?"

An unfamiliar French voice at the far end of the table said, "Bravo," and Mr Gardiner and Colonel Fitzwilliam cried "Hear, Hear!" which made Caroline suddenly shy and Anthony Tate, feeling the need to make some acknowledgement, said, "When I hear you present the argument in that fashion, Mrs Fitzwilliam, I must confess I cannot fault it. The *Review* has always supported the movement for reform and will do so in the future. Whether we can lead a campaign, I cannot say. But you are right; someone must tell the people the truth of the matter."

It was almost time for the ladies to withdraw and Caroline went with her mother, her sister Emily, and Elizabeth, while the men partook of plenty of port and even more political debate.

By the time they met again in the drawing room, however, Elizabeth, who had very little interest in matters political, had succeeded in getting them around the pianoforte, and Monsieur Antoine, Emily Gardiner, and Caroline were trying out their parts for a popular French song, the singing of which was followed by general applause and calls for more.

When coffee was taken, Richard Gardiner, who had been busy telling everyone about Paris, approached his sister and returned to the subject of their discussion at dinner.

"Very good, Caroline, I *am* impressed. Tate has already spoken to me regarding an article in the *Review* about the need for a children's hospital; my friend Paul Antoine is keen to help us establish one, and Tate is happy to give us his support. But I think I shall hold my fire until we have some word on Parliamentary Reform, eh?"

While he was younger than Caroline, she had always treated her brother Richard as if he were older than she was. His stature and the enormously responsible profession he had chosen set him on a pedestal for her. She knew also that Fitzwilliam loved and admired her brother as a fine young man with a strong social conscience.

"Richard, I do hope Mr Darcy and Sir Thomas were not angered by my speaking out; I know it is not customary, and Cousin Lizzie would never do it, but I felt I had to say something. Mr Tate is able to use his newspaper to tell the truth in a way no one else can. He reaches hundreds of people, where we probably see ten in a day if we are fortunate. Fitzy works so hard, I would hate to see him disappointed."

"Nor shall you, Caroline, I promise. I shall speak to Tate and perhaps I may convince him of the need for the *Review* to take a stand," her brother gave her his word. "As for Sir Thomas and Mr Darcy, have no fears on that score—I do not believe I am being indiscreet by revealing that after the ladies had withdrawn, both gentlemen were full of praise for your point of view, and Sir Thomas urged his nephew to consider it seriously. No, Caroline, the time is ripe for reform and I do believe you have spoken out at the right moment."

They were interrupted by their hostess, who wanted to question Richard about Mr Antoine.

"Richard, you must tell me more about your charming friend—who is he and does he intend to settle in England?" she asked and, as Richard was led away by Elizabeth, Caroline rejoined her husband.

"Fitzy, I do hope I did not embarrass you at dinner…" she began anxiously, but got no further.

"Embarrass me? My dear Caroline, it was the most important thing anyone had said on the subject all evening. Until you spoke, we were all being wary and uncertain, while young Tate was downright sceptical," he said, hastening to reassure her. "Not anymore; we now have Anthony Tate's word that the *Review* will support reform, even if he has not promised to campaign for it as yet! No, my dear, I think you did our great cause a service tonight. Mr Darcy said so."

"Mr Darcy?" She was incredulous.

"Indeed, he did. When you had left the room, Sir Thomas said, 'Out of the mouths of babes, eh, Tate?'" and seeing her outraged expression, he added swiftly, "But Darcy disagreed and said, 'Caroline is no babe, Sir Thomas, Fitzwilliam here will tell you, she is his staunchest ally and a most effective campaigner.'"

Caroline looked up at her husband, wide-eyed and astonished at such praise, and asked, "Fitzy, did you tell him I was?"

Fitzwilliam, realising that her mood was becoming more playful, matched it as he replied, "Of course, though I do believe there was hardly any need for it, my love. Your advocacy was most convincing. I have never before seen young Tate lost for words."

~❦~

The weeks and months that followed were to prove both Mr Anthony Tate and Caroline right. Social upheaval and domestic turmoil overtook many families in the land, and the enthusiasm for reform brought out the supporters of other causes as the cry went up to "end child slavery in the mills" and the working classes began to demand a "ten-hour day."

Taking over editorial policy at the *Review*, Anthony Tate, ambitious and astute, set about acquiring other, smaller news sheets and journals and used them to push the cause of reform. Always aware that those in power may act arbitrarily against the press, if they felt threatened by it, he cultivated the goodwill of influential men like Lord Ashley, a reformist Tory, Viscount Althorp, and a family of prominent Whig lawyers—the Wilsons, who had the respect of both sides of Parliament. As he grew more accustomed to it, he enjoyed the power and influence he could wield through his newspapers, and by the time the Reform Bill was introduced into the Parliament by Lord Russell, Mr Tate and his press were firmly and openly behind it. It was the first time the *Review* had become overtly involved in a political cause, and it made a significant difference.

Caroline, meanwhile, had acquired so much information and familiarity with the causes that Fitzwilliam held dear, she had no longer any fear of embarrasing him by her forays into the field of social reform. One story which became almost a legend in the family concerned her chance meeting with the powerful Viscount Althorp at a social function.

Mr Gardiner and Richard had accompanied Fitzwilliam and Caroline to London to attend the debates on the bill. While Caroline returned with ecstatic reports of her husband's speech, which had won sustained applause from an unusually crowded chamber, Richard had a far more intriguing tale to tell.

At a soireé in the salon of a leading London hostess, while everybody around them was talking of "the bill and nothing but the bill," Caroline, finding herself seated next to the influential Viscount Althorp to whom she had been introduced, had taken up a cause dear to her heart. Her brother, at first a somewhat panic-stricken listener, had been amazed to observe them as they spoke.

"You could have knocked me down with a feather," he told the family as they sat at dinner. "There was Caroline, telling Althorp that while it was very important indeed to get Parliamentary Reform, it would not be much good to ordinary people until they could get their children out of the mines and into school. He listened, paying her every courtesy, while she related heartrending stories of families whose boys went into the mines when they were barely ten years old and ended up stunted and wizened like gnomes, having worked the long hours underground, hardly ever seeing the sun. It was clear that Althorp was moved; he never once interrupted her and listened most attentively."

Mr and Mrs Gardiner could scarcely believe it themselves, when he continued, "I could not hear exactly what he said in reply and did not wish to seem to eavesdrop on them, but when I asked Caroline later in the evening, she was quite sanguine about it. Apparently, though initially surprised at her interest, he had assured her that the cause of young children in the mines and mills was a matter he intended to address very soon, by bringing in new laws to regulate working hours and conditions for both women and children. He even told her that it was a matter on which he had the support of the prominent Tory Lord Ashley as well!"

When the story came to be repeated at Pemberley, by Mrs Gardiner, Elizabeth and her sister Jane were incredulous.

"But did she not fear he would rebuff her? It could have been quite mortifying!" said Jane, and Elizabeth wondered at her cousin's apparent boldness. She herself would never have contemplated such a thing.

"Was she not afraid of offending him by such an approach?" she asked.

"Apparently not," replied Mrs Gardiner. "Caroline told Colonel Fitzwilliam she had thought that as one of the most powerful members of the new government, Viscount Althorp would be the best person to lobby on a matter of such importance, and since she found him conveniently seated next to her, she decided to do just that."

Mr Darcy put down his wine glass and laughed.

"She is absolutely right, of course, there is not much to be gained by haranguing some obscure back bencher with little or no influence in the Cabinet. Althorp and his supporters must ultimately win the day," he said. "Britain cannot for much longer preach the abolition of slavery for Africans while retaining conditions tantamount to enslavement for its own children."

Mr Bingley cried, "Hear, hear!" and Mr Gardiner could barely conceal his delight and pride in his favourite daughter. Caroline was the very apple of her father's eye, and he predicted confidently that she would eventually succeed in her campaign to free the children from the mines.

"She has set her heart on this and will not give up," he declared.

Elizabeth had a question. "Do you believe Caroline is sufficiently ambitious for Fitzwilliam to put up with the strains and vagaries of political life? It is not easy for a woman to be so deeply involved."

Darcy replied, "It is not simply a question of ambition. I do not believe Caroline is unduly ambitious for her husband; not any more than he is himself. But each time I hear her speak of such matters, I cannot help feeling that she wants to change things for the better. She is not content to be comfortable, as many of us are; she sees injustice and wishes to do something about it. Whether it is the children of the poor who get no schooling, or the widowed women who have no recourse but to the poor house when they are too old to work, Caroline is moved by their plight and draws attention to it, hoping someone will listen. Now these are important, worthy causes and her work cannot possibly do Fitzwilliam any harm with his constituency."

There was general agreement on that score, but Mrs Gardiner remained anxious. "You are right, Mr Darcy. She has a compassionate heart and I can see her, a child in her arms and another at her side, talking passionately to anyone who will listen about the evils of child labour. I know she appears to have boundless energy but I do fear she works too hard," she said, expressing a mother's anxiety.

Had she seen the note Caroline had written to her sister Emily, Mrs Gardiner may have been somewhat less concerned.

Dearest Emily,

You are the very first to hear my wonderful news, all three pieces of it.

First, Fitzy is to work with Mr James Wilson, who is in charge of the campaign for the election in December, which he says will finally set the seal of approval upon the Reform Bill. It is indeed a great honour to be invited, for the Wilsons are both important and influential reformists.

Second, I know you will be delighted to hear we are to get some money from the council for the parish school, for which we must thank young Mr Tate and his dear mother, who have campaigned endlessly in the Review for it.

And last, but certainly not least, my dear sister—you after my beloved husband are the first to know—I am to have another child in the Summer!

Is it not the most wonderful conclusion to a most successful year? With Richard home and all our family together again, it will be just the best year of all. I feel so excited and happy I have to tell someone, else I shall explode with the joy of it all!

Dearest Emmy, pray do not say anything to Mama or Cousin Elizabeth. I must tell Mama myself and let her have the pleasure of giving the family the news. I had to tell you though, for I know you will share my happiness.

I am glad most of the campaign for the Reform Bill is complete. I shall now be able to concentrate my attention upon my darling children and Fitzy for a while. I think it may be another boy; but it does not signify, since we have dear Edward and Isabella. Pray only please, Emmy, that he or she will be healthy and strong…

Emily Gardiner, who had been busy that year with her own interests, smiled as she read her sister's note.

She knew her well; Caroline might withdraw from the fray awhile and enjoy the love and warmth of her family, especially with a new baby, but Emily knew it would not be long before her sister would be drawn back into the struggle.

Single-minded and dedicated, her work would not be done, "not until we get the babes out of the mines and into school," Caroline had once said, and Emily was certain she had meant every word.

END OF PART ONE

MY COUSIN CAROLINE

Part Two

Chapter Five

CAROLINE'S THIRD CHILD, DAVID, WAS born in the Summer of 1833. A solemn little boy with deep, serious eyes, he was the very opposite of his high-spirited brother Edward, whose energy and sense of fun made him a great favourite with everyone. Thoughtful and slight, David was said to take after the colonel in his youth. Mrs Reynolds remembered and remarked upon the likeness.

"He'll be a gentle lad surely," she said, "just like his father," and his mother agreed.

The family celebrated his christening at the village church, and the entire populace turned out to congratulate Colonel Fitzwilliam and his wife. They were proud of their new member and his young family; the colonel and Caroline had, by their sincerity and passion for reform and their ceaseless campaigns on behalf of the poor and needy, convinced many who were without the franchise that he would represent them well in the new Parliament. As for his wife, there was not a single voice in the village that would speak out except in praise of her.

As the nation settled into a new era, with their new king, a new parliament, a new government, and promises of new laws to outlaw bad old practises, an air of optimism had replaced the earlier gloom. The nation basked in relatively favourable economic conditions resulting from prolific harvests, profitable trading contracts, and consequent high levels of employment. If there were impending problems, storm clouds gathering beyond the horizon, hardly anyone was aware of them.

The Gardiners were visiting Colonel Fitzwilliam and Caroline.

The topic of conversation turned, as it often did, upon the state of the nation.

"Manufacturers, tradesmen, and businessmen are all prospering and seem quite content with their lot," said Mr Gardiner to Fitzwilliam.

"Do you not believe the working class wishes to improve its conditions or demand political rights?" the colonel asked and to his disappointment, his father-in-law replied, "Not now, while trade is good, business is doing well and paying good wages; however, should there be trouble overseas or a loss of trade, your friend Tom Attwood may well be proved right. A million or more unemployed men will soon make them change their tune."

Colonel Fitzwilliam shook his head, "Why does it always have to be so? Must we wait to be pushed and shoved into reform? Can we not see that it is in all our interests to change when times are good, rather than wait for the lean years?"

Mr Gardiner, by now well aware of the principled and idealistic philosophy his son-in-law espoused, smiled and said, not at all unkindly but with the sound knowledge of a practical businessman, "We shall have to change human nature first, Colonel Fitzwilliam, before we see such an attitude prevail; but if the radicals keep at it, their turn will come round again, perhaps sooner than we think."

The appearance of Caroline with Mrs Gardiner and the two older children brought their discussion to an end, not because they had exhausted their topic, but because the favourite pastime of all grandparents, that of indulging their grandchildren, could now begin. Both Edward and Isabella were learning to please their elders with songs and poems, and there was little chance, while this was in progress, that there would be any further serious conversation.

When the children, having delighted them for almost half an hour, went upstairs to bed, however, Mrs Gardiner caught her daughter's eye and, as the gentlemen settled down with their drinks, followed Caroline out of the room.

Caroline had felt a little anxious all evening, conscious of some disquiet in her mother. Mrs Gardiner was a calm, sensible woman, not easily discomposed, but this evening, she had a somewhat distracted air and Caroline knew her mother was not happy.

They had barely reached the upstairs sitting room when Mrs Gardiner said in a rather tense voice, "Caroline my love, I fear we have had some bad news."

Even before she had finished speaking, Caroline swung round and grasped her mother's hand.

"Mama, what is it? Is it Richard? Has something happened to Richard?"

Mrs Gardiner was quick to reassure her, "Oh no, no, it is nothing like that. Richard is well and has settled into his new place in Birmingham with young Mr Antoine. No, Caroline, it is Robert who is in trouble!"

"Robert's in trouble! Whatever has he done?" Caroline could not believe what she was hearing. Robert, quiet and compliant, what trouble could he possibly be in?

Mrs Gardiner, having first begged her daughter to keep her voice low lest the servants should hear her and learn of their troubles, proceeded to explain.

"Last week, your father received a letter from Mr Bartholomew, his manager in London, alerting him to the fact that Robert had disappeared from his lodgings. No, no, do not be alarmed, Caroline, it is not as bad as it sounds; your father and Mr Darcy went to London immediately and found Robert quite safe and well; he had only left his lodgings to avoid his creditors," said Mrs Gardiner, throwing poor Caroline into even greater confusion.

"His creditors? What creditors? Why was Robert borrowing money?" she asked, desperate for information.

Mrs Gardiner then revealed a sad, foolish tale of a naïve young man and his high living, time serving city friends, who had enticed him with favours into borrowing money to pay their gambling debts and then left him to repay the entire loan.

It was clear to Mrs Gardiner that Colonel Fitzwilliam, whose help Mr Gardiner had enlisted in London, had not, on his return, revealed any of these unhappy circumstances to Caroline, hoping no doubt to keep it from her until everything was settled.

"Was it a great deal of money that was owed?" Caroline asked and her mother revealed reluctantly that the sum, though not vast, was nevertheless considerable and had meant that her father, in order to repay it, had to place some of his shares in the company with the bank as security against a loan.

Seeing Caroline's ashen face, for she had never known her father to do such a thing, being a man of sound dealings and great common sense in money matters, Mrs Gardiner tried to assuage the shock and sorrow she clearly felt.

"You must not worry, my dear. Mr Darcy has kindly offered to guarantee the loan, which is only for a very short term, though on a high rate of interest. Once your father repays the bank and the matter is settled, it will all be right again."

Caroline was incredulous. How could such a situation have come about? It seemed so unlikely. She was keen to discover the circumstances, and it was only the sound of David crying in the nursery that distracted her from further questioning her mother, who was not very forthcoming in the first place.

However, after her parents had left, Colonel Fitzwilliam did not escape her attention quite as easily.

Waiting only until the maid had left the room with the tea things, she quizzed him about Robert's predicament and demanded to be told everything. She was vexed about being kept in the dark for over a week, when he, being in London with Mr Darcy and her father, had had full knowledge of Robert's situation while she remained at home in ignorance.

"Robert is my brother, Fitzy, do I not have the right to know if he is in trouble?" she asked and Fitzwilliam explained patiently, "We were all anxious not to alarm you, dearest. Your parents, your mama in particular, begged me not to reveal the details of your brother's plight, at least until we had the matter satisfactorily settled. I believed, rightly as it turns out, that she intended to break it gently to you. Now she has done so, you may ask me anything you wish to know and I shall answer you."

"But, Fitzy, Robert is not as clever as Richard nor as industrious, but he is not a criminal. What was the need to hide it from me? He may have acted foolishly but he has not broken the law, surely?" she persisted.

"Indeed, no, my love, he has not. But he has shown a lack of sound judgment and, it seems, he is unlikely to pursue his legal studies as had been hoped. But there is good news—your papa has told me just this evening that Robert will accept the position which has been offered to him, one that will enable..."

Caroline interrupted him. "What position? Who has offered him a position?" she asked, curious and puzzled that her mother had made no mention of this.

Fitzwilliam explained, at length, "A mercantile house in the colony of Ceylon, the very same firm with whom I worked for some years, has offered Robert a position..."

"In Ceylon?" Caroline was disbelieving.

"Indeed, yes," he replied.

"But why? Surely he has not done anything so disgraceful as to require banishment to the colonies?" she protested.

Her husband was at pains to explain.

"Certainly not. It is not a question of banishment. Robert is heartily sorry for what has happened—he realises that he has cost your papa a great deal of money and much grief. He has asked to be allowed to get away from London— from England, if possible, and the company of his irresponsible friends—for a few years. It was his choice."

"But it is so far away," Caroline cried, still unwilling to accept his explanation.

"Yes, but consider this, my dearest, Robert will be with an excellent British firm, with sound credentials, and he will gain training in the management of a business, so that on his return to England, he will be ready and able to assist your papa in his company. Think, my love, I went out to the colonies many years ago and had no regrets, save that I had left my dear friends behind, some of whom I missed very much."

Ignoring his attempts to divert her attention, she asked, "Will he be safe?" and Fitzwilliam was quick to reassure her.

"It is a far more peaceful colony today than it was twenty years ago, with many opportunities for a young fellow like Robert. Do not fret, Caroline, it will do him much good, mark my words."

Caroline was not easily convinced and, despite his best efforts, she determined to see her father and discover his opinion on the matter.

꧁꧂

On the following day, she took advantage of an opportunity to visit her parents' home, taking her daughter Isabella with her. Mrs Gardiner was about to set off for the local church fair, and when Isabella attached herself to her grandmother and asked to accompany her, Caroline was more than pleased. It would give her all the time she needed. Mr Gardiner, she had been told, was in the study.

Entering the room that was her father's domain, she found him looking seriously at pages of accounts, which he put down upon seeing her. Greeting her warmly, Mr Gardiner rose and moved to a couch beside the windows. Caroline was his favourite child and she was always welcome.

They had a good understanding of one another, almost an ability to read each other's thoughts, and for all his good cheer, Caroline could see her father was troubled.

She went straight to the matter that had occupied her thoughts.

"Papa, Fitzy has told me everything. I am so sorry; is there not anything we can do to help Robert?" she asked, sitting down beside him.

Mr Gardiner was touched and took her hand in his.

"My dear Caroline, your husband has been a tower of strength. It was he helped us locate your brother in London and then found him proper lodgings until arrangements were made to release him from his debt. I could not have done it without Fitzwilliam and Mr Darcy," he said and she asked immediately, "And this debt you owe the bank, how is it to be repaid so you may reclaim your shares?"

Mr Gardiner flinched and Caroline knew why he had appeared so troubled. She knew how much his company meant to him and how hard he had striven to acquire and develop it. She, as his eldest child, also appreciated how much of the present comfortable situation of their family was owed to the success of his work.

She understood, above all, what a difficult decision it must have been for her father to place a portion of his shares as security with the bank in order to borrow the money to rescue Robert from the consequences of his indiscretion and naiveté.

She saw plainly now the anxiety upon his countenance, as he clearly contemplated the loss he had suffered and the enormity of the debt that remained to be repaid. She was determined to know the whole truth.

Mr Gardiner knew also that Caroline could not be deceived with platitudes and reassuring remarks. He would need to be open with her. She was too astute to be satisfied with some facile explanation.

"Well, my dear, it is a considerable sum and it will have to be repaid and fairly soon, even if it means selling some of my shares."

"No, Papa!" she protested. "You shall not sell any of your shares. That is not fair—it is your life's work and I shall not stand by and let you do this."

"Caroline, my child, it may not be necessary, not unless we have a very poor season or business turns down unexpectedly."

But she would not let him continue.

"Papa, please hear me out; I may have little knowledge of business matters, but I do know how very hard you have worked over many, many years, and if you sell any of those shares and subsequently lose control of the company, you will never forgive yourself, nor will you, in the end, forgive Robert for having been the cause of it."

Hearing her impassioned plea, Mr Gardiner was himself surprised, not at the intensity of feeling but at the clarity and depth of her understanding of his problem. Once some of his shares were in the hands of others, he could find himself under pressure to dispose of more and may well lose control of his business. He was sufficiently experienced in business to know that predatory buyers of profitable, well-run companies were legion and he had no desire to go down that route.

Caroline went on, "Please, Papa, let me help. Fitzy has told me how much is owed to the bank; he says you would not let Mr Darcy contribute except to guarantee the loan, so it is entirely yours to repay. Now, I have as much or more in my own trust account and I should like, I would very much wish for you to take some of it, repay the bank, and reclaim the shares you have lodged with them."

Mr Gardiner was so astonished, he was speechless for a moment, before he said, "No, Caroline, I cannot take it; that money was placed in trust to give you an independent income, if ever you should need it. God forbid that it should ever come to that, but as in the case of poor Mrs Collins, we are none of us certain of the future and I will not deprive you of it."

But Caroline was adamant. "Papa, please believe me, I know what I am suggesting. It will not disadvantage me or my children in any way. We are well provided for and indeed, I should be proud to have been of help, knowing you have done so much for me."

Mr Gardiner's amazement was not at her generosity, for he knew her nature well, she was quite capable of such a gesture, but at the calm and collected way in which she appeared to have thought through the entire scheme and the sensible manner in which she had put it to him.

"It was as if she was accustomed to engaging in this type of transaction every day of the week," he told his wife later, when describing the events of the morning to her.

Realising his daughter would not be refused, Mr Gardiner made a counter proposition, suggesting that the shares be redeemed and transferred formally to Caroline, in order that her money be thereafter invested in the company.

Caroline, after a few moments' thought, agreed, making only one condition: that the matter be kept confidential, except from the partners and her mother.

"I should not wish it to be common currency among our friends and neighbours. The fewer people who know of the arrangement, the better we shall all be," she had said and her father agreed.

Soon afterwards, she set about making the necessary arrangements to have the money made available to Mr Gardiner. Only Colonel Fitzwilliam and Mr Darcy were privy to the transaction. Both men, like Mr Gardiner, were quite astonished at the remarkable good business sense Caroline had shown, though neither were surprised by the generous impulse that had prompted it. Many years would pass before other members of the family would become aware of her benevolent gesture and the consequences that were to flow from it.

Quite unaware of all that had transpired to free him of his debt and assured of his family's support and affection, Robert Gardiner sailed for the eastern colonies, where he would work for the next few years.

Mr Gardiner, buoyed by the ease with which he had solved what might have been a far more intractable financial problem, plunged back into the development of his company, taking it to even greater levels of profitability.

But, while Britain, now perhaps the most commercially advanced nation on earth, experienced a period of bountiful prosperity, the families at Oakleigh, Matlock, and Pemberley were not destined to enjoy unalloyed happiness as their reward.

For them, the storm clouds were gathering.

Chapter Six

LATE IN THE AUTUMN OF 1833, not long after the families had attended the baptism of Sophia Bingley, daughter of Jane and Charles Bingley, news was received at Pemberley of the death of Mrs Bennet.

While this was not of itself unexpected, for Mrs Bennet had been ailing for some years, beset with a respiratory disease that had long since replaced her "poor nerves" as her chief source of complaint, it did precipitate a particularly unpleasant series of incidents. Unforeseen and therefore more shocking, it disturbed the peaceful lives of Mrs Bennet's elder daughters and their families to a considerable degree.

Caroline, who had not travelled to Longbourn for the funeral, heard most of it from her cousin Elizabeth and more later from her mother. The Fitzwilliams were in London for the Autumn session of Parliament and met with young Jonathan Bingley when they dined with Mr and Mrs Darcy at their town house in Portman Square.

Elizabeth had revealed how Mr Bennet had sagaciously, and some would say mischievously, outwitted the Wickhams, who had attempted after Mrs Bennet's funeral to insinuate themselves by devious means into Longbourn and gain a foothold there.

"They intended, under the guise of caring for Papa, to occupy Longbourn and so stake their claim for their son Henry Wickham to inherit the property," she explained, "but, by announcing his intention to leave Longbourn to Jonathan, his eldest daughter's son, with life interest to my sister Mary, as long as she is single, Papa has cleverly frustrated the machinations of Lydia and Wickham. That the couple will not be pleased is without question," said Elizabeth, "but far more satisfying is the fact that Longbourn will remain a peaceful haven for Papa and Mary; there is no means by which Lydia and her brood can invade it now. Mr Grimes, Papa's attorney, is to write to Lydia advising her of the situation, and dear Jonathan will, on his eighteenth birthday, take over the management of the estate, freeing Papa from that onerous task."

Caroline, who had had little contact with her errant cousin Lydia since her infamous elopement and marriage to Mr Wickham, was very impressed.

"It certainly does seem as though my dear uncle Bennet has been most astute, does it not?" she said and Mr Darcy agreed.

"He has indeed, Caroline, and while I have absolutely no desire to meet Mr and Mrs Wickham, I would pay to see their faces when they receive the news." There was laughter as everyone recalled that there was no love lost between Mr Darcy and Mr Wickham.

Fitzwilliam spoke for them all when he raised his glass to propose a toast to young Mr Jonathan Bingley, whose universal popularity in the family made him an excellent choice, and to celebrate "a happy and satisfying conclusion all round."

So, despite Lydia's persistent complaints, was a most vexing problem peacefully resolved.

There was, however, another matter on which Caroline was not inclined to be quite so sanguine. It concerned her younger sister Emily, who had visited her at the farm in Matlock while the rest of the family had been away in Hertfordshire attending Mrs Bennet's funeral.

Emily Gardiner, now almost twenty-five years old, spent a good deal of her time at Pemberley, where she worked in the library, cataloguing a number of valuable items that had lain unused for many years. She also helped Mrs Jenkins—her cousin Kitty, who was married to the rector at Pemberley—run the parish school.

A gentle, quiet young woman, she had escaped the inevitable matchmaking efforts of friends and family by appearing to be completely content with her present situation. Her sister Caroline could not understand it; but on the advice of her mother and her husband, she made no attempt to quiz her sister about her preference for the single state.

One morning, Emily had arrived at Matlock to visit her sister accompanied by Monsieur Paul Antoine, the young Frenchman who had arrived in England with their brother Richard. A qualified and skilled apothecary, he had joined Richard at his practise in Birmingham.

In between times, he would take in the many delights of Pemberley and its environs, with Emily Gardiner as his guide.

His natural interest and her own obliging nature combined to make for a very easy association. Besides being a keen art lover, he had also a talent for scenic drawing, and on this day, Emily had promised to let him view the breathtaking landscape of the Peaks from the comfort of her sister's home.

"The outlook from the music room is unsurpassed—nowhere, not even at Pemberley, can one command such a prospect," she had said, and Monsieur Antoine, when he had seen it, had to agree she was right. It was, he said, a vista that made him wish he was a painter, not just a scribbler. Having spent an hour or so sketching, he joined the sisters for tea, and while he made light of his own artistic talent, he left Caroline in no doubt of his gratitude for her hospitality.

In every way, a most charming and agreeable young man, Caroline had liked him very much. Observing him and her sister together on other occasions, she had detected in their behaviour towards one another the signs of genuine affection.

She had thought, at first, the attraction was only on his part, since Emily appeared not to encourage it. But, as she observed them in the more intimate atmosphere of her home, she noticed Emily's looks and expressions of pleasure, even delight, in his attentions, which Caroline did not fail to recognise and interpret appropriately.

Later, when she mentioned it to her husband, he had teased her for being such an incurable romantic; when she had insisted that this was no figment of her imagination, Fitzwilliam had accepted her judgment but advised her not to interfere.

"Do you not think, my love, that your sister, at twenty-five, is well able to manage her own romance, if that is what it is? After all, she has shown no interest in any man before. If she seems to like Monsieur Antoine, he must be different. Besides, your brother Richard must surely have vouched for his friend—he is unlikely to permit his sister to be taken advantage of," he had said, being quite logical and reasonable.

In the flurry of excitement that accompanied the passage of Lord Althorp's Factory Act, Colonel Fitzwilliam paid little attention to the possible romance between his sister-in-law and the young Frenchman. Fitzwilliam, however, like Caroline herself, was ignorant of certain salient facts. Had he but known the truth, he may well have realised that Caroline's concern for her sister was not entirely misplaced.

～❧～

It was almost Christmas when, having spent the last few weeks of Autumn in London, the Fitzwilliams returned to Derbyshire.

They were met with bad news. A coach, on its way to Staffordshire, had gone off the road into a deep gully near Kympton and several people had been injured. Some had been taken to the district hospital, but most of the travellers, having been treated at the church hall, had been removed to Pemberley, where they had been given shelter and food until they recovered and could resume their journey.

Friends and neighbours told of the excellent work done at the scene of the accident, in dreadful weather, by Dr Richard Gardiner and his assistant Monsieur Antoine. They were said to have saved the lives of many travellers that night who, already weakened by injury, might otherwise have perished in the cold.

Visiting Pemberley the following day, Caroline found her sister Emily busy attending upon some of the victims of the accident and, to her surprise, discovered that one of her patients was Monsieur Antoine himself.

"He has suffered severe exposure, working in the cold and wet with Richard," she explained, "and is under doctor's orders not to leave his room. Richard believes he has a chill on the chest."

While she sounded no more concerned than if he were any one of the others, Caroline, who went downstairs to tea with Elizabeth, heard enough from her cousin to confirm her suspicions that Emily and Paul Antoine were more than good friends. At the very least, he was in love with her, while she was still undecided.

Elizabeth had no doubts about Emily's role in his recovery.

"It was Emily's care as much as Richard's treatment that saved him from pneumonia," Elizabeth explained. "He had worked for hours with Richard, helping to treat and comfort the unfortunate travellers. Richard says he has a weak constitution and the exposure has affected his lungs. Emily insists that he does exactly as the doctor orders—she feeds him and gives him his potions and pills and he seems to enjoy it. He is certainly much improved this week," she said, her eyes dancing with merriment.

When Emily joined them for tea, Caroline invited her to spend Sunday at the farm.

Emily accepted but, as her sister was leaving, came out to the carriage to say in a whisper, "I do not think I should bring Paul; he is much better, but still not strong enough to be out and about in this weather. However, I shall come; it will be nice to see the children again. I have missed them."

Considering she had not invited Monsieur Antoine, Caroline was surprised to say the least, but she showed no astonishment at all, saying in a most matter-of-fact way, "Of course, Emmy, you are quite right. We shall look forward to having you. It is a very long time since we have had a real heart-to-heart talk. I have been away in London with Fitzy and you have been busy here at Pemberley—it is time we had a good, long talk together. I am looking forward to it very much."

Even as she spoke, Caroline thought she noticed a look of some apprehension cross her sister's face, as though, for some unaccountable reason, she did not welcome the prospect of a "heart-to-heart" talk.

Could it be, Caroline wondered, that Emily already knew Paul Antoine was in love with her and was reluctant to speak of it, because she did not return his affection?

Perhaps, she surmised, he had already proposed and she had turned him down? Her romantic imagination conjured up a dozen different possibilities, all equally intriguing. She longed to know the truth.

When Sunday came around, Caroline waited with great anticipation but in vain; for when Emily did arrive, she brought with her Kitty's twin daughters, Eliza Anne and Maria Jane. The two girls, both very like their mother and one another, were not only accomplished in their school work, they could also sing and play. Emily, knowing of Caroline's plans for a small local chamber music group of young performers, had brought them along so her sister could hear them.

"I was sure you would like to hear them perform," she explained, adding, "for ten-year-olds, they are very good indeed."

Which they were; both children could play the piano and the recorder, while Maria Jane was learning the Irish harp as well, Caroline learned, and though their voices were soft, they were sweet and harmonised perfectly. "They are taught by their father, of course," said Emily, reminding Caroline that Mr Jenkins, the rector, was himself a singer of renown.

Caroline could not fail to be impressed, as Emily had clearly intended that she should be, and the twins were delighted to be told they could join her chamber group. But this little scheme had completely upset Caroline's plan for a private *tête-à-tête* with her sister, and consequently, the subject of Paul Antoine was not mentioned at all.

Emily showed no sign of wanting to speak of him, and Caroline was afforded no appropriate opportunity of asking a single significant question on the subject.

However, Emily did bring some interesting news of a plan being hatched by their cousin Elizabeth and herself, with young Cassandra Darcy's enthusiastic support, to hold a Harvest Fair at Pemberley next Autumn.

"Cousin Lizzie says it will provide a good opportunity for the tenants and farm workers and their families to sell their produce and crafts without having to give some of their profits away to the merchants. Cassy is very excited and asked her father if we may have the Lower Meadow for the fair and he has agreed. We hoped, dear Caroline, that as the wife of our popular Member of Parliament, you will consent to open the fair."

Caroline, though compelled by modesty to suggest they ask some other more important county dignitary, was easily persuaded to accept. Delighted to be so honoured, she predicted with confidence that it would be a wonderful occasion for the entire district and especially for Pemberley and its community.

"With the loss of jobs in so many of the mills and factories, it will give many people a chance to make some extra money. Times are hard for the poor and we must help," she said.

Emily agreed, "Indeed we must. We were concerned, Lizzie and I, that Mr Darcy might be averse to the idea of letting hundreds of strangers tramp all over his grounds, but he was quite agreeable, Cassy said, so we shall be making great plans for next Autumn," she declared adding, "and, Caroline, I do believe the Pemberley Ball will be held on the day after the fair."

Caroline was amazed, not because of the Pemberley Ball, which was an annual event, but by the unmistakable excitement in her sister's voice.

Emily had never been keen on dancing and rarely attended balls except when she had to for family or charitable functions. Caroline, on the other hand, had always enjoyed the music and fun of a ball and was all astonishment to find her sister similarly affected on this occasion. Could it possibly have something to do with Paul Antoine, she wondered, and was about to ask if the gentleman would be present when Isabella and the Jenkins girls came racing into the room, pursued by an aggravated puppy that had to be rescued and comforted.

Later that evening, when Fitzwilliam returned and they sat down to dinner, Caroline told him of the planned Harvest Fair. He was most enthusiastic, claiming that many village folk, who owed their livelihood to Pemberley's prosperity, would be grateful for the opportunity and it was exceedingly good of Mr Darcy to agree to the scheme.

"We could benefit too, my dear. I believe we should set up a table to collect signatures for the People's Charter for Universal Suffrage," he said. "It is a cause that is gaining support all around the country."

Both Caroline and Emily saw the good sense of his suggestion and added it to their plans. As for the invitation for his charming wife to open the fair, "Well," said the colonel, "I cannot honestly think of anyone more appropriate, can you?"

Which compliment so pleased his wife, she spent no more time that evening worrying about her sister's romance. It was time, instead, to make plans for what promised to be an exciting new year, and Caroline was full of ideas for her community.

⁓᪲⁓

Christmas came that year with not a very great deal of mirth or revelry around the country. Ominous signs in the nation's economy and some very unpredictable weather threw a pall over the festivities at Pemberley. Several of the children on the estate had contracted croup or influenza and could not attend their annual Christmas party, while one, sadly, succumbed before the apothecary, who had been held up by the appalling weather, could arrive.

Young Cassy Darcy, whose task it was to organise the entertainment for the children of the tenants and staff, was bitterly disappointed, complaining loudly to her parents that something had to be done about providing medical attention to sick children.

"It is not enough to say that the apothecary will look after them; clearly he cannot attend upon them all. Richard believes we need a children's hospital in this area, and Cousin Caroline agrees," she said at breakfast on Christmas Eve, and turning to Mr Darcy added, "Papa, do you not think it is time we did something more for the children than pay for their funerals?"

Her father, not entirely surprised for he was aware already of Doctor

Gardiner's views on the matter, was nevertheless shaken by the vehemence of Cassandra's advocacy.

"We do more than that already, Cassy, we pay for Mr Masterson, the apothecary, and for the medicines he provides to the children," he replied, then seeing what looked like tears in her eyes, his tone softened as he told her of the plans he and Richard Gardiner had discussed following the accident at Kympton, for a hospital at Littleford.

"None of this is certain until I have Sir Thomas Camden's consent, but if he does agree, and I can see no reason why he should not, since it will benefit his people as well as ours, we may well start work on a hospital at Littleford early in the new year."

This information caused Cassandra to smile with surprise and say, "Papa, that is good news."

Her father went on, "Indeed, but what is even better news is that Richard Gardiner has told me that if we were to build a hospital for the area, he would move from Birmingham to work here."

Neither Mr Darcy nor Elizabeth could have failed to note the delight that this information seemed to cause as Cassy expressed astonishment and disbelief.

"Richard would move back to work at Littleford? That would be wonderful!" Her voice betrayed her feelings and there was a flush of pleasure upon her cheeks, which could not all be due to her concern for the health of the children of the Pemberley estate.

Mr and Mrs Darcy took note but said nothing.

Richard Gardiner was a young man for whom they had the greatest esteem and affection, besides the fact that he was the son of their beloved Uncle and Aunt Gardiner. Since his return last year from Paris, having qualified as a physician, he had been busy organising his practise in Birmingham; but when he was home, he was a frequent visitor to Pemberley, ostensibly to see his cousins and his youngest sister, Emily, who spent much of the week there.

More recently however, Elizabeth had noticed that, whenever he visited, he seemed to find Cassandra either wandering in the grounds or playing the piano in the music room, and the two would appear to have a great deal to say to one another, which, considering that Cassy was an intelligent, vivacious young lady, not yet seventeen, did not entirely surprise her. Nor did it escape her attention that Cassy had spent an entire afternoon trying out a number of gowns before deciding upon which she would wear on Boxing Day, when the family was to gather at Pemberley. When she finally appeared downstairs to greet their guests, in a becoming gown of damask rose silk, even Elizabeth was startled by her beauty. Richard Gardiner, arriving shortly afterwards with his parents and Monsieur Antoine, could not take his eyes off his charming young cousin. After dinner, when the musicians appeared and the dancing began, she was clearly his preferred partner.

It was a happier occasion than they had expected, for though the weather had been cold and blustery all week, it cleared for long enough to enable everyone to arrive in time and at least they were not snowed in, as they had been some years ago. Jane Bingley, Charlotte Collins, and Elizabeth had the pleasure of seeing their children mingle as friends, just as they had done many years ago in Hertfordshire.

As the great house filled with the sounds of music and the laughter of young voices, as they sang and danced all evening in the large room which glowed with the light of candles and a large comforting fire, it seemed to Elizabeth that everything was right with her world.

She had found great happiness here, and watching her children enjoy themselves gave her special satisfaction. Both Cassy and William brought her so much pleasure and so little anxiety, she counted herself one of the most fortunate of women. She was determined that nothing, not even the persistent unease she felt about her cousin Emily, should spoil her happiness.

Meanwhile, Caroline remained watchful of her younger sister, still unable to rid herself of her concerns. Her naturally romantic disposition, which rejoiced at the prospect of Emily and Paul Antoine being in love, had to struggle with her protective instincts towards her sister.

She was puzzled by the fact that Emily still seemed unaware of the feelings she inspired in the gentleman, feelings he betrayed often enough by his very particular attentions to her.

More than once, Caroline had tried to reassure herself that Emily was twenty-five and well able to know her own mind in such matters, but she could not shake off her feelings of apprehension.

Inexplicably, in spite of her husband's assurances to the contrary, she was too anxious to be complacent. She vowed that after Christmas, she would ask her mother's opinion at the very first opportunity. Surely, she thought, Emily must have confided in her mother—if there was anything to confide.

The New Year did not get off to a very good start.

A wet, blustery Spring kept most people at home, unless it was imperative that they undertook a journey.

The disappointment did not end with the weather. Politically, Colonel Fitzwilliam was disheartened that the great reforms of 1832 and '33 seemed to have stalled. Instead of moving quickly to bring about more changes, the government, despite its majority in the Commons, seemed to be overwhelmed with confusion and internal bickering as Lord Grey resigned and Lord Melbourne, who had no real heart for reform, became the new leader of the party. None of this was advancing the causes dear to Fitzwilliam's heart. Disillusioned, he was on the verge of resignation, only persuaded to stay on by Anthony Tate and James Wilson, who argued that the cause of reform would soon be dead if every disappointed reformist threw in the towel.

Caroline, saddened by her husband's disappointment and sharing his impatience with politicians who abandoned their principles for expediency, threw herself more passionately into her charitable work. Helping the poor and campaigning for money to get the children—who, thanks to Viscount Althorp's law, were gradually being brought out of the mines—into schools was far more satisfying.

In the time she had to spare, she persevered with her pet project of gathering together and training a chamber music group, in which task she had considerable assistance from young William Darcy, whose musical talent was already acknowledged to be quite remarkable.

He had confided in her his hopes of being a concert pianist, but wondered if his father would countenance such a thing.

"I cannot see Papa agreeing to it," he had said ruefully, as they selected the music for their first concert, and Caroline would always recall the smile that lit up his face, when she said, "Oh, I would not give up so easily, William. Your papa is a man of great intelligence and culture; if you and your mama do your best, you may well persuade him to let you try. Besides he loves you dearly and wants what's best for you. I am confident of that."

As she told her mother later, "William looked so moved, I thought he was going to weep, but he put his arms around me and said, 'Thank you, Cousin Caroline. I shall always remember that.'"

Her brother Richard, meanwhile, was hard at work in Birmingham, ably assisted by his friend Paul Antoine, who had recovered from his earlier indisposition. He remained rather pale, however, and both Elizabeth and Mrs Gardiner had expressed some concern about his health.

When he was away in Birmingham, it seemed as though Emily lost no sleep over him, confident he was well looked after by her brother.

But each time he returned, it was obvious even to the most disinterested observer that his attachment to Miss Gardiner had increased. Yet, while Emily may have been pleased by his regard, she showed no sign of reciprocating his affection.

Despite her earlier determination, Caroline's resolve failed her and she did not question her mother on the subject of her sister and Monsieur Antoine, fearing that she might unduly alarm her. Had she done so, she might have learned enough to enable her to understand the situation, for Mrs Gardiner had been in her younger daughter's confidence for several months, and her knowledge had only increased her own anxiety.

~❦~

While Spring had been a great disappointment, being mostly dull and wet, Summer arrived with a glorious burst of sunshine, luring everyone out of doors and all those with the inclination and the means to travel onto the roads. Fitzwilliam and Caroline accepted an invitation to visit Standish Park in Kent—the elegant family home of Mr James Wilson, a colleague of Fitzwilliam's in the Parliament whose reforming zeal was in every way as genuine and determined as his own.

Furthermore, the colonel had agreed to call on his aunt Lady Catherine de Bourgh, whose great estate Rosings was in the same county. Her Ladyship's fondness for her nephew's wife and a softening of her generally brusque manner with the passage of the years meant that the visit was, amazingly, more a pleasure than a tour of duty.

The Darcys and their two children, Cassandra and William, left for a tour of the Lakes of Cumbria, whither Elizabeth had often longed to go without success. On a previous occasion, her initial disappointment had resulted in a quite remarkably advantageous turn of events, but this time, Mr Darcy was determined she should have her wish.

They set off, therefore, hoping to enjoy all those natural wonders, which had so inspired Wordsworth and his fellow romantics that no anthology of poems was complete without lyrical verses in praise of the Lake District.

As they said farewell, neither Caroline nor Elizabeth were to know that, by the time they returned to Derbyshire, Emily Gardiner's life would have changed forever.

Chapter Seven

WHILE THE DARCYS WERE TOURING the lakes and Colonel Fitzwilliam and his family enjoyed the hospitality of their friends in Kent, back in Derbyshire, a series of events began to unfold that neither Caroline nor Elizabeth could ever have imagined.

Worse still, they happened with such speed as to allow no time for any of the participants to communicate with any persons, save those who were directly involved. All other members of the families and their closest friends were to learn of the matter only after the fact.

Elizabeth and Darcy had been gone but a few weeks when Richard Gardiner came alone to see his mother at Lambton, on a day when he knew his father was in Manchester on business. Mrs Gardiner, at first delighted to see her son arrive unexpectedly, was made rather uneasy by his unusually solemn countenance and his long silence while she ordered tea and his favourite cake. At first, she assumed he was tired from his journey and later supposed it might have been caused by another altercation with the hospital board in Birmingham, with whom he was forever in dispute; but when they had taken tea, he rose and, going over to stand beside the window, said, "Mama, I am afraid I have some unhappy news."

Even though she had anticipated something of the sort, Mrs Gardiner was startled by the seriousness of his tone and expression. She could not recall seeing him appear quite so solemn before.

"Why, Richard, what has happened?" she asked "Is someone ill?"

She was hoping it might be a simple matter, but he turned and, coming to where she was seated, said, "Yes, it's Paul; he is very ill. I fear I shall have to take him to London to see a colleague of mine in Harley Street. I need another opinion, but even without it, I can see his health is deteriorating faster than either of us expected. I cannot explain it."

Mrs Gardiner, who had some previous knowledge of the situation, asked, "How do you mean?"

Richard explained briefly, "Well, you know all I have told you; you are aware of his illness, as is Emily. He has inherited from his unfortunate mother a poor respiratory condition, which has troubled him since childhood, and his lungs are weak. When we discovered it was tuberculosis, we tried to treat it with medication and nourishment, and for a time, we appeared to have some success; but recently, he has grown pale and has lost weight…"

Mrs Gardiner looked apprehensive, her thoughts were of Emily.

"But Richard, Emily has been often in his company; is she not in danger of infection?"

He sat down beside her and took her hand in his. "As I explained to Cousin Lizzie when she asked me that very question, if Emily is careful and sensible, there is no danger. I have given her certain instructions for her own protection; if she follows them, she is unlikely to be infected and it was her choice to continue their association."

He tried to reassure his mother, "I explained it in every detail and Paul offered never to visit her again, for her sake, as he has done with the Fitzwilliams, where there are young children, and to continue their friendship only by letter. He is devoted to her and would not do anything that might hurt her, but Emily has insisted on seeing him."

Hearing his words, Mrs Gardiner could not restrain her tears and Richard had to spend some time comforting her.

"If his condition is worse than we believed, then I fear Paul may have to leave England for the south of France or Italy. Our Winters are too damp and cold for anyone suffering from tuberculosis—if he stays, he will not survive long," he explained.

Mrs Gardiner shuddered at the dreadful word; she knew of families where two or three had been lost to the relentless disease.

"Mama, I need you to help Emmy; if that is what she has to face, she will need all the support we can give her. As I think you are already aware, she and Paul are exceedingly fond of one another; it will be a painful parting for both if he has to leave England for good."

Richard's voice was grave; his countenance betrayed his sorrow.

Mrs Gardiner could think only of the pain her daughter would have to bear. "Must he go?" she asked.

Richard nodded, "I believe he must, especially if my colleague in Harley Street confirms my fears. If he does, I shall take Paul to Italy myself and arrange for him to stay there and be looked after by a reputable physician. There is no problem with money; he inherited most of his mother's estate. He can be well cared for, but if he does not go, he will die within a few months."

"Are you going to tell Emily?"

"I am," he replied, "she will not forgive me if I do not. I am going to call on her at Pemberley this evening."

"And Paul?" his mother asked anxiously,

"He is at the house in Littleford that Mr Darcy made available to us. He was exhausted after the journey; I gave him some medication and left him to rest. I think it is preferable that he remains there tonight. My man will stay with him."

"What about Lizzie and Caroline?" Mrs Gardiner asked.

Richard thought for a moment. "I shall inform Caroline and Fitzwilliam, when I meet them in London, but, Mama, I must leave it to you to tell Cousin Lizzie. Perhaps you should wait awhile; there is nothing to be gained by spoiling their tour of the lakes."

Mrs Gardiner knew Elizabeth would be most perturbed and said so.

"I shall write to her, after you have returned from London," she said and Richard agreed, "Yes, she will be shocked, I know. It has surprised me, even though I have observed him carefully all year. Cousin Lizzie was very concerned for Emily and questioned me closely. I had to explain that Paul and Emily have both known all the facts for as long as they have known one another. They are neither of them silly young people, but I do know that he cares deeply for her."

"And she for him, Richard," his mother interposed, "Emily told me everything some weeks ago and begged me to keep her secret. I have told no one but your father; I know she will take this news very badly. She did not expect his condition to worsen so rapidly. She has spoken of some years…"

"I thought so too, but this wretched disease is unpredictable and pitiless.

It appears to withdraw for a while and then returns with redoubled vigour to claim its victims. It's a scourge for which we have no cure," he said sadly and Mrs Gardiner could sense the despair and frustration in his voice.

"My poor dear Emily," said Mrs Gardiner and Richard spoke gently, understanding her grief, "She will need our help, Mama. It will not be easy."

"When do you go to London?"

"Tomorrow," he replied, "soon after breakfast. Mercifully, we have some fine weather. I pray it will hold over the next few days. I would rather not travel with my patient in drenching rain."

When he was gone, taking the familiar road to Pemberley, Mrs Gardiner went to her room and wept, for her daughter and for the gentle young man for whom they had so much affection and respect.

~⁂~

His curricle was less than a mile from Pemberley House, at a point where the footpath from the village of Littleford met the road from Lambton that descended into the park, when Richard Gardiner caught sight of two figures walking up the path. They were two women, and though their hats hid their faces from him, he had no difficulty in recognising his sister Emily and their cousin Kitty, the rector's wife.

Pulling up beside them, he offered to drive them home, assuming they were returning to Pemberley, but Kitty declined, saying she had to be back at the rectory in time for tea and would take the route across the park, while Emily, having first embraced her cousin and thanked her, climbed in and sat beside him.

Her face, despite the protection of her hat, was flushed and Richard spoke gently, asking if they had been out visiting the poor. He was aware that Kitty did a great deal of charity work in the parish and Emily often went with her. But this time he was wrong.

Emily's voice was quiet, "I know all about Paul; I have been to see him," and before he could say a word, she added, "Kitty and Dr Jenkins saw you arrive at the house at Littleford this morning. When she told me, I had to go to him. You were not expected today and I was afraid it may have been bad news. I was right. Paul has told me he is to go with you to London tomorrow."

Her brother tried to explain, "Emily, I was on my way to tell you. I have just told Mama and left her but half an hour ago. I did not intend to leave you in ignorance."

She nodded and said, "I know that, Richard, but I needed to see him and tell him how I felt. He has told me often of his feelings, but I have held back, fearing it would only cause more pain, but today, I had to tell him. When I knew you were going to London, I could not let him go to hear whatever dreadful news they might have in store for him; I had to say that I loved him.

"Oh Richard, what a wretched creature I am, that after all these years, during which time, I have met no man for whom I felt any deep regard or affection, I should meet the only man I could dearly love and he is the one man I may not marry."

Her voice broke and her sobbing forced him to stop the vehicle and wait, while she became calmer and wiped the tears from her face. It was, for her brother, a heart-rending sight, to see her weep and know that he could do nothing to comfort her or help his friend.

When they reached the house, he sat with her for some time in a private sitting room while she asked several pertinent questions, which he answered as best he could. She wanted to know every detail and begged him to keep nothing, however painful, from her.

When he revealed that it was most likely Paul would have to leave England and live in Italy, she wept again, softly this time, but with a despairing sadness that was unbearable to see.

"If he does go to Italy, how will it help?" she asked and Richard explained gently that it would only extend his life for some months and keep him more comfortable, since the salubrious climate would retard the progress of the disease.

"He would have greater enjoyment of the time he has left and that time may be a little longer than if he remained here."

She nodded, accepting his word, saying nothing, but the sorrow in her eyes was unmistakable. It was almost sunset when he left, embracing her and promising to do all he could for Paul's comfort.

On the following day, Richard and his patient left for London.

⚜

The weeks that followed were some of the most difficult in Richard Gardiner's life.

The physician they consulted in Harley Street confirmed his diagnosis. The disease had affected both Paul's lungs and unless he got away, out of the cold and damp of the oncoming English Winter, to somewhere warm and dry, he would not survive beyond the next few months.

"Sunshine, medication, and good nourishment can sometimes work miracles, Dr Gardiner," he said. "At the very least, it will let your patient live comfortably for much longer than if he remained in England."

Knowing well his own condition, Paul Antoine took the news with an amazing degree of stoicism and courage, agreeing with Richard that it would be best that he did as the doctor ordered. Yet, as they returned to their lodgings, he could speak only of Emily and the grief he knew she would feel at their parting.

"I am aware, my dear friend, it is my fault; probably I should never have permitted her to know my true feelings. But your sister is such a woman, a lady of such great sensitivity, she could read my thoughts before I spoke them aloud and when she came to visit me, it was in vain to pretend. It will be difficult for her, she knows I love her; I have told her so, but she knows also there is no future for us. It is my fault, I should have known better," he said.

Richard assured him that no one would blame either of them for falling in love.

"It is one of those situations in life over which we have very little control. Besides, Emily and you have been remarkable; you both knew the truth and yet grew to care for each other. Who can blame you for such selflessness? I do not know too many people who could do as you have done."

Going round to the Fitzwilliams' town house, Richard discovered that, fortuitously, they were due back in London from Kent that very night. On the following morning, he called on them after breakfast.

When he told them why he was in London and revealed the news about Paul and Emily, both Colonel Fitzwilliam and Caroline were aghast.

"I cannot believe it, Richard," she cried, saying again and again, "it is just not fair!"

"Is there no cure at all?" asked Fitzwilliam, who could not accept that such a fine young man could be struck down so cruelly.

Richard shook his head, "Sadly, there is not. If he goes to Italy, it will probably extend his life and improve the quality of it for a while."

"And if he does not?"

"He will most likely die before Christmas."

Caroline could think only of the suffering of her sister, alone at Pemberley.

"Fitzy, I believe we must return home. Emmy needs me" she said.

Her husband agreed at once and preparations were set in train to leave London the following day.

Reaching Derbyshire, having broken journey briefly for some refreshment and to change horses, they went directly to Pemberley, where Caroline, eager to see her sister, hurried upstairs to her room.

Expecting to find her inconsolable, Caroline was astonished to find Emily packing a trunk with clothes and linen, clearly preparing for a journey.

"Emily!" she cried, and as the two sisters embraced and clung together, their tears flowed, even though they had said not a word.

"Richard has told me, oh my dear sister." She got no further, for Emily placed a finger on her lips and asked, "Is Richard here?"

"Yes, with Paul and Fitzwilliam, downstairs in the saloon. We travelled together from London," Caroline replied.

In seconds, Emily had washed her face, tidied her hair, and insisted upon going down to see them.

They found the three gentlemen taking tea and refreshments, which Mrs Reynolds had thoughtfully provided for the travellers.

When Emily entered the room, she went directly to her brother and Paul. Standing beside them, she declared that she had made a decision and wanted to tell them about it.

She knew, she said, that Paul would have to leave England and travel to Italy for the sake of his health and she had decided to go with him.

Seeing the looks of amazement on every face in the room and hearing Caroline gasp, she added quickly, "Have no fear, Caroline, I am not proposing to outrage my family by doing something foolish and unseemly; Paul and I will be married by special licence and I shall go as his wife, so I can look after him in Italy. I have asked Mr Jenkins and Kitty to make the necessary arrangements for our wedding in the chapel at Pemberley next week. Richard, I must ask you please to arrange our travel and accommodation. We shall be ready to leave as soon as the wedding is over."

She spoke so calmly and with such determination that no one felt they could interrupt her. She had taken Paul's hand in hers as she spoke.

When she had finished speaking, Colonel Fitzwilliam asked, "Emily, are you quite sure?"

She smiled then and replied, "I have never been more certain of anything in my entire life, Colonel Fitzwilliam. We love each other and I cannot let him go away to suffer alone. Paul needs me and I want to be with him, to care for him for however long or short a time it may be."

There was silence in the room. Clearly, there was nothing any of them could say that would change her mind.

Looking at Monsieur Antoine, Caroline could see how he felt; unbelievably happy to know he was so dearly loved, yet in such agony that Emily was doing this for him. He tried to speak, to say something, to protest that she must not sacrifice herself, but she would not let him. Instead, she bent down and kissed his cheek and then turned to embrace her brother and sister, leaving no one in any doubt of the strength of her resolve.

Richard held her close and said softly, so only she would hear, "If you are quite sure, Emmy, I shall arrange everything for you," and she thanked him, sincerely, "Thank you, Richard, I am not only sure, I am eager for us to be married as soon as possible, so I can start caring for my husband. It is what I want to do. I have not wanted anything so much in my whole life."

That night, back at their farm, Caroline and Fitzwilliam could not resist returning again and again to the events of that afternoon. They had both been deeply moved, but the colonel was concerned lest Emily was acting on impulse, driven by compassion.

"How is it possible for her to be so certain? Is it not probable that she will regret her decision when it is too late? What consequences might flow from this for her in later life?" All these questions troubled him.

But his wife had other ideas. "What is there to regret, Fitzy?" she asked. "They love each other. She wishes to look after him for however long he lives; I think she will suffer far greater anguish were she to stay at home in England, knowing that Paul is in Italy, dying alone."

Fitzwilliam seemed to accept her argument; then suddenly, he asked, "Would you have done the same for me, Caroline?"

She was outraged that he should ask such a question. She could not believe he was other than serious at such a time.

"Fitzy, of course I would. Did you think I would say no? Had you returned from the colonies with some dreaded fever, did you think I would have let you go away and die alone in some foreign country?"

Seeing her tears and regretting his half-serious question, he reached out and held her close, knowing how deeply she felt for her sister. He apologised, realising he had been wrong to make light of it. He tried to comfort her, but in vain, for Caroline could think only of Emily's sorrow and the terrible pain it would cause her parents.

"Poor Mama and Papa, how will they bear it? And poor Richard, how will he tell them?" she cried and nothing her husband could say would assuage her grief.

When Richard Gardiner returned to Oakleigh the following morning and revealed to his parents what Emily intended to do, Mrs Gardiner cried out, "Oh, no, no!" burst into tears, and covered her face with her hands. Her husband, whose devotion to his wife and family was a byword among all who knew him, was struck dumb for several minutes.

A businessman of good sense and perception, this was not the type of crisis he had ever expected to face; he had no experience that had prepared him for it or taught him what to say or do in such a dire circumstance as this.

While Richard waited, knowing well the severity of the blow his words had dealt his parents, his mother had fled the room, unable to contain her grief.

Mr Gardiner, grave-faced, turned to his son and asked, "What is your honest opinion, Richard? Is Emily right?"

"It is not my opinion that matters, Papa. It is not for me to say if Emily is right or wrong; she is twenty-five years old and says she has decided to marry Paul. I cannot see how we can stop her. Furthermore, it is probably not in her interest that we do thwart her, since if we succeed and Paul dies alone in Italy, she will forever blame us for keeping her from going to him. Moreover, she may sink into some kind of depression and suffer a deep sense of guilt as well," he explained.

"But if she does go, if she marries him as she says she will, what problems might she face?"

Mr Gardiner was concerned with the practicalities for the future as well as their present predicament.

Richard assured his father that he would do everything possible to assist and protect her. He had, he said, good contacts among the medical fraternity in Europe and could ensure Paul was well looked after. As for their comfort, Paul had sufficient means to take a suitable house, employ some servants, and pay for all his medical requirements.

Mr Gardiner sighed. "Well, Richard, if she must go, we must provide her with everything she needs and ensure that they are both well attended upon. One of my men can travel with them to ensure they are safe. Make whatever arrangements you think fit, spare no expense. I cannot have Emily lodged in some pensione with dark rooms and no ventilation. For whatever time they have left together, they must be secure and comfortable," he said.

Richard agreed, adding quietly, "Mama will not be happy," but his father intervened, "Of course, what else would you expect? She thinks her child is throwing her life away, putting her health in jeopardy. I am not happy myself, but I would not hurt Emily by expressing my displeasure, when she has so much to bear already. I shall talk to your mother, Richard, but I must rely on you to ensure that everything is done to assist Emily and Paul. They are both fine young people and entitled to be happy; they are not to blame for the cruel blow that Fate has dealt them."

Touched by the compassionate response of his father, Richard assured him that he would do all that was required of him and left to return to the cottage at Littleford. There he found his friend, sitting up at a table in the front room, writing laboriously by the light of a small lamp.

He was making a will.

~❦~

By the time the Darcys returned from the Lakes of Cumbria, Emily Gardiner had been married and she and her husband had already left for Italy.

Alerted by a hint of disquiet in a letter from her Aunt Gardiner, received at Ambleside, Elizabeth had soon sensed that something was wrong at Pemberley. Cutting short their tour of the lakes, the Darcys had returned to find the birds had flown. Only Mrs Reynolds and Kitty remained to give them Emily's letter, until Richard arrived later to explain, clearly and without any subterfuge, his sister's decision—a decision that shocked and appalled her cousin Elizabeth.

Unable to comprehend it, she was compelled to admit to her husband that she felt Emily had blighted her life by her precipitate action; it was a remark she regretted as soon as she had uttered the words.

Mr Darcy was immediately censorious of what seemed to him like uncharacteristic callousness on her part.

"Dearest Elizabeth, that is not fair, nor is it worthy of you," he had said, and when Caroline arrived on the morrow, Elizabeth, seeing how differently she had responded, felt ashamed of her rush to judgment.

To Caroline, Emily's actions were evidence of her selflessness; she had placed love above self-interest and, in so doing, had established its preeminence in her life.

"No matter how short-lived, a marriage founded upon such genuine love could only enhance Emily's life," said Caroline.

In her heart, Elizabeth knew this to be true and wanted desperately to believe that Emily would find happiness, however briefly, in her marriage. She deserved nothing less. But her head was not so easily satisfied.

A note Richard had delivered to Caroline from their sister brought some consolation.

Dearest Caroline, Emily wrote, in a hand that was surprisingly firm:

You must not feel sorry for me, believing that I am making some terrible mistake or sacrificing myself for Paul. That would be wrong, utterly wrong.

The truth is I have experienced so much satisfaction and genuine happiness since we set out from Pemberley that I know I have done the right thing.

Indeed, feeling as I do, it would have been unthinkable that I could have let him go alone to face his fate. It would have left me bereft and miserable.

Dear Caroline, forgive my secrecy; it was well meant, to protect Paul and keep my dear family from suffering undue anxiety, but I have known for months that I loved him and even though I would not say it, despite his having told me many times of his feelings, I think Paul knew too.

Now it is acknowledged, we are both happier than ever before. Caroline, if I were to live to be eighty and never love another man for the rest of my life, I shall still have the bright memory of the love I have shared with Paul. However long or brief our marriage may be, nothing will ever eclipse the light it has brought into my life.

You must tell them all, Cousin Lizzie, Kitty, Mr Darcy, Cassy, William, and especially Mama and Papa, who have been so good to me, how very happy I am, we both are. There has not been one single moment of regret, not one!

We both send you all our love and I thank you with all my heart for your love and understanding.

> *Your loving sister,*
> *Emily.*

Caroline needed no more evidence to convince her that Emily was right.

~☙~

Throughout the Summer of 1834 and well into Autumn, Emily wrote to her brother, her parents, Caroline, and Elizabeth warm, enthusiastic letters, recounting pleasant days in the sun and recording a slow but steady improvement in her husband's health. The doctors in Italy were satisfied that the progress of the inexorable disease had been slowed at least, if not halted.

As every scrap of information gleaned from her letters was eagerly shared with every other member of the family, most began to feel more comfortable with the situation. It appeared as though Paul's condition was improving, however slowly, and there was new hope.

Only Richard had warned them that it was best not to place too much credence on the good news.

"It is typical of this wretched disease," he said as they sat together, after dinner at Pemberley, discussing Emily's latest optimistic letter,

"It seems to withdraw for a month or two, occasionally even for several months, when the patient recovers his colour and appetite; but then, with no warning, it returns, often with redoubled vigour."

Caroline and Elizabeth begged him not to tell his mother of his reservations.

"It would take away the little comfort she gets from Emily's letters, which she reads avidly two or three times over; at least they give her some hope," said Caroline and Richard agreed.

He admitted he had cautioned his father though; it would not be right to keep him in ignorance, he said.

"I hope Papa will in time advise Mama, so she will not be too shocked when the crisis comes, as it must, in the end."

Gradually, as the year moved deeper into Autumn, their anxiety for Emily and Paul abated somewhat, as they turned to the prodigious task of organising the first Harvest Fair and the annual Ball at Pemberley.

Having initiated it, Elizabeth, finding herself without Emily's valuable help, had to call upon her sisters and cousins to assist her.

Jane Bingley and her eldest daughter Emma answered her plea, and as they sat together drawing up the inevitable lists of things to be done and people who might be called upon to do them, Emma happened to ask if there had been any recent news from Emily.

A gentle, compassionate young woman herself, Emma Bingley had been deeply moved by Emily's actions. Elizabeth, in answer to her query, handed her Emily's letter and said, "Well, I must admit, I had not expected it; but there has been only good news ever since they have been settled in Italy. It is almost as though Emily and Paul have been determined to defy the disease and the generally accepted notion that he had but a few short weeks to live."

Emma could not restrain her tears as she read the letter and looking up at her mother and aunt, said quietly, "I have not heard or seen such selfless devotion before. Emily is such a strong, determined person, she seems to be able to will him to recover. I shall pray that she will succeed."

Unwilling to let young Emma, whose strength of character belied her own tender years, labour under a misapprehension, Elizabeth spoke quickly, "Richard warns us, however, that this dreadful infection can hide for months at a time, permitting the patient to appear close to recovery, then return to strike them down. I have no doubt he has cautioned his sister too, so she will not be too optimistic, but Emily is unwilling to accept these gloomy prognostications."

Jane, whose tender heart had been strained to breaking point by Emily's wedding and departure for Italy, was already in tears.

"Oh Lizzie, how cruel it is that such things should happen to the best and the kindest of people. If only Emily had been married before Richard returned from France, she, her parents, and all of us would surely have been spared this agony."

Emma, though not usually quick to contradict her mother, could not remain silent, "Mama, one cannot be sure of that. Marriage is not always a haven in which a woman may find happiness or refuge from life's sorrows. I believe Mrs Collins may testify to that."

Elizabeth agreed entirely and intervened with a light remark about marriage to the late Mr Collins being hardly a haven of happiness for their friend Charlotte, and even Jane, who had often in the past reprimanded her sister for poking fun at the reverend gentleman, had to laugh.

"Oh Lizzie, you are cruel. Poor Mr Collins...."

"Poor Charlotte," interrupted Elizabeth and proceeded to regale her niece with stories of the pompous Mr Collins and his pretentious patron Lady Catherine de Bourgh, which lifted their spirits considerably.

"There is no doubt that my friend Charlotte is far better off without her odious husband and his impossible sense of obligation to Lady Catherine. Indeed, I would go so far as to say that *there* was a marriage which could not possibly have been made in heaven, so ill-matched were the pair, so undeserving the man of such a generous-hearted and sensible wife."

"Are Mrs Collins and the girls invited to the Pemberley Ball?" asked Emma, and Elizabeth replied, "Indeed, they are, and I do believe two of them are coming. Rebecca and Amelia-Jane will attend, but Lady Catherine has taken young Catherine Collins under her wing since the demise of her father, and it seems they are otherwise engaged. Sadly, we shall not have an opportunity to see what difference there is, if there be any, between the young lady from Rosings and the two girls who are free of Her Ladyship's influence."

"No doubt Lady Catherine is particularly attached to Miss Collins, since she was named for her," said Jane, and Emma thought Mr Collins may have wished it so. At which Elizabeth and Jane broke into laughter and, abandoning their lists, proceeded to tell Emma of Mr Collins's obsequious allegiance to his patron and his determination that their eldest child should be called Catherine.

"She is also named Eliza, but there is no question which her father preferred," declared Elizabeth.

The arrival of their cousin Caroline Fitzwilliam did nothing to deter their fun, which continued through the afternoon as they made arrangements for the Harvest Fair. While the entire community looked forward to the occasion, three young women were at the centre of most of the excitement.

Emma Bingley, Cassy Darcy, and Rebecca Collins were all seventeen that year. The ball given by Mr Darcy was in their honour. As Caroline said to her husband that night, it was going to be a very special event.

OCTOBER BROUGHT GOOD WEATHER, A bountiful harvest, and more encouraging news from Italy.

Richard had had word from a colleague who, while in Europe, had called on Paul and Emily and reported that Monsieur Antoine seemed to have regained some weight and a good deal of his colour and energy. Best of all, he and his wife were both in good spirits and enjoying the company of their cheerful, friendly Italian neighbours.

It was exactly what Caroline wanted to hear. She had spent some time trying to decide how she would write to Emily and enquire after her husband's health, yet afraid of what she might hear, she had postponed writing until her brother returned from London. The news he brought cheered them all up considerably.

Caroline had other concerns too, closer to home. Fitzwilliam was becoming impatient because he had received no guarantees from his political allies that the reforms he had advocated and they had promised—extending the franchise to ratepayers in local government elections—would be introduced in the near future.

"It is not as though they had not given their word to the people," he complained to his brother-in-law. "I am ashamed that I campaigned for them but can give no assurance to the people who supported us, decent citizens who ask only for a say in their local councils, that their rights will be protected."

Caroline was keen to pursue the question of Paul's health and wanted to ask her brother's opinion on the possibility of a complete recovery.

Richard shook his head. "I must admit I have not heard of a single such case; it is a most intractable disease for which medical science has found no cure yet."

"But surely," argued Fitzwilliam, "with the kind of devoted care that Emily provides and good medication, there must be a chance?"

Richard looked very solemn.

"I am sorry to disillusion you, Colonel Fitzwilliam, but while the good work my sister undertakes is certainly improving the quality of Paul's life and there is no doubting its value, such treatment, however estimable, is not known to have affected the final outcome; delayed it perhaps, but never averted it."

At this rather gloomy prediction, Caroline, moved to tears, silently left the room. She was about to go upstairs when she heard the sound of a vehicle being driven at some speed along the road from Matlock. Going out to investigate, she saw it turn into the drive and as it approached the house, she could tell it was the Tates' carriage and wondered what could have brought them here at this hour.

It was almost sunset and the half light of an Autumn evening glinted upon the windows of the vehicle and obscured her vision of its occupants until it came to a standstill, when Anthony Tate leapt out and ran up the steps to the entrance. He seemed agitated, not his usual urbane self at all.

Greeting her only perfunctorily, he asked, "Is Fitzwilliam at home?"

Excited and out of breath, he marched into the hall and entered the parlour, without waiting for an answer. Bewildered, Caroline indicated that her husband and her brother were both within and, curious to discover the reason for this sudden intrusion, she followed him into the room. She knew Anthony Tate was a supporter of her husband's reform group and assumed his visit must have something to do with the cause to which they were both committed. Perhaps he had some urgent news.

Seeing their visitor, Fitzwilliam rose and came forward to greet him.

Anthony Tate had barely shaken his hand, when he said hurriedly, "I cannot stay, Colonel Fitzwilliam, I must get back to the *Review*. We are to print a special edition with the news—I assumed you would not have heard it and clearly I was right—the Houses of Parliament are burning!"

"What?" all three of his listeners exclaimed as one and Fitzwilliam, overwhelmed with astonishment, cried, "Look here, Tate, is this some rotten joke?"

"It certainly is not; I have the news from two of my men who are absolutely reliable. The Palace of Westminster is in flames—a fire began in one of the lower rooms during the afternoon and has since engulfed most of the old wooden buildings. The flames are spreading and can be seen for miles around; thousands of people are watching the inferno from across the Thames."

"Could nothing have been done to stop it?" asked Caroline, aghast at the news.

"Apparently not, the fire must have taken hold well before it was noticed and the old buildings burned quickly." Anthony Tate prepared to leave, politely declining any refreshment, eager to get back to his newspaper.

"I had to come, I was certain you would not have heard," he said and left, promising to send them more news of the disaster as it came to hand.

Colonel Fitzwilliam was appalled. The shock was so great he could not speak for several minutes. He sat in his chair and stared out of the window and then at the fireplace, where the small friendly flames seemed suddenly to take on quite a menacing aspect.

Richard stayed awhile, anxious for his brother-in-law, who looked pale, shaken, and drained of energy.

Trying to cheer him up, Richard said, "Those old buildings were probably long overdue for replacement anyway—we can look forward to a grand new Parliament in the future," but to no avail.

To Colonel Fitzwilliam, who had come late to both love and politics, the Palace of Westminster had a special relevance. It had been the stage for the historic struggle for constitutional and social reform, in which he too had recently participated with so much enthusiasm. Its destruction would remove from the landscape of London an important link with the most significant part of his public life.

He was devastated.

Caroline could see he was deeply shocked. When Richard finally left, she went to her husband and put her arms around him and was astonished to feel his body shake as she held him.

"I cannot believe it, Caroline. The great forum, where men of the calibre of Walpole, Fox, Wilberforce, and Burke have debated, where the battles for the abolition of slavery and our great Reform bill raged over many days and nights—reduced to ashes. How could it have happened? Who would do such a thing?"

There was no immediate news of the cause of the fire, and Fitzwilliam presumed that it was the work of arsonists, angered by some of the work of the Parliamentarians.

In fact, it was no such thing; it was an accidental fire—the result of an act of stupidity—but he was not to know that. He felt only a sense of violation and outrage at the destruction of an historic site.

At dinner that night, he said very little and when they went upstairs to bed, Caroline tried again to speak of the possible advantages of a new, larger Parliament, one more suited to the modern age in which they lived, but he would not be comforted.

"If I were to tell you what it means in terms of our life here, Caroline," he said, "it would be as if someone had burned down our home, with all our precious memories. No new edifice, no matter how grand, could replace it and a part of our lives would be lost with it."

And, loving him as she did, Caroline knew exactly how he felt.

In the weeks that followed, despite the shock of the conflagration in Westminster, life at Pemberley revolved mainly around the organisation of the Harvest Fair and the ball that was planned for the day after.

Elizabeth, ably assisted by her housekeeper Mrs Reynolds and her maid Jenny, had put in place all the arrangements for the ball, which would be carried out by the efficient, well-trained staff at Pemberley. Meanwhile, Caroline and Kitty, together with Richard, Cassandra, and Mr Darcy's steward, had worked to ensure that all was in readiness for the fair.

No one, certainly not Elizabeth, had fully realised the extent of interest in the community, and they were at first unprepared for the rush of eager participants. Tenants and their wives, craftsmen and women, farm labourers from both the Camden and Pemberley estates as well as many others from further afield—Bakewell, Lambton, and Ripley—seemed eager to bring their wares and skills to the Pemberley Fair.

Stalls, tents, and trestle tables had to be set up in the lower meadow and a myriad of local products, arts, crafts, embroidery, and farm produce were on sale.

On the morning of the fair, when the weather, which had been mild all week, improved to produce one last burst of Summer, Elizabeth was afraid that everything was going too well. Caroline, the much-loved wife of the local member, was there to open the fair, after which, the crowds poured in. The buying and selling was brisk and clearly profitable, as was evidenced by the fast emptying baskets and stalls and the general air of satisfaction.

Mr Darcy, who had encouraged his wife when she had first suggested a Harvest Fair, could not recall such a day; not since he, as a little boy, had accompanied his mother to a market fair in Staffordshire. There he remembered seeing booths and barrows on the common, containing everything from bolts of woolen cloth, silk scarves, and pottery to cheeses, soap, and candles. He had a vivid memory of a blue silk scarf his mother had purchased and a painted wooden toy he had acquired with the tuppence she had given him; it had remained a treasured possession for many years, reminding him of her. Around them had been hundreds of people: housewives, merchants, and traders buying and selling everything you could possibly imagine.

At Pemberley, there were not the merchants and itinerant tradesmen; rather, it was the working men and women of the district who filled the lower meadow with their wares. Mr Darcy was impressed. "Lizzie, there is no doubt your idea has been exceedingly popular. I had never imagined we would have so many people here," he said, as they stood together, observing the hive of activity in the meadow below.

Elizabeth was pleased to have his approval.

"I am so happy you think so; I was afraid you may object to all these strangers tramping around the grounds."

Darcy turned to her with a look of surprise. "I do not regard them as strangers, my dear, they are the people of this community. Most of them have lived and worked the land, either in their own right, as tenants, or as labourers on the estate; I am perfectly happy to have some part of the grounds used for such a good cause as this is. In fact, Sir Thomas Camden thinks it is such an excellent idea, he is looking to host a similar event at Camden Park next year. So you see, my love, your Harvest Fair has been a great success," he said, drawing her close in a gesture of warm affection that brought her even greater pleasure than his words.

Towards sundown, as the stall holders packed their carts high with their baskets and boxes and took their weary children home, the families gathered on the lawn to watch energetic young men and women engage in country dancing accompanied by lively local musicians.

Caroline, feeling rather tired and looking for a place to rest, wandered into a small sitting room overlooking the west lawn, meaning to take advantage of a conveniently placed sofa by the fire. Her feet hurt and she had lost interest in the dancing.

On pushing open the door, however, she glimpsed a couple who appeared to be in what could only be termed—in words popular with writers of romantic novellas—"a fond embrace."

There were no lamps or candles in the room; only the last rays of the setting sun filtered through the curtains illuminated the darkness, and the couple, intimately engaged as they were, did not immediately realise that someone had intruded upon them. Engrossed in each other, they failed to notice her until Caroline, who had immediately recognised her brother Richard and Cassy Darcy, deliberately pushed over a footstool to alert them to her presence.

On becoming aware they were no longer alone, they moved apart and left by the doors opening onto the lawn. Neither had glanced at her, as she stood in the shadows; clearly, they did not know who it was had entered the room and invaded their privacy.

Even as they went out into the twilight, their arms still entwined, their warm, affectionate manner leaving her in no doubt of their closeness, Caroline smiled to herself. She had recently observed that Richard was spending a good deal of time at Pemberley. That Cassandra Darcy was the chief reason for this, she had suspected, but had not known, until that moment, how far the association had progressed nor how deep and tender were their feelings for one another. The encounter set her thinking.

While Caroline's romantic heart rejoiced for the lovers she had accidentally disturbed, her mind had begun to run along quite different lines. Her brother was not only a man of learning and skill, he was also a person of absolute integrity. It was impossible, therefore, to imagine even for a moment that what she had seen was some flirtatious episode, in which he, like many other young men about town, was indulging himself without paying heed to the consequences of his actions for the young lady involved. By the same token, she had then to assume that Richard had formed a serious attachment and intended to propose marriage to Cassy Darcy.

It was at this point that Caroline began to wonder whether Mr Darcy, who she knew to be exceedingly protective of his daughter, would consider a country physician, son of a commercial businessman, the right sort of suitor for Cassandra. While she had no doubt of the esteem and affection that the Darcys and her parents had for each other, and she knew her cousin Elizabeth spoke very highly of Richard, she could not be certain that the prospect of a marriage between Cassy and Richard would be welcomed equally by both parties.

Though she would not betray them to anyone and wished them joy with all her heart, she could not help feeling somewhat apprehensive.

Clearly, they were as yet not ready to declare their intention and she hoped they would soon do so. Secrecy brought with it a multiplicity of problems, as Caroline knew better than anyone.

On the journey home to Matlock, Caroline, no longer able to hold all this within herself, attempted to draw a reaction from her husband. Without disclosing the reason for her suspicions, she remarked that she thought her brother Richard and Cassy Darcy were in love, although they were probably not ready to reveal it to their families.

Her husband, who had seemed rather preoccupied on the journey, replied in a matter-of-fact manner that it was not an unusual circumstance for young people to be in; reminding her of his own predicament before they were engaged, when he had to conceal his feelings for many months before he could summon up sufficient courage to ask her father's permission to court her.

"Do you think that Richard is similarly concerned about approaching Mr Darcy?" she asked. "Could that be the reason he has not proposed to her yet? From my observation of them, I do not think there could be any doubt about his feelings, nor any uncertainty about hers."

Fitzwilliam was surprised at her question, "Why should you suppose that to be the case, my dear? My reluctance was based mainly on the difference in our ages—you were but fifteen years old and I was almost thirty-three; I feared your father would refuse my suit on the grounds that I was much too old for you. There is no such impediment in the case of Richard and Cassy. She is seventeen and your brother is twenty-five. Why should he fear rejection?"

"You do not think then, Fitzy, that Mr Darcy would consider Richard unsuitable?"

"Unsuitable? Caroline, your brother is perhaps the most eligible young man in the county; he is a fine, honourable fellow with an excellent profession, he is good-natured, clever, and exceedingly handsome, why should Darcy find him unsuitable?"

"He is certainly all you say, Fitzy, and he is clearly in love with Cassy and she with him, but he has no estate and Cassy is Mr Darcy's only daughter. Is it not likely he would have high expectations for her?"

Fitzwilliam was silent for a few minutes before saying in a very serious voice, "To my mind, Caroline, that would be all the more reason to let her marry Richard; his character and background are known and your parents are their dearest friends. Nothing could be simpler. My dear, if Richard and Cassy love each other and tell Mr Darcy so, I cannot see him standing in their way. Darcy will have to be very hard-hearted indeed, which I know he is not, to let the matter of an estate come between his daughter and the man she loves. No, I do not believe your brother has anything to fear," he said, and Caroline, who trusted her husband's judgment implicitly on matters concerning his cousin Mr Darcy, agreed to be reassured.

"Well, if you are right, I daresay we shall all know very soon. I cannot believe they will not be engaged after the ball tomorrow," she said, her romantic heart content at last.

Fitzwilliam, well aware of his wife's tender nature, had humoured her with talk of the young lovers. But he had other matters on his mind. He was looking forward to a meeting with Jonathan Bingley, who was also attending the ball at Pemberley on the morrow. Unbeknownst to Caroline, he had written Jonathan a note inviting him to call. There were matters far more serious than a romance in the family, which he wished to discuss with young Mr Bingley.

On the morning of the ball, Caroline went to visit her parents at Lambton, quite deliberately, since she knew Richard would be there too. Finding him in the sitting room with Mrs Gardiner, she lingered awhile, hoping to discover if Cassy Darcy and he had guessed the identity of the person who had intruded upon their rendezvous the previous evening. But, despite the fact that he was alone with her in the room for fully fifteen minutes, while their mother had left them to go upstairs, Richard made no mention of the previous evening. Nor did he appear awkward or embarrassed by her presence. Obviously, Caroline thought, neither he nor Cassy had realised that it was she who had surprised them.

Like most persons of a romantic inclination, Caroline would have given anything to know the answers to a myriad of questions.

How long, she wondered, had her brother and Miss Darcy been in love?

Did her parents know of it? Were his parents aware of his intentions? Did he intend to propose or ask Mr Darcy's permission first?

These and other matters, vital to her peace of mind, plagued her. But since she had no opportunity to ask the questions, she could find no answers to them at all. It was most vexing indeed!

Jonathan Bingley called on Colonel Fitzwilliam and found him alone. Caroline, he explained, was visiting her parents in Lambton.

The two men went into the parlour, where Jonathan, who had been in London when the Houses of Parliament burned down, provided his host with a lively description of the blaze and its chaotic consequences for the business of government. Jonathan's association with the Wilsons, who were prominent Whig parliamentarians, gave him an insider's view of the situation.

"It does mean there will be a good deal of disruption, but no doubt the administration of government will go on," he said casually.

Fitzwilliam's reply was uncharacteristically cynical. "Oh no doubt at all; after all, even if the Palace of Westminster is reduced to ashes, the bureaucrats and their minions will continue to impose all their harsh laws upon the people with even greater vigour."

His sardonic tone surprised young Jonathan, who looked a little puzzled and asked, "Do you refer to the new amendments to the Poor Laws, Colonel Fitzwilliam? I am told that they are being rather strictly imposed upon the unemployed and the destitute. My sister Emma is a member of a group of ladies who are trying to help children in poverty, and she has some very unhappy stories to relate of the consequences of such action. I believe many hitherto respectable families have been adversely affected. Emma has been very distressed."

Fitzwilliam agreed. "Indeed, Jonathan, your sister is right; not only are the poor being pauperised and forced into workhouses, but those placed in charge of these grim institutions are profiteering off the backs of the wretched inmates. Coming on top of the draconian laws against the taking of game or fish in the woods and on the commons, and the recent transportation of the six union members from Tolpuddle in Dorset, I must admit that I am beginning to have serious doubts about the value of continuing to sit in the Commons in support of this government after the next election."

Jonathan was shocked. "You cannot mean that, sir," he said, taken aback not only by the vehemence of his speech but by the prospect of Colonel Fitzwilliam, who had fought assiduously for the people he had represented, speaking passionately on their behalf on every occasion, declining to stand for Parliament again.

"Indeed, I do," affirmed the colonel, and the depth of his disillusion with the Whigs, for it was their law that was being used to harass and hound the poor, was astonishing. Jonathan had had no indication of his feelings before today.

By the time they had finished their drinks and Jonathan made ready to leave, it was quite clear to him that the colonel had lost his enthusiasm for politics. A reformist at heart, he had been excited by the prospect of being part of a reforming parliament; clearly he had little interest in its present policies of penny pinching and repression.

As they stood together in the hall, Fitzwilliam asked, "Have you ever considered standing for Parliament, Jonathan?"

Even more astonished than before, Jonathan Bingley answered almost without thinking, "No, sir, I have not."

"Never? Would it not interest you, if an opportunity arose, sometime in the future?" Fitzwilliam persisted.

This time, Jonathan considered the question a little longer.

"Perhaps, I would not rule it out. But it is easier said than done, Colonel Fitzwilliam. The party does not hand out seats in the Commons to a mere nobody like me," he said lightly.

"You are far too modest, Jonathan. I can see you doing very well in Parliament in the right circumstances. My colleague James Wilson speaks very highly of you."

"I *am* interested in promoting good policy, sir, and have done some work for Mr Wilson, but as for standing myself, I have not considered it."

Fitzwilliam smiled. "But you are not set against it?" he asked.

"No, I am not, but at present..."

"I am very glad to hear it—perhaps we shall talk again, one day," Fitzwilliam said vaguely and Jonathan Bingley left, feeling even more confused than ever.

❧

The Pemberley Ball was a spectacular success, as such events usually were at Pemberley House. Its gracious proportions, beautiful grounds, and elegantly appointed apartments combined to provide an ideal setting for such an event.

Mr Darcy had spared no expense, and his staff no effort, to make this a very special evening for the three young ladies in whose honour the ball was being given.

Meticulously planned menus, exquisite crystal and chinaware, and not one but two groups of musicians to provide the music at dinner time and later for dancing made for a remarkable occasion.

Mr and Mrs Darcy and their two handsome children, Cassandra and William, stood together in the hall to greet their guests. Cassy, dark haired, vivacious, and elegant, so much like her mother Elizabeth had been at her age; William, fair, gentle, and sensitive, already at fourteen a talented pianist; they were both much admired and there was no doubt their parents were proud of them.

Some of the many guests and family members gathered at Pemberley remarked upon the sense of closeness between them, but none were aware of a secret that Cassy had shared with her mother only a few hours before they had come downstairs.

Coming in to Elizabeth's room to borrow a piece of jewellery to match her new gown, Cassy had confessed to something her mother had suspected for several weeks. Revealing that Richard Gardiner had requested the pleasure of the first two dances, at least, she had said, "Mama, I fear I have fallen in love with him. I did not mean to, but there it is. It's happened."

When her mother had asked what caused her fear, Cassy had pointed to their concern that her father might not approve.

"That would really break my heart," she had said and Elizabeth, trying to discover the reason for this, had probed further, wondering why her daughter thought her father would disapprove of one of their favourite young men—son of the Gardiners, who were so very dear to them.

There appeared to be no logical reason, except an anxiety that Mr Darcy may not consider Richard good enough for his daughter. Clearly, Cassy had no such reservations.

"He is the most intelligent, handsome, kindest man for hundreds of miles around," she had declared, and while her mother had no reason to dispute her opinion, she did try to persuade her daughter that it was best to wait until Richard had seen her father before leaping to any conclusions.

Urging her daughter, meanwhile, to be discreet, Elizabeth had spoken of the matter to no one but her beloved sister Jane, whose delight was, as expected, boundless.

"Lizzie, I cannot say how pleased I am. They are so well suited, I am sure they will be exceedingly happy together," she said, her eyes shining.

Watching the many attractive young couples dancing, the sisters recalled the time when they had both spent endless unhappy days and nights wracked by uncertainty, not knowing if the two men they had fallen in love with would return to ask for their hands in marriage.

"Lizzie, when I think how we suffered, I am happy that in these times of greater openness, our children will be spared such wholly unnecessary grief," said Jane, and Lizzie agreed. It brought back many memories, not all equally pleasant. They had endured trying times before everything was settled between them.

The music started up again, and as they watched Richard and Cassandra take their places in the dance, they enjoyed their shared secret. It was almost like being back at Longbourn and Netherfield again.

Meanwhile, Caroline, convinced that her brother was on the verge of proposing marriage to Miss Darcy, had hoped she might be one of the first to learn the news. Throughout the evening, she had sought an opportunity to speak with him, but none came. When the ball ended and the guests were leaving, she looked everywhere but could see neither Richard nor Cassy.

William Darcy had been persuaded to entertain a party of guests in the music room, from where their enthusiastic applause for his playing could be heard. Richard and Cassandra were not, however, among them, Caroline noted.

Recalling the episode of the previous evening, she smiled to herself, believing the lovers had "disappeared" for a while, but then saw them come in from the conservatory and join the Darcys at the foot of the great staircase. This time, Richard stayed with Cassy as she and her parents accepted the thanks of the departing guests.

Had he asked her? Caroline did not know and it was most vexing indeed!

On the journey home, Caroline expressed disbelief that Richard and Cassandra were not as yet engaged.

"They are obviously in love and if he has already approached Mr Darcy, I do not understand why there has been no announcement tonight. It would have saved the trouble of writing to everyone. Besides, it will not do for the entire county to be gossiping about them, as they must, if no engagement is announced. No one who has seen them together tonight can doubt they are in love."

Caroline's daughter Isabella recalled later how very anxious her mother had seemed that night about Richard and Cassy.

"It was as though Mama was impatient to share their happiness," she wrote to her Aunt Emily, who had wanted to be told all the news.

On the morrow, however, while they were having a late breakfast, the arrival of Richard and Cassy, bringing news of their engagement, put an end to Caroline's anxiety. The happy couple brought also an invitation from Mrs Darcy for the Fitzwilliams to join the family at a celebratory picnic luncheon on the grounds of Pemberley.

"You must all come, it is such a glorious day," said Richard, and Cassy added, "The very day for a picnic, is it not, Cousin Caroline?"

Caroline agreed, embracing her brother and Cassandra fondly and wishing them every happiness, "Indeed it is so perfect that you will always remember the day of your engagement. But then, how could you ever forget?"

It was to be a most prophetic remark, and in the years to come, they would all recall the moment when Caroline had said it.

END OF PART TWO

MY COUSIN CAROLINE

Part Three

Chapter Nine

I N THE YEARS THAT FOLLOWED, neither Caroline nor her husband would ever forget the moment when they knew for certain that Edward, their eldest son, was dead.

Nothing, not the passage of years, the comfort of family and friends, nor all the accumulated pleasures of life with their other children, could erase the awful horror of that instant.

Caroline had been inconsolable. A cold, unfeeling hand seemed to have gripped her heart and squeezed it until she could feel nothing but the pain. Not even the dreadful reality that Darcy and Elizabeth had lost William, their only son, had had any impact upon her except when she saw both coffins at the church and heard her cousin sobbing beside her.

It had been such an idyllic, luminously lovely Autumn afternoon at Pemberley. Richard and Cassandra had, on becoming engaged, bestowed upon the day a special magic that everyone shared and wished to celebrate.

After a delectable feast, partaken of in the shade of ancient trees beside the stream in that mellow, hazy weather which sometimes returns in mid-Autumn to remind us that Summer is not quite ready to depart, the family had been wrapped in a comfortable mood of optimism and fun. There had been so much to look forward to.

Yet, as Summer's sweet pleasures are often disrupted by inclement weather, only a few hours later, apprehension, dread, and finally total desolation had overtaken them all.

First there was the anxiety on discovering that young William Darcy and Edward had gone out riding with Tom Lindley, son of a horse breeder recently settled near Bakewell. Elizabeth had been alarmed because William never rode unfamiliar horses; they made him nervous.

There followed the agony of waiting as Darcy, with his steward and Richard, had ridden out after them, up into the wooded hills behind Pemberley, only to return an hour or more later with the news that the two boys had been killed in a horrific accident.

The disbelief and shock, followed by the appalling realisation that it was indeed true, was something none of them could forget.

Even years later, Caroline could not look back upon that day without experiencing intense feelings of hate and outrage. Hate for the Lindley brothers, who, having arrived uninvited on that happy afternoon, had enticed William and Edward away to their deaths, and outrage that whatever power guided the universe had not seen fit to save their boys from the consequences of a foolhardy adventure.

It was, she admitted freely, an irrational, illogical emotion, but she could not rid herself of it. Unable to comprehend the needless destruction of two innocent young lives, she had withdrawn from the circle of their friends and family into her own small world at the farm.

There with her children Isabella and David to care for and with Fitzwilliam to comfort and love her, her life, though lonely, was at least more bearable than when she moved among other, happier families whose contentment seemed to mock her grief.

For the rest, it seemed she did not care anymore. She wanted no part of it. It was, she told her mother, as though she had jumped off the world like it was a merry-go-round at the seaside; she could then, from the relative security of her life at the farm, stand apart from those whose happy lives continued to revolve around her.

Her mother and cousins, Jane and Kitty, tried often, without success, to encourage her out of what she referred to as her "dungeon of despair."

Her husband, himself bereft and wracked by guilt at not having been there to prevent the boys from undertaking their impetuous escapade that evening, tried too. But, though he was loving, tender, and protective, doing everything possible to share and assuage her pain, Caroline's wounds would not heal easily. The total devotion she had given her children only made her loss harder to bear.

A series of events dragged her back and forth, in and out of gloom, driving her emotions first one way then another.

The predictable, untimely, but relatively peaceful death in Italy of Paul Antoine, her sister's husband, brought Emily back to England and to Derbyshire in the Spring, where the two sisters found some consolation together. Emily's gentle acceptance of her husband's fate stood in stark contrast against Caroline's defiant anger, but it did give both women time and opportunity to help one another.

"I cannot believe that you are so accepting of it, Emmy," Caroline would say, "why should everyone else we know have their husbands fit and well and the only man you loved be taken from you and in so short a time? Do you not feel outraged? Do you not ask why?"

"I did, Caroline, often, until I tired of asking questions to which I could find no answers," Emily replied. "It occurred to me that I would do far better with my time to spend as much of it as we had with Paul. Because we always knew there was so little time left, we chose to use every minute of it in making one another feel loved and happy. It was a wise choice; it has left me with sufficient memories of him to last a lifetime."

Caroline did not always comprehend her sister's attitude.

When their cousin Emma Bingley was married in London to Mr David Wilson, a promising and popular young MP, Caroline could not be persuaded to attend, and Emily went in her place.

"To be at a wedding, amidst all that merry-making and congratulating would make me ill!" she declared when her mother tried to persuade her to join them. "I know they must get on with their lives, Mama, but let them do so without me. I am become so dull a companion these days, I doubt I shall be missed," she said, and the bitterness in her voice was inescapable.

❧

Not even the birth of another child, a daughter, Rachel, a year and some months later, changed the sombre melancholy of her mood, and when her cousin Elizabeth was delivered of a son, Julian, Caroline could not bear to call on her and see the child.

It was Emily, whose gentle persuasion and unquestioning love had succeeded where others had failed, who accompanied her sister to Pemberley to visit Elizabeth. Emily, who since her return from Italy had lived at Pemberley, cajoled and pleaded until her sister agreed.

Longing for a son, Caroline had felt a sharp stab of envy at the sight of the Darcys' child, and it had taken all of Emily's coaxing to stop her leaving the room in tears. Elizabeth did not know it, but she owed the pleasure of that day, of seeing her cousin Caroline again, to Emily alone.

Indeed, if it were not for Emily, there would have been a compounding of sorrow that Winter. For Caroline, there was now only one reality: the death of Edward, which had opened such an abyss in her life it seemed nothing would ever fill it. Each day, week, or month seemed to bring more occasions to rend her heart anew rather than heal it. Her husband and family began to despair of her ever returning to normal again.

Emily, meanwhile, threw herself into every available activity, whether it was collecting funds for the hospital for children, helping Kitty with the parish school and the children's choir, or working to ease the struggle with poverty that filled each day in the lives of many families in the community.

With the onset of a recession, unemployment was increasing and many men were returning from the factory towns and the coal mines in the Midlands without work. Those who were fortunate enough to get it, irregular and poorly paid as it was, did not make enough money to keep their families in food and pay the rent. Some, venturing further afield in search of work, were away for months on end, their womenfolk and children left to fend for themselves.

A few of the men had become involved in the machine breaking and rick burning incidents; inevitably, they were caught and hanged or transported, leaving their families destitute.

It meant that many women, who had hitherto never worked, except in domestic service when they were young girls, had to go out in search of work to feed their children. Some took their children with them while they worked in the fields and dairy farms all over the county, often toiling many hours for a pittance. They hoed, weeded, dug up and bagged potatoes, cleaned out stables and cattle stalls, and filled dung carts for hours on end.

Many performed laborious work in dairy farms, milking, churning, and loading until their limbs ached and their backs were bent with pain, all for a few shillings. Others, nursing babies or carrying toddlers in their arms, unable to take labouring work, wandered from one household to another, begging to be allowed to perform some menial domestic chore in return for food and, occasionally, a little money. For women alone, poor and with young children to raise, it was the very worst of times, an era of never-ending drudgery and humiliation.

The consequent fatigue and chronic ailments they suffered were many.

Richard and Emily saw it all at the hospitals and in their cottages, and they turned to Mr Darcy for help.

"These women are not lazy, Mr Darcy, they have a desire to work but they have young children and no one at home to care for them, and can only hope to get the very worst of menial jobs, which they must do, often carrying their babes with them. If we can set up a cottage or two, places where they might leave their children while they worked, it would be the greatest help to them. They could then get better paid work, and it would also mean the older children could go to school instead of following their mothers into the fields and farms to look after the babes," Emily pleaded as she revealed the extent of the problem.

Aware that Mr Darcy was a compassionate landlord, she had hoped for success.

She was not disappointed. Mr Darcy and Sir Thomas Camden had already permitted the establishment of a couple of soup kitchens in vacant cottages, where the hungry might be fed and the homeless given temporary shelter. Emily, with the help of her brother Richard, Cassandra, Kitty, and a few other women in the area, had made up rosters and worked at these community shelters.

Mr Darcy explained, "I have already ordered that we do not enforce rent payments or tithes upon those who are out of work. If we were to extend the assistance we now provide at the cottages and employ a few women from the area to look after the children while their mothers worked, would you and Richard promise me that the place will not become some den of iniquity and I shall not have other landholders in the district, as well as the magistrates and churchmen, complaining that we are encouraging sloth and idleness?"

The sardonic tone of his voice belied the strict implication of his words, and Emily immediately promised that no such accusation would ever be levelled at any one they helped.

"These are honest women, Mr Darcy, they would give anything to keep their families out of the dreadful conditions in the workhouse. I give you my solemn word, there will be no justifiable criticism of anything we do," she said, and her transparent goodness and sincerity, which had always impressed Mr Darcy, brought success.

"You may see Mr Grantham, Emily, and ask him to make the necessary arrangements for the cottage at Springwood. It's large enough for your purpose and is conveniently situated in relation to the villages it will serve. I shall speak to Sir Thomas; if he is keen to help, we may do more. There is another place, which has been vacant, closer to Littleford, which may be useful.

"But, please remember, Emily, you must get some more people to help you. I cannot have your father blaming me for letting you work too hard and for too long in these places," he warned. " It would be a great irony if you were to fall ill while trying to preserve the women from overwork. Why do you not persuade Caroline to join you? I am confident, if she knew how much need there was in the community and how hard you worked, she would not refuse to help."

Emily thanked him for his generosity and his concern for her before setting out to take the good news to her brother and mother at Lambton.

It was going to mean a great deal more work, but her satisfaction came from knowing that many widows, wives, and countless children would find food and shelter.

The more work she undertook and the more weary she was at the end of a day, the more easily she could sleep, or so she told her mother, Mrs Gardiner, who worried about her working too hard.

"There is nothing I like more than to be so tired at the end of the day that sleep comes quickly. I have no desire to lie awake and spend time on unfulfilled dreams," she said, explaining to her mother that Mr Darcy had suggested that she persuade her sister to join their group.

"If Caroline will come with us and see at first hand the extent of the suffering that is out there amongst the women and children, if she will agree to help us in our work, I am certain she will find herself relieved of some of her own burden of grief. I am no stranger to pain myself, and I know that helping others can alleviate it, even for a few hours. If you will speak with her, Mama, tell her how much we need her help, that may convince her."

The strategy proved most effective.

When Mrs Gardiner, while visiting the Fitzwilliams, mentioned her anxiety about Emily's health, adding she was working too hard at the community shelters, Caroline was exceedingly concerned and expressed some irritation that her sister had not asked for her help.

"She should have told me. Tell Emmy I shall be happy to help, Mama. I cannot imagine why she has not asked me before. I have a great deal of time on my hands, I may as well use it to help the poor rather than sew endless bits of useless embroidery, which profits no one. They are not good enough to give as gifts, and I never seem to find any use for them myself. I would much rather be out with Emmy, helping her women and children."

It was just what Mrs Gardiner wanted to hear.

Within the day, she had taken the message to her younger daughter, and Emily worked swiftly with Mr Darcy's steward to make arrangements for the cottage at Springwood. Bedding, tables, chairs, and rugs had to be found, doors and windows secured, and fences mended.

Caroline, with her daughter Isabella, joined Emily, and together they worked to prepare for the women, who had been told they could bring their children in on the Monday. By the end of the week, she had begun to feel something of the exhaustion that her sister had welcomed, and to her surprise, it was accompanied by a new sense of purpose and shared satisfaction. Caroline had not been unaware of the increasing levels of deprivation and misery in the community as the recession deepened.

What she had not known was that she, personally, could do something to help its victims. It was the first positive emotion she had experienced in a long while.

⁓✤⁓

Meanwhile, Colonel Fitzwilliam, heartsick and disillusioned, had decided he no longer wished to sit in the Commons and set to work to secure a suitable member to represent the people of his constituency. It was not going to be an easy task, but he thought he had found the right man, one he could recommend to succeed him.

The death of Mr Bennet had delivered to Jonathan Bingley a most timely inheritance in the estate at Longbourn, which had for many years been the Bennets' family home.

Mr Bennet's plan to leave it to Jonathan, with life interest to his daughter Miss Mary Bennet, had brought him the status and responsibilities of a country squire, which he carried out conscientiously and with dignity.

Observing him, Fitzwilliam saw a promising candidate to take over his seat in the House of Commons. Enlisting the help of friends and family, as well as the influence of Anthony Tate of the *Review*, he proceeded to encourage and persuade young Mr Bingley to consider the proposition seriously.

Jonathan, who was by now engaged to marry Amelia-Jane, the youngest and prettiest daughter of Mrs Charlotte Collins, found himself contemplating the prospect of a seat in Parliament with more sanguinity than before. His young bride-to-be expressed herself very pleased at the prospect of having a husband in Parliament.

"I am sure Jonathan will do very well indeed," she had told her mother-in-law-to-be, "he is so handsome and distinguished looking *and* he makes such excellent speeches. He is just what a Member of Parliament ought to be."

Jane Bingley was not entirely certain that young Amelia-Jane had the right understanding of the role of a Member of Parliament, but she said nothing. Jane was fond of Amelia-Jane and had no desire to hurt her feelings by contradicting her. Besides, if Colonel Fitzwilliam thought her son was suitable to stand for Parliament, that was good enough for Jane. No doubt, she thought, Jonathan would enlighten Amelia-Jane, when the time came, of his other responsibilities.

Colonel Fitzwilliam had grown weary of Westminster, especially now his old heroes "Orator" Hunt and the radical William Cobbett had both died; he could no longer summon up the enthusiasm for the fight.

But he urged Jonathan to do so. "There is still much to be done, Jonathan, and we need able young men like you, with strong principles and a social conscience, to carry on the struggle," he had said.

Jonathan Bingley did indeed have a strong social conscience. It was only the previous week he had been with his sister Emma and heard from her of the woeful state of housing and sanitation in the east London area, where her group of ladies did their charitable work. There was little doubt in his mind that Fitzwilliam was right; there was a great deal more to be done.

Travelling to Pemberley to call on Mr and Mrs Darcy before returning to his parents' home at Ashford Park, he was invited to stay to dinner and was delighted to accept. The Darcys were his dearest aunt and uncle and Jonathan was likewise their favourite nephew.

To his great pleasure, he found they were to be joined by Mr and Mrs Gardiner, whom Jonathan regarded with great affection, as well as their son Richard, who had recently moved from Birmingham to a practise in Derby.

At dinner, during which it soon became clear to him that the engaged pair, Richard and Cassy, were more than keen to be done with the meal and withdraw to the privacy of the music room, Jonathan found himself sitting next to Emily Gardiner. It was the first time he had met her to speak to at any length since the death of her husband, Paul Antoine.

After some initial awkwardness on his part, through which Emily graciously helped him, he succeeded in discovering that she was involved in a scheme to help the poor women in the district, and thereafter, their conversation flowed easily as Jonathan learned a great deal about the work of the ladies of the Pemberley estate and their friends in the surrounding district.

"Do you believe then that the poor are being disadvantaged by the new Poor Law?" he asked, and was amazed by the vehemence of her reply.

"Oh indeed they are, Mr Bingley, of that I have no doubt. None of the women, who work so hard and suffer so much privation to feed their children, will exchange that life, grinding and painful as it might be, for the indignities of the workhouse. To be poor is hard enough, to be a pauper through no fault of one's own, stigmatised and treated as one is infinitely worse," she declared with deep feeling.

Jonathan recalled that Fitzwilliam had spoken with similar conviction on the subject and said so. Emily was not surprised.

"Colonel Fitzwilliam has condemned the Poor Laws repeatedly, but the government will not pay any heed to him. Recently Caroline has joined our group, and I think you will find that the colonel's views will be even stronger in future," she said.

"I wonder if Anthony Tate is prepared to campaign on the issue in his paper. He has a great deal of influence," Jonathan mused.

Emily's reply surprised him. "He may well do; since his marriage to Becky Collins, he must know more of the matter—she is also a member of our group and has done much to help us place some of the women in less arduous jobs, replacing laborious farm work with domestic chores in the homes and gardens of some of her prosperous friends in the district. It is a wonderful way to help the women, who may then earn a little money to feed themselves and their children and not have their health ruined by inordinately heavy labour," she explained.

"Do you suppose Mrs Tate has discussed this with her husband?" he asked and Emily replied with confidence, "I should be very surprised if she has not.

For some time now, Becky Tate has been writing occasional pieces for the *Review*, which her husband publishes, using the pen name Marianne Lawrence. In them, she has made mention of the scandalous conditions of women's employment. It is unlikely that Mr Tate would not be aware of it himself. It is an issue that affects the lives of many hundreds of women and children in this county and all over England."

In later years, Jonathan was to tell Mr and Mrs Darcy that if he had doubts about Colonel Fitzwilliam's offer, they were largely dispelled by talking to Emily and afterwards, to Anthony and Rebecca Tate, who had promised him complete support. On his return to Ashford Park, he would write to Colonel Fitzwilliam, accepting the proposition.

Before Jonathan left Pemberley, Emily returned with a letter addressed to his sister Emma, who now lived in London at the Wilsons' house in Mayfair or at their family estate in Kent.

"When you see your sister Emma, Mr Bingley, may I trouble you to give her this letter from me? I had intended to send it to the post, but since you are here, I wondered if…"

He interrupted her gently and said, "Pray do not concern yourself, Cousin Emily, it will be no trouble at all. I expect to be in London on Wednesday and will hand it to Emma personally when I see her."

❧

Emma Wilson received Emily's letter from her brother's hand when he joined her and her husband David Wilson at dinner the following Wednesday. Mr James Wilson was also present and Jonathan was keen to consult him about his recent decision. After dinner, leaving the gentlemen to their discussion of party politics, Emma went upstairs to her room to read her letter; it had been awhile since Emily had written and Emma was eager for news.

The two cousins had been friends for many years despite the difference in their ages—Emily was almost thirty, while Emma Wilson was not yet twenty-one.

Dearest Emma, wrote her cousin:

> *I must immediately apologise for the lateness of my response to your kind letter; it is not for want of inclination, I assure you, merely the lack of time and opportunity to do so.*
>
> *We have been so very busy these last few weeks with the work we are*

doing to help the poor women of the district and their children, who are the innocent victims of this terrible system.

However, I must not delay giving you what must be the best news we have had in almost two years. It concerns my sister Caroline.

As you would know from your mama as well as from my letters, Caroline has been almost a recluse these eighteen months, since the death of her beloved Edward. She has consistently refused to be sociable or to travel any distance from her home, which has become her physical and emotional fortress.

It has been a source of great sorrow to us all, my parents and Colonel Fitzwilliam, who has done everything that one could ask of a husband, himself bereft and grief-stricken, to encourage and support her.

I had almost given up hope of interesting her in the work we do for the women and children of this area, made destitute by this wretched recession and the strict enforcement of the new Poor Law, when suddenly, following a visit from Mama, Caroline volunteered enthusiastically, I am told, to join us.

Emma, it is the very best thing that could have happened and I know that Colonel Fitzwilliam is very pleased. He arrived to take her home last Friday, after we had spent the day working at the cottage shelter in Springwood, and seemed delighted at the change in her. Caroline herself says little, but she works with a will and at a great pace.

I am so thankful to her and to our dear Mr Darcy for his generosity in making available the cottages at Springwood and Little Meadow, not far from the hospital at Littleford. Our women are ever so grateful that they and their children are far safer than before.

Reading between the lines, Emma could sense the relief and joy that her cousin must feel at Caroline's return to normal life. She had learned from her mother Jane of the concern they had all felt at her state of mind, and poor Colonel Fitzwilliam was desperately unhappy that he had not succeeded in helping his wife to return to a degree of normalcy, as Elizabeth had done.

Emma, who unbeknownst to all her friends and family carried a burden of sadness that she would reveal to no one, knew how both Emily and Caroline must feel. There were afflictions, she believed, that women would endure alone and not divulge to anyone.

Putting away her letter, which she would return to reply later, Emma went downstairs to join the others, only to find her husband, David, fast asleep on the sofa in the drawing room, having finished most of the port, while his brother James and Jonathan Bingley sat by the fire, clearly engrossed in their discussion. Reluctant to disturb them, Emma bade them good night and returned to her room.

Much later, she heard her brother-in-law and their guest come upstairs and retire to their rooms. Only in the small hours did her husband, awakened no doubt by the icy temperatures in the drawing room, where the fire had long been extinguished, stagger into their room and fall noisily into bed, fully dressed and very drunk.

Emma, who had lain awake for hours, pretended to be fast asleep.

As for Caroline, after a week or two of working at the cottage shelters, she had realised not just the value of Emily's work to the women and children of the area, but the inestimable worth of her sister's scheme in her own life. She had admitted this to Rebecca Tate as they worked together and to her husband when they were alone.

Colonel Fitzwilliam was clearly delighted to see her so engaged and active again. He could not do enough to help her and told her of his happiness often, demonstrating his pleasure and approval in every way and on every possible occasion.

She knew that he loved her dearly and understood the depth of the fear that had assailed him; fears for her health and reason. Caroline was pleased that she could, at last, reassure him that she was at least well on the way to recovery.

But, it was in the private thoughts, which she confided only to a little notebook with a blue leather cover which she kept locked away in her bureau, that she revealed even to herself what it had really meant to her.

Some three weeks after she had begun to travel daily to the cottage at Springwood, where groups of children arrived each morning brought there by their mothers on their way to work at the houses, where they were employed to sew, mend, wash, and iron, or on the farms, where they picked, washed, and packed fruit and vegetables for market, Caroline wrote:

Were it not for Emily, her unending goodness and selflessness, these little children and their mothers would undergo the most atrocious suffering, making barely enough to eat, and I would have continued to remain locked in the dungeon of my selfish despair.

Once again I know that I owe so much to my dear sister. Over these last few weeks, she has shown me not only how one might usefully employ the vacant hours of one's life, but she has opened my eyes to the extent of the truly intolerable suffering of hundreds of women, many in our own neighbourhood.

While I knew from Fitzwilliam that poverty was on the increase, because of the loss of jobs in the mills and mines, it was not till I saw these unfortunate women—some of them mere girls, weary and work-worn, their hair greasy with sweat, their faces grimy with dirt from the fields in which they had toiled—not until then, did I understand the true extent of a mother's suffering. As for the children, many of them so thin that one might feel their bones through their clothing, the sight of them brings tears to my eyes.

If there is a cause that one feels impelled to work for, it must be this and I am filled with gratitude for the opportunity; for since the death of my darling Edward, I have believed that my suffering and my own loss was so overwhelming I had no time for anyone else's troubles. What were they when compared with mine? I know different now and it was Emily who opened my eyes.

Since I have rejoined the world, my dear husband is happier too.

Poor Fitzy, he is the mainstay of my life; without him, I would surely have been blown so far off course, my life would have been utterly wrecked.

His patient, loving nature has meant even more to me in these cruel years just past than the ardent passion we shared when first we were married.

Then, I being young and innocent, learnt from him the ways of love, when it was easy to be happy and nothing could happen, but it would enhance our desire for one another. I had not known such happiness was possible.

But it is quite another matter to love when the heart is wounded and every circumstance conspires to hurt and bruise. I thought it had all ended for me then, that I would neither love nor care again. Even my dear parents and my precious children seemed not to reach my heart. As for those like Jane or Kitty, I could hardly bear to see them, knowing the sight of their happy, healthy children would only serve to ignite in me dreadful fires of envy and grief.

Only Fitzy remained close to me, loving, trying, encouraging always. What would I have been without him? I am afraid to think.

And Emily, dear, generous Emily, who must be the closest thing to an angel here on earth. I know I have her to thank for my sanity.

Tomorrow, she and I will join Becky Tate in making an appeal to the council for funds to start another shelter, this one for the children of Wye Bridge, the little village below the Tate property, where most of the men are out of work.

If the council will help with funds, the Tates will provide a vacant cottage and furniture, and two more ladies from Matlock will join our group at the shelter.

I shall pray that we succeed.

It will mean that I shall again have the joy of knowing that my work has truly done some good.

Chapter Ten

THE DEATH OF KING WILLIAM IV early in 1837 brought to the throne of England a very young queen, and for the first few years of her reign, at least, a new spirit of enterprise and excitement seemed to possess the nation.

Queen Victoria, though she did not actively promote many cultural pursuits, came to symbolise a growing concern with style and refinement, which included an interest in the arts and architecture, no less than the pursuit of trade and commerce.

A softer approach to those who lived and worked upon the land came to be advocated and in some cases followed by some landowners, who had begun to understand the value of providing decent housing, sanitation, and facilities for schooling and health care on their estates.

This was particularly the case at Pemberley and Camden Park, where the combined efforts of Sir Thomas Camden, Mr Darcy, and the ladies of Emily and Caroline's group had made a significant difference to the lives of the people in the surrounding villages. With the support of the Tate family, whose newspapers provided them with all the publicity they could ask for, the ladies of Pemberley and Matlock campaigned for everything from schooling for girls to shelters for vagrants.

So well did they achieve their goals that they soon caught the attention of aspiring local politicians, who would vie with one another to cut the ribbon or unveil the plaque at the opening of a school, a library, or an orphanage established by the efforts of the women.

Jonathan Bingley, supported by both Colonel Fitzwilliam and Anthony Tate, was standing for election in Fitzwilliam's seat. He readily acknowledged that he was assisted to a very great extent by his family connection with Pemberley.

Dr Richard Gardiner received what could only be called a hero's welcome when he took up his position at the new hospital at Littleford, which had been built on land donated by the Camden and Darcy families and equipped with funds raised by Emily, Caroline, and their friends.

For Richard and Cassandra it was a very special year. When they had become engaged, it had been with the intention of marrying within a year. Yet, their wedding had been postponed not once but twice, following the deaths first of young Edward and William and then, the year after, of Mr Bennet.

The couple, though quite passionately attached to one another, agreed to wait a little longer. Having proved the depth of their love by their constancy and restraint, when at last they were wed, they were rewarded with one of the loveliest days that Nature and Pemberley could provide.

No one in the large gathering of friends and relatives who saw them married could have had any doubt of their joy. For their parents there was no prouder, happier moment than that of the union of their beloved children.

Caroline and Emily, who had been privy to some of the agony that had accompanied the long months of waiting, knew how gladly Richard and Cassandra would set off on their wedding journey.

After the marriage of her brother to Cassy Darcy, Emily was drawn even deeper into the fold of the Pemberley family. Her enduring and warm friendship with both Elizabeth and her husband gave her a very special place in their home.

Meanwhile, Caroline found herself becoming more involved than before with the workings of her father's business. With his younger son Robert away in the colonies and Richard married and busy with his work at the hospital, Mr Gardiner, who had always valued Caroline's ability to grasp a problem and suggest a sensible solution, began to turn more often to his daughter for help. Her quick understanding and methodical approach to work was an asset to her busy father. She began to go regularly to Oakleigh to put his papers in order and attend to his accounts.

While initially, she had not regarded it seriously and had been rather flattered to be consulted by her father, the first realisation of the gravity of her situation came when her parents were on holiday in France. Emily, who had inherited a small property in France from her late husband, had persuaded her parents to accompany her on a visit.

Mr Gardiner had left Caroline in charge of his office, instructing her to attend to the accounts and pay the bills in his absence. Expecting not to have to do more than reconcile the weekly statements from the offices in London and Manchester, Caroline had cheerfully agreed.

"You will help me, will you not, Fitzy?" she had said rather playfully, not knowing that Fitzwilliam, though a partner, had little knowledge of the workings of his father-in-law's business.

While the first week passed without incident, the arrival of an express communication addressed to her father threw everyone into a state of confusion. It was from an attorney, Mr Culver, requesting Mr Gardiner's immediate presence in Manchester on account of his chief clerk Mr Upton being arrested for defrauding Her Majesty's Customs.

Caroline, who went immediately to Pemberley to consult Mr Darcy, found, to her consternation, that he had gone to Derby on business. There was nothing for it but to leave immediately for Manchester with her husband. Taking her father's authority and seal with her and hoping that there had been some stupid mistake, Caroline left, having begged Elizabeth to send a message to Mr Gardiner asking him to return to England at once.

"It would be best not to tell him about poor Mr Upton, Lizzie, at least not until he gets here. It would so upset him and Mama and achieve very little, for there is nothing he can do until he gets to Manchester," she said, and Elizabeth agreed.

On arriving in Manchester, they took rooms at the house where Mr Gardiner usually stayed when visiting on business and went immediately to the company office.

Caroline had been there before, with her father, but she did not recall it being so gloomy. Perhaps it was the fact that Winter was almost here and Manchester in Winter was not a salubrious spot, or it might have been the general air of desolation that hung over the narrow street that afternoon; either way, it made Caroline's heart sink.

Inside, it was not much better. Two junior clerks sat in a cold office, looking stunned, while an old man, who was supposed to be in charge in the absence of Mr Upton, sat at his desk, sighing and wiping his tearful eyes.

"Fitzy, this is ridiculous," Caroline whispered, "how are we ever going to discover the cause of the problem?"

"I think you will have to ask them, my love," he replied in a voice that was certainly not filled with confidence.

Caroline, after looking at him quickly to check if he was serious, drew up a chair and sat down at the chief clerk's desk.

The others looked at her as if expecting her to take over where Mr Upton had left off and give them their orders. Clearly everything had come to a shuddering halt when he was arrested and taken away. They were still sitting there, shocked.

The sound of footsteps on the stairs heralded the arrival of a rather smartly dressed young man, probably in his early thirties, dapper and well spoken, who on seeing Caroline and her husband said, "Ah, customers I presume? I am so sorry, sir, ma'am, but unfortunately, we are not in a position to…"

Caroline stopped him in mid sentence.

"We are not customers, sir, I am Mrs Caroline Fitzwilliam, Mr Edward Gardiner's eldest daughter, and this is Colonel Fitzwilliam, my husband and one of my father's partners. Mr Gardiner is away in France and we are here in response to your express letter about Mr Upton's arrest. I take it you are Mr Culver?"

As the meaning of her words appeared to sink in, there was an obvious diminution of the gentleman's air of confidence. By the time she asked the question, he was standing in front of her, his mouth a little open, his eyes staring in disbelief.

"Are you not?" Caroline repeated gently but quite firmly.

Like a marionette jerked into sudden activity, he nodded his head and said, "Indeed I am, ma'am, Humphrey Culver, at your service. My father is Mr Upton's attorney and I am his clerk. I have just come from the courts, where Mr Upton has been before the magistrate and has been asked to provide surety of a hundred pounds if he is to be granted bail. I have come to discover whether there is anyone here who could be persuaded to stand…"

Caroline interrupted him again and said quickly, "Colonel Fitzwilliam will go with you," then turning to her husband, assured him she would be quite safe in the office while he and Mr Culver attended to the matter of Mr Upton's bail. "We need to discover what has occurred, how has Mr Upton come to be charged, and what evidence has been produced against him. I shall stay here and talk to these gentlemen until you and Mr Culver return with poor Mr Upton." At this, another deep sigh went up from the corner of the room.

The absolute confidence with which she had spoken had surprised even her husband, but Fitzwilliam knew there was little he could do in the office; Caroline knew more about her father's business than anyone else in the family except Mr Gardiner himself.

As he left with Culver, who still looked exceedingly startled, Fitzwilliam noticed that Caroline had sat down again and opened up the large, bulging file of papers on Mr Upton's desk.

As the door closed behind Culver and Fitzwilliam, Caroline stood up and moved to the centre of the office. It was a large room, but not as tidy as it might have been, which made it seem small and cluttered.

Standing beside a table on which stood a wilting aspidistra, Caroline addressed the others, saying in a voice as convincing as she could make it, "Now, you all heard what I said to Mr Culver; in my father's absence, we must discover how it was that Mr Upton got himself into such a bother with the customs. It is not at all like him and I do not believe for a moment that he was trying to defraud them. To do this, I need your help, so you will put aside whatever you are doing and begin by telling me your names and what your duties are. You first," she said, indicating one of the clerks, a pale young man with unruly, dark hair.

He stood up and said in a low voice, "Jeremiah Jones, ma'am, they call me Jerry; I keep the order books and send out the bills to the customers."

"Thank you, Mr Jones," said Caroline and inclined her head towards his colleague, a somewhat older man, with a neat moustache and a well-pressed grey suit. He stood up but seemed so awkward in her presence; he looked down at his hands and mumbled when he spoke, so she could barely hear him. His name sounded like George Selby (she learned later it was Selbourne) and it was Jones who explained that Mr Selbourne prepared the documents on all the export orders for the shippers.

He pointed to piles of files, neatly stacked in a cupboard behind him, as proof of his industry, no doubt.

Finally, there was the elderly gentleman, who in both appearance and apparel looked more like a character from the previous century accidentally stranded in this one. He reluctantly admitted to being a Mr Perceval Adams, in charge of import accounts and bills of lading.

Upon hearing this important piece of information, Caroline decided that Mr Adams was the most likely source of the problem. He, she thought, would surely know why the customs officers were after Mr Upton for fraud.

Seating herself upon a high stool beside his desk, she began to ask questions about the reasons given for Upton's arrest and the existence of any evidence.

"Did they say what fraud he was being accused of perpetrating?" she asked and while Mr Adams looked confused and took out his handkerchief to wipe his eyes once more, young Mr Jones stepped up to say that he had understood it had to do with a consignment of fine Chinese porcelain for which there had been no documents submitted.

"They said, ma'am, there was only tea, spices, and cotton on the bill of lading, but they had found a large crate containing valuable chinaware."

Caroline turned to Mr Adams and asked, in a quiet voice, "Is this true, Mr Adams? Was not this one of your documents? Did you not prepare it?"

The poor man could not speak, he seemed to be overcome with remorse or guilt or both at first; however, with further probing, it transpired that he had in fact made a serious error in preparing the documents for the customs and had obviously omitted the porcelain.

"But why did you make no mention of this matter when the customs officers questioned Mr Upton?" Caroline asked, whereupon Adams broke down and moaned about it being all his fault, he was afraid they would arrest him too, he did not want to go to jail, and he thought Mr Gardiner would come and put it right again, as he always did.

Caroline was furious but realised that anger would achieve nothing.

It was important to get a message to Culver and Fitzwilliam and she decided to send young Jones after them with a brief note in which she explained that it had been an error, not a matter of fraud, and if they could bring Mr Upton back to the office, he would probably be able to straighten it all out.

With Jones gone, there was only Mr Selbourne to help her and the blubbering Mr Adams.

"Come now, gentlemen, we must find the documents so Mr Upton and his attorney can prove it was a genuine mistake. No doubt, there will be some fine to be paid, but that will be nothing to having poor Mr Upton locked up in jail for fraud."

She put Selbourne to work, going through the piles of papers on Adams' desk to track down the documents for the cargo of tea, spices, and cotton while she searched through the file on Mr Upton's desk for any evidence that might prove the porcelain was a legitimate part of the same consignment.

After close to an hour of searching, punctuated by groans from Adams, Selbourne triumphantly produced the documents, checked them against the ship's papers, and declared them to be the right ones.

Caroline was relieved. "Well done, Mr Selbourne, that is a good start," she said.

But how would they prove that the porcelain, which had not been included, had not been fraudulently imported? It was a most vexing problem.

Recalling that Jones had told her it was his job to maintain a record of orders and send the customers their bills, she flew to his desk and, with Selbourne's help, located the filed documents, which held an itemised list of the valuable Chinese porcelain ordered by the Duke of Devonshire.

"If only Mr Adams had included this list with the rest of the documents, there would have been no trouble at all, poor Mr Upton..." she said and as Adams groaned and moaned again, the door opened and Jeremiah Jones rushed in, followed by Fitzwilliam, Culver, and Mr Upton, looking very miserable indeed. But he did not remain so for long.

On learning that the documents needed to prove his innocence had all been found, Upton's gratitude knew no bounds. He was an old and trusted employee and Caroline had never believed him to be capable of fraud. Now, they had the proof of his innocence.

Over the next few hours and for most of the following day, the attorney, Mr Culver, and Fitzwilliam accompanied Mr Upton, as he went first to the Customs office and then to the Police and back to the Court House, where the documents proving he was innocent of the charge of fraud were produced before the magistrate. The requisite sum of money was then paid to the customs and the charge against Upton withdrawn.

His relief was indescribable. He thanked both Fitzwilliam and Caroline repeatedly, telling her how much he owed to her quick thinking and prompt action. Caroline was gratified indeed.

On the day before they were to leave Manchester, with still no sign of Mr Gardiner, Fitzwilliam invited Mr Upton to dine with them. He arrived bearing a bunch of hothouse flowers for Caroline and made another speech expressing his undying appreciation of her efforts to save him from a fate much worse than death: the disgrace of being sent to jail at his age for fraud, ending thereby an impeccable career in commerce.

As they were about to sit down to their meal, a vehicle drew up outside the house, and to their great delight, Mr Gardiner stepped out.

Exhausted after having travelled with very little rest or refreshment since arriving from France, he was plied with food and drink, while being told that all was well.

"I called at Pemberley, where Mr Darcy and Elizabeth passed on the scant information that Caroline had received before leaving for Manchester, and I set out immediately, expecting to find my chief clerk behind bars," he explained and listened as they told the tale of the consignment of Chinese porcelain, the missing documents, and how the problem had been satisfactorily settled, so the Duke would have his valuable porcelain, which might otherwise have been confiscated by the customs, causing the business an enormous loss of both money and goodwill. Mr Upton was so grateful, he could barely speak without tripping over his words, which came thick and fast as he sang the praises of the lady who had saved the day.

"Of one thing I am certain," he said, "I and indeed all of us owe an enormous debt of gratitude to Mrs Fitzwilliam, without whom I may well have been behind bars today."

Mr Gardiner, when he had heard all the details, was almost speechless with surprise, but not so that he was unable to say how very proud he was of his daughter and to thank both Caroline and Colonel Fitzwilliam for their invaluable work.

Caroline, though modestly claiming no special credit for herself, was secretly delighted. Her father's approval had always meant a great deal to her. To have satisfied his high standards was a very special achievement.

When finally they retired to bed, Fitzwilliam was even more lavish with praise for his wife, of whom he was very proud indeed.

"My dear Caroline, you were absolutely remarkable. I cannot wait to tell Darcy and Elizabeth what you accomplished here."

"Fitzy, you must not, I forbid it," she protested.

"And why should I not? There is no harm at all in their knowing how well you coped with a most difficult problem and with what tact and circumspection you involved the clerks at the office and had them working to discover the vital information that had Mr Upton freed. No, my love, I must tell them, it makes me very proud of you," he insisted and even though she protested, she would not in the end deny that it had given her a great deal of satisfaction.

"I am happy that I was able to do what had to be done to help Mr Upton and above all else to save Papa a great deal of money. Had the porcelain been confiscated, the Duke would have been furious, with justification, and poor Papa would have had to pay. As it is, everyone is happy," she said. Her husband smiled.

"It was very well done, my love," he said and she put her arms around him in a show of affection that was as warm and spontaneous as he could remember.

They returned to Derbyshire on the morrow, and during their journey, Caroline took up with her father the matter of organising the Manchester office.

Mr Upton, she told him, was excellent as a chief clerk, but he was far too busy and needed a good assistant. The two young clerks, Jones and Selbourne, were promising but needed training and careful supervision. Again, Mr Upton was too busy to attend to them. As for Mr Adams, "Oh Papa, could he not be retired? He is too old and not able to cope at all," she said.

Mr Gardiner agreed, but confessed he felt sorry for the old man.

"It would kill him, Caroline, he lives alone and has few friends; coming to the office each day keeps him alive. I will ask Mr Upton to give him some less taxing work. He is old and forgetful; there have been mistakes before, but none as grave as this one, I must admit."

Caroline, who had helped her father set up his office at Lambton when they had moved to Oakleigh Manor, knew something about managing one. She was keen to tell him how the Manchester office might be improved with better accommodation, adequate heating and lighting, well-trained staff, and some methodical routines.

Mr Gardiner was pleased not only because Caroline was showing an interest in the family business and making a valuable contribution to its improvement.

He was gratified by her interest and as her father, even happier because it meant she had finally climbed out of the well of despair and isolation that had imprisoned her for years after Edward's death.

Caroline had come through the worst experience of her life with a new sense of purpose: working now for the people she loved and the ideas she believed in. She seemed eager to be involved and her father was pleased to support her in every possible way.

Later, in conversation with Colonel Fitzwilliam and Mr Darcy, Mr

Gardiner explained that he believed they could do with some changes at the Manchester office.

"If Caroline can help bring something of a woman's skill for order and method into the running of an old-fashioned office, I think it can only improve the management of our business. I believe Upton in his present mood will welcome it and we should seize the moment," he said.

Mr Darcy concurred and a delighted Fitzwilliam agreed to take the proposal to his wife.

He had no doubt it would be well received.

Chapter Eleven

THE ARRIVAL IN THE DISTRICT of a new family was always a matter of interest. When that family was reputed to be wealthy, the level of interest was usually enhanced; when it included not just one or two, but three particularly attractive young persons, the consequent attention that they excited among the general populace was bound to be quite phenomenal.

This, then, was precisely the situation that came about in the district, when the news got around that Newland Hall was being let at last, having remained vacant ever since the demise of the last occupant, Mr John Newland, to a Mr Henderson, originally from Newcastle and lately from Jamaica. It was being said, by those who knew these matters, that Mr Henderson's origins were distinctly lowly, being the son of a tradesman in his hometown upon Tyne. However, having made a fortune in the Caribbean colonies, where sadly his first wife had died of a fever, he had apparently returned to England, remarried, and was said to be looking to purchase a suitable property in Derbyshire. The family had taken Newland Hall on a year's lease.

Becky Tate brought the news when she met with Caroline, Cassandra, Emily, and the rector, Mr James Courtney, at the Kympton parish hall. She had learned that Mr Henderson had two very pretty daughters and his stepson was a gentleman of elegance and wit.

"Upon his father's death, the boy was sent to live with relatives in Surrey, where he had benefited from the advantages of an excellent schooling as well as a full social life," she told them. "I understand he is now attached to a firm of lawyers in London."

Of Mrs Henderson, however, she had heard only that she was a quiet, modest woman, who had been governess to the two girls for several years before she married their father.

The ladies may have been interested in Becky's information, but the rector had other matters on his mind.

Despite the protestations of the politicians, who attempted to cajole the populace into believing otherwise, all the signs pointed to the onset of a severe recession. In many of the "textile towns," mills were either closing or halving their production, throwing thousands of workers literally onto the street. In Manchester and Liverpool, men and women, who lost their jobs each day, joined the hopeless queues of those who looked for work, while knowing there was none to be had.

Back in the villages, as their fathers and mothers became unemployed and breadwinners returned home empty-handed, groups of women and a few benevolent men worked hard to care for the hapless children.

James Courtney, who was no stranger to the district, having previously spent some years of study in the area before he had been appointed to the parish of Kympton, was dedicated to the protection and education of the children of his parish.

He had, from the outset, urged Caroline, Emily, and their group to do more than feed and clothe the children.

"It is incumbent upon us to seize the opportunity to educate them; these are children whose parents would rather put them to work in the mills or the fields, where they may earn a few pence, than send them to school. They see no benefit to their families in schooling. Well, now that there is less work and what there is must go first to the adult workers; we have an opportunity like never before to introduce these children to learning. I have no doubt that some will find it boring and be off as soon as they see a chance, but others will stay and learn and in the future benefit from it," he said.

Emily and Cassandra agreed it was worth trying, while Caroline was ambivalent, pointing out that the children would only continue to come if the school taught them more than Bible reading and hymns. Rebecca was completely in favour of the proposition and went so far as to say that she could garner the support of the community through her husband's newspapers if they undertook such a scheme.

"If we could raise some money from donations and persuade the council to help as well, we could improve the little parish school at Kympton. I am confident Mr Tate will support us through the *Review* and the *Pioneer*; he has long deplored the lack of public education for working-class children," she said, and the rector was delighted.

"If you could ensure that we got the support of the *Review* and the *Pioneer*, Mrs Tate, I think we would be well on the way to achieving our goal. Mrs Fitzwilliam, when I last spoke with your husband, he promised to ask Mr Jonathan Bingley to lobby the government in Westminster for funds to help parish schools expand their activities. If that could be achieved, we would be well placed indeed."

Caroline promised to ask her husband what progress had been made and, shortly afterwards, having prayed with them and asked for the Lord's blessing upon their endeavours, the rector left to call on a sick parishioner in the village.

The ladies then broke for their customary tea and cake and Becky had more news about the Hendersons.

"Well," she said, as they sat together, "who do you suppose I met this morning, taking a quiet walk in the woods around Newland Hall?"

None of the others could even guess, though Caroline suggested mischievously that it might have been Mr Henderson and his bulldog! The tenants of Newland Hall were reputed to have a number of dogs on the premises; one in particular, a pugnacious bulldog, was said to be the master's favourite. An ill-tempered animal, it had no friends in the village.

"That creature is getting quite a reputation in these parts, Becky, he chases the girls, bites the boys, and, I am told, almost ate Mrs Winslow's cat," Caroline complained.

Becky Tate laughed with the rest, but was determined to tell them her story.

"No, of course it was not Mr Henderson and his dog—he would hardly pay any attention to me. It was in fact Mrs Henderson and her son Philip Bentley, for that was his father's name and hers before she married again," Rebecca explained, gratified to note that the level of interest around the tea table had increased somewhat.

The Hendersons were her neighbours and she took a proprietory interest in their activities. None of the others had met Mr Philip Bentley and were curious to hear what he looked like.

"He cannot look like Mr Henderson," said Emily, and Caroline was scathing.

"Of course not, he is only his stepfather. Is there much resemblance to his mother?" she asked, recalling that while Mr Henderson was a large, corpulent-looking man with a double chin and a very red complexion, his wife was a slight, frail-looking woman with a small bird-like face topped with a bunch of ginger-coloured curls.

Rebecca said no, he was not at all like his mother, being very handsome.

"Indeed, you would hardly believe they were mother and son—he is such a tall, upstanding young man and she is so plain and small in stature. Though there is little resemblance, it does seem there is a good deal of affection between them, judging by the very protective way in which Mr Bentley escorted his mother during their walk together. I was much impressed," said Rebecca.

"Did she introduce him to you?" asked Emily and Rebecca replied with some pride, "Yes indeed, she did, and I might say he was most charming. I had heard, as I believe I have told you when we last met, that he was attached to a firm of lawyers in London, and I did expect he would be rather disdainful of us generally, as lawyers are wont to be; but he was exceedingly pleasant and asked about various matters as we walked, appearing quite interested in the entire district and its people."

She was clearly very impressed with Mr Philip Bentley's manners and charm.

"Is he older than his stepsisters?" asked Cassy who had seen the two Misses Henderson in church; they had appeared to be young women in their early twenties.

Becky was sure he was. "I would say he is twenty-eight or thereabouts. He may be a year or two younger, but he conducts himself as a gentleman would. His clothes were elegant, though not those of a dandy, and there was not even a trace of a swagger about him. No, I think we are fortunate to have in our circle a family with three such agreeable young persons, do you not agree, ladies?"

Everyone did agree, and Caroline rose, preparing to leave.

She had heard rather more about the Hendersons than she wanted to hear. The others followed her out, having secured the parish hall and collected their belongings.

"Becky Tate is obsessed with them," Caroline told her husband that evening. "We have heard all about their fortune, their looks, and the girls' extraordinary talents; truly, Fitzy, I am already tired of the Hendersons, even before we have met them all.

"We know the two daughters are pretty, and always very well gowned in the latest modes, and they are well taught and play and sing; there appears to be no end to their accomplishments. Now we are to hear all about Mr Bentley, their stepbrother—his wit, elegance, and charm. To listen to Becky, you'd think he was the Prince of Wales! Poor dear Emily, she must get bored with Becky's chatter."

Fitzwilliam was amused by Caroline's remarks, understanding her impatience, but tried to make light of Mrs Tate's predilection for social climbing.

"Don't be too hard on her, my dear, I think Becky feels she must assiduously pursue each and every opportunity in society. Unlike Anthony, who is quite secure in his own estimation of himself and his family connections, Becky, like her unfortunate father Mr Collins, does tend to overdo her enthusiasm for the rich and famous. She obviously regards the Hendersons in that light and is making an early pitch for their friendship. I hope she is not going to be disappointed."

Caroline sniffed, unconvinced.

"I'd rather have a few good friends who have little wealth and no fame at all but upon whom I could rely implicitly. Becky knows little of these people, except what she has heard from others or whatever they choose to tell her themselves; it may not all be true."

"It very rarely is all true, my dear, and Becky is a grown woman who will have to look out for herself. However, I have some information for you too. I saw your father this afternoon, he was back from Derby, where he had gone on business, and would you like to guess who he had met at his club?"

Caroline looked puzzled at first and then as realisation dawned, she cried out, "Oh no, not Mr Henderson?"

Fitzwilliam laughed and nodded.

"Indeed, my love, none other than the man himself. He was introduced to Mr Gardiner as an entrepreneur from the Caribbean colonies. Your papa thought he heard it was in sugar that he had made his fortune."

"In sugar?" Caroline exclaimed, apparently bewildered, and deciding that she had had quite enough of the Hendersons for one day, changed the conversation to a more appropriate subject: the raising of money for the parish school.

"We are of the opinion, Fitzy, that were the council to be persuaded to provide some of the funds, we could, with some private donations, greatly expand the education provided at the parish school. Furthermore, Reverend Courtney wishes to know if Jonathan Bingley has been at all successful in his lobbying for funds at Westminster."

While Caroline had little interest in the Hendersons, others in the area seemed quite fascinated with the family that had recently moved into their midst. Not only was Mr Henderson reputedly wealthy, but his daughters were attractive young women, which accounted for the appreciative audience gathered to witness the crowning of the Queen of the May. This year, the chosen lady was Miss Frances Henderson.

The organisers had taken over the council hall and erected a large marquee on the lawn. Every family of any standing in the community had been invited to attend, and most did, or so it seemed to Caroline and Isabella, who with Emily went along, despite a premonition that it would be all very dull.

Mrs Henderson was there of course, with the two Misses Henderson. The elder, Maria, was undoubtedly very pretty and exceedingly fashionably dressed and coifed.

"No doubt her maid spent hours on that coiffure" said Caroline, who had for many years worn her own pretty hair in a simple chignon, for which she needed no help at all.

As for Frances, the chosen May Queen, she had already informed everyone that she would under no circumstances allow herself to be called "Fanny." Though not as handsome as her elder sister, Frances had the kind of youthful glow and vivacity that makes up for beauty in the young. She too was exquisitely gowned and had her long chestnut curls cascading down to her shoulders, all tied up with ribbons. It was no wonder, thought Caroline, that all the young men present were agreed that she was a fitting May Queen and were literally waiting in line to dance with her.

After the "coronation," at which the mayor made a number of effusive remarks about Miss Frances Henderson and her family, whom he was proud to welcome into his shire, there was respite from formality, with food to eat in plenty and dancing, either on the green in country style or inside the hall, where a small orchestra provided appropriate music for more formal dancing.

Isabella Fitzwilliam was standing with her mother and aunt in front of a large bay window, which overlooked the garden, when Rebecca Tate approached them with a gentleman, whom she introduced as Mr Philip Bentley. She declared that Mr Bentley had specifically asked to meet Mrs Fitzwilliam and her sister, Emily, of whose remarkable work for charity he had heard so much. To which the gentleman added, "And of course I am delighted to meet Miss Fitzwilliam too. Indeed, I remarked to Mrs Tate how very charmingly grouped you were before this magnificent window; against the colour of the evening sky, you made a most picturesque group," he said, and Emily noticed that he spoke, without any affectation, in a very well modulated voice.

Rebecca was quite carried away by his word picture, declaring it to be a most poetic description.

Even Caroline, who had decided she was not going to be influenced by Becky Tate's recommendation, could not help being impressed by Mr Bentley's gentlemanlike manners and easy charm.

He neither flattered them nor talked endlessly of himself and, unlike some young men about town, did not presume to remain silent in the belief that there was no topic on which he might have a worthwhile conversation with the ladies.

Instead, he alternately listened and spoke, asked sensible questions, and waited to hear their answers, giving every indication of being genuinely interested in what was being said.

He had heard a great deal, he said, of the valuable charity work done by the ladies of the district, and he hoped if the opportunity arose, he too would be able to assist them in some way. He sounded quite sincere, and Emily, touched by the kind offer, thanked him with a smile and was about to suggest something he could do, but at that very moment, the musicians, who had been taking a short rest, resumed their playing. Mr Bentley looked around and, seeing several couples preparing to take the floor, bowed briefly and addressed young Isabella. "Miss Fitzwilliam, if you are not already engaged for this dance, may I have the honour?"

Isabella took only a few seconds to glance at her mother and, seeing no disapproval in her eyes, accepted, and they moved to join the others.

As he escorted Isabella into the centre of the room and then led her in the dance, Caroline, like Rebecca, could not help admiring young Mr Bentley. He was indeed a very personable young man, and though not really handsome by conventional standards, there was something quite remarkably attractive about him, she had to concede.

By the time the evening drew to a close, he had twice danced with Isabella. He had very correctly asked Emily too, but she had begged to be excused. Then she had noted with approval that, instead of turning to another of the young ladies in the room, Mr Bentley had sought out his stepsisters and danced with them.

Going home in the carriage, all three ladies had reached the conclusion that Mr Philip Bentley was indeed one of the most agreeable gentlemen they had met in a very long while.

Emily was most open in her approval. "He has none of the affectations and pretensions that I find so tiresome," she said and added, "I do believe him to be a thoroughly decent young man. Becky is probably right: Mr Bentley and his stepsisters will be an asset to the community."

Caroline was more cautious. While she agreed Mr Bentley had turned out a good deal more acceptable than she had expected, she could wish, she said, that Becky Tate would stop bragging about them, as though she were personally responsible for them being here.

Isabella alone was quite silent on the subject of the Hendersons and Mr Bentley; though both her mother and her aunt could see she had enjoyed the evening. Indeed, Isabella could not remember when she had last enjoyed herself so much.

A rather solitary young woman since the death of her brother Edward, Isabella would not often speak of her thoughts and feelings. Very occasionally, she would confide in her Aunt Emily, to whom she was very close. But, on this occasion, she said nothing at all.

❧

Not long afterwards, the Hendersons gave a dinner party, to which all persons of note in the area were invited, as well as some from as far afield as Derby, where Mr Henderson had business connections.

Newland Hall had neither the handsome proportions nor the architectural appeal of Pemberley, but as houses go, it was spacious and lent itself well to the occasion. Mr Henderson had spared no expense in the preparations for the function; it was their first opportunity to simultaneously entertain and impress the local community, and he clearly intended that they should be so impressed.

Food and drink were plentiful and of good quality, the general atmosphere appropriately convivial, even merry, with everything available that was necessary for good entertainment.

There were fiddlers playing in a gazebo, jugglers performing on the lawn, and a very fine three-piece ensemble playing indoors during dinner. For those who wished to dance afterwards, there was a large hall with musicians ready to play seated on a low dais at one end, while others, who preferred to idle away their time in less energetic ways, could lounge and talk in one of the spacious reception rooms or watch the fireworks from the terrace.

It was there that Caroline and Colonel Fitzwilliam were seated, during an interlude in the entertainment, when they were joined by Mr Philip Bentley. They had been introduced earlier and he appeared to be well-informed about Colonel Fitzwilliam's politics and professed himself honoured to meet him, referring to his career in the Commons and his reputation as a Reformist.

"I believe you have been instrumental in making some very important reforms, Colonel. I envy you," he said.

Fitzwilliam was flattered, though Caroline, believing he had obtained all his information from one convenient source—Becky Tate—was somewhat less impressed.

"No doubt," she said later to her sister, "he had informed himself well and proceeded to speak in glowing terms of Fitzy's achievements in the Commons with an air of genuine authority, merely to flatter him."

Emily was a little puzzled. "But why do you suppose he would want to flatter Colonel Fitzwilliam, even if he had some political ambitions, knowing he is no longer active in political life? Do you not think, Caroline, that he may be genuine?"

Caroline was sceptical. "Emily, you are so good yourself, you will believe good of everyone you meet. I am not so sure, although I must confess I cannot fault his behaviour, I do harbour some suspicions about his intentions."

"Do you mean he may want to ask Fitzwilliam a favour?" asked her sister, still bewildered by Caroline's line of argument. Caroline nodded. "Indeed, though I have no proof as yet, I do believe he is strongly attracted to my Isabella and is building up credit with her father for the future."

Emily's eyes widened. "Do you think he intends to make her an offer?"

Caroline, eyes dancing with mischief, replied, "Emily, I should be very surprised if he does not. I have said nothing to Fitzy, though. He is sure to think Isabella is too young!" and the sisters laughed, recalling that Caroline had been married at sixteen.

"And Isabella, do you suppose she will accept him? Have you any indication of her feelings?" asked Emily.

This time, Caroline was not so certain.

Her daughter, though a gentle, lovely girl, had a mind of her own, not unlike her mother, and her feelings were rarely openly expressed.

"Well, that I cannot say for certain. Isabella will do exactly as she pleases, but I have noticed she seems to find his company very agreeable. Why just tonight, I noted that she had just come back from dancing two dances with Captain Danvers and had barely been seated five minutes, when Mr Bentley approached, and before he could even complete his bow, which he does so well, she rose with some enthusiasm and was gone with him to dance some more."

Emily almost began to point out that a girl may enjoy dancing with a gentleman, especially if he was an accomplished dancer and an interesting companion (a combination rare enough these days), but she may not view a proposal of marriage from the gentleman with the same degree of eagerness.

She thought the better of it, however, and said nothing. She had no desire to rile her sister and hoped she might have some indication of the situation from Isabella herself.

Returning to Pemberley after the function with Mr and Mrs Darcy, Emily mentioned some part of her conversation with her sister, having urged her cousin Elizabeth to discuss the matter with no one else.

Elizabeth reacted with some enthusiasm. Isabella was almost eighteen, she said, just the right age to have some personable young man take an interest in her, even if it came to nothing.

But Mr Darcy was silent, so much so that his wife, thinking he had not heard their conversation, repeated some of its salient points for him.

This time, he did respond.

"I did hear you the first time, my dear. The reason I did not respond immediately is that I was rather surprised. Mr Bentley has only known Isabella and her family for a very short time. I mean, what does he know of her family and how much do they know of his connections?"

Seeing the expression on the ladies' faces, he added, "These are not idle matters for gossip, for when a young woman is given in marriage, she goes into the care of her husband's family; it is therefore imperative that everything possible that can be known about them is discovered before and not after the event.

"As for the young couple, how much time have they spent together to gain an understanding of one another's disposition and interests? I should imagine they have met and conversed together on some four or five occasions. On what foundation will such a marriage be built if he were to propose and be accepted so precipitately?"

Elizabeth's excitement abated somewhat at his sober words. She knew well her husband's cautious attitude to such matters, and he had, on occasion, been proven right.

She asked Emily, "Does Caroline really believe Mr Bentley means to propose to Isabella?"

Emily was unsure.

"I think she does, but she admits she has no indication of Isabella's feelings at all."

"What do you think, Emily?" asked Mr Darcy, who had the highest opinion of his wife's cousin. "Do you believe Bentley will propose?"

But if he had expected a definitive answer, he was to be disappointed.

"I am afraid, Mr Darcy, I have not had the opportunity to observe them closely at all. But, Isabella is not only beautiful, she has a very gentle and appealing nature, and I would not be surprised if Mr Bentley's feelings were already engaged. As to his intentions or her feelings, I am not privy to them," she said.

Both Darcy and Elizabeth laughed at this response. It was typical of Emily that she would not rush to judgment upon any matter. Prudent, circumspect, and sensible of the consequences of anything she might say or do, she was generally unwilling to commit herself until she had all the facts.

Only once in her life, at the age of twenty-six, when she had decided within an hour that she would marry Paul Antoine and travel with him to Italy where she would care for him until his death, had Emily thrown caution to the winds and acted, having consulted none but her own heart. It was a decision she had never regretted.

<hr>

Meanwhile, Caroline had waited impatiently to discover if her husband had had an approach from Mr Bentley, but apparently, there had been none, since he mentioned no such thing. For her part, she had resolved not to speak of the matter to Fitzwilliam unless and until Isabella spoke of it to her. Determined that she would not appear to be pushing her daughter into any situation, Caroline held her peace.

There being no communication from Newland Hall, nothing more appeared to be required of her.

However, on the following Friday, when the family, having finished a late breakfast, had each departed to attend to their own interests, Fitzwilliam to Matlock with his steward, Caroline to attend to her correspondence, and Isabella to the music room, a carriage arrived at the door and the maid came upstairs to advise Caroline of the arrival of visitors.

On going downstairs, she found Mr Philip Bentley and the two Misses Henderson waiting for her in the parlour. The gentleman was seated, perusing a book he had picked up from the table, while the ladies were studying intently a portrait of her husband and their two sons, which hung above the mantelpiece.

Clearly, Caroline thought, Becky Tate must have enlightened them about the circumstances of Edward's death, for they turned as she entered and, with great sensitivity, refrained from making any comment on the portrait.

Greeting them warmly, Caroline asked for tea to be brought and sent the maid to ask Isabella to come downstairs. On her entering the room, it was quite apparent to Caroline that Isabella was the reason for their visit, for the conversation turned immediately from comments upon the impressive views of the hills and moors that the windows afforded to their pleasure at seeing her again. Maria and Frances Henderson were both elegantly dressed for driving out, while Isabella wore a simple gown of sprigged muslin; yet the sisters remarked upon her dress, saying how well she looked, while Mr Bentley kissed her hand and expressed his delight at seeing her looking so well. Isabella blushed and thanked them for their kindness. It seemed to her mother that to Isabella, the compliments were entirely unexpected.

Caroline could not help feeling that there was some degree of embellishment in their language, yet while their enthusiasm may have been extravagant, she could not point to anything that might lead one to believe it was insincere. Indeed, the two sisters appeared to like Isabella almost as much as their stepbrother did.

As they took tea, the purpose of their visit became clear.

It transpired that the young people were planning a picnic party to one of the prettiest places in the district—indeed, some would say, in Derbyshire.

"We have been informed that Dovedale is a place of such charm and beauty, it is not to be missed," said Maria, "and my brother has expressed a desire to see it before he returns to London at the end of the month."

"We thought perhaps we might take a picnic and wondered if Isabella would like to join us next Saturday," Frances added eagerly.

Seeing the look of surprise on Isabella's face and thinking perhaps that she was somewhat unsure, Mr Bentley intervened to say that Mrs Rebecca Tate would be coming and had promised to bring along a couple of friends: Doctor Gardiner and his wife.

Caroline laughed and said it would be a brave person who believed that her brother Doctor Gardiner would be free for a picnic, but perhaps his wife Cassandra would be happy to join their party.

Only then did the Henderson girls discover that Doctor Richard Gardiner was Caroline's brother and offered their apologies, very politely.

"We have met and heard of so many people in the past few weeks, we cannot keep up with them all; please accept our apologies, Mrs Fitzwilliam," said Maria, only to be assured by Caroline that no offence had been taken.

"Well, Isabella, will you come?" asked Frances and Isabella turned to her mother, momentarily, as if not entirely comfortable with the prospect, at which point Mr Bentley, who had been standing a little apart, intervened to say, "If safety is your concern, Mrs Fitzwilliam, you need have no anxiety. Mr Henderson will let us use one of the carriages and everyone will be transported there and back with the greatest care, I assure you. Miss Isabella will come to no harm."

At that, Caroline smiled, as if to dismiss all such concerns and said, "Well, if Isabella wishes to go, I can see no objection. I am quite sure I can entrust her into your care, especially if Becky and the Gardiners are to be there too."

It seemed Isabella was not at all averse to going but had waited for her mother's response. When Frances urged, "Please do come, Isabella? I am sure it will be great fun," she said, yes, she would like to and thanked them very much for inviting her.

While both ladies greeted her reply with smiles, there was no mistaking the delight that lit up the countenance of the gentleman.

They left soon afterwards, having arranged to call for Isabella on Saturday morning.

Caroline was by now quite convinced that Mr Bentley was falling in love with her daughter. Romantic by nature, she was easily persuaded, but how else, she argued, was one to explain the most particular concern shown by him and the very special assurances he had given regarding her safety and comfort?

Still, she waited for a hint from Isabella that she'd had some indication of his feelings for her, but none came. If she had any knowledge of it, Isabella was keeping it to herself. She did not appear to be inordinately excited about the picnic either. Perhaps, Caroline thought, Mr Bentley was being a truly proper gentleman and wished to ask Isabella's father's permission first, just as Fitzwilliam had done before revealing his feelings to her.

On the morning of the day chosen for the picnic, Caroline was rather more excited than her daughter.

It was an uncommonly lovely day, following upon a cool, clear night, when the wind had blown all possibility of rain away. A sky of quite breathtaking blueness greeted them, with small, white clouds drifting lazily across it and sunlight spilling over the tranquil scene.

"A perfect day for a picnic," said Caroline and Isabella agreed, but again said little more.

When the Hendersons called for her, they came in a handsome open carriage; Mr Bentley alighted and came to the door to escort her to the vehicle, while the ladies remained within, waving to Caroline as she stood at the entrance. She was surprised to see no sign of Becky Tate but was assured by Mr Bentley that the Tates were on their way in their own vehicle and would be bringing Dr and Mrs Gardiner with them.

Reassured, Caroline wished them an enjoyable day and waved them away, believing now that she could with confidence reveal her hopes for their daughter to her husband.

She was not sure, however, that he would welcome the news.

Chapter Twelve

CAROLINE WAS RESTLESS.

She disliked uncertainty and was concerned that Isabella had said little on returning from the picnic, except to indicate that she was rather tired.

Caroline had thought she looked happy and had noted also the general expression of pleasure on Mr Bentley's countenance when he had escorted Isabella to the door. Polite and correct as ever, he had wished them good night and sent his compliments to Colonel Fitzwilliam, who had not as yet returned from a journey to Staffordshire.

Thereafter, Isabella had gone directly to her room and asked the maid to prepare her bath. Despite Caroline's desire to discover what, if anything, had transpired at the picnic, she had restrained her curiosity and left her daughter alone. Determined not to behave as their infamous Aunt Bennet had done in times past, she waited, hoping Isabella would come to her if she had something to confide.

But she did not.

Finally, unable to contain her curiosity any longer, Caroline sent for the carriage and travelled the mile and a half to the Tates' place to see Rebecca. She felt uncomfortable doing it but needed desperately to talk to someone. Though somewhat weary after the day out, Becky Tate was quite willing and able to talk.

At first, Caroline pretended that she was concerned because Isabella had returned and gone directly to her room and was ever so quiet.

"I was anxious she may have been too long in the sun out of doors or had eaten something that disagreed with her," she said, but Becky soon assured her that it could be no such thing.

"Isabella was not out of sorts," she insisted, "indeed she was in a very happy mood all day, but especially in the afternoon, when she and Mr Bentley walked along the water's edge to the stepping-stones above Thorpe, where they waited for the rest of the party to catch up with them. I have not seen her happier. Believe me, Caroline, I am convinced Mr Bentley will soon propose to her. It was quite clear to me and to anyone who saw them that they are in love; at least he is, without any doubt, and though Isabella's modesty will not let her reveal her feelings, I cannot imagine that she is unmoved by such a strong show of affection. However, I think he has to wait awhile before he can propose to her."

Caroline was greatly discomposed at having to ask young Rebecca Tate these questions, but she had to know.

"Do you mean, Becky, that he has said nothing to her yet?"

"I think he has all but said it, though not in so many words, but Mr Bentley probably intends to write to Colonel Fitzwilliam first. He returns to London next week and I think I can safely predict he will approach Colonel Fitzwilliam on his return. His sister Maria thinks so too," she declared and again Caroline was bewildered.

"Becky, how can you be so certain? Has he spoken of his feelings to you?" she asked.

Rebecca laughed out loud. "Of course not! But I have eyes and ears, Caroline; it is quite obvious he is besotted with her; ask Cassy if you do not believe me, she will tell you no different. Oh, he behaved with perfect decorum, he is such a fine gentleman," she went on. "But, I understand he needs to attend to some business matters in London before he can make her an offer. I gathered from Frances, who is a little more forthcoming than her elder sister, that Philip Bentley has no estate, only his income from the law, which is pitifully small, and a generous allowance from his stepfather."

This information set Caroline thinking and, having thanked Rebecca, she left, hoping to be home before dark. Rebecca's revelations had put a somewhat different complexion upon the matter and left Caroline even more confused.

When she reached the house, she could hear Isabella playing the piano in the music room and gathered that she must be in a better mood. She half hoped her daughter would come downstairs, but she did not.

As she waited for Fitzwilliam to return, Caroline's impatience and anxiety grew. What, she wondered, should she tell him? At first she had wanted to break the news by suggesting that he prepare himself for an approach from Mr Bentley, but now, if as Becky Tate had supposed, the gentleman was going back to London without proposing to Isabella or asking her father's permission to do so, what was there to tell?

Poor Caroline, torn between her romantic inclinations and the practicalities of giving a daughter in marriage, was completely perplexed by the situation in which she found herself. It was clearly not a simple matter of two young people falling in love. Besides, there was the business of Mr Bentley's income. If Becky Tate was right, what would Colonel Fitzwilliam say to the prospect of his son-in-law being so dependent upon the generosity of his stepfather?

Perhaps, she thought, it may be best to say nothing at this stage, and when Fitzwilliam did arrive, weary from his journey and rather irritable at having been delayed, Caroline decided that the latter path was unquestionably the more appropriate one.

The following week, Mr Bentley called to say good-bye before leaving for London, where he expected to remain a month. But, he assured them, he was delighted with Derbyshire and would return as soon as his work permitted him to do so. Invited to stay to dinner, he begged to be excused, blaming his stepfather for imposing upon him a duty he had to perform before he left.

"I would so much prefer to stay to dinner, Mrs Fitzwilliam, but alas, duty calls..." he said and Caroline replied that she understood perfectly and they agreed he would dine with them the very first Sunday after his return. Isabella, who spent some time alone with him in the parlour while her mother absented herself, ostensibly to ask that refreshments be served, had seemed very pleased to see Mr Bentley, but not so very unhappy to see him go. Caroline, who remembered suffering deeply each time Fitzwilliam and she were parted, was confused.

Could her daughter really be in love? She could not be certain.

As for the gentleman, it was quite apparent that he went very reluctantly and took as long as he possibly could over their parting, after which Isabella retired to her room again.

When Fitzwilliam returned from the markets at Ashbourne, Caroline waited until he had bathed and rested and made sure he was comfortably settled in his favourite chair with a drink before she ventured to open the subject of their daughter and Mr Bentley.

Fortuitously, Emily had come over that afternoon and taken Isabella with her to the hospital at Littleford, where some new equipment was being installed in the children's ward. Isabella had always shown a great interest in the hospital and had been pleased to go, besides which, she wished to speak with her aunt Emily, who was the closest Isabella came to having a confidante.

While Caroline told her husband, in some detail, everything she had observed and all that Rebecca had told her regarding the matter of Mr Philip Bentley and Isabella, Fitzwilliam listened very carefully, asking only the occasional question.

Once she had concluded her narration, however, his response was rather curious; at least, it was not at all what his wife had expected.

He appeared to be neither overjoyed nor unhappy. He made no immediate objection, but he gave no sign of approval either.

He said simply, "Well, I shall wait for Mr Bentley to approach me and when he does, we shall see. Meanwhile, I do not believe we should badger Isabella with questions on the matter. I do not wish her to believe that we are keen to be rid of her. She is not yet eighteen and I am in no hurry at all to marry her off to anyone."

Caroline agreed, of course, but persisted with her query to him, asking if he thought Mr Bentley a suitable husband for their daughter.

Fitzwilliam regarded her with a quizzical expression. "Suitable? I don't really know, my dear, and that is the problem, is it not? He seems a well-spoken, well-presented, and intelligent young man, with excellent manners—rare enough in this day—but what does that tell us about him, except he has had the good fortune to receive an expensive education and has been brought up in genteel circles?

"Before I agree to let him marry my daughter, I should like to know a good deal more. Who was his father? Does anyone know? I have heard some talk of him having been a ship's captain; is this true?"

Caroline had no information on the subject and Fitzwilliam continued, "And what are his prospects? What is the source of his income? What does he mean to do? I cannot believe he lives as well as he does on his earnings as a lawyer; a junior solicitor in London cannot afford such fine clothes and a town house in Belgravia. How does he propose to keep himself and Isabella in some degree of comfort? Most of all, I wish to know how much he owes to Mr Henderson, his stepfather.

"Despite the general approbation he has received around the district, which I think you will agree, my dear, is chiefly on account of his wealth and the beauty of his two daughters, I am not entirely sure that I trust Mr Henderson."

Caroline gasped, astonished at this remark.

"Not trust him? Why, Fitzy, on what evidence do you say this?" she asked when she had got her breath back.

Her husband smiled. "None, at the moment, my love, but I intend to find out if there is any. I have asked your father's advice and I shall speak to Darcy too; it would have been far quicker and simpler to have asked Anthony Tate; he is much better equipped to discover such things, but seeing that Rebecca has become intimate with the family, it will not be appropriate to draw him in. I cannot help feeling that Mr Henderson is not who he would like us to think he is."

Caroline was most disturbed by this turn of events. What did he mean, she demanded to be told, had he heard anything that had made him suspect…? But Fitzwilliam put a finger to her lips.

"No, my dearest, it is much better that I keep my suspicions to myself until we know the facts. It will not do to have you worried sick with anxiety about something which may turn out to be nothing at all. Please do not speak of this to anyone, not Isabella or your mother and most of all not Becky Tate. Trust me and your father. It is for the best, Caroline, believe me, and t'will soon be done."

Caroline had not been so discomposed, nor felt so thoroughly deflated, in years. She had started the evening feeling exhilarated in anticipation of giving her husband some good news, yet now it had all collapsed around her. She could hardly hold back the tears, but Fitzwilliam, understanding her disappointment, reassured her not only of his love for her and Isabella, which was his reason for doing what he intended to do, but also of the rightness of his quest.

"It is not because I have any objection to Mr Bentley, my dear, he seems a perfectly decent fellow; but it would be dereliction of my duty as her father were I to let our daughter marry into a family of whom we know so little without discovering the truth about their antecedents, the source of their wealth, and the nature of their business. Once I have ascertained these facts, and found them to be unexceptional, Mr Bentley is quite welcome to marry Isabella, if she will have him, of course."

"Then you are not set against him?" she asked with some trepidation.

"Certainly not, he seems a nice enough young man; but, my dear, there really is no need for any haste on our part, whilst I have had no approach from him regarding his interest in our daughter."

At this point, Caroline did try to say that Becky Tate was strongly of the opinion that a proposal would be forthcoming as soon as Mr Bentley had arranged some of his business affairs in town, but Fitzwilliam was ahead of her and Rebecca Tate on the subject.

He had already received some information that cast doubt upon the story that Philip Bentley had serious matters of business to settle in London. He proceeded to tell Caroline what he knew.

"Caroline, I do not believe Becky is very well informed on that score; her husband informed me very early in our acquaintance with the Henderson family that Mrs Henderson had been left penniless when her first husband, Bentley, died. Bentley and Henderson were business associates, and Henderson, having first employed Mrs Bentley as a governess to his daughters, later married her and had entirely supported her son, who had been judged even then to be a bright lad. He was sent to live with a titled family in the south of England and educated at his stepfather's expense. I believe the generous allowance that Henderson gives him is all the income he has, save for the small retainer he is paid for his work with a firm of London solicitors. As you can see, he cannot have much business to arrange in London."

Colonel Fitzwilliam's expression was unusually grave as he continued.

"However, that's as may be; for the rest, we shall wait and see. If, as you have said, Isabella has told you nothing, it probably means he has not proposed to her and intends to write to me first. So, there is no need for you to be anxious at all. Meanwhile, I shall proceed with some discreet enquiries. I am confident that your papa will have contacts in Portsmouth and London who will provide us with the facts about Mr Henderson's business and why, if it was so profitable, he gave it all up so suddenly and returned to England."

And with that, Caroline had to be content.

*

As the weeks passed with no word from Mr Bentley, Caroline wondered at Isabella's composure. If she loved him and was aware that he cared for her, how could she be so calm, so seemingly unaffected by his silence? It was almost as though she had no capacity for deep feeling, and *that* Caroline knew was untrue. When Edward died, Isabella's grief had been overwhelming. Losing a brother to whom she had been very close had been a shattering blow, but, in the end, she was strong and had borne not only her own but her parents' sorrow as well.

Caroline recalled, with gratitude and love, how often Isabella, though not much more than a child, had rescued her from embarrassment, when in the midst of a domestic task or a visit from friends, she had begun to weep and fled the room.

Perhaps, she thought, they had some understanding of which Isabella did not wish to speak until Mr Bentley had approached her father.

Remembering her own love affair with Fitzwilliam, Caroline knew there were times when it was enough to know one was loved; there was no need for words.

However, unbeknownst to her mother, Isabella had spoken to Emily of Mr Bentley, confiding some of her hitherto secret thoughts and feelings. Having revealed her enjoyment of his company and her appreciation of his kindness and good nature, she had said, in reply to the question, "Do you love him, Isabella?"

"I think I *could* love him, but I must know more about him. Marriage is a matter of such depth and intimacy, I could not contemplate it with any man unless I knew his character well and understood it truly."

"Do you not know Mr Bentley well enough?" Emily had asked and Isabella had replied, "I believe I do, he is both kind and amiable; but I feel I do not understand him as well as I would wish to if I were to say I would marry him. I think that would need more time."

Emily had smiled and agreed that it probably would.

~❦~

When Fitzwilliam visited Pemberley alone, having sent a message ahead to announce his intention, neither Darcy nor Elizabeth supposed it to be a private matter of great seriousness.

England was battening down the hatches against the impact of a severe economic recession that was imminent and, in view of the spate of bankruptcies and closures of enterprises around the country, Darcy assumed Fitzwilliam was there to talk business. He had admitted to some anxiety on the subject on a previous occasion, when they had met with Mr Gardiner, and Darcy supposed this visit would be taken up with similar discussions.

But Mr Darcy was mistaken.

Indeed, business was furthest from his cousin's thoughts as he sat down with Darcy, whom he had always turned to for advice when faced with difficult decisions. This time, the decision was a formidable and heart-wrenching one.

He had in his case several papers which he placed face down upon the table, save for one, a letter from Mr Philip Bentley, asking in the most polite and modest terms, for Isabella's hand in marriage.

Fitzwilliam passed the letter across the table to Darcy and sat back while he read it. Darcy was understandably awkward at having to read what was clearly a very private communication, but Fitzwilliam insisted.

Having read it, Mr Darcy returned the letter, realising that his cousin would not have produced it for his perusal unless he had some problem with it or its writer.

"What do you think of it, Darcy?" he asked and Darcy shrugged his shoulders as he said, "Well, it's a good letter, as such letters go, but that is not what you want to know, is it, Fitzwilliam?"

Fitzwilliam looked most uneasy. "Darcy, this is exceedingly difficult for me; I need your advice. I have known for some time, from my own observation and things Caroline has said, that Mr Bentley has a particular partiality for Isabella. When Caroline recently revealed that Becky Tate believed I should expect an approach from him very soon, I decided to make some discreet enquiries about the young man and his background, in particular, his stepfather Mr Henderson."

Mr Darcy nodded, appreciating the need for such action; as he had already pointed out to his wife, it was essential that such enquiries be made before a proposal was accepted.

He remarked to Fitzwilliam that Elizabeth and he had been exceptionally fortunate, in that they knew the Gardiners and Richard intimately before Richard and Cassandra discovered they were in love.

Fitzwilliam confessed that he'd long had reservations about Mr Henderson.

"He is too loud and coarse for my liking, Darcy, and to be quite honest, I did not trust the man. Mr Gardiner, at my request, made some enquiries in Derby and London and also in Southampton and Portsmouth, where he does business, and Darcy, I have been truly shocked, indeed astounded, by what he has uncovered."

Darcy leaned forward, as Fitzwilliam dropped his voice as though embarrassed by the words he was about to utter.

"I hardly know where to begin. There have always been rumours about Henderson's character; he is inordinately fond of the drink and horse racing and, we now learn, of women too. While he behaves himself in company, Mr Gardiner's informants are aware of two or three establishments of ill repute, which he visits whenever he is in Derby, where he goes often on the pretext of attending the races. There are tales also of him staying overnight at inns in the ports, carousing and gambling all night long with men of dubious reputation.

"Poor Mrs Henderson, it seems she is either unaware, which is difficult to believe, or has continued to ignore his actions in return for the material security he has given her and her son. They are both totally dependent upon his bounty and there, Darcy, lies my problem. Mr Bentley, who was entirely educated at Henderson's expense, has no estate and no income apart from the very generous allowance his stepfather allows him, unless you count the very small retainer he earns from the practise of law."

Mr Darcy was amazed by these revelations. He had had his own reservations about Henderson, based mainly upon his dislike of the man's brash and boastful ways, but had no idea things were this bad.

"And what of young Bentley's character?' he asked.

Fitzwilliam replied, "There is nothing against his character that has been uncovered, nor does he appear to be linked in any way to his stepfather's unsavoury conduct, but I am sorry to say, he is not unscathed. The story has a way to go yet and it gets worse."

Darcy raised his eyebrows, wondering how much worse it could get.

Fitzwilliam continued, "Mr Gardiner's contacts in Portsmouth and Southampton have produced further proof that Henderson was far from being just a respectable businessman who had made good in the colonies. He had let it be known that he was a sugar trader in the Caribbean colonies and the southern states of the American Union; but it is now apparent that, in fact, he was a slave trader too, or at the very least an agent for one, contracting to procure black slaves from Africa for the cotton, cane, and fruit plantations in the southern states."

"Good God!" exclaimed Darcy, as Fitzwilliam went on.

"These unfortunate men and women were being abducted and shipped in chains to America or the islands of the West Indies to be sold like cattle. Darcy, it is beyond belief, but *that* is said to be the chief source of Henderson's fortune."

Darcy shook his head, incredulous. All through the debates on the abolition of slavery, he had heard much about the dreadful fate of the slaves and the greed and brutality of the slave traders, whose ships had carried the human cargo, but never had he expected to encounter one here in Derbyshire! It was barely credible, yet the information had come from a reliable source.

"This is truly shocking, Fitzwilliam. Are you convinced it is true?" he asked, and his cousin replied, "It gets worse, Darcy, because Mr Gardiner has learned also that Mr Bentley's father was a ship's captain who worked in partnership with Henderson and others of his ilk, running guns and transporting slaves across the Atlantic and returning with cargoes of cotton to England for several years. Even after laws were passed in Britain outlawing the evil trade, he continued to defy them.

"It transpires that in the course of a particularly bad voyage, there was a mutiny and he was killed. His body was taken to Jamaica where Henderson arranged for it to be buried.

"Later, after his own wife died, he married Mrs Bentley, who was at the time employed as governess to his two daughters, and established them in a house in London. Quite clearly, he had no love for her; he returned alone to the Caribbean, where he had a Creole mistress and two more children while making many thousands of pounds. After the passage of the Abolition of Slavery act, probably realising it was too hazardous to continue his obnoxious trade, he is said to have sold his colonial properties and returned to England."

Mr Darcy's countenance betrayed his astonishment and revulsion.

"It beggars belief, Fitzwilliam. I take it you and Mr Gardiner have evidence of the truth of all this material? Is it not even remotely possible that someone with a grudge against the man, a disgruntled employee perhaps, has concocted all this to discredit him?"

Fitzwilliam laughed. "You are much too charitable, Darcy," he said. "In fact Mr Gardiner feared the same thing and had the information checked over, fearing he might have been duped, only to discover there was more, not less, evidence of Henderson's heinous conduct. He has met with men who sailed on his ships."

At that point, Fitzwilliam turned over the papers that lay on the table between them to reveal dozens of letters and documents that told their own story. In particular, the diary of a ship's purser, contacted by Mr Gardiner in Southampton, which provided incontrovertible evidence, containing damning accounts of the voyages of the slave ships.

"I shall spare you the rest of the sordid story, Darcy—it is all in the same vein. The only conclusion I can draw is that Henderson is a blackguard, a criminal of the deepest dye, and while there is no evidence whatsoever of similar behaviour on the part of Mr Bentley, his total dependence upon his stepfather's tainted money must surely give one cause to reflect. Whether he knew of his activities, I cannot tell, but it is not relevant when considering his request for permission to marry my daughter."

Elizabeth had come in while they were talking and could not help hearing the last few sentences of their conversation. As she stood there, her eyes wide with shock, Darcy urged her to be seated and together with Fitzwilliam related, in somewhat less graphic language than had been previously used, the gist of Mr Gardiner's information concerning Henderson.

She listened, appalled, but when it came to the revelation about the slave ships, Elizabeth unable to contain her disgust, exclaimed, "A slave trader! Good God!"

"Exactly, it is hardly a pleasing prospect; Fitzwilliam fears that Isabella may, in ignorance of the facts, agree to marry Mr Bentley," said her husband.

Elizabeth was adamant. "It is unthinkable, I cannot believe that Isabella, once aware of the truth, will wish to, and you would not consent, would you, Colonel Fitzwilliam?"

"Certainly not, but then I have no wish to break her heart either. If she is in love with young Bentley, as both Caroline and Rebecca believe her to be, how will she respond to my refusal? Is it not possible that she will hate me for thwarting her?"

Elizabeth had an idea.

"Not if she understands your reasons. Some means must be found to acquaint her with the truth, so she can make the right decision herself, rather than have you refuse permission. However deeply she loves Mr Bentley, and I have to say, I have seen no sign of any passionate attachment between them, I cannot believe Isabella, with her character and her tender heart, will knowingly attach herself to the family of a slave trader. It will be thoroughly abhorrent to her."

Fitzwilliam agreed it was a good plan, but how was it to be achieved?

"We shall have to find someone who could tell her gently and kindly," he said and then in a flash, Elizabeth said, "Emily, Emily will tell her, I am sure of it. They are very close."

Both gentlemen thought this was an excellent idea, but Darcy wondered if Caroline should be apprised of it first.

"Does Caroline know all this?" he asked and Fitzwilliam admitted that he had not told his wife everything for fear of upsetting her.

"She is quite fond of young Bentley; I cannot tell how she will take this news. He is, after all, innocent of any wrongdoing, tainted only by his association with others who are guilty."

Elizabeth spoke quietly, echoing his words. "I am very sorry for poor Mr Bentley—he is unfortunately the innocent son and stepson of two quite evil men. No doubt this is why the two Misses Henderson are in their middle twenties and as yet unwed. I have often wondered what impediment, apart from Henderson's coarseness, had prevented two such pretty, accomplished, and well-endowed young women from being snapped up by aspiring suitors. Their father's past must be known to their general acquaintance, surely?"

"Well, I think you have your answer, Lizzie. The children are innocent victims. But, we must now consider Isabella's future; it would destroy her to discover the truth after she has given him her word," said Fitzwilliam ruefully, well aware how difficult this was going to be.

❧

That evening, a plan was made for Fitzwilliam to convey Emily to Oakleigh Manor, where Mr Gardiner would enlighten her, so she could relate the sad and unpleasant tale to young Isabella before Mr Bentley returned from London.

Fitzwilliam knew that Caroline had invited Bentley to dine with them on the first Sunday after his return; it was very likely that he would expect to approach Isabella and essential that she be in possession of all the facts by then.

"Poor Isabella," said Elizabeth and her husband added, "Poor Emily—I would not have her task for the world. She is very fond of Isabella, which will make it all the more difficult."

And yet, when it was put to Emily and the circumstances were explained, she was so deeply affronted by the prospect of her niece marrying into such a family, in ignorance of their circumstances, she agreed immediately to their scheme, on one condition.

Her sister Caroline must be told and must agree to the plan.

"It will not only be totally wrong for me to approach Isabella without her mother's knowledge, I think it would break Caroline's heart. How would it be, Cousin Lizzie, if Jane or Kitty or Caroline had decided to counsel Cassy without a word to you? Would you not have considered it an act of intolerable arrogance?"

Elizabeth had to agree and Fitzwilliam consented. He would bring Caroline with him to Oakleigh, he promised. There, they would acquaint her with everything before Emily spoke to Isabella on the morrow.

It was not a prospect any of them looked forward to with any degree of enthusiasm, least of all Emily, whose warm affection for her young niece would make the telling of it very painful indeed.

Chapter Thirteen

THERE WAS NOTHING UNUSUAL ABOUT Sunday morning, except that Emily, who usually attended the church at Pemberley, arrived for the midmorning service at the parish of Kympton. Isabella thought perhaps her aunt had enjoyed Reverend Courtney's sermon on another occasion and had decided to change her allegiance to the parish, but her mother said, no, Aunt Emily was coming back to the farm with them because she had something important to do.

Isabella could not imagine what there was for her aunt to do at the farm, but in view of her mother's rather grave countenance, decided not to ask too many questions.

Later, after they had partaken of tea, when Emily invited Isabella to accompany her on a walk down to the lower meadows of the property, she began to believe there was more to this morning's visit than at first met the eye.

Isabella loved the wild meadows and the little river that leapt and sprang as it rushed along its rocky bed on its way to join the Derwent, beyond the steep gorge. She often used to come down here with her brother Edward and enjoyed sketching the scene, as he played at fishing. As children, it had been their special place. Their grandfather had a couple of her pictures of the high peaks rising above the tumbling water on the walls of his study and one of Edward pretending to land a fish.

When they reached a familiar spot, where a large tree overhanging the water gave them good shade, Emily said, "Bella my dear, do you think we could sit here awhile? There is something very important which you must know."

Isabella knew she had no choice; she'd had a premonition that had increased in strength as they walked that her aunt had bad news for her. They sat in the shade and over the next hour Emily told her in detail all the information she and Caroline had had from Mr Gardiner about Mr Henderson's business and the part played by Mr Bentley's late father.

As Isabella listened, Emily explained that her father had received a letter from Mr Bentley asking permission to propose marriage to her; it was news Isabella took without any show of surprise.

Emily then proceeded to tell her of Fitzwilliam's concerns and relate the sequence of events that had led to Mr Gardiner's discoveries. Taking a bundle of papers out of the small satchel in which she had placed them that morning, she gave them into her niece's hands.

As Emily watched, Isabella's expression changed from mild bewilderment to alarm and revulsion. She intervened gently, "Remember, my dear, that Mr Philip Bentley is not guilty of anything more than being the son and subsequently the stepson of men who seem to have had no limits to their greed. He had no control over the situation, nor did he ever participate in any of their evil deeds."

Isabella looked up at her aunt, and Emily, seeing tears in her eyes, braced herself for a struggle, marshalling her arguments and preparing to use her most persuasive manner, but none such ensued.

Instead, Isabella said very softly but quite firmly, "Yes, and therefore, I can see no impediment to my continuing friendship with Mr Bentley; but I suppose I could not marry him."

Emily only just succeeded in concealing her astonishment, when Isabella continued, "If I were to do so, quite apart from the sorrow I should cause Papa and Mama because I know Mr Bentley receives a generous allowance from his stepfather, I should never be able to rid myself of the feeling that everything we had, every pleasure we enjoyed together, each luxury we indulged in was purchased with money tainted with blood of slaves. It would be forever on my conscience."

Emily took her hand and held it, feeling the fingers tremble as she spoke in a voice that was surprisingly steady.

"Dear Aunt Emily, you will remember when we last spoke of Mr Bentley, I said I thought I could love him, for he is indeed an amiable and kind gentleman, but I also said I needed to know him better. Unhappily, it would appear that my enhanced knowledge has not been to his advantage, although he is not directly responsible for the impediment."

The tears that had welled in her eyes compelled her to stop and take out her handkerchief.

Emily put her arms around her. "My dear, dear Bella, if you do love him, it will surely hurt to turn him down…" but Isabella shook her head.

"If I loved him as deeply and as selflessly as you loved Paul, I would have been prepared to risk my happiness and my parents' disapproval to marry him, but clearly, I do not. I like him very much, Aunt Emily, he has been a most agreeable and engaging friend and we have spent many happy hours together.

"Nor do I deny that I have been aware of his deepening interest through the Summer and have enjoyed it, but clearly, I am not in love with him. I am deeply sorry for him; he does not deserve to be so burdened with the sins of his father and stepfather; he is kind and good-natured, and I cannot pretend that I have not felt some affection for him, but how can I marry him, knowing that it will cause my dear parents so much grief? Such a marriage will make neither of us happy."

As Emily listened, Isabella continued, "I shall tell Papa to respond but make no mention at all of the crimes of his father and Mr Henderson. Mr Bentley must not think that I have learned of their misdeeds and hold him responsible for them. Papa can convey my sincere thanks, but say I cannot accept his proposal, though I hope he will always count me among his friends. It is sincerely meant, for I do not mean to denigrate him in any way and must hope that it will be accepted by him in the same spirit."

As Emily watched, amazed at her niece's words, Isabella turned to her and asked in a voice heavy with resignation, "Will that do, Aunt Emily?"

Holding her very close, Emily replied, "My dearest Isabella, that will do very well; you are indeed a brave, kind-hearted girl. I pray that one day, you will meet someone you can love with all your generous heart and be very happy together."

Isabella gave no sign that she believed this would be the case. Her expression was grave and sad as they returned to the house.

Caroline met them in the hall. She looked apprehensively at her daughter, but Isabella kissed her mother and went to her father in his study, while Emily took her sister upstairs. When she heard of Isabella's decision, Caroline wept with relief and sorrow. Renunciation was never easy, and she hoped that it would not be a scarring experience that blighted Isabella's life. Emily's assurance that it was not likely to do so did not convince Caroline, who had observed the couple closely through the Summer and seen a degree of attachment which she had believed would not be easily extinguished or forgotten.

Recalling her own romance and the strength of her feelings, which would have precluded any possibility of forsaking the man she loved, Caroline was not as confident as Emily that they had done the right thing.

⚜

Three letters will suffice to conclude this unhappy episode.

Writing to Mr Phillip Bentley, after speaking with his daughter, Colonel Fitzwilliam took particular care to say nothing that might reflect upon his character in any way; it was what Isabella had wished him to do.

Having thanked Mr Bentley for his proposal, Fitzwilliam wrote:

> *My dear daughter Isabella also asks me to convey her thanks for your offer, which she regards as an honour. However, she regrets that she is unable to accept your proposal of marriage.*
>
> *She wishes me to say that though she cannot marry you, she will always think of you as a friend and hopes you will remain so in the future.*
>
> *Mrs Fitzwilliam and I join our daughter in wishing you good fortune, health, and happiness.*
>
> *Yours etc.*

When it was done to the satisfaction of both father and daughter, it was signed, sealed, and dispatched to the post forthwith.

Fitzwilliam rose and kissed his daughter on the forehead.

"I am so very sorry, my dear. I was thinking only of your happiness," he began, but she would not let him continue.

"Please, do not apologise to me, Papa. You did what you thought was right and I did what I had to do for my own peace of mind. I am pleased, however, that Mr Bentley need never know that the uncovering of his father's heinous deeds was the cause of it. Believe me, Papa, he is a good man, deserving of both love and respect, regardless of these unhappy circumstances of which I am quite sure he is unaware."

That night, two more letters were written in which the hapless Mr Bentley figured prominently.

Emily, writing to her cousin and confidante Emma Bingley, now Mrs David Wilson, recounted the details of Isabella's story and Mr Bentley's unfortunate antecedents, which had prevented what might well have been a perfectly happy union of two otherwise well-matched young people.

Do you not think, my dear Emma, that there must be some wretched force at work in the Universe that pits itself against the will of good people when they wish to enhance their chances of happiness?

How else to explain such a dreadful debacle as has befallen our dear Isabella and the unfortunate Mr Philip Bentley?

That a young man with all the advantages of good looks, a sound education, charming manners, and an amiable nature should have his suit refused and his happiness blighted because of the brutal criminality of his father and stepfather, of whose misdeeds he knew nothing, seems utterly unfair. Yet if you were Isabella's mother or father, how else would you respond except to protect her from such an association?

Even Isabella agreed she could not knowingly marry him and live on an income derived from the suffering of countless human beings, abducted and abused by her husband's father and stepfather. Yet, I could not help noting the tears in her eyes as she spoke of him, assuring me he was a good, kind man deserving of affection and respect.

It was a most melancholy situation, Emma, and I was glad when it was over.

Out of all this misery, there was but one shining moment—when Isabella, having decided that she could not marry him in the light of all these revelations, was most anxious that he not be humiliated by a recitation of the actions of his father and Henderson. It showed a generosity of heart and a greatness of spirit in one so young that is quite uplifting in a time of increasing selfishness and moral cowardice.

Do you not agree?

Emma Wilson did agree. Indeed, she had reasons of her own to believe exactly as Emily had done in the value of moral courage, but for Emma the time was not opportune and she could not reveal any of it, not even to her dearest friend.

Many years were to pass before the truth could be told.

In the early hours of the following morning, Isabella arose after a restless night, during which she had had little sleep and, while everyone slept in the silent house around her, wrote to Rebecca Tate.

My dear Becky,

It would not be fair to let you discover what has transpired through the vehicle of gossip and rumour; hence this letter, which I hope will reach you before any other news. I shall send it over after breakfast.

As you are no doubt aware already, Papa has received from Mr Philip Bentley an offer for my hand in marriage. Perhaps you have learned from Mr Bentley or Maria that such a situation would eventuate.

Sadly, Becky, while I have greatly enjoyed his company all Summer and am convinced he is one of the most amiable men I am ever likely to meet, I do not believe that I love him enough to marry him. Not, that is, with the devotion and unquestioning love that my mother or Aunt Lizzie or even my dear Aunt Emily loved their husbands.

I have asked myself why this is and can only conclude that neither Mr Bentley nor I can claim, with sincerity, that we were able to open our hearts totally to one another and hold nothing of ourselves back. I do not feel I know him well enough to accept him, and he, though paying me the most charming compliments, knows very little of me. We were friends, certainly, but I doubt that we are ready to become lovers. He is a man of such good nature and kindness that he deserves to be well loved.

I respected him as a friend and hope one day he will find someone who will love him as a wife should love a husband. I am sorry I could not be that fortunate woman.

I wish him well and, dear Becky, when you do meet, should my name be mentioned between you, will you do me the kindness of telling him what I have told you in this letter?

Your loving friend,

Isabella Fitzwilliam.

It was a week later the news came that the Hendersons would not remain at Newland Hall beyond the end of Autumn. The family was returning to

London, it was said, for the Christmas season. Mr Henderson had taken a house in town.

It was Fitzwilliam who told Caroline as they sat alone in the parlour after dinner. Caroline felt some relief; it had been exceedingly difficult to meet the Hendersons, even the innocent members of the family, with the knowledge of Mr Henderson's activities constantly nagging at her thoughts.

"Fitzy, how was I so wrong?" she asked softly. "I never dreamed that Mr Bentley could ever be the son of a slave trader, it's unthinkable; nor that Mr Henderson's wealth had been amassed by criminal means.

"Oh, I could see that he was uncultivated and coarse in his manners and his background was unknown to us, but I would not have suspected the truth had it not been for you and Papa. I sincerely hoped Mr Bentley would propose to Isabella and she would accept him. It seemed an ideal match. How could I have been so mistaken?"

Comforting her, Fitzwilliam was generous. "My dear Caroline, do not blame yourself; like many people with little experience of confronting evil, you do not look for it in everyone you meet. It is to your credit that you treated Mr Bentley as you did, for in truth, he is not guilty of anything. His misfortunes arise from the misdeeds of his father and stepfather, which you were not to know.

"Nor, I am sure, was young Bentley aware of the extent of their iniquity, else he is unlikely to have been so open and carefree in his dealings with everyone."

Caroline agreed, "Indeed, he could never be accused of concealment or dissembling."

Fitzwilliam continued, "Once the truth was revealed to us, however, I had to act. I was relieved that Isabella, having heard the truth, made her own decision and there was no need for me to forbid her to marry him. Yet, she was so particular that he should not be allowed to believe that we held him responsible for the guilt of others. Nothing was to be said in my letter that could belittle or offend him. Caroline, I think we can be very proud of our daughter," he said and she concurred warmly, "Indeed, we can; Isabella's conduct in this situation has been exemplary. I cannot help thinking that she at eighteen showed greater maturity in this matter than I did. Fitzy, I have been a silly romantic woman, wanting to believe that this charming, handsome young man was going to marry our daughter and all would be well, as in some fairy tale."

He would not let her continue.

"Caroline, dearest, there is nothing to be gained by indulging in self-reproach; you are in no way to blame for not knowing the hidden guilt of Henderson when half the community was proclaiming his success as a businessman and welcoming him and his family to the district."

"But you were not taken in, Fitzy? You said you had your suspicions."

"I did, but then I have lived and worked among men of his type here in England and even more so in the colonies, where honour and decency, even if they are learned early at home, appear to decrease with the distance they travel abroad. I have encountered others like him and so has your father, which is why we had the advantage over you.

"As for Bentley's father, he is long dead, and were it not for Mr Gardiner's contacts in the shipping lines, we would never have discovered his guilt.

"We must be grateful Isabella has emerged almost unscathed from this sad episode."

Caroline was not so certain. "Do you think so? I cannot help wondering if she did not care more deeply for him than she would have us believe."

"I do not think so, my dear. She made it clear to me that she regarded him as a friend but did not love him enough to marry him."

Fitzwilliam was most persuasive, but it would be quite awhile before Caroline could shake off a sense of inadequacy. Never before had she doubted her own judgment nor her understanding of her daughter. It was a humbling, disconcerting experience.

<hr />

In the weeks that followed, they were all busy again.

Autumn and harvest time meant there was much to be doing. Fitzwilliam was busy on the farm, and Isabella had gone to spend a fortnight at Pemberley, where they were preparing for the annual festivities.

On a cold, windswept day, with the leaves cascading down onto the lawn, Caroline was indoors, tucked up in front of the fire, reading, when the maid announced a visitor.

It was Philip Bentley.

Caught completely unawares, Caroline was unable to compose herself in time and he could see she was uneasy, although she smiled as he came towards her and rose to greet him warmly. She had always liked him and found it difficult to associate him with the evil reputation of Henderson. He looked thinner, and when he spoke, his voice was quiet and less confident than it had been. He saw she was embarrassed and was at pains to put her at ease, reassuring her that he had come only to say good-bye; he had received Colonel Fitzwilliam's letter, he said, and though deeply disappointed, he had accepted his answer.

"I do love Isabella very much, Mrs Fitzwilliam, but if she cannot love me enough to marry me, I must be satisfied that it is the right answer. Nothing would be worse than a marriage without the assurance of mutual love."

Caroline agreed but added softly that they hoped—all of them, including her daughter—that he would remain a friend and would visit them whenever he was in Derbyshire. He would always be welcome, she said.

At which, he smiled a wry, sardonic little smile, and said, "Mrs Fitzwilliam, I am here because I have lately discovered some quite shocking facts pertaining to my stepfather's business affairs, whilst he was in the Caribbean colonies. I realise now that even if Miss Isabella had been of a mind to accept my offer, it would not have been possible for her to do so, once the truth of these matters was known, as they will be known, very soon. It is unlikely that my stepfather's disgraceful conduct can be concealed for much longer.

"Had I any prior knowledge of the seriousness of his crimes, I would never have approached Colonel Fitzwilliam, for I am aware of the revulsion this information will arouse in Isabella and all of you."

As he related, without giving her much detail, the matters concerning his stepfather's involvement with the slave trade, Caroline said little, hoping he would believe her to be ignorant of the shameful situation. Showing some surprise and sufficient unhappiness to be credible, as his story unfolded, she was careful not to add to his distress by appearing to connect these matters with the refusal of his proposal.

He spoke with great sadness, but without bitterness, "Apart from saying good-bye, my reason for coming here today was to inform you that, following this shocking revelation, I have entirely broken my ties with Mr Henderson and his money. I shall no longer accept the allowance he has paid me, I have given up my town house for which he paid the rent, and I have accepted a position as a shipping clerk—for I am little qualified to do much else—in a French trading company operating out of the port of Marseilles."

"Marseilles?" Caroline could not hide her astonishment.

"Yes. I leave for London tomorrow morning and for France at the end of the week. I hope that, having emancipated myself from the tainted association with my stepfather, I may soon do the same for my mother. I owe her that, at least."

Caroline felt tears sting her eyes as he continued, "Mrs Fitzwilliam, my mother is a genuine, good woman, who has been his slave for years, for my sake alone, and he has treated her abominably!" His voice shook with emotion and Caroline's countenance must have conveyed the shock she felt on hearing his words.

She was perplexed. How, she wondered, had he found out the truth, which had been well concealed for so long?

Almost in answer to her unspoken question, Bentley said, "I had no knowledge of my stepfather's business, having spent most of my life in Surrey and at school or college. It was my mother who enlightened me. When I told her I had written to Colonel Fitzwilliam to ask for Isabella's hand in marriage, she revealed to me what she had learned some years ago because she said I ought to know the truth.

"She had discovered it herself, when some of his papers were mistakenly sent to England from the West Indies, but had hidden it from me and my stepsisters. There were few others in England who knew; it was not a subject that was ever spoken of in our family.

"My mother thought she should warn me in case Colonel Fitzwilliam had also discovered the truth. Clearly she felt it would ruin my chances with Isabella and hoped I could do something to avert disaster."

He sighed and walked away to look out of the window, and Caroline took the opportunity to pour out a cup of tea, which he accepted gratefully as he returned to sit opposite her.

He continued, his tone reflecting his forlorn mood, "I knew then that my suit was almost hopeless; I am aware of Colonel Fitzwilliam's work on social reform, and I knew the very thought of such a connection would be abhorrent to him and no doubt to you and Isabella. I decided I could no longer accept my stepfather's money and went to London to make enquiries about obtaining employment. I have contacts in France, where I spent some years studying art; I hoped they would help me. I wanted, above all, to be able to tell you, Colonel Fitzwilliam, and Isabella that I was no longer beholden to Mr Henderson; that I had no further need of his tainted money, and would work to earn a living in my own right.

"When I returned to London, however, I found Colonel Fitzwilliam's letter waiting for me. I knew then it was hopeless to attempt to persuade you.

"But, I came here today to tell you what I had done and, through you, Isabella. Even though what I do with my life is no longer relevant or important to her, I could not bear to feel she did not know the truth."

Caroline rose and went to sit beside him; she was filled with sadness and compassion for his undeserved suffering. "Mr Bentley, please let me say that it *is* important to us, all of us, to know that you have taken steps to establish yourself independently of Mr Henderson.

"I shall certainly tell Isabella and I know she will be very pleased to hear of it, for she truly regards you as a friend, and we will pray for the success of your venture in France. I hope too that you will be able to assist your dear mother as you intend to do."

He seemed a little more cheerful and, taking her hand, kissed it as he made his farewells, asking only that she convey his regards to Colonel Fitzwilliam and Isabella. As Caroline watched him leave, the tears she had fought hard to hold back finally spilled down her cheeks. Caroline's romantic heart felt deeply for Mr Bentley and Isabella; nothing would convince her that their separation had been entirely justified.

❦

On the following Sunday, Isabella returned from Pemberley with Emily, who broke the news she had been keeping to herself for some weeks now, not wishing to intrude her own plans into the whirlpool of emotions that had swirled around the family.

Until that morning, only Mr Darcy and Elizabeth had known that Emily had accepted a proposal of marriage from the Reverend James Courtney, Rector of Kympton. On arriving, Isabella had run upstairs to her room, leaving her mother and aunt alone.

When she heard the news, Caroline was speechless.

Never had she imagined that Emily would consider marriage again after the agony of her passionate and tragically short experience with Monsieur Paul Antoine. Caroline would never forget those terrible days when her sister had left her home to marry and care for the man she loved, a man she knew to be dying of tuberculosis.

But here she was, smiling as she said, "Caroline, are you not going to wish me happiness?"

Her thoughts wrenched back to the present, Caroline said, "Of course, I wish you every happiness, but dear Emily, are you sure? Do you love him? Can you love him as you loved Paul?"

Emily smiled. "Caroline, I could not love anyone with the same devotion I had for my dear husband. It was the first and most absorbing passion I had ever known. Not a day passes without my recalling him, nor can I ever reclaim the loss I suffered when he died. It would be deceitful to pretend that I would ever feel the same again for any other man.

"But James is a good, kind man and we share many interests, not the least of which is a common desire to do whatever we can to help the poor people and especially the children of this parish. I respect and value his goodness and the affection he has shown me. We understand and esteem one another and I know it will be easy to love him."

Caroline had bitten her lip, not wishing in any way to hurt her sister's feelings, but a marriage without the deepest love, to however good and kind a man, seemed to her unthinkable.

Emily, seeing her struggle, said gently, "Do not be disappointed for me, Caroline; I have known the best, most enduring love in marriage, nothing will ever dilute that joy; perhaps it is now my turn to give some happiness in return."

Caroline embraced her sister, hoping desperately that she was right.

The wedding was to be in October with Isabella as bridesmaid. There was little time to worry about anything else in the next few weeks, which, to Caroline's way of thinking, was indeed a blessing.

But, in spite of the bustle around her, Caroline found time to visit Rebecca Tate and suggest that they call on Mrs Henderson at Newland Hall. It was something she had intended to do ever since Mr Bentley's visit. She confessed to Rebecca that she had felt guilty at having for so long ignored the woman who most needed and deserved their support.

Now the news was out about her husband's activities, the unfortunate Mrs Henderson and her daughters had to suffer all of the opprobrium and soon found they were ignored by most of their neighbours and acquaintances. Those who had milled around them, enjoying their wealth and hospitality, were reluctant to be seen in their company now.

"I should like very much to show her that while I find her husband's activities deplorable, I do not regard her as being corrupted by his deeds. She is a sad, unassuming woman and deserves our compassion rather than censure," said Caroline and Becky agreed.

Having ascertained that Mr Henderson was away in London seeing his lawyers, they made an appointment to visit Newland Hall and were immediately asked to afternoon tea.

The family was to leave Derbyshire at the end of Autumn, but Henderson had other matters on his mind. A summons to appear before a magistrate had interfered with his plans. Exposure and dishonour seemed imminent. Quite clearly, these were the very reasons for their departure from Newland Hall.

But none of this seemed to concern a delighted Mrs Henderson, as she greeted the two ladies with such obvious pleasure that Caroline was glad indeed that they had come.

A simple woman of very modest means, who had for the sake of her son and her stepdaughters concealed the ugly truth about her husband's guilt for so many years, it seemed as though she had now been liberated from her own.

Though nothing was said directly about the matter, the openness with which Mrs Henderson conversed for an hour or more, whereas before she had been circumspect and cautious in everything she said, was astonishing.

When they rose to leave, so touched was Caroline by her sincerity as she thanked the ladies for coming, she could not help feeling some measure of shame that she had left it so long.

❧

Some days later, when they were alone in the music room, which they both loved, Caroline told her daughter of Mr Bentley's visit and of the actions he had undertaken to free himself from his dependence upon Mr Henderson.

Isabella listened, saying not a word.

"He was very keen that you should know what he had done and why he had done it. I gave him my word I would tell you," said Caroline.

The room was very quiet.

Isabella did not respond immediately; she was looking out at the setting sun, which had just dipped behind the hills, leaving the scene below them bathed in the strange half light that softened the sharp edges of the peaks and concealed the dark clefts and gorges she knew were there. Turning to her mother, she smiled, a rather melancholy little smile, and said, "I am glad that he has done it, Mama, and happy indeed that he cared enough for our good opinion and sensibilities to have come here to tell you of it. It is as I always thought: Mr Bentley knew nothing of their crimes and is entirely without guilt in this matter."

Caroline nodded, agreeing, but said nothing.

Isabella did not ask if he had said anything more, and Caroline did not tell her that Mr Bentley had declared that he had loved her dearly and was desolated by her refusal to marry him.

"I did not think it would help to tell her," she said, and Fitzwilliam agreed. They hoped very much that Isabella would soon begin to recover from the unhappy episode, now it was unlikely they would see Mr Bentley again. They would have been surprised indeed had they seen the words Isabella wrote in her diary that night.

Having recounted the story of Mr Bentley's visit, as her mother had told it, she wrote:

I know now that I was not mistaken in Mr Bentley when I judged him to be a good man; indeed he is even better than I had supposed him to be, for all his actions were undertaken without hope or expectation of any benefit to himself.

His persistence in liberating himself from the taint of his stepfather, after he had received Papa's letter in which I had indicated that I would not marry him, speaks to me of a nobility of spirit, which I had not envisaged.

Perhaps, if he had told me himself and declared his feelings when we stood together beside the river in Dovedale, on that glorious afternoon, I may well have said yes, and then, once pledged, nothing would have made me retract, for he is without doubt one of the best men I have met and has nothing at all to be ashamed of.

How different would our lives have been then!

END OF PART THREE

MY COUSIN CAROLINE

Part Four

Chapter Fourteen

CAROLINE'S LIFE CHANGED QUITE SUBSTANTIALLY in the years following
her sister's marriage to James Courtney, though not in any way because
of it. Several matters combined to effect the transformation.

Those who knew Caroline knew also that the birth of her two youngest
children, Amy and then James, had helped heal her bruised heart. While
neither would replace her beloved Edward, they kept her busy, and their affection brought the warmth of a child's unquestioning love into her life again.

There was also the realisation of the depth of suffering endured by her
cousin Emma, whose marriage had been destroyed from within, by the actions
of a selfish and cruel husband. While marveling at the extent of Emma's
courage and magnanimity, Caroline took some satisfaction from the fact that
she had played a part in the unmasking of David Wilson.

It had come about almost by chance. The Tates had invited the colonel and
Caroline to dinner, and afterwards, while Rebecca and Caroline were engaged
in a game of cards, the gentlemen—Colonel Fitzwilliam, Jonathan Bingley, and
Anthony Tate—had been involved in a discussion on the imminent passage
through the Parliament of the Ten Hour Day legislation and the Public Health
Act, for which they had campaigned over many years.

Rather bored with the card game, Caroline was paying some attention
to their conversation when she heard the name of David Wilson mentioned.

Jonathan Bingley had pointed out that Wilson had shown scant interest in the debates on these vital reform bills.

"He has also been seen quite often in conversation with Lord XXX___, and there are some who believe he is about to defect to the Tories and vote against the Public Health Bill," he said, and his companions well nigh exploded in expressions of outrage and disbelief.

"That's impossible—the Wilsons have been Reformists since the days of William Pitt!" said Tate.

At this point, both Becky and Caroline put down their cards and turned to listen more closely. Both women had an interest in the conversation.

David Wilson was one of two brothers in the Parliament from a prominent family of Whig lawyers, but even more important for Caroline was the fact that he was the husband of her cousin Emma Bingley.

They had been married some ten years, had two pretty daughters, and Mr Wilson, a personable and ambitious member of Parliament, was said to have a bright political future ahead of him. His elder brother James, a quieter, less ostentatious gentleman with strong Reformist credentials, was already a well-respected member of the government.

Neither Becky nor Caroline had found it easy to accept that the younger Mr Wilson was a potential defector to the Conservatives.

But there was no mistaking the concern expressed by Jonathan Bingley and by Anthony Tate, who, being even more suspicious about Wilson's motives, promised to have his reporters investigate the man.

"It should not be difficult to discover if he has been approached by the Tories and if he has, the plot should be exposed," declared Tate.

Caroline was perturbed. She wondered what, if anything, Emma knew of her husband's activities, and when they were taking coffee, she had approached Jonathan Bingley, hoping to find out.

"Jonathan, forgive my asking, but I could not help hearing your comments about Mr David Wilson, your brother-in-law, and I wonder, is it possible that Emma is ignorant of these matters?" she asked.

Jonathan Bingley, whose natural predisposition was to be obliging, had answered her with disarming honesty.

"I have very little reason to believe that my sister is aware of anything concerning Mr Wilson's parliamentary activities, Cousin Caroline. As you know, she lives mostly at Standish Park in Kent and comes only occasionally to

London and not at all to Westminster. I think I could safely assure you that she knows nothing of these developments."

Caroline did know that, unlike Colonel Fitzwilliam, who had encouraged her to attend the Parliament whenever he was speaking, Emma's husband did not welcome her attendance and, except on formal occasions when wives of members were invited to attend, Emma Wilson took no part in her husband's political life. She recalled Emma saying as much in answer to a question about her attendance at an important debate.

"It appears that Mr Wilson does not derive any pleasure or benefit from our presence," she had said, with a little shrug of her elegant shoulders. "Indeed, he claims it puts him off—because he does not debate with the same degree of aggression if his mother and I are in the ladies' gallery."

Caroline had thought at the time that this was an odd thing to say, but had not pursued the matter, noting that Emma had not wanted to pursue the matter either. Clearly their attitudes differed. Caroline would not dream of missing such a debate if her husband was involved.

She proceeded to quiz Jonathan Bingley. "Do you really believe he intends to defect to the Tories?"

"Well, I can only say that there is a very strong suspicion in Whig circles that he may do so," had been his circumspect reply and he added, "However, I think, Cousin Caroline, we should not speak of this matter to anyone else until we are quite certain of the facts."

Caroline had agreed at once, but persisted with her enquiry.

"What if Mr Tate's men turn up some information? Would you do some-thing about it then?" she had asked, and Jonathan Bingley had said in a voice that was suddenly very grave, "That would depend very much on the nature of the material they uncovered. If it was clear that he had undertaken a course of action that was going to damage the government, I would certainly consider bringing it to the attention of the party whip. I believe it would be my duty to do so."

And there was no doubt in Caroline's mind that he meant it.

Returning home to Matlock, Caroline had repeated their conversation to her husband, whose disillusionment and anger were further inflamed by it. He expressed his displeasure in no uncertain terms.

"I have never had much time for young Wilson; he has always struck me as pretentious and vain, using the party and the Parliament to promote himself. He lacks any commitment to the cause," he had said.

"Now James Wilson is quite different; a thorough gentleman and a sincere reformist. Caroline, it is a great pity your cousin Emma did not marry him instead of that young coxcomb!"

"Fitzy!" Caroline had exclaimed, incredulous, only to have him reinforce his provocative remark with another, "It's true, Caroline, ask your cousin Lizzie; she knows that Mrs Bingley would have preferred Emma to have married James, but David was a handsome rogue and stole a march on his brother, I believe. I know him only slightly; he never showed much interest in the work of the party, unlike James, and from what I have heard, poor Emma is being badly deceived. It is well known that he drinks heavily, gambles himself into debt, and is slow to repay his creditors. It is common talk in the Parliament—the man's a disgrace and does his family no credit at all."

Caroline had been so shocked by what she had heard that evening, she had not been able to sleep at all well that night. Quite clearly poor Emma must not know all this; but if she did, what could she possibly do about it? Her thoughts turning over in her head had driven away all hope of sleep, and by morning, Caroline had been feeling quite ill and miserable.

Her own indisposition, a variety of domestic concerns as well as Amy and James going down with measles had taken her mind right off the subject for some weeks, until one afternoon, closer to Christmas, when Jonathan Bingley and his wife Amelia-Jane had arrived to see them.

Jonathan was a regular visitor to their house; being the local member, he frequently consulted Fitzwilliam about political and parliamentary matters. But Amelia-Jane, who was not by inclination politically active, came rarely, only to be sociable. Caroline could see, however, that this was not such a visit.

Jonathan's countenance gave very little away, except to signal his general unease, while his wife wore a look of such extreme outrage that Caroline wondered what it was that had so offended her. When they were all seated in the parlour, partaking of refreshments, the purpose of their visit and the reason for their extraordinarily grave demeanour was revealed. "I have just been with Anthony Tate at the offices of the *Review*," Jonathan had explained, "and I am told that the men who were assigned to investigate David Wilson have uncovered a good deal more than we anticipated."

As the rest listened, he added with some embarrassment, "His private behaviour appears to be almost as outrageous and irrational as his public life."

When Caroline and Fitzwilliam appeared bewildered, Amelia-Jane, taking over from her husband, had provided them with the details.

"Caroline, the man is not only a traitor to his party, he has consistently deceived and betrayed his wife and family. He has a mistress who runs an illegal gaming house in Chelsea, which he attends regularly. He is both a turncoat and an adulterer and is so deep in debt, he is in the clutches of a group of ruthless villains," she declared in what sounded very much like the tone of a moral crusader.

Amelia-Jane appeared to be even more outraged by Wilson's private immorality rather than his public betrayal of faith, but Jonathan hastened to add that both were equally reprehensible.

"He has certainly gone beyond the bounds of decency in his private affairs; I have no doubt that my sister will be desolated were she to learn the truth, yet his betrayal of his party is likely to bring much greater retribution upon him. Emma may forgive him, but his parliamentary colleagues will not," he said ominously.

Caroline was so shocked she could hardly speak. She listened as her husband asked how exactly these matters had come to light.

Jonathan's explanation was patiently given, but Amelia-Jane was far more precipitate and Caroline wondered at her vehemence. Colonel Fitzwilliam, who had asked for more details, was so appalled when they were provided, by either Jonathan or his wife or both, that he had risen abruptly from his chair and left the room.

When he returned, some time later, he was calmer and had addressed them gravely.

"Jonathan, he cannot be permitted to go unchallenged; it is beyond belief that he should be conspiring with the Tories to subvert the elected government. Wilson will have to be exposed."

"But how shall it be done without harming Emma and her children?" asked Caroline, appealing to Jonathan.

He was well aware of the need to consider Wilson's family and advised caution. "Before we act, however strong the principle, we must consider the effect exposure will have on his wife, his mother, and the two girls, Victoria and Stephanie, all of whom are innocent victims in this matter. There is also Mr James Wilson, who must be one of the most respected men in the Parliament. I do not believe we should embark upon any course of action that may destroy their lives."

Amelia-Jane was less circumspect. Wild for some kind of revenge, she interrupted, "But, Jonathan, if we do nothing, tell no one, will he not get away with it and probably do many more things that will only harm his family to a much greater extent?"

Despite her own feelings of abhorrence, Caroline had agreed with Jonathan. "I believe that we should proceed with caution. It is not our prerogative to undertake some moral crusade that will create much misery for so many innocent people. But I do agree that David Wilson cannot be permitted to carry on his activities with impunity."

At which point, Colonel Fitzwilliam had remarked, "I should very much like to know Darcy's opinion on this matter. I am angered by Wilson's hypocrisy and cannot claim to be without prejudice; I dislike the man. But Darcy hardly knows him at all, and has no particular political allegiance; he will be dispassionate and fair."

This prompted Caroline to suggest that the Darcys be invited to dinner and the matter of David Wilson be discussed with them before any further action was taken. That was agreed to be an excellent suggestion, and it had fallen to Jonathan, because he was their favourite nephew, to go to Pemberley and convey the invitation.

And so it had been arranged.

The events of the next few weeks seemed to take place at a heightened speed, each following upon the other with inordinate rapidity, creating such a confusion of thoughts and feelings as to render one's recollection of them utterly unreliable, as though they were scenes from some chaotic nightmare.

Caroline, in years to come, would attempt to forget many of the sordid scenes, the shocking stories which had emerged as Fitzwilliam and Jonathan Bingley had gone to London to acquaint James Wilson with his brother's situation. Their hope of confronting David Wilson himself had been dashed when, self-indulgent to the end, he had, on being forewarned, gone into hiding at the house of a friend, where he had shot himself, rather than face exposure in the Parliament.

But Caroline could not forget the day Colonel Fitzwilliam had returned with news of Wilson's suicide. It had been very close to Christmas, yet there had been no festive atmosphere in the house while they awaited Fitzwilliam's return from London. When he did arrive, the news he brought was so shattering, Caroline had gasped and sat down at the foot of the stairs. She had been numb and cold; but, thinking at once of Emma, she had felt only an immense sense of relief.

Apart from breaking the news, Fitzwilliam seemed unwilling to talk about the details, and it was some time later, when Caroline went to visit her sister Emily at the Kympton rectory, that she discovered the hideous story of David Wilson's demise and the even more shocking revelation of his ill treatment of his wife over many years, a secret she had hidden from most of her family.

Emily, now a mother of two children and an indefatigable worker for the poor of her parish, was closer to their cousin Emma than anyone else, and there was much that Emily knew which no other person had heard.

Her compassionate heart had given Emma some comfort.

When Caroline had learned what her sister had known, she had wept.

"Knowing how cruelly she was treated, the depth of her anguish, it is difficult to imagine that Emma could go to London, attend the funeral, and accept the condolences of strangers," she had said.

"Yet, for the sake of her children, her family, and her mother-in-law Mrs Wilson, whom she loves as she does her own mother, she went through it all with grace and decorum," Emily had replied gravely.

Caroline had found it incomprehensible.

Shaking her head, she had said, "I could not have done it, Emmy, not after such cruelty."

But Emily had pointed out that none of us is able to say what we could or could not do until faced with the moment and the decision.

"We have all known sorrow, Caroline: you, I, and Lizzie, each in our own way. None of us can claim that hers is the greater agony; all of us have borne the pain and survived. But where ours has been the result of sickness or accident, of misfortune or circumstances outside our control, poor Emma made a choice to marry David Wilson. Having discovered, all too late, her dreadful mistake, for she says she knew within weeks of her wedding that life with him was not what she had hoped it would be, she then determined that she alone would bear the consequences of her error of judgment. Hers was a life sentence, self-imposed, with little relief except in her two children; we can only be grateful that it lasted but ten years. It is a blessed reprieve."

Caroline had one more question to which she sought an answer.

"Emmy, did you understand why Amelia-Jane was so enraged as to be almost vengeful towards David Wilson? Did she also know of his cruelty towards Emma?"

Emily had smiled. "No, but she knows enough of his capacity for deception and betrayal; I learned last year that he had tried to seduce her when she and Jonathan were guests of the Wilsons at Standish Park. To her credit, she gave him short shrift and threatened to expose him, but it was a dreadful shock to her and she has never forgiven him. She has not told Emma, but I think she must have known he was capable of it."

There had been tears in Caroline's eyes as Emily spoke, tears of understanding and relief. Hearing the news of Wilson's ignominy and death, she had felt only relief and been concerned at her apparent callousness. Having spoken with Emily and learned more of the truth, knowing what her cousin Emma had been through, she now believed that hers had been an entirely appropriate response.

~❦~

The arrival of Charlotte Collins at Pemberley the following Summer, to spend some time with her dear friend Elizabeth, provided an occasion for all the ladies of the family to meet and exchange news and views, while their husbands talked inevitably of business and politics.

Elizabeth gave a party, at which the main topic of conversation among the ladies was the forthcoming marriage of Jane Bingley's widowed daughter Emma to James Wilson, her well-respected brother-in-law.

Jane was delighted. It was what she had hoped for with all her heart.

"He is, without doubt, one of the finest gentlemen I have met," she said and then had to admit, on being teased, that he was perhaps just a little less perfect than her dear Mr Bingley.

Elizabeth knew her sister's heart.

"They are so well suited, it is a pity they were not married to one another in the first place," she said and everyone concurred.

The wedding was to be at the church at Ashford Park in Autumn, and Emma's sisters Sophia and Louisa were excited at the prospect of being brides-maids. There was not one person in the room who would not have wished Emma, who was a great favourite in the family, every happiness.

Following Jane's happy news, it was Mrs Gardiner's turn; her son Robert was expected home soon. Having spent several years in the eastern colonies, where he had worked for a leading British trading house, Robert, it was hoped, would now have sufficient experience and skill to assist Mr Gardiner with the management of his own company.

"Mr Gardiner is looking forward to having Robert's help in running the business," Mrs Gardiner revealed. "He thinks it would be best if Robert took over management of the office in Manchester."

There was no doubting her excitement; she had not seen her son in many years and was busy making plans for his return.

Mr Gardiner, who had been working exceedingly hard all his life, had already been cautioned by his son Richard about doing too much and putting his health at risk. Richard had even approached Mr Darcy, to plead with him. "Please, Mr Darcy, I know my father takes your advice on most things. Please urge him to take a holiday from the business, else it will make him very ill indeed. He does not pay much attention to my warnings."

Mr Darcy, who was Mr Gardiner's closest and most trusted friend and partner in business, agreed to make mention of his son's concerns.

"I shall certainly speak to your father, Richard, but I cannot guarantee he will heed my advice any more than he does yours," he said and Richard knew this to be true.

A self-made man, Mr Gardiner was a very determined and meticulous businessman, with a penchant for doing most things himself.

Which was why it did not come as any surprise when Richard was summoned by his mother to Oakleigh, late one evening, to attend upon his father, who was having a great deal of trouble breathing and complained of severe pain in his chest. Reminding his father of all the advice he had received and rejected, Richard called in a colleague, a physician with special skills in the treatment of diseases of the heart. When he confirmed Mr Gardiner's condition and strongly recommended complete rest, Richard, with his mother's support, was able to insist with greater hope of success.

Mr Gardiner had to have some help in the running of his business until Robert returned, giving him and Mrs Gardiner a chance to take a holiday from work. Mr Darcy, whose advice had been most timely and could not be scoffed at, recommended Scarborough, where his family had repaired regularly for Summer vacations, and both Richard and his mother agreed it would be ideal.

But Mr Gardiner was loathe to leave his business without supervision at what was a particularly busy time. Trading was intensely competitive and any slackness could bring disastrous losses.

Mr Gardiner had always maintained close supervision of his company, and he set about making alternative arrangements in the hope of retaining some control over the situation, in the event of any problems.

His decisions were to have far-reaching consequences.

He began by surprising everyone when he sent for Caroline and asked for her help, but not before he had decided to appoint a man to assist Mr Upton in the Manchester office.

Mr Peter Kennedy came highly recommended from his previous employer, Mr Anthony Tate. He was well qualified in both accounting and the law as it related to trade and commerce and had worked also for Mr Tate's uncle, Sir Thomas Camden, helping to put his accounts in order after the death of his brother.

Mr Gardiner had decided that Peter Kennedy seemed exactly the sort of man he needed to help Mr Upton organise the office more efficiently, as Caroline had suggested, and had sent for him. Having taken an instant liking to him, he had offered Mr Kennedy the position and, upon his acceptance, invited him to call at Oakleigh Manor on the following afternoon to make the necessary arrangements.

When Caroline received a message from her father requesting her help in a business matter, she had assumed that it was probably a missing document or some urgent correspondence that needed her attention. Her father had come to depend more on her lately to attend to such matters, because, he said, she wrote so well and expressed his ideas much better than he could. Mr Darcy had commented favourably upon it too.

Caroline had been flattered, realising that in a competitive world, the manner of conducting one's business was as important for its success as the matter of the enterprise. Her father, a plain-speaking man of great business acumen, appreciated the niceties of expression and elegance of style that Caroline brought to her task, believing that it enhanced his company's standing among the ever-growing community of commercial entrepreneurs with whom they had to deal.

On arriving at her parents' house, Caroline was somewhat surprised to see an unfamiliar vehicle standing in the drive. Within, in her father's study, she found the owner of the curricle taking tea.

A man of around thirty years or thereabouts, Mr Peter Kennedy was immediately on his feet as Caroline entered the room, and Mr Gardiner introduced them.

"Ah, Caroline my dear, this is Mr Peter Kennedy, who is to help Mr Upton with the Manchester office, just as you suggested. You do recall, we decided he needed an assistant to manage the place better?"

Caroline could barely contain her surprise, and as Mr Kennedy bowed over her outstretched hand, she met her father's eyes with a quizzical look before making some polite response to the greeting.

So astonished was she at the suddenness of her father's action, it was a while before she felt sufficiently comfortable to say more than a few words to express her pleasure at meeting him. With Mr Kennedy sitting right in front of them, she was constrained from saying anything that might set her at odds with her father. She had certainly recommended the appointment of an assistant to Mr Upton—well here, said Mr Gardiner, was the very man.

As Caroline relaxed a little and helped herself to a cup of tea, offering Mr Kennedy some fruitcake, which he accepted with alacrity, her father proceeded with the explanation of his plan.

"Mr Kennedy, as I have already explained, my daughter, Mrs Caroline Fitzwilliam, will represent me whenever I am not available, for whatever reason. She has my seal of authority and will act in my interest and that of our partners in the company. You will, therefore, report regularly to her in my absence, and she in turn will keep me informed of the progress of our plans for the office at Manchester. I know you already understand how important it is for the office to be smoothly and efficiently run at such a time as this."

"Indeed, sir, I do," said Mr Kennedy, and Caroline noted that his intense blue eyes were possibly the only striking feature in an otherwise pleasant but homely face, whose openness and lack of guile was immediately obvious to her.

"I do agree it is absolutely vital to a business if it is to succeed in these very challenging times. I am completely committed to doing my very best to achieving your goal in this regard, and to this end, I shall take all my instructions from Mrs Fitzwilliam and assist Mr Upton in every way possible. You have my absolute word on that, sir."

Now that was quite a speech, thought Caroline, amending her judgment to include his very pleasing, well-modulated voice as another feature one might appreciate in this earnest young man. But, above all, he was seriousness itself and seemed eager to begin work.

Later, Caroline was to remark to her husband that if Mr Kennedy's work was as well organised as his speech was articulated, then her father would have made an excellent appointment indeed.

"He seems a keen and honest fellow, Fitzy, his references are numerous and uniformly good, his manners are impeccable without being irritatingly so, and yet, he is not puffed up with his own importance. My father appears to have been singularly fortunate in his choice," she said and Fitzwilliam promised himself a careful look at this paragon!

He had the opportunity to do just that when Mr Gardiner requested that they travel with the gentleman to Manchester and introduce him to Mr Upton and others in the office.

Mr Kennedy went away to collect his goods and chattels, which consisted of a small trunk of clothes and a large wooden box of books, and returned the following week ready and eager to undertake the journey to Manchester.

He had expected to take the public coach and was most grateful when told he would be travelling with Colonel Fitzwilliam and his wife. They found him a quiet and pleasant companion, who spent most of the journey reading, and when they broke journey at an inn, partook only of a light meal and tea. If his abstemious personal habits were any indication of his attitude to work, Mr Kennedy was probably going to be a godsend to Mr Upton, thought Caroline.

Upon reaching Manchester, they were welcomed by Mr Upton and his wife, who were happy to offer Mr Kennedy lodgings in their house. He was as pleased with his room as they were with his offer of rent, paid in advance. Mrs Upton was most impressed.

There appeared to be no grounds for any dispute between Mr Upton and Mr Kennedy on any of the important matters relating to the work he was expected to do and the general aims they shared regarding the organisation of the office.

Mr Kennedy showed an appropriate degree of deference towards the older man, appreciating his experience and loyal service to Mr Gardiner, while Mr Upton seemed genuinely pleased to have an enthusiastic young man with the skills needed to assist him.

It was, therefore, with a feeling of satisfaction that Caroline returned to report to her father that things had gone remarkably well between Mr Upton and his new assistant. Mr Gardiner, well pleased with her news, now felt able to pursue his intention, too often postponed due to pressure of work, of taking a holiday. It was something his family and his partner in business, Mr Darcy, had urged upon him for a very long time. To this end, Mr and Mrs Gardiner left for Scarborough, where they expected to spend some weeks before returning to Oakleigh, in good time to welcome home their son Robert.

In their absence, Caroline took time to go through the books her father had left in her charge, hoping to make herself more knowledgeable about aspects of the business of which she knew little. She felt the need to acquaint herself with the administration of the offices and, if Mr Kennedy was going to send her regular progress reports of his activities, she thought it essential that she should have a clear understanding of the enterprise.

As she did so, she was surprised to discover how well she enjoyed the experience. What had started out as a chore, undertaken out of a sense of duty to her father, was becoming an interest and soon she found herself looking forward to the task. Fitzwilliam would often tease her about her new enthusiasm for figures and accounts, but even he understood the purpose behind it.

Each week she would receive a batch of papers from the offices in London and Manchester, and her regular scrutiny of reports and accounts, as well as correspondence meant for her father, drew her deeper into the management of the business.

Mr Kennedy appeared to be working well with Mr Upton, the former submitting detailed reports every week, while the latter would send her occasional private notes, presuming no doubt upon his long association with her father, praising the work and industry of his new assistant.

He wrote:

I must thank you, dear Mrs Fitzwilliam and Mr Gardiner, from the bottom of my heart for sending me this exceedingly keen and hardworking young man.

Mr Kennedy is indeed a fine young man, being both knowledgeable and disciplined (for one without the other would never do), and he is a real help to me and of great benefit to the company.

Not only has he spent several hours organising a neat and tidy system for the filing of orders and bills, he has taken it upon himself, often in his own time, to train young Mr Jones in proper procedures. It was something I had always intended to do, but for which I never quite found the time.

He has made a great difference to the efficiency of our office.

And when our work is done, he returns to our home, where Mrs Upton is full of praise for his tidiness and punctuality. Amiable but quiet in

disposition and always prompt in payments, he is indeed the ideal lodger.
I must thank Mr Gardiner again for providing me with such an excellent
assistant. I could not have chosen better had I done so myself.

No wonder then that Caroline felt quite at ease as she wrote off to her father, assuring him that the office at Manchester appeared to be humming along very nicely and Mr Peter Kennedy was proving to be a veritable treasure.

At the London office, however, matters did not seem to be quite so satisfactory. Being still the head office of the company, much of the banking was done through London. Transfers of money to and from overseas suppliers and customers was a complex matter, which Caroline had hitherto left alone, believing that her father's trusted manager Mr Bartholomew would be in charge.

Which was why it had taken her so long to realise that there were, from time to time, seemingly inexplicable discrepancies in the accounts, which were submitted for Mr Gardiner's perusal.

When at last, feeling she needed some advice, she applied to her husband, he refused to believe that Mr Bartholomew could be involved in anything dishonest.

"Caroline, Bartholomew is one of your father's most trusted men; it is simply not possible that he would fiddle the accounts," he had said.

Caroline was not so sanguine. "But are you sure it is he? Is it not possible that some other employee could be responsible? Fitzy, it is happening too often to be a mistake or an oversight. I believe we must tell Papa and let him decide what to do. I shall make a note of all the discrepancies and show him how much appears to be missing. The individual sums are not large, but they do add up, and if nothing is done, it will only embolden the culprit and he will go on to commit even greater fraud. It must be stopped."

Fitzwilliam was both amused and impressed by his wife's tenacious pursuit of what may after all turn out to be only an accounting error. He was no accountant, however, and said as much to Mr Darcy when they met.

"I must confess I cannot understand how Caroline has become so interested in the business, Darcy; she is completely engrossed and spends a great deal of time following up obscure clues and small amounts of money, until she is quite certain the accounts are correct. I doubt I should have had the patience or the skill."

Mr Darcy had laughed, "I am quite sure you would not, Fitzwilliam. But Caroline is her father's daughter, meticulous and particular in everything she undertakes. I have no doubt at all that if she believes there is something wrong with the accounts, then there is; she will pursue it until she uncovers the cause, and if that search reveals that there is fraud being committed in the London office, Caroline will find the culprit."

The return of Mr and Mrs Gardiner from Scarborough, followed soon after by the arrival of Robert, threw everyone in the Gardiner household into an unusual state of confusion.

Mr Gardiner looked rested and fit, while Mrs Gardiner was eager to have everything in readiness for her son. Rooms were aired and cleaned, furniture polished, and the finest linen brought out. Butchers and green grocers were alerted that their best produce was required; everything had to be just right for Robert. He was her youngest and she felt a special responsibility for him. Returning after several years, Robert would need to be introduced over again into the society he had left as a rather shy and callow young man, which meant dinner parties and family gatherings in every home.

All of this meant that Caroline was not able to convey to her father, with an adequate degree of seriousness, the disquiet she had felt about the accounts from the London office. She had made notes and marked documents for his attention, but Mr Gardiner, who had so enjoyed the rare pleasure of being away from the business without any of the usual anxiety, was in no hurry to revert to the routine.

Besides, Robert was coming home.

⁓ᲥᲥ⁓

The family welcomed Robert Gardiner back with warmth and affection. Having missed him terribly, his parents, especially his mother, had completely forgiven the errors of judgment that had necessitated his departure for the colonies and were prepared to put their hopes in him for the future. Much was expected of this young man.

Believing him to be now more mature and capable, his father was keen to give him an opportunity to prove himself, and his sisters and brother were delighted to discover that he appeared less shy, and more open and energetic than before. Robert himself seemed unaware of the expectations of his family and announced in a surprisingly casual manner his intention to accept a position with the Liverpool office of Mathesons, the firm for which he had worked in Ceylon.

Seemingly unconscious of his parents' hopes for him, he explained, "I was exceedingly honoured to be invited to take the position in Liverpool; it has hitherto only ever been held by a man from the district with many years of loyal service. Since I had no other expectation of employment on my return to England, it was not an offer I could refuse."

His mother immediately agreed, and even Mr Gardiner, though rather disappointed, allowed that this position would help his son become more familiar with the trading conditions and procedures in England and looked to the future with optimism.

What none of them had foreseen were the events of the next few months, which culminated in Robert's engagement and subsequent marriage to Rose Fitzwilliam—daughter of James and Rosamund Fitzwilliam, niece of Colonel Fitzwilliam—within the short space of two seasons.

Robert had made the acquaintance of the very attractive and personable Miss Fitzwilliam at a dinner party and fallen in love with her almost instantly. None of the young women he knew could compare with her for beauty, elegance, and accomplishment.

Emily, who as her brother's only confidante had been privy to the burgeoning romance between them over the Summer, had broken the news to her incredulous sister.

"Caroline, I think he means to write to her father first and ask Rose very soon afterwards," she said.

Involved in her family and her father's business—for Mr Gardiner had been so pleased with her organisation of his paperwork, he had begged her to continue—Caroline had had less time with her brother and no indication at all of Robert's intentions.

As the younger sister in the family, Emily had been closer to Robert, and since Caroline's marriage, when Emily had assumed the responsibilities of an elder sister, he had turned to her often for counsel. His confidence shaken by previous errors of judgment that had deeply disappointed his parents, Robert had sought Emily's advice on the matter of Rose Fitzwilliam before proceeding to approach her father. Having courted her through the Summer, he was ready to propose but was unsure of the response he would get from the lady in question and her father.

"I have never proposed to a lady before," he had confessed, adding that Rose was so beautiful, he felt unworthy of her and worried that he may not be considered suitable by Mr Fitzwilliam, who was expected to succeed to his ailing brother's title in the very near future.

Emily had attempted to reassure her brother that neither Miss Fitzwilliam's beauty nor his own occupation should be a reason for any objection. She had sent him away feeling buoyed by her encouragement and sound advice.

"He was unduly concerned that the Fitzwilliams would look askance at his long exile in the colonies and the fact that both Robert and Papa made their living entirely through commerce," she revealed.

Caroline, who was as yet unable to absorb the shock of the news she had just received, asked, "Emily, do you mean to say Robert, who has never been in love before, having only just this minute returned from the colonies, has within the space of one season, fallen in love with Miss Fitzwilliam and means to marry her before the year is out?"

Her sister had an amused smile whilst she nodded and replied, "Indeed, it does seem rather sudden, but it is not unlike a certain Colonel, who fell in love with someone I know within a few days of returning from the colonies and arriving in Derbyshire."

Caroline was outraged at the comparison,

"But Emily, *he* had known our family for many years and corresponded with Papa regularly. All of us and Cousin Lizzie knew him well. Rose Fitzwilliam's parents, on the other hand, know nothing of Robert and as for their disapproval of Papa making his living out of commerce, let them look to their own relations, Fitzy or Mr Darcy, who are his partners."

Clearly incensed by the implications of snobbery, she continued, "Fitzy maintains that without the valuable contribution made by men like Papa and others in trade and commerce, England would not have enjoyed the prosperity she has today. I have heard Mr Darcy say it too—'trade is the life blood of modern England,' he said the other day.

"The Fitzwilliams may have their family estate and no doubt enjoy its many comforts, but it contributes little to the common wealth of our nation, whereas trade feeds and clothes many millions of people."

It was clear to Emily that her reformist sister was not going to be easily persuaded that Robert was making the right choice in courting Rose Fitzwilliam.

She decided to try another, more acceptable, argument, "But think, Caroline, if Robert loves Rose and she accepts him, of which we cannot yet be certain, then he will have every reason to abandon this tedious job with Mathesons in Liverpool and take up Papa's offer of a position in his business. Would that not be a good thing?" she reasoned.

Caroline set down her work and looked directly at her sister.

"Has Robert told you he is prepared to do this? Can you be certain?"

"I cannot be certain, but yes, he has hinted at some such arrangement. I do know he is not averse to working for Papa," Emily replied.

"Not averse?" Caroline was affronted by the suggestion. "My dear Emily, poor Papa has been awaiting Robert's return in the hope of persuading him to take up some of his own work and offering him a partnership in the company. He will need to be a good deal more enthusiastic if he is to make a success of it. But, now there is Rose to consider. She is beautiful, accomplished, with very fine tastes and a great liking for things Parisian; how will she like living in Derbyshire with her husband running a trading company?" she challenged her sister who had no answer to this except to say that if Rose really loved Robert, she would not mind living in Derbyshire.

"It really is a matter for them, Caroline, but for Robert's sake, I confess I am pleased, for I have not seen him so buoyant since we said good-bye after that sad farewell in London, before he sailed for Ceylon those many years ago. He appeared so dejected; if falling in love with Rose means he will be happy and cheerful, I am delighted," she said and Caroline, realising that her sister was probably committed to support their brother, replied, "Indeed, Emily, and I am determined to be delighted too, for Robert's sake. If that is what he wants, I do hope Rose accepts him and makes him very happy. Do you know what Mama thinks? Does she approve? Has he told her yet?" she asked.

"I believe he hopes to tell Mama and Papa when he returns from Liverpool at the end of the week. He will write to Rose's father before then," said Emily.

Caroline recalled that her mother had remarked that Robert had been spending a great deal of time with the Fitzwilliams, but it had not occurred to her that it was more than a happy social coincidence. She knew Rose was a talented and attractive young woman but, for a variety of reasons, had never considered her a prospective sister-in-law.

"You could have knocked me down with a feather, Fitzy," said Caroline as she told her husband the news, whilst urging him to keep it to himself. "Robert has said nothing to my parents yet," she warned and Fitzwilliam laughed a very knowing laugh.

He had already heard from Mr Darcy that Rose Fitzwilliam's parents had been making anxious enquiries about Robert Gardiner and quipped that he could not understand why his brother James had not simply asked him.

"Perhaps he was embarrassed, on account of Robert being my brother," Caroline suggested. But her husband had other ideas.

"It would seem, Caroline, that when it comes to matters of matrimony, my brother and sister-in-law value the opinion of Mr Darcy more than they do mine. Well, I shall say nothing, but I am prepared to wager a considerable sum of money that young Robert, if he marries Rose, will be ruled by his wife and his father-in-law. They are both stronger and more determined than he is."

And with that pronouncement, Fitzwilliam appeared to tire of the romance of Robert and Rose and wanted to hear no more about it. Caroline, though a little disconcerted by his prediction and the certainty with which it had been made, decided to oblige him and said no more.

It was not, however, a prognostication she would easily forget.

Robert's declaration that he had resigned his position with Mathesons came a week later, and soon afterwards, there followed the announcement of his engagement to Miss Rose Fitzwilliam. If either Caroline or Mr Gardiner had expected him to take up his duties with the company immediately, they were disappointed.

Rose had planned an Autumn wedding followed by a long wedding journey in Europe, principally to Paris, which was her favourite city. Robert had never visited France, and his wife-to-be had insisted that this was a gap in his cultural education that had to be remedied at the earliest opportunity. Consequently, there was little time before and none at all after the wedding for Robert to be inducted into his role as the manager in charge of the Manchester office of his father's company.

It fell to Caroline, therefore, to continue with the work she had begun and, it has to be said, carried out to the complete satisfaction of her father. In her task, which was considerable, she was ably assisted by the experience and loyalty of Mr Upton and the almost unbelievable capacity for hard work of Mr Peter Kennedy.

Indeed, by the beginning of the new year, Mr Kennedy had become almost indispensable. Mr Upton and his staff relied upon him, Caroline trusted and respected him, and Mr Gardiner was absolutely delighted with the improvements he had made, which enabled the office to hum along with hardly a problem to speak of.

Caroline had hoped that following their return to Derbyshire, her brother's wife would involve herself with the charitable work in their communities. There was much to be done and volunteers were welcome.

The harshness of the new Poor Law, as it was administered by local authorities, the lack of schooling and health care for the children of the poor, and the cruel treatment meted out to those who fell foul of the law, even with the most minor misdemeanour, had created a whole class of people whose welfare depended totally upon private charity.

There were also the Irish immigrants: whole families fleeing the potato famine, some of whom had settled on the fringes of the moors around the district. In addition to their impoverished state, they suffered the hostility of the villagers, who regarded them as unwelcome interlopers.

The women of Pemberley and its environs had worked tirelessly throughout periods of prosperity and depression to bring some hope into the lives of these unfortunate people.

Caroline and Emily had hoped that with Robert and Rose settled at Oakleigh, where Mr and Mrs Gardiner had invited the couple to live after their marriage, they would be available to help them in their work in the community. In this too, they were to be sadly mistaken, for Rose, despite being almost completely free of any household duties, on account of the efficiency of her mother-in-law's large and capable staff, always seemed to have other things to do.

"I cannot believe she is too busy to attend a meeting of the hospital board or the school council, Mama," Caroline had complained when Rose, beautifully gowned, had come downstairs and asked to be excused from a meeting before driving off to visit her mother. With Robert away in Manchester, Caroline had hoped for his wife's assistance in a charity fair for the Irish children, but it was not to be.

"I would love to join you, Caroline," she had said, in a voice that lacked some sincerity, "but I did promise Mama I would spend the day with her. With Papa away in Derby, she will be quite alone."

It was not the first time, and Caroline's impatience had almost got the better of her, but seeing the expression on her mother's face, pleading wordlessly that she should say nothing untoward, Caroline held her peace.

Not when she met her sister, though, for she was most irritated by the fact that Rose made so little contribution to their work in the community.

"Emmy, I do believe it is time your dear husband preached another of his excellent sermons on charity and the milk of human kindness. But, let him ensure that our dear brother Robert and our sister-in-law Rose are present in church when he does so. I am heartily tired of waiting for Rose to do her share. Oh I know she is but recently married and they are still getting accustomed to their responsibilities in the community, but I cannot escape this dreadful feeling that neither Rose nor Robert has any sense of duty about the people of this district," she said, leaving Emily in no doubt of her feelings.

Emily understood her sister's anger. Caroline worked harder for the poor than anyone Emily knew, while continuing to assist her father with his business affairs. With two young children, a son who was growing up fast and a daughter who was of an age to be wed, she had her hands full, yet never failed to give of her time for the community in which they lived.

"Don't be too hard on them, Caroline, both Robert and Rose have grown up rather differently to the way we did," said Emily and even she was surprised by the sharp retort.

"Oh yes, indeed, in selfishness and the pursuit of personal pleasure, no doubt. I have no recollection that either Rose or her mother ever found the time to help with work in the parish and Robert, well, when was he ever at home?"

Emily was rather more charitable. "I am quite sure when Robert has settled into his job and Rose realises that, as Robert's wife, she has responsibilities to the people of the village, they will participate. I shall ask her to be on the committee at the library; Isabella helps but then she does a great deal of work at the hospital and doesn't have much time. Lizzie and I could do with some help. I am sure Rose would enjoy it; she is both intelligent and well read."

Caroline wished her sister luck. "She is indeed—educated and well read, and she has many interests and diverse talents, including art, music, and the like, but Charity does not appear to rate very highly on her list of priorities," she said and there was no mistaking her meaning.

Meanwhile, Robert had taken over the management of the Manchester office while he and his father considered the matter of a possible partnership. His initial response had been rather casual when his father had said, "You do realize, Robert, that it will have to be approved by all the partners, but, if you are keen and show that you are willing to contribute your time and effort to improve the business, I can see no reason why they will not agree."

"Oh indeed, Father," said Robert with barely a trace of anxiety, "I am sure it will all work out very well."

And for a while it did seem to be doing just that.

Robert began by spending some time with Caroline, as she explained the workings of the office and the role of each of its employees.

Afterwards, he went regularly to Manchester, where he seemed to get along well with both Mr Upton and Mr Kennedy. Mr Upton, who remembered him as a very young man, had welcomed him enthusiastically, hoping he would be like his father: keen and hardworking. He knew little of Robert's earlier problems or his present situation.

As for Mr Kennedy, in a brief report to Mr Gardiner, which Caroline read to her father, he detailed how he had spent some hours with Mr Robert Gardiner, explaining his own role, the systems he had introduced, and the training he had given the staff.

He concluded optimistically:

I cannot be certain of course, sir, but it seemed to me that Mr Robert Gardiner was interested in and pleased with the work I had done. I look forward very much to working with him for the further improvement of the company.

Both Caroline and her father were pleased indeed.

Then, quite without warning, some months after he had begun work, Robert complained that he was unhappy with Mr Kennedy's administration of the office and wished to appoint a man who would supervise the staff more closely and report directly to him.

"I am not convinced that Kennedy is able to maintain discipline, and since I am not at the office daily, I feel I need a man I can rely upon to do so and to keep me informed of the work that is going on. Someone who is not directly connected to the present staff," he had said, and while Mrs Gardiner thought that was reasonable enough, both Mr Gardiner and Caroline felt it was unnecessary.

"Discipline?" Caroline was amazed; she had no indication that there was any lack of discipline in the office.

"Whatever do you mean, Robert?" she asked, but her brother only talked vaguely of punctuality and too much conversation and drinking of tea in the office.

Mr Gardiner was unimpressed. "It would be an expense we do not need and cannot afford," he said, adding that Mr Upton was like a father to the younger lads and kept them working well.

"He may even be offended by the appointment," he added.

Caroline intervened to say the obvious, "And it may well cause some ill-feeling among the staff. It might appear that you do not trust them, Robert."

But Robert was determined, and soon afterwards, announced the appointment of a man recommended by his father-in-law, James Fitzwilliam, a Mr Caddick.

"John Caddick has had many years of experience in the textile industry; he is very familiar with the business of exporting cotton goods to the colonies, which is a growing part of our enterprise," Robert explained.

"I shall bring him round to meet you, Father, after which he will travel with me to Manchester."

Mr Gardiner seemed content to let him have his way, though he did warn of possible aggravation among the current staff.

To Caroline, his actions spelt disaster.

Having tried in vain to dissuade Robert, she begged her father to go with them to Manchester and reassure Mr Upton and Mr Kennedy that Caddick was not some sort of spy sent to observe and report on them.

"If you do not go, Papa, it will be seen as a vote of no confidence in Mr Upton and his staff—including Mr Kennedy, who has done such excellent work all year. It may well undo all the good we have achieved. "

Reluctantly, Mr Gardiner agreed and arranged to accompany Robert and Mr Caddick, if only to set Caroline's heart at rest.

On the day they were to travel to Manchester, Caroline had visited her parents early and was already leaving when Mr Caddick arrived complete with his luggage. She could not stay to take tea but was introduced to him by Robert as she waited in the hall for the carriage to be brought round to the front door.

Caroline's heart sank as she watched him come up the steps.

There was nothing about Caddick that she could point to which was unpleasant or awkward; indeed, he behaved in a perfectly proper manner when they were introduced, but Caroline took an instant dislike to him. It was no more than an impression, but it was enough.

He was taller than Robert and somewhat thickset, a powerful-looking man with prominent features and a low hairline, which she found most unattractive. While he was well spoken and clearly not uneducated, he walked with a swagger that Caroline found particularly disagreeable.

"He has neither the appearance nor the manners of a gentleman," she said later, complaining to Emily that Robert had clearly made a mistake in appointing him.

Declaring that he was delighted to meet her, Caddick had remarked that Mr Robert Gardiner had told him of his sisters' work for charity.

Caroline was struck immediately by the fact that Robert had probably neglected to mention her work for the company, helping her father and running the business in his absence. No doubt Robert would have been disinclined to admit that his sister knew more about the business than he did, she thought. Clearly Mr Caddick knew naught of that, or if he did, he did not set much store by it.

Caroline complained later to Emily, "I just cannot see him getting on harmoniously with Mr Upton and Mr Kennedy. As for the others, he will probably terrify poor old Mr Adams into an early grave, while Mr Selbourne and Mr Jones will detest him."

"Why do you say that, Caroline?" Emily asked, perplexed at her sister's vehemence.

"Oh I don't know, Emmy, I just feel it in my bones—he is not the right man for the job. He seems too self-important. Besides, I do not believe he will stay; the salary Robert has offered him is not large and he will soon find the office too restrictive for his ego. I am sure of it."

Emily pleaded that Robert should be given a chance to succeed. She was aware of her mother's desire to see him satisfactorily settled, now he was a married man. Mrs Gardiner had hoped to see her youngest son redeem his reputation by making a success of this position and go on to enter into a partnership with his father.

"I know our parents, Mama especially, are very anxious that he should do well in the business. If this Mr Caddick can help him achieve that, it will be good for Robert and for all of us. You do not agree, Caroline?" Emily seemed puzzled.

Caroline shook her head, "I cannot see Caddick helping Robert to succeed in the business. Mr Caddick is the type of man who is solely concerned with promoting his own interest and will use Robert to achieve his ends. I think Caddick knows more about matters of business than our dear brother; he will probably end up running the place as he sees fit and Robert will not be any the wiser.

"Sadly, he will probably bully and unsettle the rest of the staff, who have given Papa loyal service, and if we lose them, Papa, Robert, and the business will be in deep trouble."

Caroline's pessimism was unusual; usually clear-sighted and willing to look for a brighter prospect, she was the one they relied upon in times of trouble and uncertainty. This time it was quite different and Emily was seriously concerned.

If her sister was proved right, life for all of them, and especially for their father, was not going to be easy in the ensuing years.

Chapter Fifteen

OTHER MATTERS OF SOME SIGNIFICANCE concerning her younger children so concentrated Caroline's attention over the next few months
that she had little time to worry about Robert and Mr Caddick.

She did, however, find time to draw her father's attention to another
discrepancy in the accounts, this time from the office in Manchester.

The sum was larger than before and Mr Gardiner took the matter sufficiently seriously to instruct Robert to investigate it forthwith.

"I have asked him to speak in confidence with Mr Kennedy and have the
accounts checked without alerting the staff," he said and Caroline was reasonably satisfied that something would be done. It was almost a year later when she
discovered how little had in fact been accomplished by her brother.

Within her own family, Caroline's life was being complicated by young
David's desire to join the cavalry, an ambition which so distressed his mother,
she demanded that Colonel Fitzwilliam and Mr Darcy should both reason with
and counsel her son, so he may be dissuaded from this reckless course.

No member of her family had been in the wars since her grandfather on
her mother's side, and everything she had learned of it from her mother and
her husband, who had been in the campaign against Bonaparte, served only to
turn her against the idea. Having lived through a period of prosperity and peace,
Caroline could not conceive of a son of hers being trained to kill and maim,

quite apart from his own exposure to danger and death it would undoubtedly involve. The rumblings of another possible war in Europe, heard in the distance, made her even more uneasy.

Then there was Isabella, who was almost twenty-seven and showed no interest at all in marriage. Caroline was anxious for her.

Since the departure of Mr Philip Bentley some years ago, there had been one or two perfectly presentable and materially quite eligible young men who had seemed interested, but Isabella had made it plain that she was not. Devoted to her work with Emily at the hospital at Littleford, where she took special care of the children, she seemed serenely happy and fulfilled, and urged her mother not to concern herself about her lack of a husband. Matrimony, she declared, was furthest from her thoughts.

That was before the arrival of Doctor Henry Forrester as assistant to Dr Gardiner. A serious young man with a single-minded dedication to his profession, most young women would probably have found Henry Forrester rather dull and unprepossessing. While he looked pleasant enough, being tall with strong, clean-cut features, he had the type of disposition that was far more likely to be appreciated after many months of social intercourse, rather than on a casual acquaintance. Unlike most other young men, he didn't dance or play an instrument and spent most of his leisure reading and taking long walks in the woods around Pemberley.

Both Emily and Richard had nothing but praise for him, and Isabella, who took so much satisfaction from her own work at the hospital, found in him a sympathetic and appreciative colleague with whom it had become a pleasure to work.

"Miss Fitzwilliam, forgive me if I seem condescending, I certainly do not mean to be, but I have been astonished to discover that you have no formal training in nursing. I have to admit that I have never met anyone who was so good at nursing the sick, particularly the children, as you are," he had said after he had been only a few weeks at the hospital, observing her work.

Isabella had thanked him, pointing out that she had learned a great deal from her aunt Emily. Pleased to be praised, but paying not too much attention to his words, she had not taken a great deal of notice of Henry Forrester until Cassandra Gardiner's youngest daughter Laura Ann had been taken ill. With her husband away, Cassy had been desperate, depending entirely upon the skill and care of Doctor Forrester and the devoted nursing of Emily and Isabella.

During those frightening days and nights, when Laura Ann's life had hung in the balance, Isabella, who had hardly ever left the child's bedside, discovered in Henry Forrester compassion and dedication similar to her own and, in the months that followed, came to believe that he was the one man she could possibly marry. His affections were plainly engaged sooner even than hers, and the couple decided to seek her parents' blessing.

Though delighted with the news, Caroline could not shake off the memory of her daughter's warm friendship with Mr Bentley and worried, lest in marrying Henry Forrester, she was taking second best.

Unable to put the question directly to Isabella, it was to Emily she turned for advice.

"Do you think Bella is really in love with Dr Forrester?" she asked, and Emily smiled, and said, what was for Emily, a very unusual thing.

"My dear Caroline, I know you are the most romantic of creatures, but even you must admit that there are some marriages which are built not upon passion but on the assurance of mutual affection and respect. Think of all those you know among our friends and family; do you really believe every one of their marriages was sustained by love alone?"

"Oh Emily, of course I know that to be true, and more's the pity that for some women there is no other way. Self-interest is more often than not the motive, but, Emily, I should hate to think that my daughter was being married without the deepest love," she replied.

Emily reassured her that Isabella was as much in love with Henry Forrester as she was ever likely to be with anyone.

"I have watched them together at the hospital; he is a fine young man and she has the highest esteem and admiration for him. I am sure he loves her and they share many common ideals; now, that surely is a good foundation for marriage, Caroline. We cannot all be as fortunate as you, my dear sister."

Caroline, believing—incorrectly as it turned out—that her sister had been offended by her insistence that marriage should be based only upon deep and abiding love, drew back.

Not wishing to hurt Emily in any way, she declared that yes, she was probably right and Isabella did care deeply for Doctor Forrester.

"I had meant to ask Cassy about him, because Richard would know him well, but if what you have observed is true, then maybe such an approach is unnecessary."

Yet, Caroline could not resist mentioning Dr Forrester when she met Richard and Cassandra at Pemberley later in the week. She had felt some awkwardness about introducing the subject and was grateful when Mr Darcy asked a question about the hospital, giving her the chance to ask Richard about his assistant.

Unaware that his sister was seeking information about a prospective son-in-law, Richard was effusive in his praise, of both Henry Forrester's medical skills and his dedication to his patients.

"I have no doubt that we owe our daughter Laura Ann's life to Henry Forrester. Cassy will not hear a word against him," he said and his wife agreed with enthusiasm.

"Indeed, I will not. Henry Forrester is quite the best doctor I know apart from my dear husband and is surely a very good man. His modesty conceals the extent of his goodness and his remarkable skill. We are so very fortunate to have such a man working at Littleford."

It seemed to Caroline that praise was all she was ever going to hear about Henry Forrester. When Fitzwilliam revealed that he had received a letter from Doctor Forrester asking for Isabella's hand in marriage, Caroline had not yet been convinced that she liked the idea of the match. Her husband, who knew her every whim and mood, detected a certain coolness in her response to the news and asked, "You do not seem very enthusiastic, my love. Have you some objection to the man?"

Caroline responded at once, "Oh no, Fitzy, what is there to object to in him? Isabella loves him and so, it seems, does everyone else. I have not heard a single word against him from anyone I know. No doubt he is a man of exemplary character. Emily certainly thinks so and she is better placed to judge him than I am," she declared.

But he was not deceived.

"Certainly, but I see no outbreak of happiness that Isabella is to marry." He persisted, "You have complained before that she would show no interest in any other young men. I know you have been anxious about her remaining single."

"I confess I have and I *am* pleased she is to marry, but Fitzy, do you not see that she has shown none of the excitement and sparkle one expects from a young woman in love? Compare her demeanour with that of Cassy when she was engaged to Richard, and Isabella does not appear at all excited by the prospect," she said and he smiled as she continued. "When I recall my own feelings, I cannot make her out, for she is so matter-of-fact about it, I am concerned that she may not be in love at all," she complained.

Fitzwilliam laughed then and, putting his arms around her, reminded her that their daughter was twenty-seven and a somewhat more dignified young lady than she, Caroline, had been at sixteen, when they had discovered they were in love. He recalled only too well the exhilaration and happiness they had experienced; it had filled their lives and spilled over into everything they did and infected everyone they met with a strange euphoria.

The memories were sufficient to make them pause in their consideration of Isabella's feelings and concentrate for a while upon their own. Caroline had never been in love before she had discovered her tender feelings for the colonel; the sheer delight of knowing that she was as deeply cherished by him had completely absorbed her throughout the year that followed, while they waited to be married. She saw herself as the most fortunate of women, and nothing that had happened since her marriage had changed her mind. Theirs was an exceptional love, she believed.

For Isabella, she had only one wish. That she too should know similar joy. When they had met Mr Bentley, whose affection for Isabella was undeniable, Caroline had hoped they might become engaged. She was certain they were right for each other. Isabella had seemed as though she may well accept him, yet, it had all come to nothing.

With Doctor Forrester, Caroline could not be sure; she confessed she had her doubts.

But Isabella *was* sure and that was all that mattered, Fitzwilliam told her, and Caroline finally agreed that it was. While she remained a romantic at heart, Caroline's judgment had sharpened sufficiently to let her see the worth of a man like Henry Forrester. Clearly, Isabella had seen it too.

⚬⚬⚬

Between the engagement of Isabella and Dr Forrester and their wedding, Caroline was drawn, albeit reluctantly, into the problems surrounding her father's business. It was occasioned by the receipt of a confidential communication from Mr Upton, sent with the intention of acquainting her and Mr Gardiner with the unsatisfactory state of affairs at the Manchester office.

He wrote:

Dear Mrs Fitzwilliam,

I hope you will forgive me for taking the liberty of addressing this to you, but I am wary of giving offence to Mr Robert Gardiner, who may see this letter if I were to direct it to Mr Edward Gardiner's office.

While I make no specific complaint on my account, I am compelled to bring to your attention, and that of Mr Gardiner, the deterioration of conditions in the office since the appointment of Mr Caddick.

Hinting that he was less concerned, being close to retirement himself, he wrote at length of the attitude of harshness and distrust that Caddick showed to the rest of his staff. Mr Adams, he said, was preparing to retire and move away to the country to live with his son since he could no longer tolerate the constant aggravation and criticism.

As for Messrs Selbourne and Jones, they were younger and better able to cope, but the worst news for Caroline was that, according to Mr Upton, Caddick seemed bent on removing Mr Peter Kennedy.

He wrote:

I have been looking forward to the day when Mr Kennedy would take over from me and continue the excellent work he has done, but that would all be set at naught were he to be dismissed on a whim by Mr Caddick.

Caroline rose, folded the letter, and put it in the pocket of her gown. It was clear to her now why Mr Upton had sent it express.

Hardly pausing to think further, she sent for the small carriage and set out for Pemberley. Colonel Fitzwilliam was in Bakewell on business and Isabella was with Emily at the hospital. Caroline wanted some sound advice and she could think of no one better to turn to than Mr Darcy.

At Pemberley, she was ushered into the saloon, where she found Mr and Mrs Darcy, the Bingleys, the Tates, and Charlotte Collins all having tea and discussing the imminent threat of war in Europe.

Caroline had heard Fitzwilliam speak of it, too; there was concern that England might be involved. Palmerston, it seemed, was about to take the country into an alliance with the old enemy, France, and conflict with Russia.

Mr Tate claimed to have information right from the heart of the foreign office. War, he said, was inevitable!

It was alarming talk, but at that moment, war was the least of Caroline's concerns. She needed to speak urgently with Mr Darcy and obtain his advice, before she took Mr Upton's letter to her father. Elizabeth, noticing her cousin's discomposure as she sat on the edge of her chair, not entering into any conversation, approached and Caroline begged her help to consult Mr Darcy privately about an urgent matter of business.

Elizabeth obliged at once and, having placed Caroline in a small sitting room where they could speak undisturbed, sent first a footman with tea and then Mr Darcy, who had been advised by his wife that their visitor was plainly upset about something concerning the business and needed his advice.

"I have not any idea of the matter, but it is clearly important, for Caroline is very distressed indeed," she had said.

When Mr Darcy entered the room, so relieved was Caroline to see him, she did not trust herself to speak. For the first few minutes, she was able only to hand him the letter, penned in perfect copperplate, and urge him to read it. Then she asked how she should break the news to her father. She watched Mr Darcy's solemn expression deepen as he read, his countenance darkening in anger.

He put down the pages and strode away to gaze out of the window, as if uncertain of how to respond. When he returned to her, he spoke gently, but with a degree of gravity that left her in no doubt that he was taking the matter seriously.

"Caroline, this is indeed a very grave situation. I agree with you that your father must be informed and some action taken without delay.

"We should otherwise be in danger of causing a complete disruption of work at the office, which we can ill afford at this time. There is a possibility that we may lose experienced and trusted employees, whose knowledge of the business is invaluable, and for a busy trading organisation, that would be a catastrophe."

Caroline nodded, relieved that he agreed with her on the urgency of the situation in which they found themselves.

"What do you suppose we should do, Mr Darcy?" she asked. "I am quite certain that were Mr Kennedy to be dismissed, we would soon lose both young clerks. Mr Jones and Mr Selbourne have learned much from him and have worked exceedingly well together; they are unlikely to stay on to work under the harsh regime imposed by Mr Caddick."

Darcy did not need convincing; he could see the problems such a development would create.

"Indeed, it would be impossible to employ and train an entire new staff whilst continuing to trade," he said, and Caroline intervened to add, "Yet, were the business to be temporarily closed, it could mean enormous losses and, above all, a loss of goodwill with customers."

Mr Darcy was genuinely surprised at the depth and extent of her understanding of the business. He had always been aware that Mr Gardiner respected Caroline's thoroughness and dedication in the work she did for him, but this was the first occasion upon which Mr Darcy had seen it for himself.

Leaving her alone for a few minutes, he went out of the room.

When he returned, having spoken with Elizabeth, he had a plan in mind. To Caroline's great relief, he suggested that on the morrow, Elizabeth and he would accompany Caroline and her husband to Lambton to meet with Mr Gardiner.

Caroline was aware that Robert and Rose were in London to attend a performance at Covent Garden. This revelation seemed to please Mr Darcy well. "That is most fortuitous," he said, "it will give us an excellent opportunity to discuss the matter openly and thoroughly with your father; Lizzie will come with us, principally to keep Mrs Gardiner company. We should make every effort to avoid alarming your mama. I am aware she is very keen that Robert should make a success of his work in the business. Were she to hear of these matters, she is likely to be very disappointed. Elizabeth has agreed to send a message to your parents advising them in an informal manner of our visit, so it may appear no more than a social call. Mrs Gardiner would not be surprised if we talk business with your father afterwards."

Caroline agreed and left having expressed her heartfelt appreciation of Mr Darcy's involvement.

Back home, she awaited Fitzwilliam's return from Bakewell. When she showed him Mr Upton's letter and explained that they were expected at Lambton on the morrow, he asked, "Does Darcy believe Mr Upton is right in his judgment of Caddick and his effect upon the staff?" to which Caroline replied with complete confidence, "I do not doubt Mr Upton for one moment and told Mr Darcy so. If he says Caddick is doing the wrong thing, I believe him and I am sure Mr Darcy does too. It is not so much a question of trusting Mr Upton—he has worked long and hard for Papa—it is more a matter of not trusting Caddick, of whom we know nothing at all. If he were to dismiss Mr Kennedy and we were to lose the services of both Selbourne and Jones as a consequence, the business would be in deep trouble."

In the years that Caroline and he had been married, Colonel Fitzwilliam had been frequently surprised by his wife. Her passionate involvement in his reform work when he had been a member of the Commons and her fearless capacity to speak up for those who had no privileges and no voice among the powerful had both astonished and delighted him, no less than the warmth of her love for him and their children. No task was too difficult, no duty too tedious, and she would undertake it with enthusiasm if the reward was that she pleased her family.

Yet, in all those years, he had not imagined he would see Caroline become involved as she was in running her father's business with such whole-hearted dedication.

There was no question in his mind that, on this occasion, she was right.

⁓⛧⁓

The early Spring weather was unusually temperate.

When the party arrived at Oakleigh, Caroline was surprised to see Emily alight from the carriage which had conveyed Elizabeth and Mr Darcy. It transpired that her sister had been taken into their confidence and had volunteered to accompany them in order to help keep Mrs Gardiner from suspecting that anything was seriously wrong.

"We thought it best if Lizzie and I took Mama for a drive to Bakewell; there is a Spring fair at the church and I want to get some tarts for tea," Emily said innocently.

The day was to be full of surprises.

Caroline had not expected her father to respond as he did on being shown Mr Upton's letter, nor, it seemed, did Colonel Fitzwilliam. Only Mr Darcy appeared unsurprised by Mr Gardiner's reaction to the news.

Knowing how much he had hoped for from Robert and understanding how disappointed they had both been at his earlier failures, Caroline had expected some degree of shock, perhaps even disbelief. Her husband had warned her to expect Mr Gardiner to defend Robert's appointment of Caddick and to suggest that Mr Upton, being set in his ways, was probably unfair to the new man.

But he did none of these things.

Instead, having read the letter, which he put down on his desk, he opened his bureau and took out a file of papers. From it, he extracted a document which he put before them—it was the report of Robert's investigation into discrepancies in the accounts of the London office.

It was both short and superficial.

As they read it, they could see quite clearly that Robert had in fact done very little to ascertain the truth of the matter, apart from the most cursory examination of the books. He had glossed over small amounts as "slight errors" and waived much larger sums on the grounds that there was insufficient evidence to prove anything against anyone. No one was held accountable; nothing was recovered; no action was recommended. Caroline, who had detected the discrepancies and alerted her father many months ago, was stunned.

She was not, however, surprised when Mr Gardiner said, "Well, you can now see why I am not shocked by any of the matters detailed by Mr Upton in his letter. I did not support the appointment of the man Caddick, I think you will bear me out on this, Caroline—I know you voiced your objections quite forcefully, but Robert paid no attention to either of us. I had only just handed Robert the responsibility for the Manchester office; it was not possible for me to override his authority on the very first question on which we disagreed. So I let him have his head. I half hoped he would succeed, but sadly as you see, he has not.

"Neither has he brought the matters in the London office to a satisfactory conclusion. I have now placed those matters in the hands of an investigator, hired by Mr Bartholomew. "

He made a point of saying, "Neither Robert nor Mrs Gardiner knows of this; only Mr Darcy has been kept fully informed; as one of my partners, he had to know. You need have no anxiety, Colonel Fitzwilliam," he added, with a smile, glancing at his son-in-law, who was also his partner. "Mr Darcy has looked after your interest very well. I did not wish to trouble you and Caroline again; I know you have been busy with other matters. I need hardly say it; it must be plain to you all that I am exceedingly disappointed in Robert. I had hoped he would return from the colonies with greater enthusiasm for playing his part in the family business. I had great hopes for him, but he still lacks confidence to make his own decisions; he looks always for someone who will take the responsibility off his hands. It is no way to conduct a business."

Turning to his daughter, he said, "I am most grateful to my dear Caroline for her help…" he began and when she tried to hush him, he took her hand in his. "No, my dear, you must not stop me saying this. No father ever had a better daughter. She has been more to me than either of my sons; she is strong and determined and, like a terrier, never drops a problem until it is resolved."

Caroline was so mortified, she ran out of the room, returning later with tea and biscuits for the gentlemen, by which time the discussion had turned to the very real likelihood of war in Europe.

After tea, the question of how to answer Mr Upton's letter was taken up by Mr Darcy. It was, he stressed, a very sensitive and urgent matter.

Mr Gardiner seemed to have it all worked out.

He asked Caroline to write to Mr Upton and send by express a letter urging him to be patient and ensure that Mr Kennedy was made aware that moves were afoot to remedy the situation.

"Assure him, please, my dear, that Mr Caddick has no authority to dismiss either Mr Kennedy or any other member of his staff, and neither has Robert, since they were all appointed to their positions by me and can only be removed by me or by my direction. Mr Upton should make this very clear to each of the employees without alerting Caddick at all. They must also resist entering into any conflict or argument with Caddick that may give him grounds for complaint against them.

"Meanwhile, I shall write personally to Mr Caddick, asking him to report to me here in Robert's absence. When he arrives, I shall make myself very clear about the extent of his authority.

"Caroline, I know you are going to be very busy with our dear Isabella's wedding, but I should like it very much if you would send for my lawyer, Mr Jennings. Ask him to call next Friday; there are certain matters upon which I have to instruct him," said Mr Gardiner gravely, adding quietly, "Mr Darcy, if you could spare the time, I would greatly appreciate your presence when he arrives."

Mr Darcy assured him that he would be happy to be present and Caroline went away to write a note to Mr Jennings.

When Mrs Gardiner, Emily, and Elizabeth returned to the house, they found the others seated on the terrace, enjoying the Spring sunshine as though nothing serious had disturbed them at all.

Two things occurred on the following morning, which threw their agreed plans into disarray.

Richard called at the house to advise Caroline that Mr Gardiner had been taken ill during the night; he assumed it was a recurrence of an incipient heart condition, exacerbated no doubt, he said, by overwork and anxiety about Robert and the business.

Caroline was immediately eager to go with him to see her father and, during the journey, confided in her brother about the troubles with which the business was beset.

"If only Robert had not appointed this man Caddick—everything was running quite smoothly until then," she grumbled. "It has created a problem where there was none."

At the mention of Robert, Richard recalled that their mother had received a message from him to the effect that their return from London would be delayed by a week because Rose had taken ill.

"It's nothing serious, probably a bad cold, but it is expected to confine her to bed for a few days and will delay their departure from London," Richard explained.

He was rather surprised that Caroline did not appear very concerned about the change in Robert's plans or his wife's indisposition.

In truth, she was rather pleased. Her father's illness and Robert's delayed return would necessitate a change of tactics, but it was to their advantage, Caroline believed.

Instead of summoning Mr Caddick to Lambton, as previously planned, the letter from Mr Gardiner, containing his strict instructions and admonitions, would now have to be delivered to him by Caroline. It was an errand she looked forward to with some relish.

Later in the week, after some hurried consultations with her father and Mr Darcy, Caroline left Fitzwilliam and Isabella to keep her parents company while she travelled to Manchester with Mr Darcy and her son David, who was down from college for the vacation.

Mr Upton, who had already received the reassuring note she had written him, welcomed them, and Caroline noted with satisfaction that in the office, Messrs Adams, Selbourne, and Jones all appeared to be in good spirits. Mr Kennedy, who came in moments after they'd arrived, was positively beaming. The explanation for this atmosphere of good cheer was not hard to find.

"Mrs Fitzwilliam, I have conveyed to the staff the message from Mr

Gardiner contained in your note to me," Mr Upton explained, and Caroline looked around and asked, "And Mr Caddick?"

"Mr Caddick has been away in Liverpool these two days. He is expected back this afternoon," he replied.

Mr Darcy had another appointment in town and David was hungry. Caroline left a message for Caddick.

"Please tell Mr Caddick I have a letter for him from my father," she said and they left to find an inn or an hotel where a meal might be had.

When Caroline returned to the office with David, Mr Caddick, emerging from behind the glass partition he'd had erected to separate his space from the rest of the staff, approached them with a most amiable smile. Caroline returned his greeting with a degree of cordiality she did not feel, but she was unwilling to give anything away before handing him her father's letter. When she had done so, he invited her into his office, but she did not follow him there; instead, she sat by the window looking out at the rather grimy view whilst he read the letter.

It was not a very long letter, but it was a particularly carefully worded and pointed communication, which made Mr Gardiner's meaning abundantly clear. Caddick took so long, he must have read it through at least twice, Caroline thought.

When he finally came out of his room, his countenance betrayed his injured feelings. Clearly, Mr Gardiner's words had been unexpected; he was angry but had probably decided it would not be in his interest to say anything adverse to Caroline. He seemed to want to pretend that Caroline knew nothing of the contents of the letter she had delivered to him, and she neither did nor said anything to contradict that impression.

The appearance of Mr Darcy, who had concluded his business in town, seemed to considerably increase Mr Caddick's discomfiture. Caroline noticed him mop his brow and loosen his collar. When at last he spoke, he said only that he would respond to Mr Gardiner's letter in due course.

It was time to leave and after speaking briefly with Mr Kennedy and commending him quite openly and warmly on his "excellent and detailed reports, submitted with unfailing punctuality," Caroline left the office with David and Mr Darcy.

Mr Upton accompanied them to their vehicle, wished them godspeed, and thanked Caroline from the bottom of his heart for setting his mind at rest. He asked also that she convey his gratitude to Mr Gardiner.

Mr Darcy reinforced his partner's words, "Mr Caddick has no authority to dismiss anyone, so if he gives Mr Kennedy or anyone else notice or tries to bully Mr Adams or either of the clerks into leaving, they should take no notice of him," he said.

"Indeed," said Caroline, enjoying the irony, "you are all employed by my father, except of course Mr Caddick, who was appointed by my brother and so may be dismissed by him!"

Looking up at the windows, David noticed Mr Caddick staring down at them even though he could not have heard their words. Seeing them look up at him, he withdrew.

When they were all within the vehicle and just about to drive away, Mr Kennedy came running down the back stairs and into the street. He handed Caroline a sheaf of papers, which he said may interest Mr Gardiner. Caroline thanked him, took them, and placed them in her case, promising to pass them on to her father when they returned to Derbyshire.

It was a promise she was unable to keep.

~❦~

Returning to Oakleigh, they found the household in turmoil.

Mr Gardiner had suffered another attack and was confined to bed. Richard had ordered that he was not to be disturbed under any circumstances. He intended to call in another physician for a second opinion.

"Doctor Gardiner has called twice today," said the parlour maid, "and Miss Emily," (she would always be Miss Emily to her mother's servants), "is here to stay all night to look after the master."

Mrs Gardiner, when she appeared, seemed so tired and worn out that Caroline decided to say nothing of their journey except to assure her everything had been accomplished as planned. Mr Darcy had advised this was the best course.

Having ascertained that her father was sleeping comfortably, Caroline returned home and, in telling her husband of the encounter with Mr Caddick, expressed the hope that things would settle down, now the staff had been reassured and Mr Caddick put in his place.

Fitzwilliam smiled and said, "I would dearly love to say you are right, my dear, but I doubt it."

Caroline was too tired to contest the point but hoped for the best. After all, she thought reasonably, everyone was now quite clear where they stood. It was unlikely that Caddick could do any damage now.

But she had calculated without the wily Mr Caddick and the response of Robert and his wife.

Their return from London had been further delayed by a problem with transport, caused by some roads in the south being flooded as the rivers burst their banks with the Spring thaw. When they arrived, Rose, apparently exhausted by the trying journey as well as her illness, went directly to her room, while Robert found time only to gather up a pile of letters, which he took away upstairs to read.

Caroline had arrived early to help her mother and relieve Emily, who had stayed all night again. It being Sunday, Emily had a number of parish duties to attend to.

Several hours slipped by and the house was quiet as the weary travellers slept undisturbed. Tea and other necessities had been delivered to their room, but there had been no sign of them since.

Caroline and her mother were seated together in the parlour, and Mrs Gardiner was asking about Isabella's wedding. She was eager to know everything about the arrangements.

"Isabella tells me it is to be at Pemberley," she remarked, and Caroline explained that, on hearing the news of Isabella's engagement to Dr Forrester, Elizabeth and Darcy had offered to host the wedding at Pemberley.

"That is so like them; both Mr Darcy and our dear Lizzie are so generous," Mrs Gardiner began, but before she could continue, they were startled by the sound of someone running down the stairs. The door of the parlour was flung open and Robert appeared, still it seemed in a great hurry, as though he was late for some appointment.

However, it was not Robert in haste, but Robert in anger that confronted them.

In his hand he held a sheet of paper, which Caroline immediately recognised as her father's letter to Mr Caddick, to which was also pinned a smaller piece of note paper. It was obvious to her that Caddick had sent the letter that had so mortified him to Robert with his own comments attached.

And Robert was furious! His eyes flashed as Caroline had never seen before, and his voice rose as he demanded to see his father. He was, he declared, outraged and insulted and wanted a good explanation, or else…

He did not enunciate what he would do but adopted a distinctly threatening tone. For a generally mild-mannered man with no record of precipitate action or intemperate language, it was quite a performance.

Unfortunately for Robert's newfound self-importance, neither his mother nor Caroline was impressed. He was most insistent that he had to see his father, but Mrs Gardiner told him quite firmly that he could not.

"Your papa is too ill to be troubled by such matters, and I must ask you to keep your voice down, Robert. Richard has said he must not be disturbed," she said and it was quite clear that she was seriously displeased with her son. Even as a child, he had never been permitted to get away with tantrums; she would certainly not allow it now!

Caroline was amazed at how determined her mother could be. Despite Robert's fuming and fulminating, she stood her ground.

"I will not have him badgered about matters concerning the business—that is for you to settle with Caroline and Mr Darcy. They know your father's wishes exactly," she said with a degree of finality that left Robert no hope at all.

Frustrated, he turned to Caroline. "I demand to know why my father wrote this letter to Mr Caddick. Who was it suggested this letter? Was it you, Caroline, or Mr Darcy? I am told he went with you to Manchester to deliver this letter, what business has Mr Darcy to interfere?"

At that point, Caroline felt constrained to speak. Having denied that she had anything to do with her father's letter, except to deliver it to Mr Caddick as instructed, she did feel the need to point out that Mr Darcy, like her husband Colonel Fitzwilliam, was in fact Mr Gardiner's partner in the company.

"Mr Darcy is as entitled as Fitzwilliam is to take an interest in the management of the company. He will not thank you for referring to his concern as 'interference,' Robert. Indeed, they have more right to intervene than you or I, since we are beneficiaries but not partners in the enterprise. Should the company suffer losses due to bad management, it is they, together with Papa, who will have to bear the brunt of it."

Robert seemed to have been temporarily silenced by her remarks and looked as though he was to about to leave the room when Rose appeared in the doorway. Her earlier languid aspect had vanished, as she strode over to Robert's side, accusing Caroline and the rest of the family of trying to undermine her dear husband.

Looking directly at Caroline, she declared, "It must have been Caroline's idea; it was you, was it not? I am quite confident dear Mr Gardiner would not have written such a discourteous letter to poor Mr Caddick, who has done much good work for Papa, unless his mind was poisoned. Why, he as good as tells him to mind his own business!"

Caroline felt she could not stand by listening to this irrational tirade without coming to her father's defence.

"Rose, that is unfair and you know it. Papa is never discourteous to anyone, no matter how angry he may be. If Mr Caddick has told you otherwise, it is not true. Nor is it correct that I have turned Papa against him. My father is quite able to compose his own letters, and I merely carried out his instructions exactly; you may ask Mr Darcy or Mr Upton, Robert, they will tell you no different," she said in a voice whose calmness belied her feelings.

But Rose was clearly in no mood to be reasonable and railed on until Mrs Gardiner rose and said very firmly, "I am sorry, Robert, I must ask you to take Rose to your room. She is plainly tired and overwrought and does not know what she is saying. I cannot have this bickering going on while your father lies ill upstairs. It is most unseemly."

Caroline stood trembling as her brother escorted his wife out of the room and up the stairs. She had been falsely accused of undermining her brother, her father had been maligned, and she was being held responsible for the tone of Mr Gardiner's letter to Caddick.

It was outrageous and Caroline had never before experienced such an affront. Never had she heard Rose use such intemperate words before; nor, it seemed, had Robert, for he had looked most embarrassed by her intervention and absolutely dejected at his mother's admonition.

That night, Caroline returned home and, having rested awhile, prepared to dress for dinner. Unwilling to worry her husband with details of Rose and Robert's outburst, she said nothing, and Fitzwilliam, though he sensed the strain in her and knew she had something on her mind, decided to let her tell him about it in her own time. He had missed her and was happy to have her home.

There was a storm brewing on the moors, but Caroline deliberately adopted a bright, cheerful mood and even found time to sit at the pianoforte. Her husband was pleased, hoping he had misread her mood; perhaps, he thought, she had been tired and was feeling better.

After dinner, they took coffee in the parlour and curled up on a sofa by the fire, by which time the storm was at its height. Over its sounds, they heard a vehicle, its urgent clatter and rattle growing louder as it turned into the drive and approached the house. Soon afterwards, they heard footsteps coming swiftly up the steps to the door.

Moments later, the maid announced Mr Kennedy.

Caroline rose at once; she knew it had to be an emergency of some sort. Mr Kennedy was unlikely to arrive late at night in inclement weather unless something was very wrong.

As he walked into the room, she gasped; he had handed his dripping overcoat and hat to the servant, but he was still a strange bedraggled sight, and his boots were sodden.

"Mr Kennedy, what on earth has happened to bring you out in this weather? Look at you, you will catch cold or worse; you must get out of those boots at once."

She hastened to send for a manservant who took him upstairs, where he divested himself of his outer garments and boots. These were taken downstairs to the kitchen to be dried while he was helped into some of Fitzwilliam's clothes, which, though too large, were at least dry and warm. When he joined them downstairs, he thanked them profusely and apologised for intruding upon them.

In the hours that followed, fortified with a drink and some hot food, Peter Kennedy revealed an amazing story of deceit, in which Mr Caddick was the main player.

He reminded Caroline of the sheaf of papers he had given her in Manchester. She confessed with some feeling of guilt that she had had no opportunity to peruse them herself, much less to hand them over to her father, whose sudden illness had precluded any discussion of business matters.

"I did not expect them to be of immediate significance, nor did I believe they would require urgent attention," Caroline admitted.

But their importance was now to become clear, as Mr Kennedy explained that they were faithful copies he had made of bills of lading, which proved beyond doubt that Mr Caddick was using the company to carry on an illegal enterprise.

"He has been importing tobacco and rum from the Caribbean to be sold privately to a merchant in Liverpool with whom he does business regularly. They are being brought in as part of the company's consignments from the Indies," said Mr Kennedy and when Caroline gasped in astonishment, he added, "It is a deception in which he has engaged for quite a long time, well before he came to work for Mr Gardiner. He has probably used every company he worked for in the same way; it is amazing that he has not been caught," Kennedy explained.

"And have you confronted him with it?" Fitzwilliam asked.

"Oh no, sir, I would be reluctant to do such a thing without the protection of the law and preferably in the presence of witnesses. I believe Mr Caddick, if he were roused to anger, would be quite a dangerous man. Besides, I did not wish to alert him before we had informed Mr Gardiner."

"You were right not to get into conflict with him, Mr Kennedy," Caroline said and then asked, "Does Mr Upton know of this?"

"Not all the detail of it, ma'am, but he is aware that I have evidence of something untoward. However, I thought it best to reveal it to you and Mr Gardiner first."

Caroline looked at her husband, wondering what was to be done next. It was unthinkable that her father should be involved; Mrs Gardiner would not hear of it. Yet, Robert would probably refuse to believe Mr Kennedy's story. She wished with all her heart that her father had not been so ill. She longed for his sound, sensible advice.

She went upstairs and retrieved the bundle of papers from her travelling case, and when they studied them, it was exactly as Mr Kennedy had described it. Small consignments of spirits and tobacco were being received along with the regular imports of cotton, sugar, and other goods. Yet there was no record of any customer placing orders for them. Clearly Caddick must have a partner in crime on the docks, who was letting them slip through undetected.

Caroline was amazed at the audacious scheme. As she pondered, Mr Kennedy spoke gently, intruding upon her thoughts, "Mrs Fitzwilliam, if I may be so bold as to make a suggestion..."

Caroline turned to him at once, "Please do, Mr Kennedy, I am at a loss to know how best to deal with what is clearly a criminal matter."

He continued, "If Colonel Fitzwilliam and Mr Robert Gardiner would accompany me to Manchester tomorrow, together with Mr Gardiner's lawyer, we could confront Caddick with the evidence and he could then be handed over to the police. Should we not report this matter, the office, indeed the entire company, could be held responsible for his crimes. In this case, Mr Caddick has defrauded both his employer and Her Majesty's customs while using the name of Mr Gardiner's company."

Caroline turned to her husband to ascertain his opinion. She could tell from his countenance that he was, as she was, astounded at what they had heard.

"Do you agree with Mr Kennedy, Fitzy? Can it be done?"

"Well, my dear, there is nothing for it, it must be done," he replied, "and to borrow a line from the bard, *then 't'were best done quickly.'* Mr Kennedy, you had best stay the night here. I shall send a note to Robert asking him to be ready to travel tomorrow on urgent business, and we can leave at dawn. I need give him no explanation at this stage.

"I agree that it is best if we have Mr Gardiner's lawyer with us, but if he is unavailable, I am confident Mr Upton will recommend a reputable man in Manchester. Our aim must be not to alert Caddick in any way, to catch him red handed as it were, and confront him. Does he know you are here?"

Mr Kennedy smiled, "Certainly not, sir. I was given leave of absence on account of my mother's serious illness, sir. Mr Upton was most obliging. You will be happy to hear, ma'am, my mother is perfectly well."

They laughed as he recounted the subterfuge he had used to avoid suspicion, then Caroline asked, "Do you think Robert will agree to hand Caddick over to the police?"

Fitzwilliam was quite firm, "My dear, Robert will have no alternative and Mr Caddick no refuge. He has broken the law and once the police have seen these papers and heard Mr Kennedy's evidence, there will be but one course open to them." Peter Kennedy nodded agreement.

It was late as Caroline left the men together. There was less than a month to Isabella's wedding and everything was in turmoil. Her father's health and peace of mind were in jeopardy, and the very enterprise to which he had given the best years of his life was in danger of being corrupted by the greed of a stranger and her brother's neglect.

Caroline could not but be depressed.

On the morrow, she bade them farewell, praying it would turn out well. She wished Robert would do the right thing and thanked God for the conscientious and honest Peter Kennedy, without whom all might have been lost.

❧

Isabella Fitzwilliam was married to Dr Henry Forrester a few weeks later.

Although neither had wished for a grand wedding, there was little chance they could escape the celebrations. Their own popularity in the community, the affection and regard that so many felt for the Fitzwilliams, and the generosity of Mr and Mrs Darcy ensured there was a large and appreciative party gathered at Pemberley for the happy event. The excellent food and fine late Spring weather contributed to make a memorable day.

Significantly, however, the main topic of conversation among the majority of guests at the wedding was not the lovely bride and her groom, but the possibility of war with Russia. Not even Colonel Fitzwilliam, whose loyalty to Palmerston had been unswerving, could deny that this time, he was wrong. Mr Darcy and Anthony Tate had both made their views on the prospect of war very clear.

"It is a wasteful exercise for which England is ill prepared, nor is she likely to benefit in any way whatsoever," said one and the other was so impressed with the sentiment expressed, he asked permission to use it in his next editorial on the subject.

Not long after Isabella and her husband had left on their wedding journey to Wales, a letter reached Caroline from Manchester. It reported that Mr Caddick had been brought before the magistrate and confessed to his crimes, some of which had been committed many years before he had moved to Derbyshire.

"It is generally expected that he will soon be on his way to New South Wales to serve out a long term of imprisonment," wrote Mr Kennedy, to whom had been returned all of the responsibilities previously held by him which Robert had needlessly and unsuccessfully transferred to Mr Caddick.

Now, everyone was pleased with him, even Robert, albeit somewhat chastened and subdued as a result of his unhappy experience with Caddick. Thereafter, he seemed content to entrust the majority of the work to Mr Kennedy, which was good news indeed, for the company and Mr Kennedy, who was recommended for promotion as a consequence.

Not so good was the news from Westminster that England after some forty years of peace and relative prosperity, was at war again in the year 1854, this time in the Crimea—and it was to drag on for four dreadful years.

In the years that followed, the lives of Caroline, Colonel Fitzwilliam, and many other members of their family were affected by circumstances and events that could not have been foreseen.

Some, as in the case of the engagement of Julian Darcy to Josie Tate, surprised everyone, including the parents of the young couple, while others, like the gradual disintegration of the marriage of Jonathan and Amelia-Jane leading finally to her death in a dreadful accident on the road to Bath, left the entire family aghast. No one who knew either Jonathan or his young wife could ever have foreseen such a disaster. It was much later that the truth was revealed.

Caroline's disappointment that Julian Darcy had chosen to marry Josie Tate, instead of her own daughter Amy, had been shared by his mother Elizabeth, who had long hoped for such a match. Amy had seemed to her a natural choice as the wife of the heir to Pemberley. But it was not Julian's choice.

At least for Caroline, the distress was assuaged when a few years later, Amy was very happily married to Frank, the son of Dr and Mrs Grantley. The genuine goodness and good humour of Mr Grantley had clearly helped him supplant the more *jejune* infatuation Amy had felt for her cousin. The couple had moved to Oxford and were clearly enjoying their life together. Letters received from Georgiana Grantley suggested that Amy was a great favourite with her in-laws as well.

However, the same did not apply at Pemberley.

Sadly, Caroline thought, her cousin Elizabeth seemed unable to forgive young Josie Tate for marrying her son.

Throughout this period, for Caroline one continuing source of anxiety remained: the health of her father, Mr Gardiner.

In spite of the best efforts of her brother Richard and several of his colleagues in the medical fraternity, there appeared to be little they could do to retard the progress of the disease, to which Mr Gardiner finally succumbed in the Autumn of 1864.

END OF PART FOUR

MY COUSIN CAROLINE

Part Five

Chapter Sixteen

C AROLINE HAD NOT SLEPT ALL night, and Colonel Fitzwilliam feared she would not be fit to face the ordeal of the morning. Despite this, she had risen early from their bed and addressed herself to the task of preparing to attend the melancholy ritual of the reading of her father's will.

The week just gone had been difficult enough, with Mrs Gardiner so bereft that her daughters had to set aside their own sorrow to console and support their mother through the days and nights following their father's death. Then, there had been the unhappy matter of Julian Darcy, who was supposed to read the lesson at the funeral service, arriving too late at the church. Mr Darcy, himself deeply grieved by the loss of a dear friend and mentor, had stepped into the breach.

Colonel Fitzwilliam, who had always had the highest opinion of his cousin, was not surprised; it was exactly the sort of thing one expected of Darcy. More astonishing was the fact that it was Caroline who had asked him, at the very last minute, in the same way that she had organised her family, so everything that had to be done was carried out in a proper manner. Yet, loving her as he did, Fitzwilliam knew the depth of her grief and the strength she had had to summon up to carry her through the day. Only at the very end of that sombre day, when they had returned home and retired to their room, had Caroline, weary and grieving, wept as he had held her, trying to comfort her.

There was little to be said, for speech at such times is often futile; there was no need for words.

Caroline had been her father's favourite, supporting his views, adopting his ideas, and following his characteristically commonsensical advice; she had been closer to him than any of her siblings. Unabashed, she, more than any other member of the family, had declared openly to many of their acquaintances that, without her father's business acumen and great good sense, they would never have been more than the family of a small trader, living within sight of his warehouses in Cheapside.

"Our family owes everything we are and have to Papa's good nature, skill, and diligence," she would say with characteristic candour, and she was right.

When Fitzwilliam went downstairs to breakfast, Caroline was already dressed and ready to face the day. Soberly and appropriately clad in soft black silk with a hat that cast a benign shadow over her face, disguising the unmistakable signs of weariness and grief, she was standing at the open window, looking out at the hills, their rough peaks still softened by mist. He went to her and, as he kissed her cheek, saw the tears in her eyes, but she smiled and held on to his hand, knowing she would have need of his support through the day.

What neither of them knew was the extent to which the business of this day would inevitably and forever change their lives.

There was nothing unusual about the day on which members of the family and partners in the Commercial Trading Company, summoned by Mr Gardiner's attorney, Mr Jennings, were gathered at Oakleigh. On a mild morning, the late Autumn sun poured in at the windows of the parlour, where refreshments had been served, while they waited to be joined by the Darcys and Mr Bingley. When it was ascertained that everyone who had been asked was in fact present, they repaired to the library.

Elizabeth looked around the room and noticed that the only person not in the formal colours of mourning was Robert Gardiner's wife, Rose, who for some inexplicable reason had a daffodil yellow scarf swathed around her throat. It was only a wisp of silk, but in that quiet room, it caught the eye like a banner in the breeze.

"I cannot imagine why she chose to wear that colour," said Elizabeth, recounting the day's events to her sister Jane. "I have no doubt at all that it must have upset my dear aunt to see it."

Cassy had noticed it too, but except to catch her mother's eye and exchange a silent communication, she had said nothing.

Mr Jennings, meanwhile, had readied himself, arranged his papers, and, clearing his throat, stood up to do his solemn duty.

No one expected any surprises on this occasion. Mr Gardiner was, above all, a stable, steady businessman, without the slightest tendency towards eccentricity or aberration. His industry and sound common sense had steered his company and his family from modest beginnings to great success, giving his wife and children the security and respectability he had sought for them.

The first bequests to his grandchildren and to faithful staff and servants were all anticipated. He was a generous man, and those who had served him well were appropriately rewarded. His children, all four of them, and their spouses were likewise granted substantial endowments of cash and shares. The property at Oakleigh was, as expected, bequeathed in its entirety to his wife, to pass upon her demise to whomsoever she chose, but with a codicil that the inheritor may not subdivide or sell it without the consent of all four of her children.

Caroline, who had been seated with her husband in a place behind her mother, breathed a sigh of relief. She had of late been concerned that Rose had been taking over most of Mrs Gardiner's duties, almost as if she were the mistress of the house. Caroline, though she had never mentioned it to either of her parents, had wondered if her father had indicated to Robert that he may inherit the property on condition he let his mother continue to live there.

"I have some apprehension on this score," she had written earlier to her friend and confidante Emma Wilson, *"as I do not believe that my sister-in-law Rose will be satisfied with such an arrangement. She is a person with artistic talents and tastes, which will inevitably result in her desiring to change and redecorate the old place; a scheme, I am sure you will agree, unlikely to find approval with Mama."*

As Mr Jennings read out the stipulation attached to the bequest, Caroline noticed her mother's shoulders relax as if a burden had rolled from them; clearly Mrs Gardiner had not been altogether certain of her husband's intentions, either. Glancing sideways at Rose, it was plain to Caroline that she was disappointed. Caroline saw her lean over to Robert, and though she did not catch her whispered words, it was obvious she had had other expectations. There was dismay written upon her face.

"She must surely have believed Papa would leave Oakleigh to them," thought Caroline as Mr Jennings coughed and cleared his throat again and picked up a final document.

Caroline's hand crept into her husband's, and as his fingers closed around hers, she heard the attorney's next pronouncement, spoken in that dry, ordinary voice that lawyers seem to reserve for their most dramatic revelations.

Mr Gardiner, he explained, had recently made an amendment to his will handing control of all of his remaining shares and the management of his company to his eldest child, Mrs Caroline Fitzwilliam, adding once again a single condition that prevented her from selling any portion of the enterprise without the consent of her mother, her brother Richard Gardiner, and at least two of the three partners in the business.

Caroline gasped audibly, and Elizabeth, glancing at her, saw her turn very pale as she looked up at Fitzwilliam, whose considerable astonishment matched her own. She saw too the shocked faces of Robert and his wife Rose, whose flushed countenance betrayed her severe discomposure.

A few minutes later, she left the room, claiming she needed some fresh air but leaving no one present in any doubt of her feelings. Her husband Robert did not flinch nor show outwardly his disappointment, but it was quite clear that both he and Rose had, like many others in the family, taken it for granted that Mr Gardiner would leave his youngest son in charge of the business.

No one had expected it would be Caroline.

Well, not quite no one, for it was revealed later, when the documents were placed upon the table for all to see, that Mr Darcy had known all along, since his signature had been placed at the bottom of the paragraph as a witness to the will.

Looking at Mrs Gardiner seated with her daughter Emily, Elizabeth could tell from her aunt's expression that she had been as ignorant of these details of her husband's will as the rest of them.

Significantly, only Mr Darcy had seemed unsurprised, and indeed, when later they were all taking a glass of sherry together, he had come over to congratulate Caroline and tell her he was sure she would do very well in her new role. Cassy was surprised and so was Elizabeth. Mr Darcy had kept his counsel very well indeed.

Back at Pemberley that evening, Cassy felt she had to ask her father about Mr Gardiner's decision. "Do you suppose, Papa, that Mr Gardiner thought

Caroline was better able to manage the business than Robert?" to which he replied, "I am quite sure he did, Cassy, and with good reason," pointing out quite firmly that Robert did not appear to have his heart in the business.

"He has made no effort to equip himself for his role, spending more time in London and Paris than in Matlock or Manchester," he said.

To Cassandra's further enquiries, Mr Darcy would provide even more precise answers, revealing for the first time to his family details of the discrepancies in the accounts of both offices, which Caroline had uncovered.

"Although Robert was advised of the problem by his father, he claimed to have found nothing wrong with the books. It was Caroline's meticulous work that led to an investigation, prosecution, and the recovery of at least some of the monies. It was her perspicacity, with the help of Mr Kennedy, that resulted in the conviction of Caddick, who had completely gulled both Robert and his wife. They had apparently no inkling of what he was doing. His illegal activities had placed Mr Gardiner's business and his reputation in jeopardy.

"To say Mr Gardiner was disappointed is an understatement; he had great hopes for Robert and they had come to naught. On the other hand, he was most favourably impressed with Caroline's tenacious pursuit of the matter. I am prepared to believe that his mind was made up on the subject of his will soon afterwards."

It was an explanation that, by its content and the tone in which it was given, convinced both Elizabeth and Cassandra that Mr Darcy had not only understood Mr Gardiner's purpose in amending his will, he had probably supported it as being both prudent and sensible.

Before leaving Oakleigh that afternoon, Mr Jennings had approached Caroline and placed in her hands a sheaf of documents, a locked cash box, and a personal letter in her father's hand.

Taking it upstairs into a private room, Caroline read the letter, which detailed among other things his continuing anxiety about the new manager at the Manchester office—a Mr Stokes, who had once been appointed by the disgraced Caddick as his assistant but had escaped dismissal by sheer luck and his assiduous cultivation of Robert's goodwill. A quiet, unobtrusive man, he had done Robert's bidding well enough to be placed in a position of some responsibility by him.

Mr Gardiner urged caution before he was entrusted with too much authority, and Caroline took careful note of his opinion. Her father's judgment had rarely been proved wrong.

In addition to several affectionate expressions of farewell, the letter contained also words of advice urging her to trust her own judgment, but if ever she needed counsel, *"ask the advice of your husband, your brother Richard, or Mr Darcy, in whom you can place your trust implicitly."*

> *Remember my dear child, that your mother's continuing comfort and peace of mind and the income that will flow to your brothers, sister, and my valued partners are all now in your care. I know you will not let them down.*

Despite the pride she felt at being so chosen, Caroline was daunted by the responsibility her father had placed in her hands. His words had underlined the extent of his trust in her, but they had also laid out quite clearly the magnitude of her task.

> *Remember, dear Caroline, it is with you I leave the most valuable part of my life's work... Apart from the property at Oakleigh, which I purchased for your dear mother, the Commercial Trading Company is my entire fortune. Bound up in it are the prosperity and happiness of several people, including my beloved family and those faithful employees who have worked for us for many years. Now, it is in your hands...*

Caroline had put the letter away and returned to the parlour. On the stairs, she had met Rose and Robert. While her brother stopped and kissed her cheek without saying anything significant, his wife seemed as yet unable to cope with her disappointment and hurried away to her room. Her sullen countenance betrayed her mood.

It was not, thought Caroline, an auspicious beginning to their new relationship.

Later, she had revealed the contents of her father's letter to Colonel Fitzwilliam and Mr Darcy as well as her brother Richard and his wife.

"I know I shall have to call on you for help to carry out Papa's wishes," she had said. "While I am quite familiar with the accounts of the company, I know much less about the business of commerce and trade. I feel quite inadequate to the task."

She was assured immediately of their support, especially by Mr Darcy.

"Never forget, Caroline, your father loved you very much, but he was also a very good businessman, the best I have known; he is therefore unlikely to have placed this responsibility in your hands, unless he was certain you were capable of carrying it out successfully. May I say, here and now, that I share his confidence absolutely," he had said, making quite certain that his expressions of confidence in her were heard by members of her family. As her father's partner, an investor in the company, Mr Darcy would hardly endorse someone he thought was incapable of managing it successfully.

Sadly, Caroline thought, neither Robert nor Rose had been there to hear his words, though she could not help wondering if they would have believed any of it if they had.

Returning home very late on what had been a day filled with so many conflicting emotions, she was both weary and elated. Fitzwilliam had reassured and supported her through the day, and the warmth of his loyalty and affection had sustained her. She was grateful and said as much.

He sensed, however, a change in her attitude from the previous evening, for despite the inevitable melancholy and fatigue the day had generated, she seemed exhilarated by the prospect of the task entrusted to her.

Caroline had done with grieving and appeared eager to begin work on what was without any doubt a difficult and demanding undertaking.

As they prepared for bed, she asked, almost casually, "You believe I can do it, do you not, Fitzy?" and his swift response was meant to reassure her.

"Dearest, of course I do. I am in no doubt that you would manage the enterprise well; far be it from me to criticise your brother, but clearly both Darcy and your father were in agreement that you would do a better job than Robert. In doing it, you shall have my total support. But then, I do not need to tell you that, Caroline, for you know it already. You can call upon me at any time. You have given me so much help and happiness for so many years, this will be an opportunity for me to be of some assistance to you."

"Did Papa not speak of it to you?" she asked, as she brushed and braided her hair.

Fitzwilliam grew serious. "No, my dear, he did not, and I can well understand his reticence—he must have wished to save me any embarrassment. Were Robert and Rose to discover I had played any part in your father's decision, they may accuse me of manipulation or worse."

"They would not dare! If they did, they would have me and Mr Darcy to reckon with!" she declared, her eyes flashing with anger. "It beggars belief that Rose, who has hitherto shown little interest in my father's affairs, should be so concerned about the disposition of his property. As for Robert, he may be resentful, but he will not say or do anything that will hurt us; he has more sensibility than her, I think."

Reluctant to provoke her further, Fitzwilliam said nothing; yet even as he rejoiced that her mood had changed from grief to determination, he hoped she would not be disappointed in her assessment of her brother.

He did not share her confidence in Robert's judgment.

An undistinguished though generally agreeable young man, Robert had always sought the approval of those he acknowledged to be his superiors. Overjoyed when he had been accepted by Rose Fitzwilliam, whose striking beauty and elegance had taken his breath away at their first meeting, he had since then walked adoringly in her shadow, his weakness of will and lack of ambition providing his wife with every opportunity to enhance her own personality, often at the expense of his. Both Darcy and Elizabeth were of the opinion that Rose, not Robert, decided their response to any situation, and it was unlikely to be different on this occasion.

Though he knew all of this, not wishing to spoil his wife's mood and eager to encourage her new confidence, Fitzwilliam acquiesced for the moment, preferring to offer her comfort and affection rather than the distasteful truth. The warmth of his love had sustained her before in times of great sorrow and did so again.

Chapter Seventeen

ELIZABETH WAS UPSTAIRS WHEN A carriage drew up at the entrance to Pemberley House, and Mr Darcy's cousin James Fitzwilliam and his wife, Rosamund, were shown into the salon. By the time she went downstairs, Mr Darcy had already been apprised of their arrival and had joined the visitors. A bright fire and ample refreshments kept them occupied awhile, but presently, they came to the point of their visit.

James Fitzwilliam began by addressing his cousin with a degree of forthrightness that Elizabeth found quite surprising. He was not generally renowned for the directness of his approach, being somewhat vague and circumlocutory in his speech. Nor was he a particularly forceful man; perhaps, she thought, his cause had stiffened his resolve, because on this occasion, he was being very outspoken indeed.

"Darcy, this is a most unsatisfactory state of affairs, I am sure you will agree," he declared and then, assuming his cousin's acquiescence, went on, "We are all at a loss to understand the reason for the exclusion of Robert from his father's business."

Mr Darcy seemed quite taken aback by this remark. "Exclusion? Why, what has given you such a notion, James? Robert is certainly not excluded, surely?"

"Ah, but he is. I am advised that Caroline, not Robert, is to manage the Commercial Trading Company."

Darcy smiled, comprehending his concern. "Manage it, indeed yes, but it does not mean that Robert is excluded. He and Rose have received bequests of generous parcels of shares to add to those he already held, from which they will derive income, and as shareholders, they will not be excluded from the business at all. In fact, it is to protect the profitability of the company that Mr Gardiner has nominated Caroline to manage its general administration, a task for which she is far better fitted than Robert."

"How so?" asked Rosamund. "After all, Robert was trained at Mathesons, was he not? Why was he overlooked? Rose has informed me that Robert believes he has been replaced by his sister because Caroline probably inveigled her way into Mr Gardiner's confidence during her brother's absence from Derbyshire. I am told she was forever in his study, going through the books…"

At this point, Mr Darcy, who had been standing in a fairly relaxed manner propping up the mantelpiece, strode purposefully over to where his cousin and his wife were seated. Placing his glass carefully upon the table, he spoke in a voice that brooked no interruption.

Elizabeth, observing from her seat on the sofa, hardly knew what to expect. It was clear her husband was very vexed indeed.

"Rosamund, you have no right nor has Rose any reason to make such a cruel accusation. Not only is it uncharitable and unfair, it is downright libellous. I assure you Caroline knew nothing of her father's intentions; only Mr Jennings the attorney and I were privy to the change Mr Gardiner made to his will placing her in charge of his interest in the company, and I must, in all honesty, declare that as a partner in the business, I entirely approved of his choice."

For a few minutes, neither spoke, then James Fitzwilliam asked, "If that was so, Darcy, what reasons did you and Mr Gardiner have?"

To Elizabeth's surprise, Darcy did not spare their sensibilities, pointing out with astonishing candour the clear, cogent reasons Mr Gardiner had provided for his decision.

"Since Mr Gardiner had been unwell for some time, Caroline had been asked by her father to assist him by undertaking a number of routine administrative tasks; these she carried out in an exemplary manner. Where Robert and Rose spent many months away in Europe or London or Bath, Caroline spent several days and weeks poring over the accounts, travelling to Manchester, confronting swindlers like Caddick, who had completely deceived Robert, and reorganising the work of the office after his sudden departure. Though Robert returned to work, he made little progress. Mr Gardiner had no choice; he had long desired to set his son up in charge of the company, but Robert, despite his many protestations, seemed to have lost interest in the business. He'd left most of the work to Caddick, whose criminal actions may well have ruined the reputation of the company. Now, in view of all these matters, I am sorry to have to say that I fully concurred with Mr Gardiner's decision."

By the end of his recital, the Fitzwilliams, whether they agreed or not, had clearly decided that it was fruitless to press their arguments upon Darcy. They had obviously hoped to use their family connection to influence him, perhaps to make some accommodation with Robert. Now it was clear they could not, they rose to take their leave.

Darcy and Elizabeth were all politeness, but James Fitzwilliam and his wife appeared to feel that their daughter Rose and her husband had been slighted and treated unjustly by Mr Gardiner and nothing would change their minds.

Rosamund Fitzwilliam was very close to her daughter and being especially aggrieved, determined to say her piece.

"My dear Rose is of the opinion that Mr Gardiner also expected Robert to move to Manchester in order to take charge of the office there," she said, adding, "which of course, would have been intolerable for Rose. Our daughter is accustomed to a style of living with a level of culture and gentility that cannot possibly be found in a town devoted totally to the pursuit of industry and trade."

Elizabeth thought she said "industry and trade" in a manner so like that of Lady Catherine, it was quite uncanny!

"Rose," she went on, "enjoys pastimes such as may be found in the salons and theatres of London and Paris, rather than the public assemblies and work-men's institutes of Manchester and Liverpool. Besides, where would they live? There are few suitable residences in Manchester, and Rose cannot be expected to live above the shop!"

There was an implication in her words that she thought perhaps Caroline, in view of her father's background in commerce, could be so accommodated.

Elizabeth bit her lip, unwilling to ignite an undignified argument, though she clearly understood the point of the remark and was inwardly very annoyed. Darcy, sensing the slight, intended or otherwise, to the Gardiners, for whom he had the utmost regard and affection, did not take the bait either. He did, however, intervene with a riposte of such levity that it made Elizabeth smile.

"Ah well," he said, "in that case, both Rose and Robert should feel mightily pleased at being relieved of the need even to visit Manchester, much less live there," and as the Fitzwilliams looked puzzled, added, "They can now draw upon the income derived from their share of the business without feeling any obligation to contribute towards its creation in any way. While Caroline is unlikely to have 'to live above the shop,' as you put it, she will certainly have no compunction at all about visiting Manchester or London, if that were necessary, to ensure the business is being conducted efficiently. To that end, I have assured her, as I did Mr Gardiner, that I will do everything in my power to assist her and ensure her success.

"Neither Rose nor Robert need have any qualms about their shares; the company will be in excellent hands, you may assure them of that. Indeed, it is a most felicitous outcome, you must agree."

Writing to her friend Charlotte Collins later that day, Elizabeth said:

The finality with which he completed his sentence and moved to escort our guests to the entrance left them in no doubt that Darcy had had the last word.

It left me gasping with astonishment, while I tried valiantly not to laugh, for it was clear that Darcy, for all his civility, had lost patience with his cousin James and his wife.

Their partiality and concern for their daughter is understandable, Charlotte, but to proceed from that relatively benign position to one of animosity and innuendo against Caroline and the Gardiners is insufferable. My dear husband, whose affection for my uncle and Caroline far outweighs his familial feelings for his cousin James, made it plain he was, in the words of his departed aunt, 'seriously displeased'!

Sadly, Charlotte, Rosamund has, over the years, become more deeply enmeshed in the old ways; the modes and manners of people like Lady Catherine de Bourgh, whose snobbery and smallness of mind are plainly obsolete. It is a pity, for her family, the Camdens, were Darcy's close friends as well as our good neighbours. It is to be hoped that Rose will not lead Robert down the same path.

Later, Elizabeth, noting that her husband was in quite good humour despite the *contretemps* with the Fitzwilliams, took up the matter of Caroline's new role with him.

"You must know that the Fitzwilliams and more particularly Rose will continue to carp and criticise. Do you think Caroline will cope?"

Darcy, taking her arm and tucking it beneath his own, smiled.

"My dear Lizzie, I am more certain that Caroline will cope with these petty problems than I would have been had Mr Gardiner delivered the responsibility to Fitzwilliam or myself. She is keen, dedicated, and unencumbered by jealousy or viciousness; I am confident she will manage very well." Elizabeth smiled as he went on, "It will, however, be an onerous task, and to ease her burden, I have a suggestion to put to the meeting of the partners next week. If it is accepted, I believe Caroline will have far fewer problems than we imagine, and the cause of efficiency will be better served."

Elizabeth was eager to discover what plan he had in mind, but Darcy, ever scrupulous, declared that he could only reveal it to her after it had been put to the partners.

"Oh Darcy, you are vexing!" she cried impatiently, but there was no changing his mind. In such matters he was scrupulous to a fault.

※

At the meeting of the partners, held at Oakleigh, Caroline sat for the first time in her father's place at the head of the table with Messrs Darcy and Bingley to her right and her husband at her left. Feeling the full weight of her new responsibility, she was at first understandably nervous and tentative, but soon got into her stride. Having attended meetings during Mr Gardiner's long illness, she was familiar with the routines and was further assisted by the consideration of the partners.

Caroline had summoned Mr Peter Kennedy to present the accounts of the Manchester office and Mr Garfield from London to do likewise for his establishment. Both men attended, explaining in some detail, and to the satisfaction of the meeting, the state of the business.

There was, however, one reservation; Mr Kennedy had brought with him a packet of documents, which he had presented to Caroline before the meeting, urging her to peruse the contents herself before revealing them to the partners.

"It would be best, ma'am, if you saw the material, which is of a highly confidential nature, before Mr Darcy and the other partners are apprised of its existence. I believe also that it would be best kept from the gentlemen of the London office at this time," he advised.

Taking advantage of a break in the proceedings for tea, Caroline withdrew to her father's study to examine the documents.

What they contained so startled her that she had to summon first Mr Kennedy to request an explanation of their significance and then Mr Darcy and Colonel Fitzwilliam to look at the material.

Their astonishment was no less than hers had been.

The documents revealed that Mr Stokes, who had been placed in charge of the office by Robert, had over the past year been defrauding the company by paying himself various sums of money for his personal use in no way related to his work. Not only was he involved in misappropriating funds, he was also forwarding small amounts to a woman, who Mr Kennedy had discovered was Caddick's mistress, left impoverished without her protector since his departure on a convict ship bound for the antipodes. It was exactly as Mr Gardiner had feared; Stokes was a henchman of Caddick's and not to be trusted.

For Mr Darcy, this was the last straw!

"Caroline, this is intolerable. We have to be rid of this man. I suggest that as a matter of courtesy, we advise Robert of this information and have him write a letter to Stokes, dismissing him from his present position," he said, and Caroline could not but agree. While she had the authority to dismiss Stokes, she would have preferred to have Robert do so.

But, unhappily, the matter was not able to be settled quite so simply, for Caroline had learned from her mother that Robert and Rose had already left for London.

"I know they have plans to spend a fortnight in London before proceeding to Europe, where I believe they are invited to spend the Winter," Mrs Gardiner had explained, adding sadly, "I think, my dear, that Rose is exceedingly disappointed that your papa did not arrange to leave Oakleigh to Robert. I cannot help wondering whether it would not have been better had he done so—it would have pleased both Robert and Rose very much and I should have liked that. I cannot bear to think that he feels unfairly treated by his father."

Caroline had been appalled. "Mama, I have no doubt it would have pleased Robert and even more particularly Rose, but I am just as certain that pleasing them was not Papa's main preoccupation when he made his will. He clearly intended for you to have this property. It was purchased for you and it is yours to enjoy and not so as Robert and Rose, who spend little enough time here anyway, should be pleased."

Seeing a look of some anxiety upon her mother's face, Caroline added, "Should you ask Mr Darcy, he will tell you how much Papa wanted for you to have the peace of mind and security of your own place. He knew well the hazards of leaving the house to Robert or Rose and expecting them to accommodate you. There are too many examples, some well known to us, of sons and daughters whose best intentions of providing for a parent or unwed sister have evaporated when property and money were involved. You know that Rose would have been the mistress of this house and I cannot believe, Mama, that you would have been happy with such an arrangement. Oakleigh is your home."

Poor Mrs Gardiner, though many years younger than her husband, had not been very well in the last few years and would have preferred to avoid the unpleasantness of offending her youngest son and his wife, who had made their disappointment with Mr Gardiner's will quite plain. She could not deny, however, that Caroline was right; living as a permanent houseguest in her in-law's home would not have appealed to her at all.

❦

When Caroline returned to join the gentlemen, who had made good use of their time by helping themselves to some of Mr Gardiner's excellent sherry, she broke the news that her brother and his wife were probably in London already. Neither Mr Darcy nor Fitzwilliam seemed surprised, and Bingley offered the opinion that he had heard his wife speak of their intention to spend Christmas in France.

"Jane met Rose and her mother in Derby last week, and she said they were all very excited about it—though I must say I cannot think why. When we were over there some years ago, I could not comprehend a word of what they said in church in either France or Italy!"

The rest of the party laughed as Caroline pointed out that, while Robert knew not a word of French or Italian, Rose was fluent in both languages and would probably be quite at ease in either place.

Getting back to business, after Mr Garfield had left to get the coach to Derby and thence to London, discussion returned to the case of Mr Stokes. It was clear that some action had to be taken and soon.

"We have to act before Stokes becomes aware that he has been discovered, else he may destroy documents and attempt to hinder the work of the company," said Colonel Fitzwilliam.

Caroline agreed there was such a danger, but Mr Kennedy intervened to reassure them.

"Mr Stokes is away in Liverpool until Tuesday, and I have taken the liberty of removing all important papers and files from his desk and storing them in the locked safe, to which I alone have the key. Were I, on Monday morning, to deliver a letter to his house before he arrives at the office, he would be none the wiser and have no opportunity to do any damage at all."

The gentlemen looked relieved and Caroline exclaimed, "Well done, Mr Kennedy."

"A capital scheme," said Mr Bingley, who had been absolutely stunned by Kennedy's revelations.

It was decided that a letter should be drafted, copies made and retained, and the original signed by the partners and delivered to Mr Stokes. With the help of Mr Darcy and some technical advice from Mr Kennedy, an appropriate communication was produced thanking Stokes for his services, enclosing his wages for the remainder of the month, and terminating his employment forthwith.

A thinly veiled threat that any attempt to create trouble may result in a report to the police was included, mainly to alert him to the fact that his petty theft and misappropriation had been exposed.

Colonel Fitzwilliam, who had been much impressed by Mr Kennedy, asked if he could "hold the fort" for a while, but Mr Kennedy, though an obliging and hardworking fellow, stated that he could deal with all of the accounts but had no experience in matters of shipping and commerce.

"Since the retirement of Mr Upton, we have missed very much the services of a capable man to take charge of our main business, which is trade," he explained. "It is a complex area, growing larger each year, and we must have someone well versed in the detail of it. None of us has the knowledge and experience of Mr Upton, and we have struggled since his departure to keep abreast of the work that is coming in. The two clerks work hard but could benefit from an experienced manager."

It was at this point that Mr Darcy decided that his plan could be put to the meeting with a high level of certainty that it would be accepted. The time, he judged, was right. He suggested that they advertise in the commercial papers in London and Manchester for a well-trained, experienced man to take charge of the shipping business of the Manchester office and do as Mr Upton and Mr Bartholomew had done.

"He would be carefully selected and, once appointed, would move to Manchester and take charge of the office, reporting regularly to Caroline and the board," said Mr Darcy.

Having explained his proposition, he sought their responses.

Mr Kennedy was immediately enthusiastic. "I think it is an excellent idea, sir. It is exactly what we need. The London office is now in good order because Mr Bartholomew, before he retired, appointed and trained Mr Garfield," he said.

Both Bingley and Colonel Fitzwilliam concurred, and Caroline, though she did point out the additional expense involved, was, with very little persuasion, convinced of its value and practicality.

When the meeting ended, a specific advertisement was drafted which Mr Kennedy was to take to the post and dispatch for publication in the appropriate journals in London, Manchester, and Liverpool. He did warn them that good shipping managers were very rare since most trading houses did their best to keep them on.

"If we are fortunate enough to get ourselves a good man, it will make all the difference to the business," he declared.

Turning to Mr Darcy, Caroline asked, "Mr Darcy, may I rely upon you to assist us with the selection of the right candidate, should we have several applicants?" to which Mr Darcy replied that it would give him much pleasure to do so.

"I shall write tonight to Mr Bartholomew and ask him to collect the applications from the post office and arrange for a convenient date when you could see the applicants and decide, with his advice, upon a suitable candidate," she said, and Darcy was obviously pleased to have been asked. It was the least he could do to keep his promise to Mr Gardiner.

"At last," said Caroline to her husband, as they drove home to Matlock, "I feel we are able to achieve something because we are all of one mind. I know for certain that Mr Darcy will not make the same error of judgment that Robert made when he appointed Caddick, and there will be no interference from anyone unconnected to the business."

Fitzwilliam agreed; he had felt very proud of Caroline as she conducted her first meeting of the partners and participated in their discussions.

"You can count on that, my dear. First Caddick, now Stokes; I cannot imagine what Robert was thinking. But of one thing you can be quite certain: Darcy will pick the best possible candidate. I am confident that with his help, you will succeed very well."

Chapter Eighteen

Mr Kennedy was right. Finding the best man for the position was no easy task.

It was almost Spring when Mr Darcy travelled up to London, taking with him some of the applications received at the Manchester office. They were not particularly promising. Mr Kennedy had apologised as he handed them over, as if he were to blame for the paucity of the talent. None of the candidates had experience in managing a trading company but expressed the hope they might be given an opportunity to do so if they promised to work hard, which, Mr Darcy said, was not quite the same thing! Meanwhile, Mr Bartholomew had received what he called "a few good letters" and had arranged for Mr Darcy to interview three gentlemen, whom he considered appropriately qualified for the position.

Caroline was particularly grateful to Mr Darcy for undertaking this rather tedious task, while she was being kept busy with a variety of domestic and family matters that demanded her presence.

Her daughter Isabella was making preparations to accompany her husband on a journey to Wales, where he hoped to study the health problems of the poor. Information received from Mr Jenkins, the former rector of Pemberley, had suggested that the poor who had the misfortune to be incarcerated in the workhouses when they fell ill, got very short shrift indeed. Doctor Forrester had obtained a commission to write a report on the subject and was taking leave from his position at Littleford Hospital to do so. He hoped, with the evidence he would gather, to convince the state of its responsibility to care for the sick when they had not the means to do so themselves.

Caroline was anxious because Isabella insisted on taking her little boy with them. "Mama, you must not worry, I shall take good care of him. Besides, Henry is a doctor and unlikely to place us in any danger of contagion," Isabella argued, but Caroline could not help being concerned.

"Will you not let us look after him, Bella my dear? Rachel will keep him amused, and my maid Harriet is very good with children. He would be no trouble at all. It is only for three months."

Her mother's pleading and some of her own misgivings about the uncongenial places in which they would have to stay combined to change Isabella's mind, and to Caroline's delight, it was decided that little Harry Forrester would move in with his grandparents.

Later in Spring, Isabella and her husband were to leave on their journey and there was much to be done before then. Caroline was glad that some of her responsibilities were soon to be taken over by the new man appointed to the office at Manchester. While she enjoyed her work, she could not deny it took a great deal of her time and often left her exhausted. Looking after her little grandson would not be half so onerous a task, she supposed.

≈≋≈

When Mr Darcy returned from London at the end of the week, he went directly to Pemberley. Having rested and enjoyed the pleasures of his beautiful estate and the company of his wife, whom he always missed when he went to London alone, he had dispatched a note inviting Colonel Fitzwilliam and Caroline to dine at Pemberley on the day following.

Reading the note, Caroline was most excited. "Fitzy, do you think Mr Darcy has been successful in selecting a shipping manager for the Manchester office? He doesn't say so in his note, but I cannot believe we would be asked to dine at Pemberley so soon after his return from London unless he had something of consequence to disclose. Do you not agree?"

Fitzwilliam shrugged his shoulders; it was a general rule with him that he did not speculate on the actions of his cousin. Even though they were very close and had known one another since childhood, Darcy always had the capacity to astonish and frequently confound him.

"I would not care to wager much money on that proposition, my love; it is quite within the realms of possibility that Darcy has returned having found no one suitable among the applicants, but wishes to put to us another scheme even better than the last. I do not mean to suggest that he will let you down—far from it—but he may have decided to do something completely unpredictable."

"Do you mean like he did when he proposed to my cousin Lizzie, having let you all believe he thought she was his inferior and so beneath his notice?" asked Caroline, whose childhood memories of the beginnings of the great romance between Darcy and Elizabeth were still very clear in her mind. After her own marriage to Fitzwilliam, they had often spoken with some amusement of Mr Darcy's inopportune and ill-judged proposal and all that had proceeded from it.

This time, Colonel Fitzwilliam laughed heartily and said, "I doubt that it will be as dramatic as that unforgettable event, Caroline, but an invitation to dine at Pemberley will never be dull. Mark my words, Darcy has something up his sleeve."

When they arrived at Pemberley House the following evening, they found that the only other guests were Mr Bingley and Jane. It was, quipped Bingley, almost like a social meeting of the board of the company. In the event, he was not far wrong.

With dinner out of the way, the three couples withdrew to the drawing room where wine, cheese, and fruit were served as well as tea and coffee. The long, mild evening allowed for the great doors to the terrace to stand open, and while the gentlemen conversed, the ladies moved outside to enjoy the prospect.

With the new Spring growth hardening on the trees and the soft blush of pink flower buds pushing out among the leaves, the park around Pemberley House was looking especially lovely, and they were reluctant to return indoors.

It was Colonel Fitzwilliam who came to invite them in.

"Caroline, my dear, Darcy has some good news," he said as they went inside. Caroline, looking up at her husband and across at Mr Darcy, who was standing by the fireplace, asked, "Is this true, Mr Darcy? Have you found us a suitable manager?"

He smiled and bowed, but said nothing until they were all seated, Caroline somewhat nervously, on the edge of her chair.

When he spoke, it was lightly, without any drama. "I think we *have* found him; he seems to me to be the right man for the position. Mr Bartholomew agrees with me, so if you approve of my choice, I shall advise him that he has been successful and he will take up duties in Manchester on the first day of May."

There were cries of astonishment. Everyone wanted to know more. Who was he? Where did he come from? What were these qualifications that so fitted him for the position?

As these and other questions swirled around him, Mr Darcy carefully refilled his glass.

"Well," he said quietly, "first, let me say he is a mature man in his forties or thereabouts, highly educated, well presented, and single."

As the ladies looked at one another, puzzled by at least one item in that list of attributes, Mr Darcy went on to catalogue a few more.

"He has worked for several years in the shipping business and knows it well. Experienced in managing commercial offices both in Europe and London, he comes highly recommended by his former employers and has excellent character references; one from a man we all esteem and respect, Lord Shaftesbury, and another from our own Jonathan Bingley."

At this, there were more exclamations of approval, while Jane and Charles Bingley looked at one another, delighted. A man recommended by their son must be close to perfect, they thought.

"Perhaps," Darcy continued, "best of all, he is prepared and able, being unencumbered in any way, to move to Manchester and live there. If I advise him that he has the position, he will do so almost immediately, as he has expressed a wish to become acquainted at the earliest opportunity with the office and its present staff."

Caroline and Elizabeth could hardly believe their ears.

"Who is this paragon?" asked Elizabeth and Caroline exclaimed, "Wherever did Mr Bartholomew discover such a man?"

Mr Darcy smiled. "Have patience, ladies, and all will soon be revealed." He went to sit beside his wife on the sofa and continued, "The gentleman is known to us; well, not intimately to me, but he has been, in years past, a close acquaintance of your family, Caroline."

"A friend of ours!" she cried, looking very puzzled indeed, until Mr Darcy, feeling he had tantalised them long enough, announced in a very quiet voice, "It is Mr Philip Bentley."

This time the reactions were even more incredulous, as each one recalled Mr Bentley and his attractive stepsisters, his gentle mother, and somewhat less likeable stepfather, Mr Henderson.

The family had leased Newland Hall for a short period some years ago. Mr Bentley had been perhaps the most well-liked member of the family.

Now, everyone remembered him.

"Philip Bentley?" Caroline was astounded. "Surely, it cannot be the same?"

"Indeed it is, for he recalls very well the many happy days he spent in Derbyshire. However, that was a long time ago and I am sure you will find him very changed now."

"I recall he was a very handsome, elegant young man about town," said Elizabeth, "a bon vivant, one would almost say."

Her husband agreed and added, "He still is very elegant and well spoken, but there is a greater degree of sobriety and moderation in his presentation, I think. He strikes me as a resolute and intelligent man with a good deal of common sense and exactly the right experience for the job."

Mr Bingley could not recall him at first and had to be reminded by Jane of the Hendersons and the grand ball at Newland Hall to which everybody had been invited.

Colonel Fitzwilliam, however, had more cause to remember Mr Bentley and recalled also the reasons for the departure of the family from Derbyshire all those years ago. He asked, "Did he mention his stepfather, Mr Henderson? There was that dreadful business of the slave trade, remember?"

"He did indeed, without any prompting at all on my part—not that I would have, but that's beside the point," Darcy replied. "In fact, Mr Bentley appears to have sought to put as much distance between the disreputable Henderson and himself when he discovered the truth about his past. Which is why, he explained, he had chosen quite deliberately to work in France. He spent almost ten years at the port of Marseilles, working his way up from the position of a shipping clerk to the management of an important shipping firm."

Caroline, who already knew some of this information, listened eagerly as he went on.

"After Henderson's death, Philip Bentley returned to England and made a home for his widowed mother and his stepsisters just outside of London. They live there today, and Mrs Henderson has used her husband's money, or whatever was left of it, to set up a home for orphans in the east end of London. This has been attested to by Jonathan Bingley, in an excellent character reference.

"Lord Shaftesbury, for whom Mr Bentley worked for some time, also mentions his charitable work and praises his dedication and compassion as well as his capacity for hard work. As you see, he is well qualified."

"Did you get any indication of his feelings towards us? Did you have the impression he was angry or bitter about what happened?" asked Caroline, and Darcy shook his head.

"I detected no such sentiment. He asked after everyone he had known— Fitzwilliam and you, Caroline, and David," he replied, adding casually, "He had some knowledge of family matters—presumably through his association with Jonathan—such as Isabella's marriage and, of course, Mr Gardiner's death, but I would doubt that he has any animosity towards you at all; he seems a remarkably sensible man."

Caroline knew she could rely upon Darcy's judgment.

"Would it worry Isabella, do you think, if Mr Bentley were to return?" asked Elizabeth. "They were close friends, after all."

Caroline smiled, recalling her last meeting with Mr Bentley; she knew how deeply in love he was with Isabella and how much she had regretted that they would never marry.

"They *were* good friends but I do not believe it will affect Isabella now; after all, Mr Bentley will be chiefly in Manchester, and even if he were to visit us, it is unlikely Bella will meet him. She is too busy with her work at the hospital. Besides, she is preparing to accompany Henry Forrester on his tour of workhouses in Wales; they will be gone in a few days, long before Mr Bentley takes up his duties."

She sounded very certain and Darcy said, "Well, that's settled then. You have no other objections, Caroline?"

"Objections? No indeed. I agree that Mr Bentley will probably make an excellent shipping manager. I confess I have always felt some unease about our treatment of him, when it was his stepfather who was the villain of the piece."

At this Fitzwilliam intervened. "That was a very long time ago, my dear, you acted for the best and need feel no guilt at all."

But Caroline could not forget, even after they had agreed that Mr Darcy could write to Mr Bentley confirming his duties as well as his salary and conditions of service in the position. On the drive home, Fitzwilliam nodded off to sleep, but Caroline's mind kept returning to that unhappy meeting when Mr Bentley had come to say farewell. Though neither of them had said it, it had been always there between them—the sense of injustice, the unfairness of it all.

That he dearly loved Isabella was never in doubt. Caroline believed her daughter would have loved him in return, yet Isabella had refused him, persuaded that she could not possibly marry a man, however good and amiable, whose father and stepfather had links with the pernicious slave trade, even though he was in no way connected with any of their actions.

For many years, as Isabella remained unwed, Caroline had suffered feelings of remorse as it became clear that Isabella, having decided not to marry Mr Bentley, had little interest in any other man. They had been such good companions, shared so many interests, it could have been a very happy marriage.

Caroline had often questioned her own part in the matter.

Now, in a strange twist of fate, Mr Bentley was coming back into their lives. Caroline wondered how it would all turn out. Could there be problems for Isabella, if they should meet? She thought not.

Isabella was married to Henry Forrester and there was little Harry and perhaps another child when all this business of visiting poor houses in Wales was over. It was very unlikely that Isabella and Mr Bentley would even meet.

But, above all that, Caroline was happy to give Mr Bentley a chance, an opportunity to return and reclaim the regard and esteem he had been deprived of by an unfortunate past over which he'd had no control.

If Isabella had a say in the matter, Caroline was certain she would have agreed.

Chapter Nineteen

CAROLINE WOULD REMEMBER THE SPRING of 1865 as one recalls a moment of quiet before a storm.

She wrote later, to Emma Wilson:

> *I have heard that sailors on the ocean speak of nights when there is a strange calm that feels as if it will last forever; then, on the morrow, unexpected swells rise up without warning and break upon the deck with such ferocity as would confound the mind.*
>
> *Likewise, I had no inkling of what was to follow our peaceful Spring…*

In the middle of a week of fine, warm weather, Isabella and Doctor Forrester had left for Wales, promising to write often, leaving Harry, their young son, to bring unalloyed joy to his devoted grandparents.

A week later, Mr Bentley called by appointment.

Their meeting, on a resplendent May morning, was both cordial and enlightening. Caroline had wondered whether they should ask him to dinner, but he had written to say he was staying with friends in Derby and would call at four o'clock if that was convenient, which meant it had to be afternoon tea. Memories from years past were bound to crowd around such an occasion, and

Caroline prayed she would cope well with the situation. She need not have suffered any apprehension at all.

When he arrived in a hired vehicle, Caroline, who had been watching from one of the upstairs windows, hurried down to the parlour. He was punctual and tea was ready to be served.

Entering the room, he came directly to her and, taking her outstretched hand, kissed it without fuss as he used to do. His manners were pleasing and elegant, as they had always been.

"Mr Bentley, how very nice to see you again, and may I say how glad I am that you have accepted the position in Manchester," Caroline said. He bowed as he acknowledged her greeting and replied that he had the greatest pleasure on both counts.

"I never knew when I applied for the position in Manchester that it was Mr Gardiner's company; not until I met with Mr Darcy, who enlightened me, did I become aware of it. I would not be exaggerating were I to say I was overjoyed to receive his letter confirming my appointment."

He smiled and seemed to gather his thoughts as he looked around the room, where they had last met some years ago, before continuing, "As for returning to Derbyshire, it is I who have been remiss and it must be my loss, for I remember enjoying such happy times during the year we spent in this part of the country."

Caroline, pleased to find him so little altered in manner at least, invited him to be seated and made to pour out the tea.

"It is still tea?" she asked, adding lightly, "You have not been converted to coffee or chocolate after all those years in France?"

"Certainly not; though I am partial to a good cup of coffee after dinner, I could not do without my tea at breakfast and through the day," he said. "My French friends think me mad! The tea in France is such a weak brew, it is not worthy of the name. I used to have mine sent over from England."

She watched him as he partook of tea and cake, not quite as eagerly as before but with genuine pleasure. He looked fit and well but a good deal older; greying hair and a deeply tanned complexion spoke of many years working in a climate which afforded greater warmth and sunshine than England. He was still a very handsome man.

"Your mother and sisters are well?" Caroline asked and he replied that they were, except his mother was rather frail and did not go out a great deal.

One of his stepsisters, Maria, lived with her, he explained, while the younger girl, the one who would not allow herself to be called Fanny, was married and living in France.

"She married a Frenchman?" asked Caroline, not entirely surprised.

"Yes, Mrs Fitzwilliam, he is the only son of a famous French family that manufactures fine porcelain. Frances met him on a visit to France; he became so besotted with her, he followed her to England and would not take no for an answer," he explained, adding, "My mother misses her, for we see her rarely, but there are consolations, for when she visits, she brings my mother so many gifts, she now has a cabinet filled with exquisite pieces of fine china, which she adores."

Caroline laughed, noting that he had not lost his sense of humour either.

She did, however, make a point of advising him, before he could ask, in as casual a voice as she could manage, that Isabella and Doctor Forrester were visiting Wales over the next few months. She noticed an initial spark of interest as Mr Bentley nodded to acknowledge her information, but he smiled and asked no further questions, and apart from indicating that it was a matter of medical practise, she said no more on the subject.

After the initial pleasantries, their conversation progressed logically to the business at hand, and Caroline found him an interested and perspicacious listener. He was keen to learn as much as possible about the work of the office and discover any of its problems before he took up his position there.

Later, when they were joined by Colonel Fitzwilliam and David, who had been out fishing all day, the conversation became much more animated. Having expressed pleasure at seeing what a fine gentleman young David had become, Mr Bentley entered easily into conversation with him and, watching them together, Caroline could scarcely believe that so much time had passed since they had last spoken.

"David will be travelling with us to Manchester," she explained during a break in the conversation while more tea was taken. "He has decided to take an interest in the business, since his grandfather left him a substantial parcel of shares."

"I'm afraid I've dumped my ambition to join the cavalry," David confessed, a little sheepishly.

Mr Bentley seemed completely unsurprised. "A very sound decision, if I may say so, Mr Fitzwilliam. The career of a cavalry officer is a highly overrated one, to my mind; I cannot believe there is much satisfaction to be had in charging across a battlefield in the face of cannon fire on a horse that is likely to be shot from under one, leaving its rider floundering in the mud to be trampled upon by others. The French are fanatical about cavalry charges, as Colonel Fitzwilliam will verify, and it has not done them much good."

Everyone laughed at this and Fitzwilliam felt much more at ease. Soon they were discussing fishing and politics and, for two men who had not met in many years, appeared to get on very well indeed. At the risk of incurring his father's wrath, David declared he was tired of Lord Palmerston and was delighted when Mr Bentley readily agreed.

"It is a sentiment widely held within his own party as well as among the general populace, I think," he said.

When the time came for him to leave, he thanked them for their hospitality and it was arranged that they would meet and travel together to Manchester in a fortnight.

Mr Peter Kennedy was informed of their plans, and when they arrived in the city, he was there to meet them and convey them to their lodgings. Later, he invited the entire party to his home, where they met his wife, took tea, and rested awhile before proceeding to the office.

To her very great satisfaction, Caroline saw that the two men, within a very short time of being introduced, were engaged in amicable and thoughtful conversation.

Other arrangements were agreed upon as Mr Kennedy and his wife invited Mr Bentley to stay at their home until suitable lodgings could be found for him. It was a generous and kindly gesture that augured well for their professional association in the future, Caroline thought.

When afterwards they attended the office, where Mr Bentley met the staff, she had more reason to hope that here at last was a reasonable resolution to the difficult problem she had inherited through her father's will and Robert's unfortunate inertia.

Leaving the two men and David together to continue their discussion, Caroline and her husband stepped out of the building and walked the short distance into the town. Colonel Fitzwilliam had seen, displayed upon a hoarding, notice of a meeting of the Reform Union set up in Manchester to campaign for the extension of the franchise. He was eager to discover more about it. Caroline did not object; it was almost like the old days when they had campaigned together for the passage of the Reform Bill.

"Do you believe the time is right for it?" she asked as they crossed the street, and he answered with conviction, "Yes indeed, with Gladstone's weight behind it, the time is far more propitious than before. If only Palmerston could be persuaded..." he said almost wistfully, and Caroline took his arm and drew him towards her. She knew better than to say what everyone knew to be true—that the success of any campaign for reform would depend upon the death of Lord Palmerston.

Instead, she reverted to the resolution of their present difficulties.

"I cannot tell you how relieved I am today, Fitzy; with Mr Bentley in charge and Mr Kennedy to work with him, we can at least be certain that all Papa's hard work will not be in vain. I have feared very much these last few months that it would all go awry and I would fail you and Mr Darcy and dear Mama. It has been my greatest concern. I could not bear to let Papa down."

Fitzwilliam hastened to reassure her that he had never shared her fears, confident that she would succeed. But Caroline knew in her heart that despite his touching faith, she still had much to prove.

Complacency was out of the question.

Returning to Derbyshire, Caroline looked forward to reporting to Mr Darcy on the successful introduction of Mr Philip Bentley to the staff of the Manchester office and, by this information, to reinforce her appreciation of his part in the resolution of a most intractable problem.

Mr Darcy, she believed, should take most of the credit, for having in the first place suggested such an appointment and then selecting the best man for the job. Of the suitability of Mr Bentley for the position, Caroline had no doubts at all.

On arriving home, however, they were overtaken by events in London and elsewhere.

Caroline's nephew, Darcy Gardiner, called in a state of high excitement, declaring that "the old fox Palmerston, having won a vote of confidence by the skin of his teeth, intends, at the venerable age of eighty, to fight yet another election!" This time even Fitzwilliam, for all his past loyalty, could see the problem inherent in such a strategy. After young Darcy left, promising to send them reports from Westminster, whither he was going post haste, Fitzwilliam decided to visit his friend Anthony Tate, confident he would have all the news on recent political events.

Caroline went upstairs to bathe and dress in preparation for a visit to Pemberley, but her husband was barely gone twenty minutes when she heard the curricle returning and, looking out, saw Fitzwilliam getting out in what seemed like inordinate haste. He could not have reached the Tates' place, nor even the office of the *Matlock Review* in so short a time, she thought. He must have had some extraordinary news; perhaps Palmerston had resigned.

Throwing on a wrap, Caroline hurried downstairs to find her husband standing in the hall with an expression upon his face that left no room for any doubt. A catastrophe had occurred! She was sure of it.

Perhaps, thought Caroline, Lord Palmerston was dead. But when he saw her, he placed a finger on his lips to warn her against exclaiming too loudly and, putting an arm around her, took her upstairs to their room. Clearly the news was not for the ears of the servants.

Caroline was wild to know what all this secrecy was about.

"Fitzy, what has happened. Is it Lord Palmerston? Is he dead?"

"If it were only the case—Caroline, my dear, this is nothing to do with Palmerston or any other politician," he said, having seated her upon the bed, in a voice so hoarse she could hardly hear his words. "I have just met your brother Richard. He was on his way here to inform us that Julian Darcy has arrived from Cambridge. His wife, Josie, has left him and their son, and gone away with some man in the book trade who has promised to publish her book!"

"What?" Caroline was incredulous. "Fitzy, are you sure?" she cried, her face ashen as she realised that, if the source of his information was her brother Richard, the story had to be true, however incredible it might sound. Richard would never retail gossip.

When her husband nodded, she asked, "When did this happen? And what is to become of their little boy?"

"I believe Julian has brought young Anthony with him and proposes to leave him in the care of Richard and Cassy. Young Lizzie Gardiner was spending some time with them in Cambridge, and Richard says she saw it happening but could do nothing to stop it," said Fitzwilliam.

"And have they told Mr Darcy and Cousin Lizzie yet?" she asked, her mind racing as she thought of the effect this news would have on them.

"No, not yet. Julian is very exhausted, Richard says, but I gather he will go over to Pemberley with Cassandra tomorrow. My God, Caroline, what on earth will Darcy do? This will be a dreadful blow!"

"It will indeed," said Caroline. "Poor Cousin Lizzie, how will she bear this? After the loss of William, she had placed all her hopes in Julian. I know she never approved of Josie, but she would not have expected anything like this!"

All week long, Caroline's one desire was to go to her cousin, but she was dissuaded by Fitzwilliam, who explained the need to give Darcy and Elizabeth time with their son.

"Julian's grief must surely take its toll upon them. They must want to help him and each other, Caroline. Then there's Cassandra too; no doubt she will feel the shock of this terrible thing. There will be time enough for us to see them."

She knew he was right and yet longed to go to Elizabeth, who had always been like an elder sister to her. As the days passed, they received scraps of news from Richard and Cassy, but there was little that could explain how this disaster had come about. Caroline was impatient to know more.

Following the return of Julian Darcy to Cambridge, Caroline went to visit her sister-in-law and found Cassandra with Anthony and her own son James in the sunlit garden they had created for the children. Cassy rose to greet her, and as they embraced, both women wept.

As the boys played amidst the swings, the rocking horse, and other colourful toys, oblivious of the circumstances that had brought them together, it was difficult to believe that Josie had left her child and her husband for some stranger who would publish her book. To Caroline, it seemed like an incredible tale, taken from the pages of a "penny dreadful."

There was little they could say in the hearing of the boys; Cassy sent for a maid to sit with the children while she took Caroline indoors.

"Cassy, did Julian know why? I cannot believe it was just so she could have a book published!" Caroline asked, but Cassandra could tell her little more than she knew already.

"I know only what Julian and Lizzie have told me," she said. "Josie, in her note to Julian, claimed that she did not love Mr Barrett, and Lizzie, who has spent most of Spring with them, says she saw no sign of any special affection between them. It is such a waste of a life, Caroline, I cannot believe she has done this."

She sobbed and Caroline went to comfort her. "My poor mama and papa—it is so unfair. Have they not suffered enough?" asked Cassy. There was no sympathy here for Josie, and not much more would be forthcoming at Pemberley either, thought Caroline, still unable to wholly comprehend the wretched situation they faced.

~~~

The rest of Summer seemed to pass like a succession of scenes in a melo-drama upon the stage, as the saga of Julian and Josie's disintegrating marriage engulfed them. Each day, they waited eagerly for news, and every household, save that of the Darcys at Pemberley, hurried to exchange what little informa-tion was to be had, gleaned generally from visitors and occasionally from letters that came from London or Cambridge. For many weeks there was no news at all of Josie, and Julian Darcy, dejected and sad, left Cambridge and went to work in Paris.

Then, early in Autumn, word came that Josie had been found and recovered by Richard and Cassandra. She had left Mr Barrett but was so ill and under-nourished, they feared she may never regain her health. Julian had rushed to her side as she was seen by the best doctors in London, summoned by Richard to treat her. "Lizzie says Julian has forgiven her completely and wishes only for her to be well again," Caroline reported, returning from a visit to Pemberley, and later, they heard that Josie had rallied and there was hope.

In all of this time, there had been a singular dearth of good news.

Even the return of Dr Forrester and Isabella in Autumn brought Caroline little joy, for Isabella revealed that Henry had been so moved by the poverty and suffering of the children of the pit villages, he intended to resign his position at Littleford in the new year and return to help Mr Jenkins establish a clinic in the valley.

"Mama, the children are all afflicted with chest and stomach infections as a result of the insanitary conditions in which they are forced to live. Their cottages are dank and dirty with no provision for sewerage or clean water; Henry and I agree that some thing has to be done. Reverend Jenkins has started to collect donations; if we can help, we must. Henry says it is only a matter of time before there is an epidemic of typhus or cholera and many children will die," she declared.

Knowing it was useless to argue when Isabella and Dr Forrester were determined upon a plan, Caroline wondered when their lives would return to normal again.

Perhaps in the New Year, she thought.

There was some talk that young Lizzie Gardiner, Richard and Cassy's lovely daughter, would soon be engaged to Mr Carr, an Irish-American gentleman who had purchased Will Camden's property at Rushmore.

That *would* be good news, thought Caroline, but since Cassy had said nothing when they last met, she had been reluctant to ask.

During a visit to Pemberley, however, her cousin Elizabeth was certain Mr Carr and young Lizzie Gardiner were in love.

"He is a fine man, very gentlemanlike, and devoted to Lizzie," Elizabeth had said. "I have observed them together and I am quite sure they would have been engaged already if it were not for this terrible business with Josie and Julian. No doubt he thinks it is the wrong time to approach Richard with a proposal for young Lizzie, but I doubt it will be far off. Young Darcy admires and likes him and Mr Darcy is very impressed with him," she had added.

"Well, at least that will mean a happy occasion at last," Caroline said to her husband, "I am so weary of all this misery and gloom."

Caroline did not know it then, but there was more to come.

News broke of Lord Palmerston's death in October, not six months after he had won an historic election. Fitzwilliam, loyal to the end, went to London for the funeral, but young Darcy Gardiner was heard to say, "Now, perhaps, there will be a chance for change and perhaps some progress on reform," adding that, "Lord Russell and Mr Gladstone have promised reform of the franchise; Palmerston was the only immovable obstacle."

Meanwhile, Josie, it was reported, was stronger and there were great hopes of her recovery, even though the prognosis was still pessimistic. Julian's letters to his parents were full of plans for their future together. He spoke always of her increasing strength and good spirits.

But, despite his faith and the prayers of their families, as the New Year dawned, Josie's unhappy spirit fled her enfeebled body, taking with it the last of her husband's hopes. Desolate and unable or unwilling to remain in England amidst all the painful memories, Julian renounced his inheritance in favour of his son and went back to work in France.

Young Anthony Darcy was now the heir to Pemberley, and his aunt Cassandra was the child's legal guardian.

The good news came in small helpings.

First, Lizzie and her Mr Carr became engaged in the Spring, and later in the year, Mr Darcy announced the appointment of young Darcy Gardiner to take over the management of the Pemberley estate.

"Our community needs a young, active man to be working with it, and I can think of no one better than my grandson," he had said.

Caroline too was hopeful that their run of bad fortune had come to an end. A letter from her daughter Amy in Oxford brought news that she was expecting her first child, and her son David was showing a commendable grasp of the business, making no further mention of joining the cavalry. When, in the Autumn, young Lizzie Gardiner and Mr Carr were married, it was one of the happiest days she could remember in years.

Meanwhile, Henry Forrester returned to Wales to work on the proposed clinic for the children of the pit villages. This time, to her mother's great relief, Isabella remained at home. Little Harry was an active and demanding child and Isabella was loathe to burden her mother with his care for a further period.

Doctor Forrester wrote, though fitfully and not at very great length, to assure his wife that matters were progressing well. Money, he said, had been collected and a temporary clinic had been set up. He wrote:

> Bella, my dear, there are many sick children in urgent need of care and I am doing my best. You cannot imagine the appalling lack of hygiene and sanitation for both adults and children. It is a disgraceful state of affairs. Mr Jenkins has managed to get a couple of useful helpers and we hope to make some changes soon.

His dedication was remarkable.

Isabella was pleased he could, in the midst of all this work, find the time to write. Not only was she delighted that he was well, but she noted with great satisfaction that he appeared to feel contented at being able to help the poor. He had an almost missionary zeal about him—it was a quality she had found hard to resist.

One morning, however, the mail brought a letter from Mrs Jenkins, which sent Isabella hurrying to her parents' home.

"Mama, I fear there is bad news; Kitty writes that Henry is ill. She writes that he is too ill to travel and is not aware that she has written to me. What can it be? Is it possible he has caught some contagion?"

Caroline felt very cold and fearful as she read Kitty's brief note.

We are not able to move him from his lodgings because he has a high fever and has much pain in his joints. Mr Jenkins has summoned the apothecary, but I am writing to ask you to come as quickly as you can and, if it is at all possible, to bring Dr Gardiner with you. I believe that he is the only person who may know what treatment Dr Forrester needs.

…she wrote, plainly not overstating the urgency of the situation.

Isabella was anxious. "I must go to him, Mama," she cried.

In minutes, Caroline had run downstairs and dispatched a servant for Dr Gardiner. Richard came at once; when he read Kitty's letter, he was very afraid of what it might mean.

They left immediately, travelling through the night in the hope of reaching their destination before the patient's fever reached its crisis. None of them, not even Doctor Gardiner, could know the cause of Henry Forrester's illness, and neither Caroline nor her daughter was fully aware of the seriousness of his condition. When, after travelling for what had seemed an interminable period of time, during which their anxiety did not let them eat or sleep, they arrived at the house where Doctor Forrester lay ill; he was in delirium.

The village practitioner, who had been summoned, could not give Dr Gardiner sufficient information to help him understand what had caused the high fever except to suggest it might be "putrid fever."

Richard was at a loss to explain how Henry might have been infected with what appeared to be typhus when he was a doctor with high standards of hygiene.

Working with little knowledge and no other assistance, Richard tried everything he knew, but nothing they did seemed to bring down the fever and reclaim the patient from his delirium. Occasionally, he seemed a little more lucid, but that did not last and soon, he would relapse again into ramblings and groans which were dreadful to witness. Isabella sat beside him throughout the night, moistening his lips with water or soothing his brow with lavender. She neither ate nor slept, and Caroline feared for her daughter's health.

After three days and nights, Henry Forrester opened his eyes; he was bathed in a terrible sweat and the fever had abated.

Richard was hopeful and they rushed to change his linen and make him comfortable. He seemed to rally a little, but his heart had been so weakened by the struggle, he lasted but a few hours, long enough to see and recognise his wife and hold her hand while he lay upon his pillow, until exhausted, he slipped gently back into a state of unconsciousness from which he never emerged.

Isabella wept.

"Oh Mama, if I had been with him, if only I had come too..." she cried, and nothing Caroline could do or say would comfort her.

Chapter Twenty

EMMA WILSON HAD COMPLETED A list of people who were to be invited to a dinner party at Standish Park to celebrate the elevation of her husband James to judicial office.

His retirement from the House of Commons following the resignation of Lord Russell and the return of the Tories to office had come at a time when England was once again going through a turbulent Summer of discontent. The crash of financial houses combined with poor harvests, the scourges of rinderpest, and cholera all helped create an atmosphere conducive to public disorder and riot. In London, to the consternation of its citizens, it even caused Hyde Park to be closed!

The previous year had been a difficult one.

With her husband no longer embroiled in the machinations of getting legislation through the Parliament, Emma looked forward to a calmer, less uncertain life. Spring was already making its presence felt in the farmlands and gardens across the Weald of Kent; Standish Park with its great orchards was at its prettiest, and as she contemplated the prospect, Emma Wilson hoped for happier times ahead.

The maid brought in her letters, and among them was one from Caroline Fitzwilliam. The cousins had grown very close over the years, and Emma opened up her letter quickly. Caroline wrote:

My dearest Emma,

I must apologise for the delay in responding to your kind letter; it has been a comfort to know how many dear friends and relatives have us in their thoughts.

Even after all these months, it is not easy to write of my dear Isabella's misfortune and the deep sorrow it has caused us all.

Unlike my sister Emily, whose uncommon strength was a source of inspiration to everyone, especially Cousin Lizzie and myself, Isabella is not a thinker or a reader. She needs activity and companionship, and at the moment, she has withdrawn from both and often denies herself food and sleep.

Emma, she blames herself, unreasonably, for not accompanying Henry Forrester on his second journey to Wales, claiming that had she been there, he would not have become infected with typhus. (Richard now believes that it was typhus, probably carried by the lice on the children Henry treated and the neglect of the condition that killed him.) It is possible Henry never realised he had been infected until it was too late.

If only he had not returned to Wales; he had so much to do at Littleford, where he has worked these many years, he would still be alive and my poor Isabella would not be in this state today. They enjoyed working together, Emma; they loved working at the hospital, especially caring for the children. He was devoted to them.

Richard speaks very highly of Henry; he was a most dedicated physician and a good husband.

Poor little Harry, he misses his father too… oh Emma, I would give anything to see my Isabella smile again. I fear for her health. She continues to live at the house with Harry and the servants. She is in no trouble financially, since Henry was very prudent and left her well provided for, but she is so very lonely and unhappy…

Emma put the letter down, disturbed by its contents.

"This will not do," she said to herself as she hastened downstairs to her husband's study to consult him on how young Isabella might best be helped. She was determined that something must be done.

Not long after receiving Caroline's letter, Emma Wilson wrote to Isabella, inviting her and little Harry to Standish Park. She wrote:

You must feel free to bring your maid and Harry's nurse; they will not be in the way and it will help Harry to have someone familiar with him. I have no plans to travel in Spring, and since James will be away from time to time for the sittings of the court, I should very much welcome your company.

Though Isabella was at first reluctant to accept, her parents and her uncle Richard persuaded her that it would be beneficial both to her and Harry. Colonel Fitzwilliam, who welcomed the chance to meet his friend and former Parliamentary colleague James Wilson again, offered to accompany them to Kent on the railway, and she finally agreed.

Caroline was overjoyed. If anyone could comfort Isabella and help rebuild her life, Emma Wilson could. She hoped fervently that Isabella and Harry would remain at Standish Park throughout the Spring. Emma's kindness and the salubrious surroundings of Standish Park could only do them both a great deal of good.

❧

The New Year had brought more good tidings when Richard Gardiner's work in medical research was rewarded with a knighthood. Cassy and he moved to Camden House on the Camden Estate, which Mr Darcy had purchased for them.

From Manchester, Mr Bentley reported of new contracts and increased business activity, resulting from the improvements made at the office.

It was with some optimism that Caroline set about preparing for the regular meeting of partners and shareholders in June of that year. At Fitzwilliam's suggestion, she decided to combine it with a small dinner party to celebrate the success of their efforts.

"It will not be anything grand," she explained to her sister Emily, who had offered to help, "just a simple function to which I can ask the partners, shareholders, their husbands and wives of course. I do believe we deserve to congratulate ourselves on our achievements in the face of much tribulation and difficult trading conditions. You do not think I am being immodest, do you, Emmy?" she asked, frowning a little.

Emily was absolutely certain she was not.

"No indeed, Caroline. I have often wondered how you carried on in the face of all that has happened. It could not have been easy."

"It was not, but then I have to confess that I could not have done it alone.

I am profoundly grateful to Mr Bentley and Mr Kennedy, who have worked so hard this last year, and to dear Mr Darcy for having the foresight to advise me to appoint Mr Bentley in the first place."

Colonel Fitzwilliam, who had gone up to London to attend the debates on Disraeli's new Reform Bill, had sent a message by telegraph to say he would be back to attend the meeting and the dinner that was to follow. He had asked that the carriage be sent to meet the train but had made no mention of seeing Isabella.

Caroline had received a letter from her daughter a week ago in which she had seemed particularly pleased with the success of her efforts at sketching the various vistas available to be seen at Standish Park.

Aunt Emma is determined that I should learn to paint; I would dearly love to, but fear I have not the fine talent that she and her daughters are blessed with. But my sketches please her and Harry, which is all I ask. I shall look forward to having your opinion when we return.

There being no mention of a date of return, Caroline did not concern herself about it.

❦

On the day of the meeting, Messrs Kennedy and Bentley arrived early, having travelled from Manchester on the previous day and stayed overnight at the inn at Lambton. They had come bearing plenty of good news with figures and charts showing increasing volumes of trade, larger contracts, more orders, and greater profits forecast for the rest of the year.

"I think we can promise the partners a much better result this Christmas," said Mr Kennedy, proudly laying out the statement of accounts, which were now in exemplary order.

In all of the excitement, Caroline, who had despatched the carriage to meet the train that morning, forgot the time until the sound of wheels and hooves on the drive brought her to the window. Thinking it must be the party from Pemberley arriving early—Mr Darcy was always insistent upon punctuality—Caroline went down to the hall just as the vehicle came to a standstill and Fitzwilliam alighted. He then picked up young Harry and set him down before turning to help his daughter out of the carriage.

Caroline saw and scarcely recognised her, so remarkably changed was Isabella, as she smiled and came directly into her mother's arms. They embraced, but this time the tears were all Caroline's.

"Bella, my dear, dear girl, how well you look. I knew Aunt Emma and Standish Park would be good for you, did I not tell you so?"

Isabella was more at ease than her mother, who almost burst into tears as she looked at her daughter and turned to reproach her husband.

"Fitzy, why did you not tell me Isabella was coming home?" she asked and as mother and daughter gazed at each other, Colonel Fitzwilliam tried to explain that they had wanted to surprise her.

Meanwhile, Harry, who had run through the hall and into the parlour where the men from Manchester were preparing for the meeting, raced out again, a sheaf of paper in his hand, pursued by a gentleman intent on retrieving his notes.

When Mr Bentley saw Isabella standing in the hall, he stopped and seemed unable to speak. Caroline watched as Isabella took a while to recover from the shock of seeing him there before she stepped forward, her hand outstretched, and said in a quiet voice, "Mr Bentley, what a surprise to see you here. I thought you were in France."

His confusion even worse confounded, Mr Bentley came forward immediately and took her hand.

"Mrs Forrester, why, I have been in England for some years and in Manchester since last Summer, employed by the Commercial Trading Company to manage the Manchester shipping office. May I say what a pleasure it is to see you again after all these years."

As they stood there, he lifted her hand to his lips and Caroline looked at Fitzwilliam.

"And this is my son Harry, who appears to have purloined some of your papers," said Isabella, retrieving the material and handing it to Mr Bentley, who bent down and gravely shook the boy's hand.

No one said another word until suddenly, young Rachel came bounding downstairs to embrace her sister and tell her how lovely she looked.

Mr Bentley, who had recovered his missing papers, excused himself and returned to his work in the parlour, and the travellers went upstairs.

When they returned later to take tea in the sitting room, Isabella had changed her dark travelling dress for a soft lavender and grey striped gown, whose style so reminded Caroline of Emma; it was clear she had chosen it for her niece.

Mr Bentley meanwhile had composed himself sufficiently to make a more successful attempt at communication, and Isabella seemed very interested in what he had to say, though as they were seated at some distance from the others, Caroline could not hear what it was about. She assumed it would be about his travels and his work in France.

By the time the rest of the party had arrived and they were ready to start the meeting, it seemed as though they were old friends, which of course they were, although both Isabella and Mr Bentley were surprised at the ease with which they had slipped into casual conversation.

At dinner that evening, Caroline waited to see if Mr Bentley would move towards Isabella as they entered the dining room, but he did not, choosing rather to sit across the table from her, from which vantage point he could both hear and observe her without drawing attention to himself. Very astute indeed, thought Caroline.

When they were joined in the drawing room by the gentlemen, however, amidst all the bustle of taking tea, coffee, and sweets, it seemed to Caroline that the pair had secured the only position in the room, to the right and a little behind the pianoforte, where they could not be overheard.

As a small procession of performers, adults, and children entertained the party, Isabella and Mr Bentley listened attentively, applauded politely, and then became engaged in an absorbing discussion; one must suppose it was to do with the merits of each performance, but one could not be certain. Afterwards, when the guests had gone home, Isabella embraced both her parents and asked to be excused. She was a little weary from travelling, she said, and wished to go to bed.

Isabella was too tired and Harry too excited by their return home to allow her much time for contemplation. But, after she had put him to bed, she did sit down at the desk in her room and make a note in her diary, recording there both her surprise at seeing Mr Bentley in her father's house and her pleasure that he had remembered her so well. It read:

> *I had not thought ever to see him again, when having left for France all those years ago, he never returned to Derbyshire nor wrote ever again. When I did see him, the shock of it was no greater than the pleasure of*

knowing that he had not forgotten me; indeed, as we spoke later, it seemed he recalled very vividly our friendship, as I did. How very strange that he should be back in England working for my grandfather's business.

Such a happy coincidence.

Not surprisingly, he appears much older than I remember him, as I no doubt must seem to him. It is a long time since we last met, though it did not feel so when we spoke together. He is still a very agreeable gentleman.

Though I doubt we shall meet often, it is good to know he is here in England, even if Manchester is many miles from Matlock.

When Caroline wrote, some days later, to thank Emma Wilson for the transformation she had wrought upon her daughter, she could not resist relating the story of the meeting between Isabella and Mr Bentley.

Forgive me, dear Emma, she wrote:

...if I sound too much like our dear departed Aunt Bennet, whose chief hobby in life is said to have been matchmaking, but it was a revelation to see them as they stood in the hall looking at one another, each as if the other were a phantom they had never expected to see again.

While I am not suggesting it was a case of love rekindled, for indeed these two are mature persons and not of an age or disposition to be over-taken by such romantic raptures, had you been there, Emma, you would understand what I mean when I say there was something very remarkable about that meeting.

Now, pray do not berate me for sounding like some silly, romantic woman with her head buried in the pages of a novella from a circulating library, but, Emma, I would give ten years of my life to see my Bella happy again.

Mr Bentley did love her dearly—he told me so himself—and they were such good friends, and of course, he has never married! I live in hope...

Emma smiled and tucked her letter into the pocket of her gown.

"Ah Caroline, ever the romantic, who knows, you may yet be right. For Isabella's sake, I hope Mr Bentley is as deeply affected as you think he is," she thought, as she went downstairs.

She was glad to have contributed to the reclamation of her niece. Recalling how dreary and unhappy Isabella had been when she came to

Standish Park with her tearful little boy hanging about his mother's skirts, she admitted it had been quite an achievement to draw her out from the depths of her self-rebuking gloom. If it had helped set her on the road to a new life, Emma would be quite content.

～✦～

The following week brought heavy rains and the possibility of floods in the valley. Happily, Isabella had allowed herself to be persuaded to stay on at her parents' home rather than risk returning to the cottage with Harry. Word had come that the lower meadows were inundated from the overflowing creek, and both Caroline and Colonel Fitzwilliam had urged her to stay.

"There will be work that needs doing before you can return, having been away so long," said her mother, and Isabella agreed.

When the weather cleared and the roads were dry again, Caroline and Isabella set out to walk to the village. They had both felt the need of some sunshine and exercise, as well as the chance to talk privately together. There were matters Caroline wished to discuss and something Isabella wanted very much to ask her mother.

They had not gone far when she asked, quite casually, why she had not been told of Mr Bentley's appointment to the position at the Manchester office.

"Did you not think I would wish to know?" she asked, gazing at her mother, with wide, clear eyes. "Or perhaps, did you fear I would be upset at knowing he was in the area?"

Caroline replied quite truthfully that it had not seemed important at the time because of everything else that was happening around them.

"I knew there was very little chance of your meeting him. We had not heard from him in years, nor had you ever spoken of him with any degree of interest. Besides, preparations were afoot for you to travel to Wales with Henry."

Isabella looked quickly away, her eyes suddenly filling with tears at the memory.

"Yes, yes of course. I understand, but even so, Mr Bentley had been a friend; no doubt he had reasons for his silence as I had. But I should have liked to have known he was back in England, that he was working for the company and he was well and happy," she said in a very soft voice that was barely audible.

Caroline smiled. "He certainly looks well, despite the passage of years, but as for being happy, of that I am not so certain," she said, causing her daughter to ask, "Why do you say that, Mama?"

"Well, for a start, he has never married and..." she began.

"Ah, but a man need not marry to be happy," said Isabella. "It is only women who believe that we *must* be married and have children to ensure our happiness. Men are able to find pleasure and satisfaction in many other pursuits and have no compulsion to marry at all unless it pleases them to do so."

Her mother expressed some surprise at this remark but was unwilling to argue the point. Instead, she said, "Well, my dear, I do think Mr Bentley *was* very disappointed when you refused his offer of marriage, and I believe that his unmarried state is a consequence of that disappointment."

Isabella seemed sceptical. "How do you know this, Mama? Has he spoken of it to you since his return?"

"Certainly not," she replied, but she did proceed to relate the gist of their conversation when Mr Bentley had come to see her before leaving for France those many years ago.

Her mother's revelation of Mr Bentley's strong expressions of affection for her astonished Isabella. While she had believed him to be partial to her, perhaps even a little in love with her, she had not fully appreciated the strength and depth of his feelings. It had undoubtedly been a factor in her decision to refuse his proposal.

"Why did you not tell me at the time, Mama? Did you think I would change my mind?"

Caroline's denial was emphatic. "No, my dear Bella, I did not, but I feared it would place a burden upon you, of remorse, even guilt. I know you are tender-hearted and kind, and I thought you would regret your refusal and feel it was your fault if you knew how he loved you and how deeply he felt your rejection."

Isabella smiled. "Did you not trust me to cope with the knowledge that he loved me? I had turned down the only man for whom I felt I could have had any strong feelings; did you fear that if I discovered how he felt, I may not be able or willing to resist?" she asked.

Caroline was at a loss for words. She had not thought that after so many years, Isabella would still recall with such clarity her feelings for Mr Bentley. But it was clear that she did. When she admitted that despite her refusal, she had genuinely admired and liked Philip Bentley and had been willing to consider marriage if he had asked her until it had been revealed to her that his family had made their money from the abhorrent and illegal slave trade, there were tears in her eyes.

"We were such good friends, Mama. I have never enjoyed such companion-ship, nor felt such warmth of feeling with any other person, before or since."

Caroline could not now deny that she had herself noticed their close association and had hoped for their engagement before the revelation of Mr Henderson's infamous past. Yet, she had to ask, "But what about Henry, Isabella? Did you not love him?"

"Of course I did. How could one not love Henry for his goodness and kindness? We did a great deal of wonderful work together," she replied. "But though there *was* love between us, there was none of the adventure, the fun of discovery, and the sense of delight I had known during that year when Mr Bentley and I had been friends.

"I was so young, so foolish as to believe that we could go on being friends, even after I had turned him down, giving him no explanation. How could I have been so blind, so self-centred, so insensitive to his feelings? I know now how utterly foolish I must have seemed to him when I made such a suggestion. I feel ashamed."

So forlorn did she seem, Caroline had to stop and urge her to rest awhile; she put her arms around her as though she were still the young girl who had been so easily persuaded that to accept a proposal of marriage from Mr Bentley would not be in her interest or that of her family.

"Bella, my love, please do not blame yourself; there is no need. Mr Bentley feels no bitterness towards you or your family; it was a long time ago, you were very young, and he understood and accepted what was done without question. Now, you have met under completely different circumstances and may well be good friends again."

Isabella shook her head. "Friends? Surely not. With Mr Bentley in Manchester and me in Matlock, I doubt we shall meet again."

"Isabella, tell me, do you wish that you could?" Caroline asked gently and the expression on her daughter's face left her in no doubt of the answer. No words were necessary.

As they resumed their walk, both women were acutely aware of the feel-ings that had been openly acknowledged that day, though neither returned to the subject. A meeting with Emily Courtney and her daughter Jessica in the village ended the possibility that it may be reopened on the way home. Neither

Isabella nor Emily had forgotten her aunt's part in Isabella's decision to refuse Mr Bentley's proposal.

Caroline spent many hours thinking over the events of the day. She was not sure she had understood everything Isabella had said, nor did her daughter subsequently return to the subject to elucidate.

But of one thing Caroline was certain: Isabella had neither forgotten nor forsaken her feelings for Mr Bentley; feelings doubtless suppressed over the years of her marriage to Henry Forrester, which had surfaced after their chance meeting. Caroline was unsure whether to be pleased or concerned by her discovery. She was in a quandary of her own making.

She wanted, with all her heart, for her daughter to be a happy and contented woman again. She worried that she ought to do something about it but knew not what. She reflected upon it for some days before deciding that she would consult her cousin Lizzie, even before speaking of the matter to her husband.

On a bright morning, when Isabella had gone with Rachel and Harry into the village to purchase a new pair boots for her son, Caroline sent for the curricle and set off for Pemberley.

Elizabeth was alone. It being a particularly fine Summer's day, Mr Darcy had taken his two grandsons, James and Anthony, down to the river for a spot of fishing. The sun was almost too warm to tempt her into the garden, which was why she was seated on the west lawn, within the cool shadow of the house, when Caroline arrived to see her.

Delighted to have such an unexpected and totally welcome visitor, she ordered refreshments and invited Caroline to sit beside her on the low wicker divan.

"Caroline, it is such a delight to have you call. I was preparing to be very bored all morning until Darcy and the boys returned. It is far too warm to walk in the garden, though the roses are beautiful again this year and this soporific weather does not allow one to read for very long. As I said to Jane, I am very spoilt because dear Jessica reads to me every evening before dinner, unless we have company. We are, just this week, reading Mrs Gaskell's 'Cranford'—are you familiar with it?"

Caroline had to confess that she was not. Mrs Gaskell was not a favourite of hers. When she had the leisure and the inclination to read, she preferred the tales of Mr Dickens, she said.

By the time the servants had brought them trays of fruit and cool, refreshing drinks, which were placed upon a low table beside the divan, both women had agreed that Mr Dickens was the superior writer, though Elizabeth complained that there were so many interesting characters in *David Copperfield* she could never remember all of them.

"That is a common complaint," Caroline acknowledged, "but it has not deterred me from enjoying it."

When the servants had left them, Caroline decided the time had come to declare the real reason for her visit. "Cousin Lizzie," she began, a little tentatively, taking advantage of the first break in the conversation, "I have come to you for advice about Bella," and immediately, Elizabeth turned with a concerned look to regard her cousin.

"Why, Caroline dear, what has happened?"

She was very aware of the plethora of problems that had beset her cousin since the death of her father but had hoped matters were settling down well.

Caroline plunged in, reminding Elizabeth of Isabella's friendship with Mr Bentley, she related in some detail the meeting that had taken place between herself and Mr Bentley, when Isabella had, upon the advice of her family, refused his proposal of marriage. She then described the recent meeting between Isabella and Mr Bentley, concluding with a careful recital of her subsequent conversation with her daughter.

Elizabeth listened attentively. She had always been particularly fond of Caroline, and despite a tendency among some members of their family to dismiss her romantic disposition, Elizabeth had recognised the value of her cousin's strength of character and affectionate nature.

As Caroline told it, it became clear to her that Mr Bentley's feelings for Isabella were unchanged despite their long separation, and it now appeared that Isabella was, at the very least, pleased to recognise this and may even welcome it.

When Caroline had concluded her tale, Elizabeth asked, "Do you believe, Caroline, that Isabella loves him?"

Caroline's answer was unambiguous. "If she does not, then she very soon will, for I have not heard her speak with such warmth and fondness of anyone before. She believes they are still good friends, but Mr Bentley cared deeply for her once, and should they have the opportunity, I am convinced they will both discover that they are much more than friends."

"And you believe this would be good for Isabella?" asked Elizabeth.

"I do, but it is not for me to answer for her, Lizzie. I wish, I should very much like, this time, to give Isabella the opportunity to decide for herself, free of my influence or that of any other member of our family.

"If this is a chance for her to find happiness, I would wish with all my heart that she would take it."

Elizabeth was thoughtful for a while, then sitting up very straight, asked, "And what are Mr Bentley's present circumstances?"

Caroline answered directly, "To the best of my knowledge, he is now a gentleman of independent means, with a substantial house and property outside London where his mother and stepsister live. He has the position in the company, of course, with an income sufficient to keep a wife and family in comfort. Needless to say, Isabella will have her own income too; Papa and Henry Forrester both saw to that."

"If that is the case," said Elizabeth, in a decisive voice, "my dear Caroline, we must create the opportunity you speak of. I agree, it is often only a question of time, and people discover for themselves how much or how little they mean to one another. Dear me, Caroline, I fear I am beginning to sound just like my mama! Let me think on it a day or two and we shall find a way, I promise."

❦

Elizabeth was as good as her word.

After Caroline had left, she rose and went upstairs to her room, where she consulted her diary. She noted that they were engaged to dine with the Bingleys later that week and to visit Netherfield, at the invitation of their nephew Jonathan Bingley and his wife, before the end of Summer.

With a full six weeks before they were due to travel south, there would be plenty of time, she decided, to plan and prepare for one of Pemberley's dinner parties. A letter from her niece Emma Bingley, mentioning the possibility of their being in this part of the country early in Autumn, confirmed her resolve. It would provide a good excuse, if one were needed, for a family gathering. She began to make a quick list of possible guests and, sending for her housekeeper Mrs Grantham, set the preparations in train.

By the time Mr Darcy and the two boys returned with not many fish but plenty of tales of the ones that got away, Elizabeth's plans were well advanced.

That evening after dinner she revealed them, gently but with genuine enthusiasm, to her husband. Darcy, not always the most ardent supporter of dances and parties, was on this occasion ready to listen and be convinced. Hearing Elizabeth's account of her conversation with Caroline, he made no comment nor lodged any objection, realising, no doubt, that his wife had many excellent arguments to support her case.

However, when she asked directly for his opinion on the possibility of a match between Isabella and Mr Bentley, he was quite frank.

"My dear Lizzie, you are not unaware, I know, that it has been my practise these many years not to intervene between young people in matters of the heart. I am even more resolute about cases where there have already been some unhappy consequences as a result of such intervention, however well intentioned. Attempts to undo what has been done before can often involve one in a tangle that may make matters much worse."

Seeing her expression of concern, he added, "This does not mean that I disapprove of Bentley or the prospect of Isabella marrying him—seeing that he is now a man of completely independent means; it is simply a preference on my part for leaving such matters entirely in the hands of the two people concerned. In this instance, I have no doubt that both Isabella and Bentley, if their feelings have remained the same after all these years, will need little manipulation or encouragement from us."

Elizabeth looked askance at her husband; she feared he was going to be difficult and object to her plan.

"But, Darcy, I do not intend to manipulate or inveigle these two people into an engagement, but merely provide an appropriate and congenial occasion for them to meet and perhaps make up their own minds on the matter. There cannot be any harm in that?"

"No indeed, and if that is so, I should have no objection to it, as long as you do not expect me to dance with all the ladies in the room who have no partners, Lizzie!" he said, and seeing her eyes brighten at his words, added quickly, "Let me, however, caution you and Caroline to be aware that both Mr Bentley and Isabella are likely to have their own plans, which may not fall conveniently within your design."

Elizabeth agreed. "Caroline and I are aware that may be the case, but being so far apart as Manchester and Matlock, they are not likely to have many opportunities to meet and decide if they are still of the same mind as before," she explained, at which Darcy laughed and said, "My dear Lizzie, such a distance is unlikely to prove a major obstacle to a man in love if his affections are genuinely engaged."

And on that prophetic note, they retired to their apartments.

～✣～

The early onset of Autumn following upon a warm Summer proved to be a blessing. The gathering in of the harvest was always a propitious occasion for thanksgiving and celebration in the district, and Elizabeth's plans could come to fruition without causing any undue comment.

There had always been celebrations at Pemberley at harvest time. Apart from Harvest Home and the traditional church festivities, balls and parties were customary. This one was to take the form of a soireé followed by a dinner party, rather than a formal ball, which was a source of much relief to Mr Darcy.

Cassandra and Caroline were both drawn in to assist in its organisation, selecting the programme of music and the performers for the evening. Letters were sent out early, and David Fitzwilliam carried the all-important invitation to Manchester to be placed in the hands of Mr Bentley.

A polite and elegantly worded note of acceptance was received at Pemberley a few days later, which news was swiftly conveyed to Caroline. Isabella, who was not privy to her mother's discussions with Elizabeth, received the news that Mr Bentley had been invited to Pemberley with pleasure but little show of emotion, except to say, "Although Mr Bentley has never visited Pemberley, we have spoken of it often; I am sure he will look forward to seeing it."

Since their first chance encounter, they had met again on other occasions. First on a visit to Manchester with Isabella's parents, when the gentlemen had spent most of the day in the offices of the company's solicitors and they had all met only for a meal at the hotel, during which there had been little time for anything more than general conversation about the office and the weather.

Mr Bentley had, however, paid the ladies the courtesy of accompanying them to church on Sunday morning while David and Colonel Fitzwilliam slept. Caroline had been impressed and said so.

Then, at the very end of Summer, Mr Bentley had arrived, hoping to see either Colonel Fitzwilliam or Mr Darcy in order to obtain a signature upon a new contract. It so happened that both gentlemen were away, one in Birmingham and the other at Netherfield Park. Rather than return to Manchester empty-handed, Mr Bentley had decided to stay on at the local inn until Colonel Fitzwilliam returned from Birmingham.

This fortuitous arrangement had resulted in several meetings, for Caroline had insisted that Mr Bentley take dinner with them at the house while he stayed in the area.

"It's the very least we can do, Mr Bentley. Colonel Fitzwilliam will be here in two or three days at the most, and if you will accept our hospitality, I am sure he will feel less guilty at having kept you waiting."

Mr Bentley expressed profound gratitude and accepted the invitation, one might almost have said with alacrity, and Caroline had the satisfaction of noting that Isabella seemed particularly well pleased.

Clearly, both Isabella and Mr Bentley enjoyed the opportunity for private conversation. What was said between them when they met on those days, Caroline did not discover until much later, but she was able to speculate that the early signs of a reclaimed friendship were promising.

Mr Bentley spent most mornings in the town but always arrived around tea time and spent most of the afternoon and all of the evening with them before returning after dinner to Lambton.

Some days he sat with them in the parlour after tea, making conversation on a variety of topics; at other times, Isabella and he would walk in the garden or down by the river, returning to the house in time for dinner.

Isabella, whose calm exterior must surely have concealed some inner excitement, seemed to accept the amicable relationship that evolved between them with equanimity and pleasure.

When at last her father returned and the required signatures were obtained, Mr Bentley said his farewells and departed, leaving Isabella in such good humour as to convince Caroline some new understanding had been reached between her daughter and Mr Bentley.

Although nothing was said, a few days later, a note arrived for Caroline, expressing his appreciation of their hospitality. Both mother and daughter read it eagerly, each looking perhaps for some hint of meaning beyond the polite phrases.

Caroline was pleased with the proof it gave of his continued exemplary manners, and Isabella, who had not expected to find herself singled out, was gratified that he had made special mention of the many pleasant hours of entertainment and conversation they had enjoyed. It had made, he said, the time spent waiting for Colonel Fitzwilliam pass all too swiftly. *At least,* she thought, *of his regard, I need have no doubt at all.*

Caroline, meanwhile having finally broached the topic with her husband, had been at pains to ensure that he did not take up the matter with their daughter. Fitzwilliam had, at first, expressed some concerns about Bentley, anxious that Isabella should not be hurt again, but Caroline, having observed the couple closely, reassured him, "I have no doubt of his feelings, Fitzy. It is Isabella who has to decide; once she is certain, they will be engaged soon enough," she had said and he, trusting her judgment in these matters, made no further objection except to express the hope that they would not leave it too long.

"All this uncertainty is doing me no good, Caroline; it must be my age. I like things neat and tidy," he said.

Unfortunately for Colonel Fitzwilliam and his predilection for certainty, some days before the function at Pemberley, Mr Bentley arrived unexpectedly and looking very anxious indeed. His mother's health, always a source of some anxiety, had taken a turn for the worse, and he was required to go to London immediately, he said.

He was to travel by train and while he waited for the hour to arrive when the hired vehicle would convey him to the railway station, he spent the morning with them at Matlock. Isabella, though composed, was plainly concerned, and Caroline could see that Mr Bentley was doing his best to reassure her. When it was time to leave, his obvious reluctance was matched only by her efforts to conceal her unhappiness.

Caroline could not tell from observing them if they had spoken of their feelings for one another, but she was determined not to interfere.

In the end, Mr Bentley summoned up sufficient good humour to make them all smile as he bade them good-bye.

"I would not want to miss my first opportunity to see the remarkable attractions of Pemberley, of which I have heard so much. Miss Rachel would not forgive me. I have given her my promise," he said and, with a wave, was gone, carrying with him their best wishes for a safe journey and his mother's recovery.

The intervening days were so busy and filled with so much activity that Caroline gave little thought to Mr Bentley. On the day before the function, a message arrived by telegraph to say he would be on the train and hoped to be in Matlock by midday on the following day.

❧

When the day arrived, everything was in readiness at Pemberley.

Nothing was left to chance; the food, the musicians, and exquisite porcelain, glass, and silverware were all arranged well ahead, and the small army of servants was perfectly practised in their roles.

At Matlock, however, there was no such certainty. It was past midday and Mr Bentley had not arrived. Isabella stayed in her room all morning, not wishing to be further discomposed by the innumerable questions of her sister and father. She had chosen with care a favourite gown and some simple jewellery, and had looked forward to the evening. Now, she was anxious beyond bearing, afraid that the delay, with no news from him, meant an accident on the railway.

Unable to conceal her concern, she decided to remain at the house with her sister Rachel and asked that the carriage return for them.

"If Mr Bentley arrives, we will proceed with him to Pemberley. If he does not, Rachel and I will join you later. Please explain to Aunt Lizzie that we cannot leave until we are certain he is not coming; it will embarrass him greatly to arrive late and find us all gone," she pleaded, and Caroline agreed she was right. Mr Bentley was their guest and had never been to Pemberley before; they could not abandon him. She was sure Mr Darcy and Elizabeth would understand.

Not long after the rest of the party had left for Pemberley, Rachel, who had eaten not wisely but too well, claimed she was feeling sick and went upstairs while Isabella walked up and down the hall listening for the sound of a carriage.

A sudden cry of "Bella, Bella! Come up here, quick!" emanating from her sister's room at the top of the house caused her to run upstairs, fearful that Rachel was in pain. But, as she reached the open door of her room, she could see her sister standing on her bed and looking out of the window, towards the road that curved up from Lambton, and pointing as she called out, "Look, look, Bella, there he is!"

Isabella flew to window in time to see a vehicle, approaching at great speed, turn into the drive.

"Thank God," was all she could say, before Rachel uttered a scream and fell from the bed onto the floor.

Aghast, Isabella picked her sister up and placed her on the bed, trying to discover whether she had injured herself. Rachel's scream had attracted the servants, who informed Isabella that Mr Bentley had arrived and was waiting in the parlour.

Hurrying downstairs, she sought to explain what had occurred, while he was anxious to apologise for being late, all of which was overwhelmed by the cries of Rachel, clearly in severe discomfort.

"I fear we shall be further delayed; I cannot leave for Pemberley until Rachel has been seen by a doctor," she explained and Mr Bentley agreed that there was no question: a doctor had to be summoned. Fortuitously, he said, he had kept the hired vehicle in which he had arrived in case it was required to take him to Pemberley.

"I was unsure if your party had already left. But now, it means I could use it to go directly to Matlock and summon a doctor to attend your sister."

Isabella was so relieved he was here, so delighted to see him, so pleased with his swift offer of help, she could have hugged him; but she did nothing of the sort. Instead, she agreed immediately with his suggestion and, as he left to get the doctor, went upstairs to comfort Rachel. Her swelling ankle, evidence of the damage done by her fall, had been swathed in cold cloths doused in vinegar, and she was being urged to take a concoction of chamomile tea and willow bark for the pain and shock. Poor Rachel was not much impressed with either.

Isabella sat with her until Mr Bentley returned with the doctor and was very relieved when he examined the ankle and declared there was no break. He prescribed hot fomentation, an application of liniment with wintergreen, and complete rest. He then went, promising to call on the morrow.

Shortly after the doctor had departed, Isabella left her sister in the care of the housekeeper, Mrs Grey, and her maid, who was urged not to leave Rachel's bedside. She returned to her room to complete her toilet before going downstairs, where Mr Bentley waited. As he helped her into the carriage waiting for them at the entrance, she sighed. It had been a gruelling day.

They started out and had not gone far when she turned to thank him.

"Mr Bentley, please let me say how grateful I am to you and how very appreciative my parents will be when they learn what you have done today. I do not know how we would have coped without your help." Casting caution aside for once, Isabella was determined to let him see how glad she was of his presence. "We are going to be late, and I fear we will have missed much of the musical programme, but at least you are here. We were concerned that you would miss the function altogether; my parents and Mr and Mrs Darcy will be very pleased to see you."

He seemed almost surprised as he said, "I am very glad to hear it and I must apologise for causing you concern: I too was anxious not to be late, lest it seemed rude, but events outside my control overtook me." Then, his tone deepening, he asked, "But, Isabella, are you quite sure they will really be pleased to see me?"

She was quite indignant. "Of course, why should they not be?"

In the silence that followed, she recalled that he would surely have guessed that her family had persuaded her to reject his proposal all those years ago. She was flustered and embarrassed. Seeing and comprehending the somewhat sardonic smile on his face, she tried to explain, to apologise, but he stopped her.

"There is no need to explain, Isabella, no need to apologise either. Your family did what they thought was right," he said in a quiet, steady voice. "Indeed, when I discovered the truth about my stepfather's activities, I knew immediately that it was a body blow to my chances with you," he said and she could scarcely look at him for the distress she was feeling. "No respectable family would have wished to be associated with us at the time, even though I had had no connection at all with Mr Henderson's infamous business. Of course, I lost all hope when I received your father's letter, which gave no reason for your rejection. Clearly, you did not wish to cause me further torment by detailing the distasteful facts, but I could read between the lines, and my loathing of my stepfather was greatly increased as I realised what I had lost."

Isabella tried once more to say something that would assuage the hurt he had felt, to find words that would convey with sincerity her regret, but none came. As she stammered and stopped, tears welled in her eyes and, feeling utterly foolish, she hid her face in her hands.

At this, he was so appalled, fearing that his words had been too harsh and had caused her grief, he could do no less than put his arms around her and beg her not to weep. He pleaded with her to believe that he loved her still and asked only that she listen to him.

"I love you, Isabella. I always have. Indeed, I had thought, on the day of our picnic in Dovedale, that there was a chance your feelings were not very different from what mine were," he said and Isabella was left momentarily speechless.

She had not expected such a declaration, certainly not in the carriage en route to Pemberley! She had no other course but to listen. Her own handkerchief was sodden as she tried to dry her eyes; she took the one he proffered and blew her nose before she spoke.

"Do you mean that your feelings are unchanged since those times?" she asked hesitantly.

"Oh no, I do not mean that at all. My feelings have certainly changed, but only to become deeper and more constant. They have made me determined to persuade you, dearest Isabella, and I hope your parents, that I am worthy of you. Will you let me try?" he asked and this time there could be no uncertainty about his intentions.

Isabella smiled and spoke slowly, "Mr Bentley, are you asking me to listen to a proposal of marriage?"

He replied with another question. "Dearest Isabella, if I were, may I ask if I would be entitled to entertain some hope of a favourable answer?"

"Only if I thought you loved me as truly and as dearly as I love you," she said, and of course, there can be no doubt at all of his response.

Not only did he declare his love in the most ardent manner that their present situation would allow, but he told her also of the many years when he had lived in Europe, alone, longing for her, hoping he could perhaps return to England and see her again, having established his complete independence from his stepfather, whose disgrace had wounded him sorely and cost him so much.

"But then I met Mr Jonathan Bingley, who told me of your marriage to Doctor Forrester, and I abandoned all hope. I thought Fate had decreed that you were never to be mine. Dearest Isabella, I was for a very long time a most unhappy man."

At these words, which he had spoken while holding both her hands in his, she said, "I am so sorry. I wish with all my heart that it could have been different..." and to his great delight, she leaned forward and kissed him.

Afterwards, she was silent, wanting to enjoy the special satisfaction of hearing him declare again his feelings for her. He explained, when she asked why he had not proposed upon that happy afternoon in Dovedale, that he had already heard from his mother of Mr Henderson's iniquitous business dealings and had hoped to change his own circumstances first, establishing his independence before approaching her father.

"Isabella, if I had asked that afternoon, would you have accepted me?" he asked and she answered simply, "I believe I would," and his countenance reflected the pain of knowing how sadly awry his plans had gone. He told her too why he had never married, knowing no other woman would ever have his total loyalty as long as he loved her.

Isabella listened, delighted. Nothing in her life so far had brought such unalloyed pleasure. She listened, then, slowly, she found words, carefully chosen and spoken with great gentleness, to tell him how she had married and loved Henry Forrester.

"He was a good, kind, and compassionate man, easy to love. We did a great deal of good work together for the children of this district, but I have never forgotten that happy Summer when we became good friends, you and I. Such memories are too rare in my life to be forgotten. I have treasured them all these years."

He tried to tell her that she had no need to explain, but she was determined that he should know how she had felt.

"I do not wish to deny that I loved my husband, but you, my dear Phillip, you always occupied a special place in my mind and were sorely missed. Often I was too busy to have much time to contemplate what might have been had things been different and I was glad of that; but when I did think of you, it was always with affection."

"Did you not blame me for my stepfather's actions?" he asked. Her response was emphatic.

"Never, but I was too young, too easily overwhelmed by the hideous truth, which was revealed to me quite suddenly, to rely only upon my own judgment. I wish I had known then what I know now, but I had had little experience of the world outside of my family.

"Still, I did not see you as tainted by his reputation, which is why I asked if we could be friends as before. When you did not respond, I believed you were unwilling or unable to agree," she said, and this time, it was his turn to be wracked by remorse.

"Isabella, my darling, do you not think if I could have, I would have wanted us to be friends? How was it possible for me, with the feelings I had for you, to agree to be friends when my dearest hopes for us had been dashed? Every meeting would have brought only greater grief. Can you not understand my situation?" His anguish was unmistakable.

She could of course, now, with the maturity of her years and life experience, see more clearly, and seeing, she not only understood but loved him for it. She also found it easier than before to say so and enjoy his pleasure when she did. Perhaps it was because they were both older now and had endured more of the slings and arrows of life's struggle, or it may have been that having been married and widowed, she felt less inhibited with him and he with her. Whatever the reason, it made for an openness and ease in their association, which was both fresh and compelling. Between them, all pretence was abandoned.

He confessed then that when he had learned he was being employed by Mr Gardiner's company, it had been partly the hope of meeting her again, however fleetingly, that had brought him into Derbyshire.

"I thought perhaps after all these years, it may not be quite so painful to meet and, perhaps to be friends. I recalled that some years ago, I had heard from Mrs Tate that you had spoken of me in kind and generous terms, even though you had refused my offer of marriage and that you had wished me to know this. I hoped that you may not have changed your opinion of me. It was all I hoped for. I knew very little of your life and was reluctant to ask.

"However, when some months after I had accepted the position at Manchester, I heard from Mr Kennedy the terrible news of Doctor Forrester's death, I was deeply shocked. Much as I longed to see you, I feared that any approach from me, however well meant, may be rebuffed as indelicate. Which is why, my dear Isabella, I stayed away from the funeral and for months afterwards. Indeed, I was glad when I heard you had gone to stay with your aunt, Mrs Wilson, in Kent."

Isabella assured him that she understood and appreciated his reserve. While she denied she would have rebuffed him, with disarming candour she acknowledged he was right not to attempt to see her then.

"I did not know then that you were back in England, much less that you were working for the company in Manchester. I was so remorseful about Henry's death, I felt I should have been with him; my feelings were so confused, I may well have said things which I did not mean and you would have gone away believing them and we may never have discovered our true feelings."

It was a prospect too terrible to contemplate, which was immediately dismissed; assurances of love and esteem were given and received, with mutual agreement that they were the sweeter for being so long delayed.

❦

Having taken some time to prepare themselves for the company they would presently face, they finally arrived at Pemberley some two hours later than they had expected to be. Strangely, neither of them had been at all perturbed by the need to explain the lateness of their arrival to their hosts.

Pemberley looked splendid against the night sky. With lights in all its rooms, its handsome façade was an imposing sight.

Mr Bentley was pleasantly surprised, as much by the generous hospitality of his hosts as by the beauty of their home. He admired everything and acknowledged to Isabella that he had rarely seen such elegance and good taste as was evidenced here. But all evening, nothing could surpass the sense of astonishment and delight he felt at the events of the afternoon, which had completely changed his life much more than he had dared to hope.

The soireé, with its fine presentation of music, was almost over as they were ushered into a reception room across the hall. Presently, Jonathan Bingley entered the room and, seeing Isabella seated by the window, came towards her with a welcoming smile.

"Isabella, there you are. We have been wondering where you had got to. Aunt Lizzie has been worried all evening," then seeing her companion, he greeted him warmly. "Bentley, I was told you were expected. How very good to see you again. I believe you are well settled in Manchester. Look, you must meet my wife…" he said turning to present Anna.

They went out together into the main hall, and Caroline emerged from the drawing room as a burst of applause signalled the end of the main entertainment. Seeing her daughter with Mr Bentley, she rushed to her side.

"Bella, my dear, you are so very late! You have missed all the best performances. What was it kept you and where is Rachel?" she asked.

When she was told, briefly and without undue drama, so as not to alarm or distress her, the tale of Rachel's fall and her sprained ankle, Caroline was concerned.

"How is she? Poor child, she is forever climbing upon tables and chairs, going where she should not, and getting into scrapes. Is she in great pain?"

Isabella explained, "No, Mama. Mr Bentley was very kind; he went at once for the doctor, who recommended treatment. Rachel was much more comfortable afterwards. Mrs Grey is looking after her and Mary will sleep in her room tonight."

Caroline turned to Mr Bentley. "I cannot thank you enough, Mr Bentley, how very fortunate that you happened to be there. Now, I can tell Cousin Lizzie that it was Rachel's fall that kept you. She was most anxious. Isabella, your aunt Lizzie does not trust the railways; she thought it might have been an accident that had delayed Mr Bentley. Thank goodness it was not."

Then, recalling the reason for Mr Bentley's journey to London, she asked, "And your mother, Mr Bentley, is she recovered from her illness?"

He thanked her and replied that Mrs Henderson had been ill with a respiratory condition but was now out of danger.

"It was my keenness to ascertain that she was on the way to recovery that led to the delay in my return, else I should have been back in Derbyshire yesterday," he explained.

Before Caroline could ask any more questions, Isabella drew her mother towards her, placed a hand on Mr Bentley's arm, and said simply, "Mama dear, Mr Bentley and I have some news for you. We are engaged and you are the first to know!"

Standing in the middle of the great hall at Pemberley, Caroline looked at her daughter, who appeared to her more radiantly lovely at that moment than ever before. They embraced and there were tears in their eyes, as Mr Bentley stood by, smiling but looking a little helpless.

Caroline could not hide her delight. She embraced them both right there. Then they went together to find Colonel Fitzwilliam, Mr Darcy, Elizabeth, and all the others who had to be told.

In the next little while, the news circulated quickly among members of the family and their closest friends, all of whom came to congratulate and admire the handsome couple and wish them well for the future.

Jonathan Bingley and his wife Anna were among the first, while Emma Wilson was perhaps happiest for them; having helped Isabella through the most difficult time of her life, she was especially delighted. Knowing in her own life the extraordinary happiness of love discovered and enjoyed in maturity, she had hoped Isabella might do likewise with a man as worthy as her own husband James.

That Mr Bentley, for whom Isabella had admitted a strong attachment, had returned to claim her love was especially pleasing. From her brother Jonathan, Emma had received only the best reports of Mr Bentley, while both her daughters, who had made his acquaintance in London, had remarked upon his good looks, distinguished appearance, and exemplary manners. She could not deny they made a most attractive couple; she hoped, with all her heart, they would also be a happy one.

Later, as the rest of the party moved out of the dining room where a splendid repast had been served, Elizabeth found her cousin in the vestibule, still seemingly amazed, unable to say a word. Caroline had not quite taken in the good news for which she had waited so eagerly and for so long.

Elizabeth drew her gently into an ante-room, where with tears in her eyes, Caroline expressed her delight at Isabella's engagement to Mr Bentley.

"I cannot tell you, Cousin Lizzie, how much this means to me. It has been for years like a deep ache in me, seeing Isabella alone and unhappy when I knew how happy she could have been had she followed her heart instead of our advice and accepted him in the first place.

"I do not mean in any way to denigrate dear Henry Forrester, who was a good man, but Isabella did not know her heart when she refused Mr Bentley. She had been persuaded that it was right to refuse him because of his stepfather's shameful connection with the slave ships; but I have known for some time that it was cruel advice and the wrong decision. I know it was all very shocking, but, Lizzie, Mr Bentley had no involvement in any of it at all and we had no right to influence her as we did. He loved her dearly and they could have been so happy together."

Elizabeth, who recalled her own contribution to the furore at the time, tried to comfort her cousin.

"Dear Caroline, you did what you thought was right; we all thought it was right to protect Isabella from what was deemed to be a most unfortunate connection. Henderson was exposed and went to prison and his entire family suffered as a consequence. You wanted to protect Isabella from all that," she said.

"And indeed I did, but only by destroying her prospect of happiness," replied Caroline. "It was stupid and arrogant. I have regretted it for some time now and am very grateful that she is to have another chance. Mr Bentley loves her still and I know she loves him. Lizzie, you and I and Jane have all known such happiness with the men we chose to love; it is so unfair that Isabella has been denied it for so long."

They repaired to the drawing room, where they found Mr Darcy and Colonel Fitzwilliam deep in conversation. There could be no doubt of the subject of their discussion. Mr Darcy, thought Caroline, looked especially pleased. Elizabeth thought she knew why; he had always been uncomfortable with their interference. Soon, the guests were gathered together and Mr Darcy proposed a toast to the newly engaged pair, wishing them happiness—a sentiment echoed by all present.

Not everyone knew Mr Bentley; those who did regarded him as worthy of the fine young woman they all knew Isabella to be. Most of them had known her since childhood and had great affection for her. Her work, together with her late husband's, at the hospital, and her generous, unassuming nature were recognised and loved. While it was not generally known that she had long cherished an affection for Mr Bentley as he had for her, their present happiness was so manifest, few doubted their union would be a felicitous one. Caroline, for one, was convinced that her daughter, in making her own decision, had followed her heart as she had done all those years ago. Fitzwilliam was glad it was settled at last. Despite his earlier reservations, he told his wife, he had always liked Bentley, and his wife encouraged him to believe it. Clearly his discussions on the subject with Mr Darcy had convinced him.

The party ended late and Mr and Mrs Darcy together with their daughter Cassandra and their son-in-law Richard Gardiner bade their guests farewell.

"Congratulations, Lizzie, it has been a most remarkable evening," said Mr Darcy, and his wife agreed. "It has indeed and I must confess, in some quite unexpected ways!"

As they retired upstairs to take tea and talk over the events of the day, as the sisters were wont to do, Jane Bingley summed up her feelings, "Lizzie dear, I think Isabella is going to be very happy with her Mr Bentley, don't you? I do not mean to suggest she was unhappy with Doctor Forrester, who was such a dear, good man, but I must confess, I have not seen her so radiant ever before. I do believe, Lizzie, that like my Emma, she has been blessed with the chance of a very special felicity."

To which sage remark, Elizabeth could only add, "Indeed, Jane, I think you are right, as usual. For my part, I am very pleased that Isabella and Mr Bentley are to wed; but even more importantly, that our dear cousin Caroline's romantic heart will be content at last."

END OF PART FIVE

An Epilogue . . .

IN THE NEW YEAR, ISABELLA'S family came to visit.

After a quiet family wedding, which was the particular wish of both parties, Mr Bentley had taken his bride home to Manchester. While they certainly did not have to live above the shop, as Mrs Fitzwilliam had supposed, the house he had acquired for them could not be compared in spaciousness or style to those of her late grandfather or her father, Colonel Fitzwilliam.

Indeed, there was not to be had, within sight of the city of Manchester, such a property as Oakleigh or the farm at Matlock, where Isabella had spent most of her life. Much of the surrounding rural land was being swallowed up by expanding industry, spreading like an unpleasant rash upon the countryside.

But with the help of a friend, a Lancastrian born and bred, with useful connections in the building business, Mr Bentley had secured a very acceptable, detached villa, in a quiet, respectable street. Comfortable and simple in design, it stood in its own small garden, shaded by a group of fine old trees, the like of which many of the inhabitants of the surrounding factory towns, with their back-to-back terraces and shabby alley ways, may never see in a lifetime.

To Caroline, who had spent most of her life within view of the great peaks of Derbyshire and a short journey from the magic of Dovedale, it was difficult to believe that anyone could live happily in Manchester. But to Isabella, it seemed it could have been perfection itself.

Writing to her cousin and friend Emma Wilson on her return from Manchester, Caroline expressed her surprise.

There is such a remarkable change in Isabella as to make her almost a different person. She was always patient and kindhearted and remains so today, but there is an unmistakable sense of joie de vivre in her, which is quite new.

Before, even whilst she was married to Henry Forrester, she was earnest and eager to attend upon others, making very little time for herself. Today, though she continues to be compassionate and thoughtful of others, she seems keener still to enjoy her own happiness, which to the observer seems quite considerable. I believe Mr Bentley has certainly made her happier than she has ever been before.

Their home, being situated off a city street, has not the grace and beauty of a country residence, nor can it be as spacious as a similar house in London, for it appears land is at a premium here; but it is a handsome villa with well-proportioned rooms and tastefully furnished. I do believe much of the furniture was transported from London.

When I asked Isabella if she does not miss the countryside, in which after all she has lived all her life, she laughed and said, "Dear Mama, I think if I were to say yes, you would worry that I was not happy here; so I must say no, because I have been so very happy since we have come to live here. I hardly notice that we are in Manchester."

By which, I assumed that she meant she was so happy in herself since her marriage to Mr Bentley that her surroundings do not matter greatly.

Dear Emma, you and I must recall that this is not an unusual condition when one is first married to a man of strong affections; it seems that is how it is with Mr Bentley and Isabella. He is clearly devoted to her and though there is certainly no lack of decorum in their public behaviour, it is easy to see that the depth of their feelings sometimes quite overwhelms them; it is as if no one and nothing else matters.

Isabella did not have the benefit of knowing the contents of her mother's letter, yet if she had, she would have been hard put to it to disagree with the sentiments expressed therein. Her life had altered so profoundly since her marriage that there were moments when she was, herself, surprised at its felicity.

Apart from her son Harry, who was soon to attend a private day school having quite worn out a succession of tutors, the most important person in her life was the man who had for many years loved her in vain, while she had loved him without admitting it even to herself. Her marriage to Henry Forrester had given her affection and security and a beloved child. But she could not deny to herself that she had never forgotten Philip Bentley, whose association had filled the best part of a year with the unexpected pleasures of a most engaging companionship.

For his part, Mr Bentley, who had long believed he had no hope of securing her affections, was delighted to discover how easily and with what warmth Isabella learned to express the love that had lain dormant in her heart. With him, she enjoyed a mature and passionate union, as he had evolved from being her "very good friend" whom she had recalled with guiltless affection into the husband who had won her heart and sublimated in their marriage all her deepest needs. So complete was her contentment, she wanted for nothing and sought no material enhancement of her situation.

Nothing else did matter. Not the distance from her family, not the ugliness of industrial Lancashire, of places like Bolton and Bury, which scarred the road leading to the small green oasis in which they lived, and certainly not the derision of her uncle Robert's wife, Rose, and her mother Rosamund, now Lady Fitzwilliam.

Robert Gardiner had come from France to attend Isabella's wedding; Rose was indisposed, he had said, trying to sound convincing. Though not a particularly ungenerous man, Robert was unfortunately too weak-willed to withstand the persuasive pressure of his wife and mother-in-law. Hence, instead of the silver tea service he had proposed to give them as a wedding gift, he had arrived bearing a very small French clock, which he presented to his niece with such an apologetic air as to be thought mean.

Moreover, his mother-in-law, Lady Fitzwilliam, who had attended in her daughter's place, had made some disdainful comments on the fact that the Bentleys were to live in Manchester. She had remarked that they would not have much use for a silver tea service in Manchester and a clock would be much more practical and appropriate. Indeed, had the choice of such a clock been left to her, they would surely have received a far more serviceable piece than the ornate model Robert had chosen.

Young Rachel, having overheard the remarks, had hitched up the skirts of her bridesmaid's gown and raced upstairs to convey them to her mother and sister with a mixture of anger and glee!

"Lady Fitzwilliam thinks that Rose would not be able to breathe in the polluted air of Manchester," she reported, affecting a lugubrious tone of voice. "I heard her tell aunt Jane she has only once driven through the place on her way to Blackpool and almost choked, the air was so foul."

Rachel was a good mimic and Isabella, who was being helped out of her wedding gown into a travelling dress, had smiled tolerantly and said, "Ah me, then it's just as well that my uncle Robert did not inherit the business, is it not, Mama? It would have been a sad day if his wife and his mother-in-law had both choked to death on the foul Manchester air.

"I cannot help but wonder though," she had continued, "how very salubrious are the towns of France and Italy where they spend much of their time. Mr Bentley, who has lived many years in Europe, tells me there is not such a deal of difference in the air at all."

Mr Bentley, who had come to escort his bride down to the carriage that waited for them, had overheard her remark. "Ah but dearest, the air across the channel has that particular distinction of being French, no matter how foul! That is the material difference!" he had said lightly, making them all laugh. Quite clearly this couple were not about to let such taunts dilute their happiness.

Isabella soon forgot Lady Fitzwilliam's jibe, but Caroline did not, recalling that the same snobbery had been at work when the Fitzwilliams had queried her brother Robert's credentials during his courtship of their daughter Rose. Caroline's loyalty to her family was absolute. She determined that if and when an opportunity presented itself, when she could deliver an appropriate riposte, she would do so and as it happened, she did not have long to wait.

Some weeks later, the two women were present together at a family gathering at Camden Park. Elizabeth, who had heard the exchange between them, wrote of it later to her friend Charlotte Collins.

She wrote:

My dear Charlotte,

I trust you are well and that Summer at Longbourn is as pleasant as it has been here in Derbyshire. We have enjoyed excellent weather and much entertainment, including a church fair, a circus, and a cricket match which was easily won by the team from the Pemberley and Camden Estates, ably led by my dear grandson Darcy Gardiner.

Speaking of young Darcy, I know you will forgive me if I say that he is proving an exemplary manager of the estate and a fine young gentleman in every sense of the word. He grows more like his grandfather Mr Darcy with every passing year: handsome, kind, and devoted to Pemberley.

That said, Elizabeth proceeded to give a lively description of the day's events and the party that had gathered at Camden House for tea after the cricket. The Fitzwilliams, Sir James—as he now was since the demise of his elderly and ailing brother—and Lady Fitzwilliam, obviously feeling the weight of their title and the loss of the match by their team from Staffordshire, had joined the rest of the party in one of the handsome reception rooms that opened onto a terrace overlooking the park.

Elizabeth had noticed that Rosamund Fitzwilliam was pointedly ignoring her sister-in-law Caroline, even though their husbands had been deep in conversation. Sir James Fitzwilliam, having inherited a somewhat impoverished farm together with a thriving pottery in Staffordshire, appeared to be in need of advice from his younger brother.

I think you already know, Charlotte, that the two sisters-in-law have never been close. Well, recent events have set them even further apart.

…wrote Elizabeth, determined to give her friend all the news.

Speaking of which, I have a story to relate that will put you in mind of your days at Rosings and the pronouncements of Lady Catherine de Bourgh!

While I do not mean to imply that Rosamund Fitzwilliam is to be compared in stature, wealth, or pomposity to Lady C., she is certainly making a very good fist of emulating her Ladyship's talent for giving offence.

Rosamund still appears disgruntled by the fact that Caroline rather than Robert was entrusted with the management of Mr Gardiner's business. Caroline, despite all the predictions of gloom emanating from Rose and her family, has successfully steered the business through some quite troubled waters and into what Mr Darcy tells me is an enviable level of prosperity.

Of course, she has had the help of excellent staff, Mr Kennedy and then Mr Bentley, whom Mr Darcy himself selected, but it has meant that Robert, like the rest of the beneficiaries and partners, has received a substantially improved income from the enterprise.

Unaware of or choosing deliberately to ignore these facts, Rosamund continues to criticise and did so to Mr Darcy when they met after the cricket. She complained loudly that Rose and Robert had been hard done by being deprived of Oakleigh and were consequently forced to pay an exorbitantly high rent for their modest apartment in Paris.

Mr Darcy expressed surprise that they had chosen to live in France if it was so very expensive, and inviting Caroline who was passing to join them, he repeated for her ears Rosamund's complaint.

(Charlotte, I have since accused him of making mischief, but he denies it. I am not so sure I believe him!)

Elizabeth had heard the rest of the story and enjoyed the telling of it.

To Rosamund's consternation, Caroline remarked, in a voice replete with sweetness and concern, "Is this true, Lady Fitzwilliam?" and before there was time for an answer, added, "Poor Robert, I am very glad we were able to send him such a good cheque out of the company at the end of last year. It does seem a pity, though, that he must pay it all out to the French in rent! Now if only Rose could bear to live in Staffordshire, they would surely save most of it and she would have much more pin money! Is that not so, Mr Darcy?"

Elizabeth continued:

I do not exaggerate, dear Charlotte, but at this, Rosamund went so red with anger and embarrassment that I feared she was about to have a seizure of some sort. She muttered something about Rose having her own very generous allowance and sought to make a hurried exit, but not before Caroline got in the last word.

"Of course," she declared, still all innocence, "Isabella and Mr Bentley have been very fortunate to acquire a most comfortable villa for a reasonable price in a part of town where the air is far fresher than in Staffordshire," knowing, of course, that the estate James inherited lies in the very heart of the Staffordshire potteries.

Colonel Fitzwilliam has told us that it includes several potteries where the dust and chalk and the ash from the kilns lies over everyone and everything. This would surely be unbearable to some one as sensitive and delicate as Rose.

Touché! I think you will agree, Charlotte?

Although I confess I was surprised at the sharpness of Caroline's riposte, I have to say that I was certainly not sorry, and my dear Darcy was genuinely pleased. He has grown weary of Rosamund's pretensions since James succeeded to the title and has little time for Rose and Robert, with whom he maintains polite contact only on account of my dear aunt Gardiner's feelings.

Besides, as you know, my cousin Caroline is a favourite of his and he will not hear a word against her…

Elizabeth's account did not include particular mention of the happiness which Isabella and Mr Bentley enjoyed, but of this Charlotte had heard much from both Jonathan and Anna Bingley. Having visited the couple in Manchester, they had returned to Hertfordshire convinced of their felicity.

"It is as though two people who are so completely right for each other have at last been brought together, and their delight in one another is unmistakable. Having been with them, one is left with a great sense of joy," Anna had declared and her husband had agreed without reservation.

Postscript

DESPITE HER DEEP CONTENTMENT IN her marriage, it was not long before Isabella began to feel the need to do something for the community outside her home.

She could not visit the markets or walk in the public park without seeing the children of the poor, those who were not working in the mills themselves, playing in the gutter, begging for coins, or scrapping among themselves for food. The numbers of young girls whose grimy little faces looked older than their years shocked her and she longed to help them.

Returning from the grocer one grey morning, she complained, "If they are not to be educated, not taught to read or write or count, what else will they grow up to be but skivvies and slaves, dependent upon the whims of others for their very existence?"

Her husband heard in her voice a discordant note for the first time since they had been married. Always sensitive to her feelings, attentive to her needs, he asked what she had in mind.

"I should like very much to set up a school for little girls where they may learn cleanliness and good manners as well as letters and numbers. I know I have not the skills to be a teacher, but I could run the school and hire a teacher with whom I could work."

Seeing perhaps some uncertainty upon her husband's countenance as he listened, she bit her lip.

"Do you think I am being too ambitious, Philip? I must do something for the children. Would you prefer it if I just went down to the church and helped with the soup kitchen at dinner time each day?"

He was immediately contrite. "Most certainly not, my dearest, I think a school for girls is a wonderful idea, I am only concerned that we may not have the money to pay a teacher and you, my darling, would wear yourself out with work."

"Apart from your concern on that score, you have no objection to it?" she asked eagerly.

"None at all if you will promise me that I will not find you doing all the work yourself." She gave him her promise and was rewarded with a warm embrace. His love for her overwhelmed every other concern in his life; having almost lost her forever, he was afraid to disappoint even her smallest wish.

Having assured herself of his support, Isabella wrote away to her parents, her aunts, uncles, cousins, and her grandmother asking for donations for her school and, within the year, had collected sufficient funds to make a start. The offer of a vacant cottage, two helpful neighbours who provided some furniture, and a kindly parish priest who found the rest, and she had things organised to open the school with eleven little girls and one enthusiastic young teacher.

Mr Bentley was amazed at the enthusiasm and energy Isabella could generate in herself and others, working tirelessly with the children, while maintaining the warmth of her affection for himself and her son. He was surprised to find that her exertions on behalf of the poor increased rather than exhausted her energy, inspiring similar charitable feelings among other families in the parish and bringing more donations of money and furniture as well as offers of help.

When Caroline next visited the Bentleys in Spring, she took back good news of Mrs Bentley's school for girls, which had opened with one teacher and Isabella as her helper, and was growing by the week with more volunteers and children appearing every week.

She also had much more exciting news to impart to her husband.

Isabella, after eight childless years since the birth of Harry, was expecting a child.

"You cannot imagine how happy she is—they both are," said Caroline.

Colonel Fitzwilliam was delighted at the prospect of becoming a grandfather, of course, but had not anticipated the next part of the conversation.

"The doctor says it will be in the Autumn, which means I shall have to be there and I mean to take Rachel with me… there will be much work to be done…"

He stopped her in midsentence. "Caroline my love, what do you mean? Surely you are not intending to spend all that time in Manchester? Cannot Isabella come to us? All our children have been born here," he argued, but in vain.

"For shame, Fitzy, Isabella will not leave her husband, no more than I would have left you and gone off to Lambton to have our babies. Besides, she will not want to leave the school and her little pupils so soon after they've begun work. You should see them, all scrubbed and brushed and learning their letters! I would not dream of asking her to leave them. It would make Bella most unhappy and you would not want that, would you, dearest? I am sure you would not. No, I am afraid there's nothing for it, Fitzy, we must go. I have given her my word."

Fitzwilliam shook his head; there was not much he could do. He knew her well and when she had decided upon on a course of action, she would cajole, argue, and persuade relentlessly until she had achieved her object. For the most part, these were not self-indulgent demands; they were usually matters concerning the welfare of others, but that made little difference to the intensity with which Caroline would pursue her goal and promote her purpose. During his own political career, Fitzwilliam had often had reason to be grateful for her persistence and charm.

He had been attracted by her beauty and sweetness of disposition and loved her for her passion, her loyalty, and her determination. She had frequently astonished and delighted him and sometimes, very rarely, exasperated him.

But, he loved her dearly and had never tried to change her. He would not do so, now. "Caroline," he said, reaching for her hand, "you are quite incorrigible!"

A list of the main characters in *My Cousin Caroline*:

Caroline Gardiner—eldest daughter of Mr and Mrs Gardiner, wife of
Colonel Fitzwilliam—cousin of Mr Darcy of Pemberley
Edward, Isabella, David, Rachel, Amy, and James—children of Caroline and
    Colonel Fitzwilliam
Emily Gardiner—Caroline's younger sister
Richard and Robert Gardiner—Caroline's brothers
James Fitzwilliam—cousin of Mr Darcy, elder brother of Col. Fitzwilliam
Rosamund (neé Camden)—his wife
Rose—their daughter
Cassandra, William, and Julian Darcy—children of Mr and Mrs Darcy
Jonathan and Emma Bingley—son and daughter of Mr and Mrs Bingley
Edward and Darcy Gardiner—sons of Cassandra and Richard Gardiner
Lizzie and Laura Ann—daughters of Cassy and Richard
Anthony Tate—owner of a local newspaper, nephew of Sir Thomas Camden
Rebecca Tate (neé Collins)—his wife (daughter of Charlotte Collins)
Josie—their daughter
Mr and Mrs Henderson—the new tenants of Newland Hall
Mr Philip Bentley—a newcomer to Derbyshire, son of Mrs Henderson

Maria and Frances Henderson—his stepsisters, daughters of Mr Henderson

Mr Peter Kennedy—an accountant, employed by Mr Gardiner's company

From the pages of *Pride and Prejudice*:

Fitzwilliam and Elizabeth Darcy

Colonel Fitzwilliam—Mr Darcy's cousin

Charles and Jane Bingley

Mr and Mrs Bennet—parents of Jane and Lizzie

Mr and Mrs Gardiner—uncle and aunt of Jane and Lizzie

Charlotte Collins (neé Lucas)—childhood friend of Jane and Lizzie

Reverend Collins of Hunsford—Charlotte's husband

Acknowledgments

The author wishes to thank all those who have written to her or emailed reviews and comments on the books of The Pemberley Chronicles series, which have been a source of much encouragement and pleasure.

Special thanks to Ms Claudia Taylor for help with research and Ms Marissa O'Donnell for the artwork. Ben and Robert for technical assistance, Beverly for her wonderful website, and my dear Rose for her untiring efforts in the office.

To Miss Jane Austen, my heartfelt gratitude for enjoyment and inspiration, and to Ms Susannah Fullerton of the Jane Austen Society of Australia, many thanks for her interest and support.

—Rebecca Ann Collins, www.geocities.com/shadesofpemberley

About the Author

A lifelong fan of Jane Austen, Rebecca Ann Collins first read *Pride and Prejudice* at the tender age of twelve. She fell in love with the characters and since then has devoted years of research and study to the life and works of her favorite author. As a teacher of literature and a librarian, she has gathered a wealth of information about Miss Austen and the period in which she lived and wrote, which became the basis of her books about the Pemberley families. The popularity of the Pemberley novels with Jane Austen fans has been her reward.

With a love of reading, music, art, and gardening, Ms Collins claims she is very comfortable in the period about which she writes and feels great empathy with the characters she portrays. While she enjoys the convenience of modern life, she finds much to admire in the values and worldview of Jane Austen.

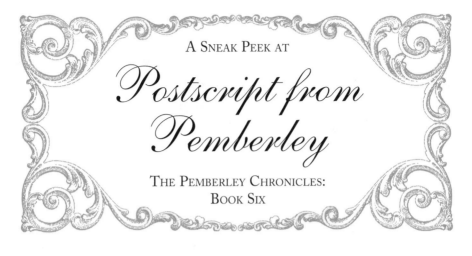

A SNEAK PEEK AT

Postscript from Pemberley

THE PEMBERLEY CHRONICLES:
BOOK SIX

Chapter One

JESSICA'S MEMORIES OF LIZZIE GARDINER'S wedding day were filled with a myriad of impressions that crowded upon one another.

The happy lovers and their contented families predominated, coming together for a great celebration at Pemberley, where Mr and Mrs Darcy watched with pleasure as their grand daughter was married to Mr Michael Carr, a gentleman they had come to admire and respect. There were other recollections too, not all of which she wished to share with the rest of her family.

Jessica had dressed with some care for the occasion, in a becoming but simple gown, resisting the temptation to have a new one made. She knew that Julian was expected, although there had been some concern that he may not arrive in time, since he had to travel all the way from France; nevertheless, she was confident he would be there.

Several months had passed between the time of his departure from Derbyshire and Lizzie's wedding in the autumn of 1866. To her surprise, not long after he had left Pemberley, a letter had arrived for her from Cambridge and upon her having sent a short reply, she had received another from Paris, whither he had gone to attend an urgent meeting of the medical board.

Both communications had been completely devoid of any descriptions of experiments, successful or otherwise, or microscopic bacteria, for that matter. Instead they contained references to many matters of mutual interest, including quite a detailed description of the part of Paris in which his lodgings were situated. Jessica had been delighted.

The first, which had arrived barely a week after his departure, began with the usual courtesies but then went on to speak of the arrangements he was making at the university as well as his attendance at a concert of chamber music, which he had greatly enjoyed. She recalled that he had confessed to a growing interest in music, which, he said apologetically, he had neglected all his life. Jessica, a proficient and keen student of music, had encouraged him.

"I cannot imagine life without music; I lay no claim to great talent but I have an abiding love of music that sustains me at all times; without it my life would be poor indeed," she had said and he, inspired by her enthusiasm, had promised faithfully to maintain his interest.

His letter had concluded with a paragraph of such warmth and sincerity that she returned to read it again and again.

He wrote:

> *Finally, I cannot send this away without telling you of the happy discovery I have made, when packing my things to be sent over to France. There among my personal papers and books was a collection of poems presented to me by your aunt Caroline Fitzwilliam and in it is Keats' Ode – To a Nightingale, which instantly brought back delightful memories of your reading it at Pemberley.*
>
> *It was a recollection replete with feelings of gratitude for your generosity and kindness to me, during a time that was particularly painful for me and indeed, distressing for us all.*
>
> *I shall be happy to take it with me to France and look forward to the day when I may have the pleasure of hearing you read it again.*

In her response, which had taken Jessica quite some time and many sheets of notepaper to compose, she had striven to appear detached though friendly. She had written of their preparations for the start of the school term and the arrival of the new schoolmaster, Mr Hurst, who was to teach the older boys.

She wrote:

> *Mr Hurst is an interesting man, though he must surely be quite old (Mama thinks he could be forty five, but I believe he must be fifty years*

old at least) he is surprisingly unlike any of the teachers one reads of in Mr Dickens' books. He is soft spoken and considerate and does not appear to have that accessory of all school masters: a cane.

What is more, he is a veritable treasure house of information on every subject under the sun. For instance, I did not know that Mr Darwin who wrote the "Origin of Species" had married the daughter of Mr Josiah Wedgwood, the owner of the great Staffordshire potteries. Did you? Nor was I familiar with the name of his ship, The Beagle. *Is that not an odd name for a ship?*

Mr Hurst knows all the details of the ship's amazing voyage to the other side of the world and the excessively weird and wonderful creatures they saw there!

In answer to a question, he informed Mr Darcy very gravely that he intended to teach the boys more than reading, writing and numbers—he plans to satisfy their natural curiosity by introducing them to Science and Nature through everyday things in their lives, he says. Mr Darcy seemed rather puzzled by this approach, but I must admit I look forward to seeing the results of Mr Hurst's work.

Thank you for reminding me of Keats' Nightingale, I am glad to learn that you have a copy to take to France; it is a beautiful piece and a favourite of mine, as you know. I am sure you will find time to read it yourself in Paris; it will remind you of home.

I trust you are well, as we all are

God Bless you,…

Jessica Courtney

Then, as if suddenly deciding to abandon the pretence of being cautious and impersonal, she had added a postscript, in which she said she had heard he was arranging to travel from France to attend Lizzie's wedding in the autumn.

If this is the case, I expect we shall meet at Pemberley. I did so enjoy our conversations when you were last here and hope there will be time to talk some more, she had said, hoping it would not be considered too forthright.

To this there had been no response for some weeks, leaving her anxious and concerned lest she had offended him, however unwittingly.

She had waited daily for the post in a state of anxiety and no letter had been delivered, until a few days before young Lizzie's wedding day, when it had arrived, postmarked from Paris.

Late, short, but to her exceedingly sweet, it brought an apology for the delay in responding to hers and assured her that he would indeed be seeing her at Lizzie's wedding, adding also that afterwards, he expected to stay a few weeks at least at Pemberley before returning to France, during which time, he supposed, there should be plenty of time for the happy conversations they had both enjoyed so much.

It was a prospect that filled her with a confusion of delight and trepidation.

❧

Julian Darcy's stay at Pemberley, at first set to be a fortnight, was extended to three weeks and more, as he surrendered to the persuasive arguments of his parents and the ambient pleasures of Pemberley in late Autumn. He spent much of the time with Mr and Mrs Darcy and his son Anthony, thereby bringing much happiness to all of them.

Elizabeth was especially pleased to see how much calmer and more confident her son had become since the previous year, when beset with a plethora of troubles, he had appeared to lose both direction and interest in his life.

As his sister Cassandra wrote to her cousin Emma Wilson:

Since Lizzie's wedding, Julian has been at Pemberley and he is a man transformed! He seems far more at peace with himself and at times appears almost happy to be here with us. I can only pray he will remain so…

As for Jessica, the period of his stay proved to be one of particular pleasure. While her days were spent chiefly at the school, she would frequently return in the afternoon to Pemberley, where Julian would join her for tea in the sitting room. The hours were filled with long, relaxed conversations on every subject available for discussion or readings from books which they selected at random, mainly to please one another, often continuing until the servants came to light the lamps and it was time to dress for dinner.

At dinner, when they were joined by Mr and Mrs Darcy and occasionally, the Bingleys, Fitzwilliams, or Cassy and Richard Gardiner, Julian would be the centre of attention, called upon to satisfy their guests' curiosity and answer questions about his work and the political situation in France, while Jessica listened. Later, however, he would join the ladies in the drawing room, usually leaving the gentlemen to their port and discussions of political and commercial matters, which seemed not to hold his interest at all. Then, his attention was all hers, as she played or read to please the company.

Jessica had many happy memories of these evenings, of conversations all invariably interesting to her, filled as they were with tales of people and places she had never seen or heard of before. He had told her so much about France, which she had not known before. She was as much enthralled by its recent bloody history as by its ancient culture and current sophistication.

Julian had detailed to her the idealism as well as the ferocity of the French revolution, yet balanced them with pictures of French music, art and architecture that were the envy of Europe.

"It is indeed a place of great contradictions, Jessica, yet one that has an undeniable grasp upon me. I realise that it is not fashionable in some circles to profess admiration for the French—we have had some bitter battles in the past—but the country fascinates me like no other place on earth."

"It is well that it does, since you are determined to live and work there," she had remarked, and asked, "Do you expect to spend much more time in France?"

He had replied, "No, not unless something untoward occurs to thwart our plans. We expect to leave for Africa in Spring, before the rains begin. Arrangements are already afoot for our journey and I expect to know a firm date for our departure very soon."

"And you are looking forward to it, of course?"

"Yes indeed, it will be the culmination of more than a year's preparation."

Jessica had expressed some apprehension. "Will it be a dangerous expedition?" she asked.

His reply, though calculated to allay her fears, had been honest.

"All expeditions to places such as Africa or South America, where so little is known of the environment, are fraught with some danger. But I am assured by my French colleagues that the native peoples of the areas we intend to study are generally friendly. They are familiar with foreigners and unlike some of the coastal tribes, whose experience of Europeans is tainted by the memory of the slave trade, these places are free of that scourge, thank God."

Despite these assurances, Jessica remained concerned.

One afternoon, when they had met as she had walked home through the park to Pemberley, she asked, "I cannot help wondering if you will be safe in

Africa—I know your mama worries, too. Will you write, if only to reassure us that you are well?"

He had smiled and replied, "Of course, it is kind of you to be concerned; but be aware there is no penny post and letters must be carried to the ports and be shipped out to England. I mention this because I should not wish you to think, if there were to be a long delay in the arrival of a letter, that I had not kept my word."

She had protested strenuously, "I should never think that—but I am glad to be forewarned of the difficulties, else I may have thought that the letters had gone astray and been anxious. Now, I know I shall just have to be patient."

"Are you always so patient, Jessica?" he had asked, with some degree of amusement, to which she replied candidly, "Indeed, I am not. Not always, at any rate. I am patient when circumstances are so fixed, there is no help for it and nothing will change the situation. But I have to confess I am impatient when unnecessary obstacles arise; I am eager to learn and discover new ideas and long to see and experience what I have read. Yet it is often impossible. I am far from being patient about such matters."

"Such as?' he persisted.

"All sorts of things—things that excite my imagination, I suppose. I should love to feel the salt spray of the sea in a storm or the bustle of London streets, perhaps to walk those beautiful boulevardes of Paris with their elegant buildings and see the great works of art in their galleries. You and others have spoken of these things—I long to know how it feels to be there. Men are so very fortunate, to be able to travel and work where you please. I do envy you and I am impatient that we have not the same freedom."

Julian had seemed fascinated as he watched her eyes shine and heard her voice rise gently as she spoke. Clearly, Jessica was growing a little restless with the sheltered existence she led in Derbyshire and he sensed a desire for something new and perhaps a little more exotic than her present life afforded her.

He understood her inclinations but was conscious of the need to be cautious in encouraging such yearnings. Remembering another young woman, whose desire to break out of the narrow confines that had circumscribed her life had led not to satisfaction and happiness as she had hoped, but disappointment and disaster, he had paused awhile before speaking.

His memories of Josie, still too fresh and painful, had made him somewhat more circumspect in his response. Reminding Jessica that she was young enough to look forward to all of those things she had mentioned and many more experiences besides, in the years that lay ahead, he had said, "There will be time enough for you to enjoy all these experiences and more; I do not doubt that you will find time in your life to do so. Remember only, dear Jessica, that life is best enjoyed at leisure, without undue haste or desperation, with time for judgment and discrimination as well as enjoyment. We are not all blessed with the capacity of John Keats to drain life's cup to the lees in a single draught."

Surprised by his words and the quiet intensity with which they were spoken, Jessica had asked, "Do you merely advise me in a general sense against haste, or do your apprehensions arise from a perception that I am too bold in dreaming of discovering and experiencing what is new? Is it because you think I would act rashly in attempting to grasp what is outside my reach?" and her voice trembled a little, as though she had felt chastised.

He responded directly, "Certainly not. Your dreams are not too bold, far from it. What would we be if we did not dream, however impossible the goal? Much of my own work is built upon a dream that we may find something that is hidden from us; something that might change the lives of millions of people. I merely wished to remind you of the great gifts of youth and enthusiasm, which are yours, which I pray you will hold on to for many years, expending them sparingly and with care as you enjoy all that life will offer you in the future."

She looked unconvinced. "And do you really believe that my life lived here, in Derbyshire, is likely to hold such promise in the future?" she asked, with an astonishing degree of frankness that compelled his own reply to be equally honest.

"It could, but if it did not, it does not follow that you should remain all your life in Derbyshire. Jessica, our lives are circumscribed not by geographical boundaries, but by the limits of our minds and our capacity to persevere in pursuit of an ambition. There is no obligation that we should continue to live out our lives only in the place of our birth, is there?

"Nor is there any reason to suppose that your life will be so constrained— after all, mine was not. I was born and bred here and rarely left the county except to accompany my parents to London or Scarborough or some such place, until I went to Cambridge. Well, you see me now..."

"I do indeed, on the verge of a great adventure in the unknown depths of the African continent! A considerable transformation by any measure! Would that we might all aspire to such an exciting achievement," she declared, making him laugh and breaking the tension of the moment.

Postponing any further argument that she might have mounted, as they approached the entrance to Pemberley House, Jessica threw one last pebble into the pool of their discussion and waited for the ripples.

"If it had been at all possible, I should have wished very much to go to Africa with you," she said in a teasing kind of voice and was surprised when he said, quietly but very seriously, "If it had been possible, Jessica, I should have liked it too, very much."

When she turned to search his face, she saw not a trace of equivocation upon it. She had then to accept that he had meant every word.

That night Jessica recorded her thoughts in her diary, admitting to herself for the first time that she was falling in love with Julian Darcy.

The Pemberley Chronicles

A Companion Volume to Jane Austen's Pride and Prejudice
The Pemberley Chronicles: Book 1

REBECCA ANN COLLINS

"A lovely complementary novel to Jane Austen's *Pride and Prejudice*.
Austen would surely give her smile of approval."
—BEVERLY WONG, AUTHOR OF *Pride & Prejudice Prudence*

The weddings are over, the saga begins

The guests (including millions of readers and viewers) wish the two happy couples health and happiness. As the music swells and the credits roll, two things are certain: Jane and Bingley will want for nothing, while Elizabeth and Darcy are to be the happiest couple in the world!

Elizabeth and Darcy's personal stories of love, marriage, money, and children are woven together with the threads of social and political history of England in the nineteenth century. As changes in industry and agriculture affect the people of Pemberley and the surrounding countryside, the Darcys strive to be progressive and forward-looking while upholding beloved traditions.

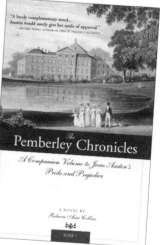

"Those with a taste for the balance and humour of Austen will find a worthy companion volume."
—*Book News*

978-1-4022-1153-9 • $14.96 US/ $17.95 CAN/ £7.99 UK

The Women of Pemberley

The acclaimed Pride and Prejudice *sequel series*

The Pemberley Chronicles: Book 2

REBECCA ANN COLLINS

A new age is dawning

Five women—strong, intelligent, independent of mind, and in the tradition of many Jane Austen heroines—continue the legacy of Pemberley into a dynamic new era at the start of the Victorian Age. Events unfold as the real and fictional worlds intertwine, linked by the relationship of the characters to each other and to the great estate of Pemberley, the heart of their community.

With some characters from the beloved works of Jane Austen, and some new from the author's imagination, the central themes of love, friendship, marriage, and a sense of social obligation remain, showcased in the context of the sweeping political and social changes of the age.

978-1-4022-1154-6 • $14.96 US/ $17.95 CAN/ £7.99 UK

Netherfield Park Revisited

The acclaimed **Pride and Prejudice** *sequel series*

The Pemberley Chronicles: Book 3

REBECCA ANN COLLINS

"A very readable and believable tale for readers who like their romance with a historical flavor." —*Book News*

Love, betrayal, and changing times for the Darcys and the Bingleys

Three generations of the Darcy and the Bingley families evolve against a backdrop of the political ideals and social reforms of the mid-Victorian era.

Jonathan Bingley, the handsome, distinguished son of Charles and Jane Bingley, takes center stage, returning to Hertfordshire as master of Netherfield Park. A deeply passionate and committed man, Jonathan is immersed in the joys and heartbreaks of his friends and family and his own challenging marriage. At the same time, he is swept up in the changes of the world around him.

Netherfield Park Revisited combines captivating details of life in mid-Victorian England with the ongoing saga of Jane Austen's beloved *Pride and Prejudice* characters.

"Ms. Collins has done it again!" —BEVERLY WONG, AUTHOR OF *Pride & Prejudice Prudence*

978-1-4022-1155-3 • $14.95 US/ $15.99 CAN/ £7.99 UK

The Ladies of Longbourn

The acclaimed **Pride and Prejudice** *sequel series*

The Pemberley Chronicles: Book 4

REBECCA ANN COLLINS

"Interesting stories, enduring themes, gentle humour, and lively dialogue." —*Book News*

A complex and charming young woman of the Victorian age, tested to the limits of her endurance

The bestselling *Pemberley Chronicles* series continues the saga of the Darcys and Bingleys from Jane Austen's *Pride and Prejudice* and introduces imaginative new characters.

Anne-Marie Bradshaw is the granddaughter of Charles and Jane Bingley. Her father now owns Longbourn, the Bennet's estate in Hertfordshire. A young widow after a loveless marriage, Anne-Marie and her stepmother Anna, together with Charlotte Collins, widow of the unctuous Mr. Collins, are the Ladies of Longbourn. These smart, independent women challenge the conventional roles of women in the Victorian era, while they search for ways to build their own lasting legacies in an ever-changing world.

Jane Austen's original characters—Darcy, Elizabeth, Bingley, and Jane—anchor a dramatic story full of wit and compassion.

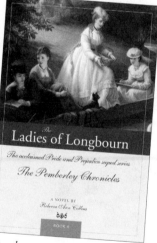

"A masterpiece that reaches the heart."
—BEVERLEY WONG, AUTHOR OF *Pride & Prejudice Prudence*

978-1-4022-1219-2 • $14.95 US/ $15.99 CAN/ £7.99 UK